PRAISE FOR

THE

DAMNE

A *Seventeen*
MOST ANTICIPATED PICK FOR SUMMER 2020

"Forbidden romance and harsh consequences set up this highly anticipated sequel that will leave you wanting so much more."
—*Seventeen*

"I loved this book. Beautiful, tortured Bastien . . . The stellar worldbuilding, the lurking presence of the Otherworld, and VAMPIRES. A clear win." —Roshani Chokshi, *New York Times* bestselling author of *The Gilded Wolves*

"A worthy sequel that builds upon the world set up in book one and takes our characters to far darker places than before." —*Culturess*

"Expansive worldbuilding . . . Romantic . . . Steamy . . . Decadent escapism." —*Kirkus Reviews*

"*The Damned* continues the thematic elegance and glamour found in *The Beautiful* and manages to take it up another level . . . There is a deep and seductive ambience that weaves throughout the story and leaves you feeling like you are reading the novel while lounging in a richly appointed New Orleans drawing room . . . The supernatural world that Ahdieh builds in this series is nothing short of fantastic." —*The Nerd Daily*

"Forbidden love, sultry romance, and clashing immortal factions fill this sequel . . . [and] will keep readers engaged . . . For fans of vampire love stories." —*School Library Journal*

PRAISE FOR

THE
BEAUTIFUL

"*The Beautiful*, which kicks off a new series, returns the vampire novel to popular form, evoking the style of Anne Rice and breathing fresh life into the genre." —*Entertainment Weekly*

"Ahdieh's New Orleans is lushly atmospheric, permeating this series opener with an undercurrent of violence within a seductive underworld around Mardi Gras . . . Readers will champion Celine's wit and incredible grit—even surrounded by powerful supernatural protectors, Celine fights for herself and those she loves . . . Fans will clamor for the continuation to this captivating volume." —*Publishers Weekly*

"It's true: Vampires are back, and they're more seductive than ever." —*Bustle*

"Ahdieh brings New Orleans vibrantly to life, particularly when exploring the complicated racial and gender restrictions of high society through main and supporting characters of mixed-race origin. Sure to please fans of the author and of the vampire-romance genre." —*Kirkus Reviews*

"Darkly glamorous . . . Compelling." —*The Bulletin of the Center for Children's Books*

"It's intoxicating. *The Beautiful* has that decadent, slow-moving horror that feels like a dream slipping to nightmare. It's like walking alone down a twilight street and feeling the snap of a branch behind you and that acidic heart-in-your-throat rush of knowing that you're being followed. Stalked." —Roshani Chokshi, *New York Times* bestselling author of *The Gilded Wolves*

"An action-packed third act and a final reveal will have readers grasping for the sequel . . . Vampires never stay dead for long, and best-selling Ahdieh's approach—part homage to the classics, part fresh-eyed revitalization—will intrigue all but the most committed skeptics."
                                                                    —*Booklist*

"An incredibly ornate, lush New Orleans; characters who imprint themselves on your memory forever; a story that is nail-biting and swoony and satisfying and tense ALL AT THE SAME TIME. And of course . . . VAMPIRES."   —Sabaa Tahir, *New York Times* bestselling author of *An Ember in the Ashes*

"The first in a series, this mystery novel shines when it focuses on Celine and her struggle to fit into society while trying to be true to herself."   —*School Library Journal*

THE DAMNED

RENÉE AHDIEH

G. P. PUTNAM'S SONS

G. P. PUTNAM'S SONS

An imprint of Penguin Random House LLC, New York

First published in the United States of America by G. P. Putnam's Sons,
an imprint of Penguin Random House LLC, 2020
First paperback edition published 2021

Visit us online at penguinrandomhouse.com

THE LIBRARY OF CONGRESS HAS CATALOGED THE HARDCOVER EDITION AS FOLLOWS:
Names: Ahdieh, Renée, author.
Title: The damned / Renée Ahdieh.
Description: New York: G. P. Putnam's Sons, [2020] | Series: The beautiful; book 2 |
Summary: In 19th century New Orleans, Sébastien Saint Germain, cursed and forever
changed, and Celine, recovering from injuries sustained during a night she
cannot remember, uncover the danger around them, including their love. .
Identifiers: LCCN 2020002295 (print) | LCCN 2020002296 (ebook) |
ISBN 9781984812582 (hardcover) | ISBN 9781984812599 (ebook)
Subjects: CYAC: Vampires—Fiction. | Supernatural—Fiction. |
Love—Fiction. | New Orleans (La.)—History—19th century—Fiction.
Classification: LCC PZ7.1.A328 Dam 2020 (print) | LCC PZ7.1.A328 (ebook) | DDC [Fic]—dc23
LC record available at https://lccn.loc.gov/2020002295
LC ebook record available at https://lccn.loc.gov/2020002296

Printed in the United States of America

ISBN 9781984812605

1 3 5 7 9 10 8 6 4 2

Design by Suki Boynton
Text set in Warnock Pro

To all those who braved new worlds
in search of something more

And to Victor, always

THE
DAMNED

Every Night and every Morn
Some to Misery are born.
Every Morn and every Night
Some are born to Sweet Delight,
Some are born to Endless Night.

From **Songs of Experience**
by William Blake

Comme au jeu le joueur têtu,
Comme à la bouteille l'ivrogne,
Comme aux vermines la charogne
—Maudite, maudite sois-tu!

As gamblers to the wheel's bright spell,
As drunkards to their raging thirst,
As corpses to their worms
—Accurst be thou! Oh, be thou damned to hell!

From "Le Vampire"
by Charles Baudelaire

The Awakening

———⟆———

First there is nothing. Only silence. A sea of oblivion.

Then flashes of memory take shape. Snippets of sound. The laughter of a loved one, the popping of wood sap in a fireplace, the smell of butter melting across fresh bread.

An image emerges from the chaos, sharpening with each second. A crying young woman—her eyes like emeralds, her hair like spilled ink—leans over him, clutching his bloodstained hand, pleading with him in muffled tones.

Who am I? he wonders.

Dark amusement winds through him.

He is nothing. No one. Nobody.

The scent of blood suffuses his nostrils, intoxicatingly sweet. Like lechosa from a fruit stand in San Juan, its juice dripping down his shirtsleeves.

He becomes hunger. Not a kind of hunger he's ever known before, but an all-consuming void. A dull ache around his dead heart, a blast of bloodlust searing through his veins. It knifes through his stomach like the talons on a bird of prey. Rage builds in his chest. The desire to seek and destroy. To consume life. Let it fill the emptiness within him. Where there was once a sea of oblivion, there is now a canvas painted red, the color dripping like rain at his feet, setting his world aflame.

My city. My family. My love.

Who am I?

From the fires of his fury, a name emerges.

Bastien. My name is Sébastien Saint Germain.

BASTIEN

———— ≈ ————

I lie still, my body weightless. Immobile. It feels like I'm locked in a pitch-black room, unable to speak, choking on the smoke of my own folly.

My uncle did this to me once when I was nine. My closest friend, Michael, and I had stolen a box of cigars hand-rolled by an elderly lady from Havana who worked on the corner of Burgundy and Saint Louis. When Uncle Nico caught us smoking them in the alley behind Jacques', he sent Michael home, his voice deathly quiet. Filled with foreboding.

Then my uncle locked me in a hall closet with the box of cigars and a tin of matches. He told me I could not leave until I finished every single one of them.

That was the last time I ever smoked a cigar.

It took me weeks to forgive Uncle Nico. Years to stomach the smell of burning tobacco anywhere in my vicinity. Half a lifetime to understand why he'd felt the need to teach that particular lesson.

I try to swallow this ghost of bile. I fail.

I know what Nicodemus has done. Though the memory is still unclear—fogged by the weakness of my dying body—I know he has made me into one of them. I am now a vampire, like my uncle before me. Like my mother before me, who faced the final death willingly, her lips stained red and a lifeless body in her arms.

I am a soulless son of Death, cursed to drink the blood of the living until the end of time.

It sounds ridiculous even to me, a boy raised on the truth of monsters. Like a joke told by an unfunny aunt with a penchant for melodrama. A woman who cuts herself on her diamond bracelet and wails as drops of blood trickle onto her silken skirts.

Like that, I am hunger once more. With each pang, I become less human. Less of what I once was and more of what I will forever be. A demon of want, who simply craves more, never to be sated.

White-hot rage chases behind the bloodlust, igniting like a trail of saltpeter from a powder keg. I understand why Uncle Nico did this, though it will take many lifetimes for me to forgive him. Only the direst of circumstances would drive him to turn the last living member of his mortal family—the lone heir to the Saint Germain fortune—into a demon of the Otherworld.

His line has died with me, my human life reaching an all-too-sudden end. This choice must be one of last resort. A voice resonates in my mind. A feminine voice, its echoes tremulous.

Please. Save him. What can I say that will make you save him? Do we have a deal?

When I realize who it is, what she must have done, I howl a silent howl, the sound ringing in the hollows of my lost soul. I cannot think about that now.

My failure will not let me.

It is enough to know that I, Sébastien Saint Germain, eighteen-year-old son of a beggar and a thief, have been turned into a member of the Fallen. A race of blood drinkers banished from their rightful place in the Otherworld by their own greed. Creatures of the night embroiled in a centuries-long war with their archenemy, a brotherhood of werewolves.

I try to speak but fail, my throat tight, my eyelids sealed shut. After all, Death is a powerful foe to vanquish.

Fine silk rustles by my ear, a scented breeze coiling through the air. Neroli oil and rose water. The unmistakable perfume of Odette Valmont, one of my dearest friends. For almost ten years, she was a protector in life. Now she is a sister in blood. A vampire, sired by the same maker.

My right thumb twitches in response to her nearness. Still I cannot speak or move freely. Still I am locked in a darkened room, with nothing but a box of cigars and a tin of matches, dread coursing through my veins, hunger tingling on my tongue.

A sigh escapes Odette's lips. "He's beginning to wake." She pauses, pity seeping into her voice. "He'll be furious."

As usual, Odette is not wrong. But there is comfort in my fury. Freedom in knowing I may soon seek release from my rage.

"And well he should be," my uncle says. "This is the most self-ish thing I've ever done. If he manages to survive the change, he will come to hate me . . . just as Nigel did."

Nigel. The name alone rekindles my ire. Nigel Fitzroy, the

5

reason for my untimely demise. He—along with Odette and four other members of my uncle's vampire progeny—safeguarded me from Nicodemus Saint Germain's enemies, chief among them those of the Brotherhood. For years Nigel bided his time. Cultivated his plan for revenge on the vampire who snatched him from his home and made him a demon of the night. Under the guise of loyalty, Nigel put into motion a series of events intended to destroy the thing Nicodemus prized most: his living legacy.

I've been betrayed before, just as I have betrayed others. It is the way of things when you live among capricious immortals and the many illusionists who hover nearby like flies. Only two years ago, my favorite pastime involved fleecing the Crescent City's most notorious warlocks of their ill-gotten gains. The worst among their ilk were always so certain that a mere mortal could never best them. It gave me great pleasure to prove them wrong.

But I have never betrayed my family. And I had never been betrayed by a vampire sworn to protect me. Someone I loved as a brother. Memories waver through my mind. Images of laughter and a decade of loyalty. I want to shout and curse. Rail to the heavens, like a demon possessed.

Alas, I know how well God listens to the prayers of the damned.

"I'll summon the others," Odette murmurs. "When he wakes, he should see us all united."

"Leave them be," Nicodemus replies, "for we are not yet out of the woods." For the first time, I sense a hint of distress in his words, there and gone in an instant. "More than a third of my immortal children did not survive the transformation. Many were lost in the first year to the foolishness of immortal youth. This . . . may not work."

"It *will* work," Odette says without hesitation.

"Sébastien could succumb to madness, as his mother did," Nicodemus says. "In her quest to be unmade, Philomène destroyed everything in her path, until there was nothing to be done but put an end to the terror."

"That is not Bastien's fate."

"Don't be foolish. It very well could be."

Odette's response is cool. "A risk you were willing to take."

"But a risk nonetheless. It was why I refused his sister when she asked me years ago to turn her." He exhales. "In the end, we lost her to the fire all the same."

"We will not lose Bastien as we lost Émilie. Nor will he succumb to Philomène's fate."

"You speak with such surety, little oracle." He pauses. "Has your second sight granted you this sense of conviction?"

"No. Years ago, I promised Bastien I would not look into his future. I have not forsaken my word. But I believe in my heart that hope will prevail. It . . . simply must."

Despite her seemingly unshakable faith, Odette's worry is a palpable thing. I wish I could reach for her hand. Offer her words of reassurance. But still I am locked within myself, my anger overtaking all else. It turns to ash on my tongue, until all I am left with is *want*. The need to be loved. To be sated. But most of all, the desire to destroy.

Nicodemus says nothing for a time. "We shall see. His wrath will be great, of that there can be no doubt. Sébastien never wanted to become one of us. He bore witness to the cost of the change at an early age."

My uncle knows me well. His world took my family from me. I think of my parents, who died years ago, trying to keep me safe. I think of my sister, who perished trying to protect me. I think of Celine, the girl I loved in life, who will not remember me.

I have never betrayed anyone I love.

But never is a long time, when you have eternity to consider.

"He may also be grateful," Odette says. "One day."

My uncle does not reply.

ODETTE

———— ≈ ————

Odette Valmont leaned into the wind. Let it buffet her brunette curls about her face and whip her coattails into a frenzy. She reveled in the feeling of weightlessness as she stared down at Jackson Square, her right hand wrapped around the cool metal spire, her left boot dangling in the evening air.

"Ah, it's just you and me again, n'est-ce pas?" she joked to the metal crucifix mounted above her.

The figure of Christ stared down at Odette in thoughtful silence.

Odette sighed. "Don't fret, mon Sauveur. You know I hold your counsel in the highest esteem. It is not every day that a creature such as myself is fortunate enough to count you among her dearest friends." She grinned.

Perhaps it was blasphemous for a demon of the night to address the Savior of mankind in such a familiar fashion. But Odette was in need of guidance, now more than ever.

"I'd like to think you hear my prayers," she continued. "After all, when I was alive, I made it a point to attend Mass regularly." She tilted her ear toward the cross. "What was that?" Laughter bubbled from her pale throat. "Mais oui, bien sûr! I knew it. You embraced the sinner. Of course you would welcome me with open arms." Affection warmed her gaze. "It is why we will always be friends, until the bitter end." She paused as if she were listening to a reply intended for her ears alone. "You're too kind," she said. "And I would never fault you for the sins of the men who have turned your pure words and generous deeds into instruments of power and control." Once more, Odette whirled around the spire. "Forgive them, for they know not what they do!" she sang, her eyes squeezed shut, a gust of wind rushing toward her face.

Odette took in the world of the Vieux Carré far below, her attention catching on the cameo pinned beneath her throat, the creamy ivory surrounded by a halo of bloodred rubies. Her fétiche, which served two purposes, much like the two sides of her life. It worked as a talisman to protect her from the light of the sun while also serving as an ever-present reminder of her past.

The sight of it sobered her. Along with the slew of remembrances gathering in its wake.

New Orleans' high society believed Odette Valmont to be the carefree sort of jeune fille who thrived in the company of others. A young lady whose greatest joy was standing center stage in a roomful of people, their gazes rapt.

"But who wouldn't adore the attention?" Odette asked. "Am I to be faulted even for this most human of emotions? After all, beauty such as ours is meant to be admired!" It was one of the things that made vampires such dangerous predators: their beauté inégalée, as she liked to call it. With this unparalleled beauty, they drew their victims into a lasting embrace.

But not long after the appreciative sighs faded, Odette would don her favorite pair of buckskin trousers. She would climb the back of the cathedral under cover of night, her fingers and toes sure as they clawed their way up the center of the edifice to the tallest of the three spires, the dark gift coursing through her veins. Once she reached the tower's apex, she would glory in the silence of solitude.

In the splendor of being alone, under the watchful eyes of her Savior.

It always struck her as odd, how people believed exciting things were bound to happen at parties with loud music, raucous laughter, and flowing champagne. This surety was what drew them to such events in the first place. Odette thought the most exciting space was the one within her own mind. Her imagination was usually much better than real life. With a few notable exceptions, of course.

Like her first real kiss. The taste of spun sugar on Marie's soft lips; Odette's mortal heart racing in her chest. The way their hands trembled. The way their breaths quickened.

She turned toward the young man on the cross. The Son of God.

"Is my love a sin?" she asked him without flinching, as she had on countless other occasions. Again he gave her the same response. Odette nodded with satisfaction and repeated the mantra. "Your message was one of love. And hatred should never prevail over love."

Once more, her memories wavered at the edges of her mind. She recalled her first brush with death, the day her father was led to the guillotine, jeers accompanying each of his steps. How he still wore his powdered wig, even when the blade fell. The slick sound of his blood splashing across the stones, which brought to mind her first kill, the night after welcoming her maker with open arms. The thrill of holding such godlike power in her grasp.

Odette's fingers turned white around the metal spire. Contrary to popular opinion, she was no longer angry. Not at the bloodthirsty men and women who'd left her a shivering orphan. Not at her parents for being unable to fight back. Not at Nicodemus for stealing Odette away from the dregs of her former life. Not at Marie, who had broken Odette's heart in the way of so many first loves.

"Because of everything that happened, I've learned to love myself more," she said. "And is that not the best gift any trial in life can give you? The power to love yourself today better than you did the day before."

Odette angled her chin into a violet sky spangled with stars. The clouds above shifted like feathers of mist in a passing breeze. Nigel used to say the skies over New Orleans were filled with the smoke of the city's misdeeds. The lapses in judgment so often celebrated by the Vieux Carré's well-heeled tourists, who helped make New Orleans one of the wealthiest cities in the entire country, despite the recent War Between the States. Whenever Nigel would sit down to share his most salacious bit of weekly gossip, his Cockney accent would deepen with prurience.

Something clenched around Odette's dead heart.

This time, she hesitated before glancing toward the metal cross in her periphery.

"I know I have no business thinking of Nigel Fitzroy with anything resembling warmth," she whispered. "He betrayed us." She swallowed. "He betrayed *me*." Incredulity flared across her face. "To think this happened only one day ago. That the rising and setting of a single moon has changed all our lives in such an irrevocable fashion." In that single night, Odette had lost a brother she'd loved for a decade to a bone-chilling kind of treachery. This loss was keenly felt, though she dared not mourn it in the open. To do so would be une erreur fatale, especially in Nicodemus' presence. The loss of a traitor was no one's loss at all.

And yet . . .

She'd cried in her room this morning. She'd drawn the velvet curtains around her four-poster bed and let blood-tinged tears stain her ivory silk pillows. No one had seen hide nor hair of Boone all day. Jae arrived not long after sundown, his black hair wet, his expression somber. Upon returning to Jacques', Hortense took to playing Bach cello suites at inhuman speed on her Stradivarius, while her sister, Madeleine, wrote in a leather-bound journal nearby. In short, every member of La Cour des Lions mourned in their own way.

On the surface, it had been business as usual. They exchanged stilted pleasantries. Acted as if nothing were amiss, none of them wishing to give voice to their anguish or breathe life into the worst of Nigel's offenses, the proof of which was soon to follow.

Nigel's worst offense?

The loss of Sébastien's soul. The unmaking of his humanity. Nigel might have betrayed them, but he had *killed* Bastien. He'd torn out his throat in front of the only girl Bastien had ever loved.

Odette shivered, despite the fact that she hadn't felt truly cold in decades. She let her vision glaze as it spanned across the square toward the glittering waters of the Mississippi. Past the twinkling ships along the horizon.

"Should I tell them about my role in this sordid tale?" she asked.

The figure on the cross remained contemplative. Silent.

"You would probably say honesty is the best policy." Odette tucked a sable curl behind an ear. "But I would rather swallow a handful of nails than face Nicodemus' wrath. And it was an *honest* mistake, so that should count for something, non?"

Again her Savior remained frustratingly quiet.

A mere hour before Bastien's death, Odette had allowed him to strike out on his own, knowing full well that a killer nipped at their heels. She'd gone so far as to distract her immortal brethren so they would not waylay him in his task to find Celine, whose safety had been threatened moments prior.

Should she confess her role?

What would Nicodemus do to her once he found out?

The last vampire who dared to cross Nicodemus Saint Germain had had his fangs torn from his mouth.

Odette swallowed. Not necessarily a fate worse than death, but then again not exactly one to inspire honesty. It wasn't that she feared pain. Even the idea of the final death did not frighten her. She'd born witness to the rise and fall of empires. Danced with a dauphin beneath the light of a full moon.

Hers was a story worthy of being told.

"It's just . . . well, I *like* the way I look, damn it all!" She liked her smart nose and her impish smile. Missing fangs were sure to mar the effect. "I suppose at least I will not starve," she mused. "That is the gift of family, among other things."

If gluttony and vanity made her evil, then tant pis. She'd been called worse things by worse creatures.

Odette reeled around the metal spire, the crucifix at its top creaking with the shift in weight. Gas lamps danced in the shadows below. Her vampiric senses flooded with the scent of a New Orleans spring evening. Sweet blossoms, sharp iron, sultry wind. The beating of hearts. The whicker of horses, the striking of hooves against pavers.

Dark beauty, all around her. Ripe for the taking.

A mournful sigh flew past Odette's lips. She never should have permitted Bastien to go, even if Celine's life did hang in the balance. Odette had known better. Where blood flowed, murder followed. She'd simply allowed sentiment to get the better of her.

Never again.

For years Odette had eschewed the use of her special gift, one unusual among immortals. The ability to foresee glimpses of another being's future, with nothing more than the touch of her skin to theirs. She avoided it because she often saw flashes of misfortune in those rash enough to indulge their curiosity.

Just as she'd seen when Celine Rousseau asked her to look the day they first met.

History had taught Odette that informing a person of their impending doom did not exactly endear them to her. Often the individual in question would demand how they might avoid their fate. No matter how hard Odette tried to explain that her gift didn't work like that—that she was not, in fact, a worker of miracles—they would continue pressing her to the point of exasperation. Twice she'd been accosted. Threatened with bodily harm, a knife flashed before her face, a revolver pointed at her chest.

The audacity!

A bitter smile curled up one side of her face. The fools in question had met with fates befitting their folly. Jae, La Cour des Lions' resident assassin, had helped her. He stalked those men through the darkness. Terrorized them for hours. Made sure their last moments were soaked in fear.

"They never suspected it was me who orchestrated their deaths," she murmured.

Of course, knowing whether something unfortunate was going to happen was all well and good in theory. But what if that knowledge pertained to someone Odette loved? Bien sûr, she could push a friend out of the way if a carriage with a spooked horse was careening toward them. But it was rarely that simple.

For this and many other reasons, Odette lied when asked about what she'd seen in Celine's future. Celine would indeed be the tamer of beasts, as Odette divulged. But Odette would never forget the muffled words that followed after, whispered in her ear like a wicked secret:

One must die so the other may live.

Putain de merde. Another ridiculous prophecy, the kind Odette hated for most of her immortal life. They were all unforgivably vague. Why couldn't they just say what they meant? *This connard will be killing this connard at this specific time and place. Here is how you might spare them this fate. Allons-y!* Would that be too much to ask?

To whom did this prophecy refer? Celine and Bastien? Or Celine and someone else entirely? It was impossible to be certain. So, in Odette's opinion, they were all better off not knowing.

But Odette's opinion had changed last night. Even if it caused her pain, she would help those dear to her avoid disaster.

Her brow lined with determination, Odette looked to her silent guardian and made a promise. "I will set things right," she swore. "Not for Bastien alone. But for *me.*"

Failure of any kind had never sat well with her.

Odette wrapped her fingers tighter around the metal spire at the cathedral's apex. "C'est assez," she said. It was time for her to do as she'd been bidden. To sate her hunger before Bastien woke in truth, for Nicodemus would need all his children at full strength when that time came.

She could only guess what kind of newborn vampire Bastien would be. He'd been difficult as a boy, prone to outbursts in temper. Likely to resolve disagreements with his fists rather than with words. This tendency had caused his expulsion from the military academy at West Point, a position Nicodemus had labored for years to make possible. After all, the son of a quadroon and a Taíno did not sport the necessary pedigree for such a lofty institution.

If Bastien survived the change, Nicodemus believed he would be the strongest of his children, simply for the fact that they shared blood in both their lives, mortal and immortal. Blood sharing was like the flipping of a coin. On some occasions, a brilliant and powerful immortal would rise from its ashes.

On others?

A murderous madman like Vlad Țepeș. Or Countess Elizabeth Báthory, who had bathed in the blood of her victims. Or Kato Danzo, who'd terrorized the skies on giant wings resembling those of a bat.

Odette wanted to believe none of this spoke to what might become of Bastien's *character*. Would he be bookish like Madeleine? Hedonistic like Hortense? Morose like Jae or playfully malicious like Boone?

"Assez," she announced to the night sky.

Odette let her attention drift across Jackson Square, her eyes flitting over the many through streets nearby, searching for a lone figure embarking on a solitary stroll. Her gaze locked on someone traveling past a flickering gas lamp along Rue de Chartres.

Without hesitation, Odette bid her Savior farewell before letting go of the spire. She shut her eyes as she fell, relishing the rush of cool air and the wind whistling in her ears. Just as she was about to strike the pavers, her body curled on itself, tucking into a roll. She hit the ground with a muffled thud, her shoulder taking the brunt of the force, allowing her to spin to standing in the next breath. Straightening, she glanced about before thrusting her hands in the pockets of her buckskin trousers. She hummed as she sauntered down the dark lane known to locals as Pirates Alley. The words of "La Marseillaise" graced the night sky, the clip of her booted heels echoing through the darkness.

"Allons! Enfants de la Patrie," Odette sang softly.

She glided past the iron bars along which the famed pirate Jean Lafitte had been known to sell his ill-gotten gains in the earlier part of the century. Dark stained glass glinted in her periphery. Inside the church, Odette swore she could see the ghost of Père Antoine swinging his thurible, the smoke hazing about him. Or perhaps it was an apparition of the monk who'd resided beneath its cavernous roof a hundred years ago, often heard chanting the Kyrie on stormy evenings.

"Le jour de gloire est arrivé," she continued singing.

The stories of this haunted alleyway nestled in the heart of the Vieux Carré had always fascinated Odette. Much like the countless tales about this shining land known as America, they often cloaked the darkest parts of its history. In the case of New Orleans, they masked hundreds of years as a port city in the slave trade. The untold deaths of those who had lived and breathed and loved along this strategic crescent of land long before the conquistadors had sailed through its harbor to stake their flags in the ground and declare it their own.

A seething darkness. Shadows shifting, lengthening behind all the glimmering beauty.

Odette repeated the next line of the song twice, her voice

clear as a bell. *"L'étenard sanglant est levé!"* She rounded the corner and hastened her steps, veering in the direction of the lone figure two blocks ahead in the distance.

When the woman heard the sound of Odette's steady footfalls behind her, she paused. Canted her head, the silver at her temples flashing in the light of a flickering flame. Then she stood straight, her elegant bonnet tipping up to the sky as if she were offering a prayer to God in heaven.

The silliness of mortals, Odette thought. *Your God will not help you now.*

It wasn't that she found the notion of God silly. She counted Christ among her closest confidants. Besides that, hope was a powerful force.

Just not as powerful as Odette Valmont. Not for this woman. Not in this moment.

She waited until the woman continued walking. Then Odette moved into position behind her. Many vampires would prolong the hunt until the last possible second to allow the terror to mount in their victim. To make them wait until they were panting, tripping over their feet, begging for reprieve. Boone enjoyed doing this. But Boone was a hunter by trade. And Odette had never been that kind of immortal.

Instead she took a final glance around to make sure they were alone. Before the woman could blink, Odette blurred forward and grabbed her from behind, covering the woman's lips with one hand and yanking her into a narrow alleyway with the other.

Odette tilted the woman's chin back so she could meet her gaze. "Don't be afraid," she whispered, allowing the dark gift to weave through her words and imbue them with soothing magic. The woman's panicked eyes softened at the edges. "I promise you won't remember a thing," Odette crooned, steadying her in an embrace.

"Who—who are you?" the woman breathed.

"Who are *you*?"

The woman's eyelashes fluttered as if she were on the cusp of falling asleep. "Francine," she said. "Francine Hofstadter."

"Bonsoir, Madame Hofstadter." Odette shifted her hand from beside Francine's mouth so she might cup her jaw. She paused to study her warm brown eyes. "You remind me of my mother, beautiful Francine."

"What is her name?"

A thin smile twisted Odette's lips. "Louise d'Armagnac."

"Such a *lovely* name," Francine drawled. "So lovely . . . just like you."

"She was a duchess."

"Are you a duchess?"

"Perhaps I might have been." Odette stroked an index finger along Francine's chin. "But my mother likely would have objected. She would never have relinquished the title, not without a fight. You might say she . . . lost her head for it."

"I'm—sorry," Francine said, her body going lax in Odette's arms. "It sounds like she didn't love you as a mother should."

"Oh, she did. Of that I am quite certain." Amusement rounded Odette's tones. "She just loved herself more. For that, I have no objections. My mother is a hero to me. Until the bitter end, she remained true."

"But how could she love herself more, when she has a daughter like you? That's not right." Francine mirrored Odette's gesture, bringing her right hand to frame Odette's face. "I wish I had a daughter. I could have loved her. I could have loved you." She marveled, her eyes twinkling like pools of water. "Perhaps . . . I *do* love you."

"Who doesn't, ma chérie?" Odette wove Francine's fingers through hers. Brought their joined palms toward her lips. "I love you, too," she whispered into Francine's warm, vanilla-scented skin.

Before Francine could blink, Odette sank her teeth into the delicate flesh along Francine's wrist. A gasp punctured the night air, but Francine did not struggle. Her limbs went languorous. Dangerously soft. Odette breathed through her nose as she took in another hot draft of blood. Her eyes flashed closed. Images wavered through her mind. Francine's memories. Her entire life story, colored by countless remembrances, which—Odette knew—could be unreliable, even among the most earnest of mortals.

People tended to recall things not as they were but as they wished them to be.

A memory of a birthday celebration when Francine had been a young girl, praline icing smeared across her lips. The death of a beloved grandmother, Francine following the funeral carriage down a wide lane in the Garden District, a lace parasol filtering the hot light of the sun. A wedding to a boy she'd believed to be her one true love. Years later, another man who'd dashed that belief to smithereens.

Between these vignettes, Odette saw glimpses of a possible future. Of a son who visited each year at Christmas, along with his wife who wished to be anywhere else. Of a distant husband who died clutching his chest, and of twilight years spent in regret.

It broke what remained of Odette's heart. This life that once held such promise.

No matter. This woman's fate was not her concern.

Through it all, Francine remained the heroine of her own story. It was as it should be. At the very least, every mortal should be the hero of that particular tale.

But the best heroes possessed flaws. And the best mortals never forgot that fact.

She drank deeply, letting Francine fall back in her embrace, like a lover overcome with emotion.

Unlike Odette's second sight, this ability to glimpse behind the curtain of a victim's life was one shared among all blood drinkers in possession of the dark gift. As such, Odette never drank from men. It was too intimate for her, the action of entering the mind of her prey. Once, when she'd been a newborn vampire herself, she'd thought to drink from a man who killed others for sport. She'd thought it fitting, to let him meet his match in her.

But the man's memories were violent. He had delighted in the horrors he committed. The images flickering through Odette's mind had knotted in her throat, choking her, burning her from the inside out.

That night, she'd sworn never to enter a man's mind again.

Men were the worst kind of heroes. Riddled with flaws they refused to see.

The instant Odette felt Francine's heartbeat begin to slow, she pulled back. It would not do to drown in Francine's death. Many a vampire had lost their minds in that slip of darkness between worlds.

Odette licked her lips, the motions languid. Then she pressed her thumb to the puncture wounds along Francine's wrist, waiting for the flow of blood to stanch. "As soon as we part," she said, "you will forget what happened tonight. I will never haunt your dreams. You will return home and spend tomorrow resting, for a critter has bitten you and made you feel a bit piqued. Ask your family to prepare steak and spinach for you." With care, Odette folded the cuff of Francine's sleeve over the wounds. "When you walk these streets alone at night, walk with your head high, even if you believe death might be around the corner." Her grin was like the curved edge of a blade. "It is the only way to live, lovely Francine."

Francine nodded. "You are an angel, dear." Tears welled in her eyes. "And I could never forget you."

"I am no angel. Angels bore me. Give me a better devil any day."

"You *are* an angel," Francine insisted. "The most beautiful creature I've ever seen." When Odette released her, Francine gripped Odette's arm tightly, refusing to let go. Tears slid down her cheeks, confusion etching lines across her brow. "Please," she said, "take me with you."

"Where I go, you cannot follow."

"I can if you take me with you. If you make me an angel like you."

Odette tilted her head, the musings of the beautiful creature she was now warring with the beliefs of the mortal girl she'd once been. In her hands, she held the power to give life. To take it.

To savor it. Slowly.

Francine smiled at Odette, her gaze tremulous, her fingers still twined in Odette's shirtsleeves. "Please, angel. Please. Don't leave me alone in the dark."

"I told you already, ma chérie." With her free hand, Odette caressed the side of Francine's face. "I am no angel." With that, she snapped Francine's neck. Felt the brittle bones break between her inhumanly strong fingers. Let Francine's body slide in an inglorious heap, lifeless, to the cracked pavers at her feet.

She stood that way for a time. Waited to see if Francine's God would smite her down. After all, Odette deserved it. She could justify her actions however she wanted. She could say she'd spared Francine the disappointment of a sad future. She could say it was a kindness. Some type of twisted mercy.

But who was she to offer mercy to anyone?

Odette waited, staring up at the moon, wincing away from the long shadow cast by the cross high above. No hail of fire and brimstone rained down around her. Everything was as it had always been. Life and death in a single breath.

"I'm sorry, ma chérie," Odette whispered. "You deserved better." She stared at her feet, letting regret roll down her spine toward her toes, to vanish between the cracks in the pavestones. What she'd done—this life that she'd stolen—it was wrong. Odette knew it.

It was just . . . sometimes she was tired of trying so hard to be good.

With a sigh, Odette began strolling away, her hands in her pockets.

"Ils viennent jusque dans nos bras," she sang, the tune tinged with sweet sadness. *"Égorger nos fils, nos compagnes."* The echo of "La Marseillaise" filtered above, mingling with the smoke of Odette's endless misdeeds.

BASTIEN

―――――≈―――――

As a boy, I often dreamed about being a hero, like the ones from my favorite stories. D'Artagnan joining the musketeers, fearless in the face of danger. King Leonidas and his brave three hundred, standing firm against impossible odds. Odysseus on an epic journey, battling mythological monsters and saving maidens fair.

Then I learned that I lived among the monsters. And that such stories were often written not by the heroes themselves, but by those left standing to tell the tale. Perhaps there wasn't much to recommend a character like d'Artagnan. After all, wasn't he only ever lucky?

Luck is not a skill. Uncle Nico said this to me time and again, when I lamented being drilled in my studies in warfare, in marksmanship, in riding, in all the talents expected of a so-called gentleman.

Maybe I should have revered Athos, a paragon of mystery. Or Aramis, a lover of life. Or Milady de Winter, the shrewdest of spies.

In the end, the monsters did possess the better stories.

My eyes open with a start. Dust motes hover in the air above me, spinning about in the amber glow of a single candle. I watch them dance for a moment, studying each of their shapes as if they were stars in an infinite sky.

The infinite captivates us because it allows us to believe all things are possible. That true love can last beyond time.

Celine said that to me the night I first realized I had true feelings for her. It was no longer as simple as being drawn to her beauty, pulled like a tide toward the shore. It had become more than that. A comfort. An understanding. Some kind of magic.

I watched her dance a quadrille in the middle of a carnival parade. It did not take long for the melody to win her over, as music so often does. She missed many of the steps and did not care. The sight caught me unawares. It was not just because of how she looked. It was how she made the people around her feel. Her smile lightened those of her partners. Caused the men and women who reeled about her to laugh with abandon.

For a breath, I lost all sense of time and place. It was just her, a lone candle in a darkened room. But behind that beguiling smile I saw something more. A world of secrets, concealed behind a pair of haunted green eyes.

As a boy with secrets of my own, an ache unfurled in my chest. I knew at that moment how much I wished to share our truths. No matter that they both might be riddled with monsters. A week later, the word *love* teased at the edges of my mind. I disregarded it. Considered myself too world-weary to fall prey to the foolishness of young love.

I was wrong. Disastrously so.

But it doesn't matter anymore. For ours is not a love story.

The ache around my dead heart spreads into my throat.

Enough.

I sense Toussaint before I see him. My entire body tenses as if coiling to spring. The giant Burmese python slithers over the tabletop, winding from my feet toward my head. I watch him move from where my family has laid me out on the table, like a body in an Irish wake. His tongue flicks the air in front of him, his yellow eyes narrowed, uncertain. He pauses on my chest, his head hovering above my sternum. I stare up at him. He glowers down at me.

Two predators appraising each other, deciding whether to strike.

After a beat, Toussaint sighs with resignation. Then he glides over my shoulder, the rest of his long body trailing behind him, his scales glistening over the bloodstained silk of my ivory waistcoat. I've always thought snakes to be prescient. The kind of all-knowing creature that thrives in the space between worlds.

At least my oracular pet seems to have accepted this unfortunate turn of fate.

I sit up, my motions blurred. Inhumanly fast. It would have been disconcerting were I unaccustomed to seeing immortals move about in such a fashion. The next instant, I douse the lone candle between my fingertips, longing to feel the fire singe my skin.

I feel nothing. Not even a whisper of pain. Nor do I need time to acclimate to the darkness. Without the light—through layers of shadow—I see every detail of my surroundings, down to the gold foiling on the wallpaper and the sixteen sparkling rubies in Odette's cameo brooch. Each strand in my uncle's black hair and all forty-eight brass rivets in the gleaming wooden table beneath me.

Revulsion grips me as the truth settles on my shoulders like a leaden thing. I am no longer of the living. I am a demon cursed to the shadows. There is nothing I can do to alter this twist of fortune. No prayer to chant. No quest to take. No bargain to strike.

I suppose this has always been my fate.

My uncle clears his throat and steps forward.

The sight of the seven otherworldly creatures gathered in a circle around me should be alarming—to mortals and immortals alike—but I keep a cool head, taking measure of my immortal brethren with the gaze of a vampire for the first time.

Odette Valmont, with her brown hair and sable eyes, watches me closely, her expression guarded. She is dressed in the garments of a gentleman, her silk cravat loose about her pale throat, her fétiche dangling from it. At first blush, she appears to be a girl of no more than twenty with a face to charm the devil.

But looks are deceiving by design.

Wrath threads through my veins, my cool-headedness lost to the winds. If Odette possessed any knowledge of my fate and kept it from me, there will be hell to pay. She's done this once before, in some misguided attempt to steer me down the path she deemed correct, as if she were judge, jury, and executioner.

Before I lash out at Odette, I look through her, willing myself numb.

Shin Jaehyuk, Nicodemus' foremost assassin, lingers in a fall of darkness at Odette's back. The second vampire Nicodemus ever turned, Jae ruled the night in the heyday of Korea's Joseon dynasty. A master of weapons and sleight of hand, this vampire—with his penchant for blades of all shapes and sizes—frightened me the most as a child. The way he loomed ever present, his pallid skin marred by countless scars, from a story told to me in pieces.

"Welcome to forever, my brother," another voice intones with its characteristic Carolina drawl. Boone Ravenel leans his left shoulder against the damask wallpaper as he sends me an insouciant grin, his features tan, his expression the portrait of charm. But beneath his angelic mien skulks a fiend with a shark's sense of smell and a hawk's eye for tracking. Fifty years ago, Odette dubbed him the Hellhound, for a variety of reasons. As with many such things, the name stuck.

To Nicodemus' immediate right stands Madeleine de Morny, her eyes and skin the color of dark teak and her expression culled from quartz. The first of my uncle's undead children to be turned, Madeleine is also the vampire Nicodemus consults before any other. Over the last hundred years, she's become his equal in many things, though I would never dare to say so in my uncle's presence. Alas, I know very little about Madeleine's past along the Côte d'Ivoire, beyond the fact that she begged Nicodemus to turn her younger sister, Hortense, in exchange for her eternal loyalty. And that her greatest passion in life—aside from her family—is to lose herself in the pages of a good book.

Hortense de Morny lounges on a chaise of tufted velvet, toying with the ends of her long, thick hair, groomed like the mane of a lion. Amusement ripples across her face, a wicked sparkle in her russet eyes. She wears a gown of translucent tulle dyed the exact color of her dark skin. Of all Nicodemus' undead children, Hortense relishes immortality the most. A lover of the arts, her favorite pastimes include an evening in Nicodemus' box seats at the French Opera House—scandalizing the lily-white members of New Orleans society with her presence—followed by a sampling of the city's finest musicians. She favors the violinists the most. *Their song is like spun sucre,* she likes to simper.

One immortal among them remains outside the circle. Though it is not readily apparent—for his hazel eyes possess a similar inhuman luster, his brown skin the same subtle sheen—Arjun Desai is not a vampire. He came to New Orleans last year at Jae's behest. Trained as a barrister under the auspices of the British Crown, Arjun was denied access to the profession's hallowed halls as a result of his heritage. Born nineteen years ago in Maharashtra, a state in the East Indies, Arjun is an ethereal, the son of a mortal man and a fey huntress of the Sylvan Vale. Another being straddling the line between worlds. His arrival to the Crescent City solved two problems: that my uncle's interest in New Orleans' hotelier industry necessitated a lawyer with a particular set of skills and that the Fallen was forbidden from bringing any more vampires into the city, following their treaty with the Brotherhood a decade ago. In less than a year, Arjun has established himself as a proper member of La Cour des Lions.

There they all stand, from all parts of the world and all walks of life. Each of them a lion in their own right. Two of my blood brothers, three of my blood sisters, and one half fey.

Gangly Nigel Fitzroy, the vampire responsible for my death, remains glaringly absent from this twisted tableau.

Rage riots through me. I swallow as it burns through my veins, my teeth gritted in my skull. Everything around me sharpens. Becomes clearer, like a point of light in a haze of darkness.

It is not an unwelcome feeling. I want to lose myself to it. To abandon all sense of logic, caring about nothing but destruction. There is purity in such a sentiment. Reason in its simplicity.

I roll back my shoulders and take in an unnecessary breath. When I gaze about the space once more, my sight fixes on my uncle, his golden eyes shining through the shadows like those of a panther.

Nicodemus studies me, his face hewn from marble. A single devilish whorl of black hair grazes his forehead. "Sébastien," he says. "Do you know who I am?" He analyzes me as he would one of the many winged specimens in his collection. Like a butterfly with iridescent stripes, a long metal pin stabbed through its abdomen.

Again the rage spikes in my chest. "Were you truly concerned I would not remember you, Monsieur le Comte?" I expect my voice to sound gruff from disuse, but the dark magic rounds its tones, making a rich melody of it.

No trace of relief flashes through Nicodemus' features, despite the proof that my mind survived the change. "It was a distinct possibility. You were dangerously close to death when I began turning you." He pauses. "And it is always a gamble to mix mortal blood with that of an immortal ancestor, as you well know."

I do. I blink back the memory of my mother, who was consumed by madness. Poisoned by grief. Obsessed with the desire to be unmade and return to her mortal form. I say nothing in response. Those remembrances serve no purpose now, except to goad my anger.

"How do you feel?" Nicodemus takes a step forward. Everything about him—from his slicked hair to his shining shoes—epitomizes the look of a gentleman. The kind of gentleman I aspired to be from boyhood. But there is an odd hesitancy in his question.

My uncle is not one to waver.

It puzzles me. Unwilling to show him any sign of my own confusion, I say the first thing that comes to mind. "I feel powerful."

I expect my brothers and sisters to laugh at the triteness of my reply.

"Are you not . . . angry?" Odette's voice is gentle. "I know this is not what you—"

"No," I lie without even considering it. "I am not angry."

More silence.

Madeleine blurs toward me, then stops short as if catching herself, her palms held in a placating manner. "Do you have any questions? Anything you need? Il y a des moments où—"

"I believe I understand the general gist of things, Madeleine."

I suppress another wave of wrath, bitter amusement quick to take its place. "Drink blood and live forever." I grin at my immortal family, then straighten my stained cuffs.

"Stop it," Jae says, the two syllables cracking through the darkness like warning shots.

Madeleine glares at Jae, attempting to silence him with nothing but a glance.

He is unmoved. Unapologetic. "Be angry," he grits out. "Be sad. Be anything but this."

I quirk a brow at him.

"Afraid," Jae clarifies. "You are so afraid, I could cut your fear with a knife. Slice it to ribbons." With his chin, he gestures toward Odette. "She can wear them in her hair."

I swallow, struggling to hold fast to my smile. Weighing whether or not to attack Jae.

He is quick to respond to my unspoken challenge. Like a ghoul, Jae glides forward, his greatcoat swirling around him. He draws two blades from hidden sheaths in his jacket. Twirls them once, daring me to answer his silent threat.

I stand straight, my hands curling into fists, the fire purifying me from the inside.

He'll win. Of that there is no doubt. But I won't tuck tail and run. I'll come at him until he's forced to cut me down. Maybe if he cuts me deep enough, I will find what remains of my humanity. Or maybe I will simply succumb to another one of my uncle's lessons: destroy or be destroyed.

Afraid? Jae thinks I'm afraid? Let him see what fear truly is.

Just before I make good on these promises, my uncle claps

his hands like a judge with a gavel, demanding order. It almost makes me laugh, for Le Comte de Saint Germain is anything but the proper gentleman he wishes the mortal world to see.

Nicodemus is renowned in all circles of the Otherworld, as much for his wealth and influence as for his brutality. He was there at the beginning, when vampires and werewolves resided in castles carved from ice, deep in a forest of perpetual night. When blood drinkers and shapeshifters lived among their fey brethren, like the gods atop Mount Olympus, toying with humans for nothing but sport. He cavorted with the nymphs, the goblins, the ogres, the phoukas, and the sprites far apart from the mortal world, in a place of endless winter known as the Sylvan Wyld. Nicodemus still remembers a time when they did not hide their elven nature, but instead basked in it. Until— in their quest for power—the vampires allied with the werewolves and made a great error in judgment: they attempted to trade their most precious commodity with humans.

Their immortality.

Nicodemus is one of the few remaining vampires to witness the events of the Banishment, the time in which vampires and werewolves were exiled from the Wyld's Winter Court for these transgressions. Forced to cede their holdings to the Summer Court of the Sylvan Vale.

"Jae," Nicodemus says, his tone weary, "that's enough."

Jae restores his blades with two quick flicks of his wrists. It rankles me how quickly he obeys, his affect cool, as if he were about to remark on the weather. My uncle looks to me, expecting me to behave in kind.

"Bastien," he says. "You will do as your maker commands, in this and in all things." Though his tone brooks no reproach, I sense another test. Another round in the proverbial ring.

I was small as a child. More comfortable around books and music than I was around people. In an attempt to teach me to stand tall in a crowded room, my uncle paid for me to train with New Orleans' best pugilist. Despite my protests, I learned to box. To feint. To dodge. To take hits and dole them out in equal measure.

I have not entered a ring in years, but my uncle has traded figurative jabs with me since I was a boy. If I obey without hesitation, I am a sheep, like Jae. A creature meant only to serve. If I resist, I am a child throwing a tantrum. A wriggling worm who knows nothing of respect.

The terms of this battle change like the seasons, without warning.

It is an impossible fight. One I usually lose.

Perhaps it is because only moments ago Jae accused me of being afraid. Perhaps it is because I don't give a damn about the consequences. Perhaps I only wish to trade more jabs, until my opponent cries mea culpa, his blood staining my fists.

I laugh, the sound bounding into the coffered ceiling.

Something akin to approval glints in Nicodemus' gaze. My uncle disdains any hint of weakness. At least I have not failed in that respect. My brothers and sisters exchange glances. Raise eyebrows. Bite back their retorts.

Before the strains of my laughter die down, I attack.

BASTIEN

───────≈───────

Bedlam erupts the instant my fist cracks against the side of Jae's jaw.

Our resident assassin is so stunned that it takes him a second to react. But only a second. He dodges before I manage to land my right hook. When Boone and Madeleine attempt to intervene, Nicodemus stays them in their tracks.

The next breath, Jae winds away from me, grabbing the back of my bloodstained frock coat. He yanks it over my head, attempting to disorient me. With a twist, I relinquish the garment and aim a series of punches at his midsection. There is no time for me to marvel at the quickness of my reflexes. At the inhuman strength in every strike. Even before I make contact, Jae flips through the air—thumbing his nose at gravity—then veers toward me until we crash onto the plush Persian carpet. I blink and his arm is around my neck, his knee pressed into my spine.

It is over in less than five seconds. I consider grappling. Instead I laugh again like a madman.

The next moment, Toussaint erupts from the darkness, his fangs shining, his aim precise.

Hortense blurs in the snake's path, positioning herself in

front of Jae, her eyes wide with warning. "Non," she commands. "Tu ne vas *pas* lui faire mal."

Toussaint coils back with a resentful hiss.

I always suspected that damned serpent loved Hortense more than he loved me.

My uncle steps forward, his expression unreadable, his eyes glittering. The scene before me is almost comical. My clothes are covered in dried blood, the remnants of my white masquerade costume a mockery of everything that followed. My face is pressed into a silk carpet that cost more than most men earn in a year of honest work. A vampire holds me in a vise. A giant snake thinks to avenge my honor.

Last night, I loved and lived. Tonight, I dance in a ring with Death.

My emotions roll through me once more, punishing in their severity. Near impossible to control. Like tongues of fire licking at pools of kerosene.

"Get off me," I demand in a low voice, struggling to maintain my composure. Again Jae waits for my uncle's permission, ever the sheep in need of a shepherd.

The instant Jae eases his grip on me, I elbow him away, refusing Odette's assistance as I rise to my feet. I take a deep breath, hating the force of habit. How the air filling my lungs no longer calms me. "What did Celine give you in exchange for turning me?" I ask my uncle.

He says nothing.

My hands flex with rage, unsettling in its potency. "I already know what you did. I want to hear you say it. What price did you exact from the girl I loved in life?" My words stab through the darkness with vicious precision, causing both Odette and Arjun to wince.

"Good," Nicodemus says. "You are angry. Let the anger console you. I hope it one day grants you purpose."

Madeleine frowns as if she wishes to say something. Jae glances her way and shakes his head. They're all sheep. Every last one of them.

"But you will need to hone it first," Nicodemus continues. "At present, it is the anger of a spoiled boy, not of a man." His smile is derisive. "Are you angry you were not permitted to die on your own terms, Sébastien?" He scoffs. "Who among us is granted such a bounty? It was Celine Rousseau's choice to make a deal with me. Her sacrifice granted you the power to overcome death. She deserves your gratitude, just as I deserve your respect."

Bitter laughter rushes past my lips. "Don't think to evade my question, Monsieur le Comte." I move toward him in a fluid motion, my face a hairsbreadth from his. *"What did Celine give you?"*

"A chance for you to learn from your mistakes and begin anew. She offered her memories of your time together in exchange for a fresh start for you both." Nicodemus' eyes narrow. "Honor her choice. It is the least of what she deserves."

I want to taunt him for pretending to care about Celine. To lambast him for forcing a decision upon her, under duress. My uncle does not bargain with anyone unless he is certain he has the upper hand. But I see no point in baiting him. I know what

Nicodemus wanted. It is the same thing he wants from any mortal unfortunate enough to form an attachment to any of us: complete surrender. The veins along my forearms flex, my fingers resembling claws. I need to destroy something before these truths destroy me.

"Forget and be forgotten," I manage to say.

My uncle nods.

Another tense moment passes in silence. Something rustles in the shadows on the other side of the room. It is likely Toussaint, but my neck stretches in its direction anyway. Madeleine's eyes become slits. Boone pushes away from the wall, a feral gleam in his gaze.

Each of us is itching for a fight. Itching to tear something apart with our bare hands, like the killers we are.

"Well, this has been un rendez-vous charmant," Odette says, drawing out the French with her particular flourish. "But if there are no objections, I'd like to shed a bit of light on all this gloom." With that, she strikes a match and begins touching the flame to all the candles throughout the chamber, the scent of sulfur infusing the air. "I must say I'm unsurprised that your first worry is for Celine, mon petit frère," she says to me. "But I went in secret to check on her earlier today. She was surrounded by friends and in the care of the best doctors in the city, who have assured me she will make a full recovery," she babbles as she works. "Rest assured she is safe. One day soon she will undoubtedly be . . . happy . . . again." She catches herself, her slender brows gathering at the bridge of her pert nose. "Or at least—she will find a measure of mortal contentment." The flames grow long and lean, bathing the chamber in a warm glow.

Boone's laughter is rich as he steps into a pool of spreading candlelight. "Amen to that. Truly it's all for the best, my brother. I know the wound has yet to scar, but you know as well as any that Celine could never have made a place for herself in our world. Lord knows what might have happened to her."

"Something did happen," Jae says in a quiet rasp. "Nigel almost killed them both."

"As a point of fact, he *did* kill me." My face hardens, my grief far too close for proper reflection. I stop myself from taking another unnecessary breath, again frustrated by my inability to control the tempest in my mind. I know why I keep turning to this tactic, which often gave me solace as a mortal.

Not long after I lost my sister and my parents, Madeleine told me that whenever I was on the cusp of losing control, I should close my eyes. Breathe in through my nose. Exhale twice as slowly through my mouth.

Though I know it is an exercise in futility, I turn to this approach once more. This final gasp of my humanity. I close my eyes. Focus as I breathe.

A slew of scents floods my nostrils. The citrus wax used to polish the furniture; the rose water in Odette's perfume; the expensive myrrh oil Hortense smooths through her long hair; the sharp brass of Nicodemus' walking stick; even the musty smell of the dust collecting above the velvet drapery. But one aroma rises to the forefront, winding through my mind, ensnaring all my senses, beckoning me forward in a trance.

Something warm and salty and . . . *delicious.*

Before I can think, I blur toward the windows facing the street and tear back the heavy indigo curtains, without a thought for safety.

Thankfully it is dusk, the last rays of sunlight waning in the distance. On the pavers across the street, a boy of no more than five is sprawled across the stones after tripping on his overlarge shoes. He looks to his mother, then proceeds to wail as if in the throes of death. Bright crimson drips from his scraped knee, trickling toward the grey stones at his feet.

The smell of it bewitches me. Sears all else from my mind. I am Moses in the desert. Jonah in the whale. It is not redemption I seek. Lost souls do not seek redemption.

My mouth waters. Otherworldly energy flows beneath my skin. Something inside me begins to take shape. A monster I cannot contain. Incongruously it is like fighting for breath. Like clawing to the surface of the sea, every second all the more precious. My teeth lengthen in my mouth, slicing through my lower lip. My jaw and fingers harden to bronze. If I had a pulse at all, it would be hammering in my chest like a Gatling gun.

I press a palm to the glass of the mullioned window. It begins to crack under the force of my touch, splintering from my fingertips like a spiderweb.

Boone flashes to my side and takes hold of my arm. I snarl at him like an untamed beast. With a thin smile, Boone digs his hand tightly into my biceps, to root me to the earth. "Brother," he says in a soothing tone. "You have to control the hunger before it consumes you."

I tear my arm from Boone's grasp with a force that takes him by surprise. He shifts half a step back before grim determination settles onto his face. Again he reaches for me, but I snare my brother by the throat and slam him into the wall beside the window, causing a gilt-framed portrait to crash to the floor.

Dark blood falls from the back of Boone's head, two drops staining his pristine collar before the wound heals, the sound like the rending of paper. Though he appears nonchalant, I cannot miss the shock that flares across his face, there and gone in the blink of an eye.

Even I am taken off guard. Injuring an immortal like Boone is no mean feat. I am . . . strong. Stronger than I first realized. My anger has become a creature too large for me to contain. I should let him go. Apologize.

Instead I tighten my grip, the rage unfurling over my body like a second skin.

Apologies are for sheep. Let them all see what I've become. Let them fear *me*.

Something stirs at my back.

"No," Madeleine demands. "Stay where you are, Arjun. A blow like that could kill you."

"I can help," Arjun replies carefully. "At the very least I can buy us some time."

"You can try," I whisper without glancing toward the half fey.

It's foolish for me to bait an ethereal. Arjun's touch could immobilize me. Leave me at my siblings' mercy. But I am more focused on what will follow, should he bother to make the attempt.

They cannot corral me forever.

"I know you think yourself unafraid," Arjun says. "That we should all fear you instead."

I say nothing, though a twinge knifes through me.

"My mortal father used to say that anger and fear are two sides of the same coin," Arjun continues. "They both make us behave outside our nature."

"Or perhaps they simply distill us down to our essence. Maybe this *is* my nature now." I glower at Boone, who raises his arms like Leonardo's Vitruvian Man.

"I don't believe that." Boone's voice is hoarse, but gentle. "Not for one minute."

Madeleine blurs closer, pausing to my left. "Sébastien." Her tone is laced in warning. Her teeth begin to lengthen, commanding me without words to stand down. "Don't do this, mon enfant."

Mon enfant. My child. Madeleine is the closest thing to a mother I have known since my own mother perished ten years ago. Nevertheless I ignore her, the bloodlust raging through my veins. The desire to kill and consume of utmost importance.

Tulle rustles to Madeleine's right. "Écoute-moi, mon petit diable," her sister, Hortense, commands in the singsong of a medium conducting a séance. "Nous ne sommes pas vos ennemis."

"Listen to her, brother," Boone says, his hands inching toward his temples. "Our enemies are real. If we waste time squabbling among ourselves, there'll be nothing left for the true fight to come."

The rational part of me knows Boone is right. But I respond by tightening my grasp until he can no longer speak. The plaster around his head starts to powder, causing a shower of white dust to descend on his cherubic curls.

Another flicker of movement. "Let him go," Jae demands, taking hold of my right shoulder. Each of his words is the point of a dagger at my back. *"Now."*

"Do you still think me afraid?" I level a cool gaze at the assassin. One meant to convey nothing but contempt.

His scowl deepens.

It is all a lie. Everything I've done or said to this point is for show.

I *am* afraid. Deathly afraid. From the moment I first understood what had happened to me. But fear cannot be all I know. *I will not let it be all I know.*

Jae remains silent. My fear threatens to eclipse all else. I stoke my anger until it burns everything else away. The color leaches from Boone's skin, the ink in his eyes swirling, spreading until the whites are completely black. His fingers turn into fists.

I know he is preparing to fight back. I should release him before the situation worsens. But the wrath continues flowing down my arms, surging through my stomach, burrowing into my bones. It makes me feel powerful. As if I am in control. I do not want to lose this feeling. I cannot be afraid. I cannot be weak.

What kind of beast surrenders to its basest nature?

The kind with nothing to fear.

So be it.

I squeeze tighter, feeling the bones in Boone's throat begin to splinter in my grasp.

I don't see Madeleine move until she has shattered my wrist with a single swipe of her arm. I roar and fly backward, slamming into the far wall. My body lands in a position of defense, crouched like a panther. Toussaint coils at my feet, his fangs bared, daring any of my siblings to tread closer.

I clutch my injured hand, feeling the crushed bones knit back together like torch fire through tinder. The sensation should feel marvelous, for it is further proof of my indestructibility; instead it only emphasizes my monstrousness. The utter loss of my humanity.

All the while, no one moves. Madeleine stands guard before a fallen Boone, who grips his throat and coughs, blood spewing from his lips. His eyes flash as Madeleine bares her fangs at me and hisses through her teeth.

Beside her, Arjun waits with his hands in his pockets, his monocle swaying from its gold chain. Hortense hovers behind Madeleine, her lips forming the beginnings of a smirk. Jae stares at me, his expression like that of a disapproving father. Odette looks . . . sad.

"It is as I suspected," Nicodemus says. A casual observer might believe he is troubled by this turn of events, but I know my uncle far too well. He did nothing to stop me from injuring Boone, nor did he attempt to intervene when the rest of his progeny moved against me in force. There is a gleam in his amber eyes. One of supreme pleasure.

Nicodemus wanted to see what might happen. I suspect he is

thrilled to witness how strong I am. How invincible his immortal blood has made me.

With Nicodemus Saint Germain, everything is a test.

I ignore the world around me, squeezing my eyes closed.

In through the nose. Out through the mouth.

The smell of the blood beyond the window taunts me again. Surrounded as I am by other vampires—my brothers and sisters—I know I cannot break free and sate my hunger. Though I have attacked one of their own, still they take on the mantle of responsibility. Still they fight to save me from myself.

Even though I almost crushed Boone's throat in my fist a moment ago.

I look around the room. I search within me for something more. I find nothing. It is not gratitude I feel for my immortal brethren. Only despair.

Choking through a haze of bloodlust, I recoil. My chest heaving, I settle my sights on my uncle, who has not moved from his position beside the burl-wood table. Who continues to watch the scene unfold with a disconcerting gleam.

"Tonight, you will go with Jae and Boone to hunt," Nicodemus says as if he were prescribing a tincture for a common cold. "They will teach you how to mark your victims. Then they will show you how to dispose of all traces, so that you do not put any of us at risk with reckless behavior."

"No," I reply. "I am not going anywhere with any of you."

"If you refuse to learn our ways, then you will be forbidden from leaving this place," Nicodemus counters without missing a beat. "I cannot risk you causing a scene."

Disgust grips me for a moment. My uncle is more concerned with me drawing attention to our coven than he is about the plight of the humans in my vicinity. I could kill every last one of them and he would not care, provided I cleaned up after myself.

I make my decision without even considering it. "Then I will remain confined here."

At least at Jacques'—ensconced in the tri-storied building my uncle owns on Rue Royale—I will not be a threat to any of the hapless mortals unfortunate enough to wander too close. Were I left to roam the streets of the Crescent City, that boy and his mother and every person nearby would be killed before I wasted a single breath reflecting upon the consequences.

Nicodemus' cheeks hollow. He arches a brow. "And what will you do for food?"

I almost blanch. "Bring me what I require to survive. Nothing more." If I sound imperious enough, perhaps he will not argue.

Anger clouds his expression. "That is not the way of it, Sébastien."

"It is now."

"The bloodsacs below should not—"

"Never call them that again in my presence," I interrupt, incensed by the slur. One he never before used in my presence.

His eyes narrow further. "And what will you do then? You are only beginning to understand what you are. Will you crush them in your arms? Listen to them scream and beg for mercy? Or will you learn our ways and subdue their emotions, never forgetting to stay to the shadows?"

The revulsion in me grows. Already I am being taught to see

mortals as lesser beings. Only last night, I wandered among them, a young man with the promise of a future filled with light. A boy with a soul. Now I am demon of the shadows, subsisting off stolen blood.

I don't want to be reminded of the price paid for my immortality. The price Celine paid. The price I paid. "Keep them away," I say. "If they don't know what I've become, I want them nowhere near me."

Nicodemus takes a step closer. There is danger in the way he grips the roaring lion carved into the brass handle of his walking stick. He thinks me weak.

Nevertheless I refuse to cow beneath his scrutiny.

"I can bring him blood for the time being," Odette interjects. "It is no trouble to me. First thing tomorrow, I'll put in an order for a new case of the Green Fairy's finest."

I glance her way, puzzled.

"A capful of absinthe prevents the blood from becoming too thick to drink," she explains. "When blood grows cold or is left standing too long, it congeals." She speaks in soothing tones.

Of course. A detail I never had occasion to consider. Nicodemus looks to Madeleine.

She nods in turn.

"Very well," Nicodemus says. "But I will not permit this accommodation for long. You *will* learn our ways, no matter how much you may disdain them." He points the end of his walking stick at my chest. "And you *will* obey your maker without question, as your brothers and sisters do, or you will be banished from the city." With that, he exits the room in a swirl of darkness.

After a time in stilted silence, Odette sighs. Then a bright smile cuts across her face. "Charades, anyone?"

Jae grunts. "You are . . . tiresome."

"And you are an incomparable wordsmith, Jaehyuk-*ah*." Odette simpers.

"Don't bait him," Madeleine commands before their bickering can continue, her expression weary. "We've had enough of that for one evening."

Odette crosses her arms, her lips pursing. "Le chat grincheux started it."

"I was hoping to appeal to your better nature," Jae says.

"Silly boy," Odette snaps back. "You know I don't have one."

"Enough!" Madeleine says. She looks to me. "Sit, Bastien. You are due for a lecture, tout de suite."

Hortense yawns. She throws herself on the closest chaise, pausing to cross her bare ankles on the edge of a carved tea table. "Ça sera un grand ennui," she sings to no one.

"I am in no mood for your lecture," I say.

"You damn near took Boone's head off, old chap." Arjun's British accent rounds out his words. "Learn from today's mistakes so you won't make them again tomorrow."

"I have no intention of making mistakes today, tomorrow, or any day thereafter," I retort, biting back the taste of my own blood. The hunger that thrashes in its wake. "I suppose I need only to accept"—I stare at my hands, my fingers still curled like bronze talons—"this fate. My new future. No matter how much I might wish it were not the case."

"Even if that meant you had died the true death?" Odette's voice is small.

I do not hesitate to respond. "Yes."

For a time, none of them says a word.

Then Jae moves forward. "It does no good to dwell on things we cannot change." The muscles in his jaw work. "And you should learn the ways of a vampire sooner rather than later. The rules are clear, Sébastien. If you cannot rein in your appetites—if you draw undue attention to us with indiscriminate violence—then you will be banished from New Orleans. Our peace is paramount."

Boone feigns a cough, as if to clear his throat. "Can't have a repeat of what happened in Dubrovnik or Wallachia hundreds of years ago, when so many of our kind were lost to superstitious mayhem. Why, I even recall when . . ."

I let his words fade into a drone as I stare at the cracked window across the room and the damaged plaster beside it, noting how the hem of the blue velvet curtain continues to sway like a pendulum. I let it lull me into a trance. Out of habit, I shift my fingertips to the side of my neck to check my pulse, an action that always served to remind me of my humanity.

The absence of a heartbeat rocks through me like a blow to the chest. I turn in place and retreat into the recesses of the chamber. In my periphery, the edges of a gilt-framed mirror glisten in the glow of the candlelight. I stride toward the silvered glass like a mortal, one foot in front of the other, my fingers flexing at my sides.

"Don't, mon cher," Odette warns, trailing in my shadow. "Not today. Give it some time. Un moment de grâce." She smiles at our shared reflections, a suspicious shimmer in her eyes. "We could all stand to be a bit more forgiving of ourselves, n'est-ce pas?"

I disregard her. Something about her sisterly affection grates my nerves like it never has before. I take in my appearance, refusing to turn from the mirror, no matter how disturbing its truth. My canines shine like ivory daggers; my eyes burn lambent, suffused with an otherworldly light. Thin rivulets of blood trickle from my lower lip where my fangs pierced through my brown skin.

I look like a monster from Hell. A creature from a Grimm fairy tale, come to life.

I . . . *hate* what I have become. Despise it as I have never despised anything before. I want to shed this new reality like a snakeskin. To leave it in the dust so that I might stroll in the sunlight and breathe in the air with the lungs of a mortal man. I want to love and hope and die with all the limitations that make such a life worth living.

What I wouldn't give for a chance to be a mortal boy again, standing before the girl I love, hoping she will take my hand and walk with me toward an unknown future.

Bitterness seeps through to the marrow of my bones. I let the bloodlust fill me again, watch my eyes swirl to obsidian, my ears lengthen into points, and my fangs unfurl like claws, cutting through my flesh once more, until the wet crimson trails down my neck to stain my collar.

"Bastien," Madeleine commands over my shoulder, her expression like stone. "Too many newborn vampires lose themselves to the hunger, drowning their sorrows in blood, destroying all sense of who they were in life," she says. "Rarely do they survive a decade before walking into the sun or being obliterated by their elders. Turn away from this path of destruction, no matter how tempting it might be." She leans closer to the mirror, watching me all the while. "The best among us never forsake their humanity."

"The higher hatred burns, the more it destroys," Arjun says. "My father is proof of that."

"Feel your anger, but do not succumb to it," Madeleine continues, "for it will be your end."

"And what would you have me embrace in its stead?" I ask my reflection, my words a coarse whisper.

Odette gestures to the handful of immortals gathered before me. "We would have you embrace love."

"Love?" I say, gripping the edges of the gilt mirror in both my hands, my eyes blacker than soot.

Odette nods.

"This is not a love story." My fingers fall from the mirror, leaving dents in the gold filigree. I want nothing more than to rage about like a demon unleashed. To defy the moon and the stars and all the torments of an infinite sky.

But most of all I want to forget everything I've ever loved. Each of the immortals standing guard around me. My cursed uncle for bringing this blight upon our family. Nigel, for betraying us and leaving me to drown in a pool of my own blood.

But mostly I curse *her*. I want to forget her face. Her name. Her wit. Her laughter. How she made me hope and want and wish and feel. As far as I am concerned, Celine Rousseau died that night in Saint Louis Cathedral. Just like I did.

A true hero would find a way back to her. Would seek a path of redemption for his lost soul. A chance to stand once more in the light.

There is no such path. And I am no one's hero. So I choose the way of destruction.

ÉMILIE

———❧———

They were called Romeo spikes.

Beneath the light of the mother moon, they looked like iron crowns mounted close to the top of the narrow columns supporting the balcony. Pieces of twisted black metal—their barbs pointed heavenward—meant to deter unwanted intruders.

Émilie smiled to herself.

In truth, they weren't meant for just any kind of unwanted intruder. Specifically, they'd been designed for Romeos on a mission to court their fair Juliets. Just imagine . . . a hot-blooded young man looking to scale the balcony, eager to win his young lady's affections. Those spikes would catch him by the ballocks, literally. A gruesome, altogether fitting punishment for a city with a gruesome, haunted past.

In other words, Émilie found them utterly delightful.

She waited until the sounds of the last passersby faded in the distance. Until all that remained was the rustling of branches and the chirruping of cicadas. The symphony of an early March evening.

These spikes would not deter her. She was no foolish Romeo,

and Juliet was a weed among the roses, especially when compared to some. Émilie gripped the slender column of sun-warmed metal and began her climb. Once she reached the first balcony, she crouched in the shadows behind the railing, the leaves of dripping ferns tickling the back of her neck and snagging her dark brown curls. Inside the home behind her, the scent of servants bustling about in preparation for tonight's repast, the tang of their sweat both salty and sweet, wafted out toward her.

Taking care to make less noise than a ghost, Émilie climbed the next set of narrow iron columns toward the third floor of the structure. Again she waited in the shadows until she was certain she remained beyond notice. Then she stood and stared at the building across the way, studying it intently.

Two weeks had passed since the incident in Saint Louis Cathedral. According to reports, her younger brother, Sébastien—the only living heir to the Saint Germain line—had been grievously injured in the skirmish, his throat all but torn from his body. A week ago, gossip in the Quarter hinted that the monsignor had come and gone after administering last rites, though preparations for a street procession typical of a New Orleans funeral had yet to be made.

The entire situation made Émilie uneasy, a feeling she abhorred. She wanted her questions answered, so that she might proceed to the next phase of the plan. Which was why she'd taken to standing along the deserted balcony, watching Jacques' from across the way. Hunting for any signs of her brother. Any possibility he might have survived his injuries.

After an hour passed, Émilie's eyes tightened. Her arms

crossed over her slender chest. It would have been impossible for Bastien to survive a near beheading by a vampire as strong as Nigel. No mere mortal could weather such a storm. Perhaps it would have been more poetic for Bastien to perish in a fire, but that was a fate Émilie did not wish on her worst enemy. Fire did not kill as one would expect. It was a slow death of smoke and choked screams.

Her fingers grazed the puckered skin along the side of her neck. Even the dark magic of being made into a she-wolf could not heal this kind of wound. Her resolve hardened.

Some injuries were not to the skin but to the soul.

No. Her brother could not have survived the attack she'd orchestrated with Nigel Fitzroy. And Nicodemus would rather die the final death than turn Sébastien into a vampire. The risk of her brother going mad was simply too great, especially given what had happened to both their parents. Not to mention the Fallen's treaty with the Brotherhood. If her uncle brought another vampire into the city without first asking for Luca's permission, there would be war.

Nicodemus could not risk war. That was a lesson he'd learned the last time. One that made him weak. Predictable. Full of fear. A shame her uncle still had yet to learn life's greatest lesson: a creature without fear is a creature capable of anything and everything.

Movement caught Émilie's eye from the uppermost floor of the building across the street. The blue velvet curtains drew back, revealing a figure she recognized in passing.

Odette Valmont.

Anger gripped at Émilie's insides like an icy vise. She took in a draft of jasmine-scented air, willing herself calm. What a precious gift it would have been to count among her confidants a vampire as loyal as Odette. How much it would have assuaged Émilie's mortal fears, to have such a formidable immortal nearby to protect her in life.

Perhaps if she'd had a guardian like Odette Valmont, none of this would have happened. She wouldn't have risked herself to save her little brother from a fire. She wouldn't have been trapped in his stead. She wouldn't have had to forswear the family of her birth for the one she'd chosen in death.

Sébastien didn't deserve such devotion. He'd done nothing to merit it, save being born beneath a lucky star.

For nigh on a decade, Émilie's little brother had taken for granted Odette's protection and loyalty. The service of so many vampires at his beck and call. Bastien had everything Émilie had ever wanted for herself: loyalty; the best education money could provide; a future filled with promise. A chance to rule his uncle's kingdom, though he claimed never to have desired it.

Fitting. For he certainly didn't deserve it.

The fool had even gotten himself expelled from West Point, all for the sake of his ego.

Émilie would never have squandered such opportunities. She could have led them all, had she been granted the chance. But such a position was never meant for her. It was only ever intended for the favored son. Everything was for Bastien. In the end, her very life had been given in exchange for his.

For more than ten years, Émilie had kept her distance.

Watched and waited to see what her brother would make of himself. As she traveled the world, she'd read the reports Luca passed along to her, and they stoked her anger. Hardened her bitterness.

Sébastien was destined to become everything Émilie despised in their uncle. A man concerned first and foremost with money and influence, all the while taking for granted his family and the myriad opportunities afforded to him.

Émilie's brow furrowed while watching Odette's lovely silhouette move about the opulent chamber. The sable-haired girl turned toward the window, her expression sad. Troubled.

A smile turned up the corners of Émilie's lips.

She would be happy to comfort the beautiful leech. Mollify her concerns. Smooth any ruffled feathers. Just before tearing out her swanlike throat.

A moment later, the resident assassin of La Cour des Lions moved into Émilie's sight line, just over Odette's shoulder.

Émilie's amusement faded. Shin Jaehyuk worried her. The research Luca's contact in Crete had done in the bowels of the Brotherhood's Greek archives indicated that the assassin from the Far East posed a significant threat. He was skilled in all types of blades, yet knew how to kill in countless ways, using nothing but his two hands. Already three different factions of wolves had tried to dispatch Jae, only to have their packs wiped out in return, the masked assassin vanishing without a trace. If Jae were to learn of Émilie's involvement in Bastien's death—and that the Brotherhood provided her refuge—no treaty would spare them from his wrath.

Émilie continued watching Odette and Jae, the jealousy a yawning pit in her stomach.

She forced her shoulders back. Stretched her neck from side to side.

Jealousy was a petty emotion. Powerful people did not succumb to it.

Instead they leveled the field.

She scanned the three floors of the structure, as she had for the last week. Still no sign of Bastien. No trace of a reckless newborn anywhere in the vicinity of Jacques'. No bodies in need of disposal in the dead of night. No cadre of immortal creatures waiting in the wings, ready to teach Bastien their soulless, blood-drinking ways.

If her brother had indeed been turned, he would be confined to the darkness. The evening following the events in the cathedral two weeks ago, Émilie had posted werewolves along the streets near Valeria Henri's parfumerie, the only place in all of Louisiana where Bastien could obtain a fétiche, a talisman fashioned to protect him from the light of the sun.

At no time did her brother venture anywhere near the shop.

Everything told Émilie that her plan had been met with success. Her uncle no longer had an heir upon whom to bestow his legacy. He'd been undone by the hand of the niece he'd dismissed at his own peril.

Then why had Nicodemus failed to inter Sébastien's bones in the family crypt? And why did Émilie still feel so uneasy?

If Luca knew what she had done, he would tell her she had nothing to fear. Her erstwhile lover would say that her uncle knew better than to violate their treaty. But Émilie could not tell him. Not yet. He might agree that it was past time for her to wreak her revenge, but he would disagree with her methods. And he would be angry at her for provoking the Fallen after a decade of peace, putting the Brotherhood at risk.

In any case, what was done was done. Though Nicodemus possessed many faults, she'd never known him to defy his own twisted principles. Indeed he'd watched her burn with his own eyes, not once lifting a hand to save her. He'd stood silent the night her father had been executed. Though a single tear had slid down his cheek when Émilie's mother, Philomène, succumbed to the sun, he'd not stopped her from surrendering to the final death.

Émilie wanted to believe that Nicodemus had not turned Sébastien into a vampire.

But exceptions had been made for her brother before.

And until Émilie could stand before Bastien's grave beneath the hot New Orleans sun—until she knew he was moldering within the stone mausoleum, his body left to burn in the heat to come—this feeling of unease would not leave her.

So she would return again tomorrow night. And the night after.

Until the last of her questions was answered.

ODETTE

―――≈―――

T he scene before Odette was a cheerful one.

Three young women were framed in a shop window, the glow of the late-afternoon sun gilding everything it touched. Muffled laughter filled the air, followed by the unwrapping of parcels, brown paper flung to all corners of the sparsely decorated space. Occasionally a corgi puppy with a high-pitched bark would snag a bit of loose string or discarded wrapping, only to fling it into the air with a joyous yip.

The petite blond girl with the heart-shaped face and the bright blue eyes—one Philippa Montrose, by name—had assumed the position of authority, hands perched on her hips and a determined set to her brow, while the unfamiliar girl with the copper skin and rich brunette hair hummed to herself as she moved efficiently behind the makeshift counter, taking stock of unboxed ribbons and skeins of colorful fabric. Though both young women stayed busy, they managed to keep watchful eyes on the pale figure seated in the corner, a tired smile on her bruised face.

Odette sighed to herself as she watched the tableau unfold from beneath the shadow of an awning across the street.

Celine had much improved in the week since Odette came in secret to check on her. But the lovely young woman had lost even more weight, her curves shrinking further into nothingness. She still moved with care, wincing every so often, the wound on the side of her neck held together by neat stitches, her right arm bound in a sling.

"It's only been two weeks," a male voice said from behind Odette's shoulder. "Give it some time." Shin Jaehyuk came to stand beside her. "Despite appearances, she *is* healing. Humans are more resilient than we like to believe."

"Was it you who asked after Celine at the hospital last week?" she murmured.

He said nothing.

Odette smirked at him. "I was told an unnamed gentleman made inquiries regarding Mademoiselle Rousseau's health." Though amusement tinged her voice, her sable eyes were kind. "I would not have expected such a display of concern for a mere mortal, Jaehyuk-*ah*."

"She means a great deal to Bastien." The knuckles on Jae's left hand turned white. "And Nigel never should have been able to do what he did, to either of them."

Odette swallowed, guilt gnawing at her insides. "It wasn't your fault."

"Nonetheless." He inhaled. "Is she sleeping better?"

"She still has nightmares. The orderly at the hospital told me she woke up screaming at least every other night before she was discharged three days ago."

Jae frowned. "Nicodemus personally glamoured her. The girl should not be haunted by memories of her ordeal."

"I've heard of men on the battlefield who lost a leg or an arm and still felt the ghost of their limb haunting them after the fact." Odette stared as Celine stood to help Pippa with an unwieldy parcel, only to be soundly criticized by her friend for daring to do so much as lift a finger. "Perhaps she lost too much," she finished.

They both turned as a young boy darted between them, rustling Odette's organdy skirts and the hem of Jae's greatcoat as he passed. A peal of silvery laughter fell from the boy's lips, his friends chasing after his heels. Across the way, the humming brunette inside the shop peered outside to witness the commotion.

"We should go before anyone takes note of our interest," Jae murmured.

"One minute more."

His expression softened. "Of course. However long you wish."

Odette arched a brow. "Careful, mon chat grincheux. One of these days, I might accuse you of sentimentality."

"It isn't for her benefit that I wait."

"Is that so?" she teased.

He stared down at the scars on the backs of his hands. "Do you remember the night I went to find Mo Gwai?"

Odette nodded, her expression somber.

"You said you would scour the earth with me. Burn the warlock to dust for what he did," Jae continued. "Because I was your brother."

Odette nodded again, a lump gathering in her throat.

"Celine Rousseau mattered to you." He paused. "You are my sister, Odette Valmont. Until the end of time."

Without a word, Odette reached across the space between them and took his hand. He flinched, but threaded his scarred fingers through hers. A gesture so uncharacteristic of Shin Jaehyuk that it touched Odette in the place her heart used to beat, the magic of the dark gift moving the blood through her chest.

"Do you ever wish you could take something back?" she asked as they resumed watching the three young women in their quest to set up shop. "Something you regretted."

"An immortal life is too long to dwell in regret."

"I welcomed Celine into our world." Odette sighed. "Perhaps if I had not, none of this would have happened."

"Perhaps. But it was the girl's choice to relinquish her memories."

"Was it?" she asked quietly. "Bastien said he would have preferred the true death."

"He is yet a boy. A man does not hide from his fears. He faces them."

"I wish I could make him a boy again."

"You wish to unmake him, then." Jae's voice was harsh.

"Haven't you ever wished to be unmade? To return to simpler, easier times?"

"No." He met her gaze, the light in his dark eyes fierce. "Because then I never would have found my family. My purpose. To me, that is worth a hundred thousand cuts and every piece of my lost soul."

Odette squeezed his hand. "See?" she said. "So sentimental."

The suggestion of a grin ghosted across Jae's lips. Then—arm in arm—they walked from their street corner into the comfort of the growing darkness.

JAE

---≈---

Shin Jaehyuk glowered at his charge from across the room.
Correction. No longer his charge. Now his brother in blood.

Sébastien Saint Germain. The Court of the Lions' newest vampire, barely a month young.

A pity corporal punishment was frowned upon between their siblings. Jae could think of none more deserving of it.

As if Bastien could hear Jae's thoughts, a surly smile curved up one side of the young vampire's face, his eyes half-lidded. Glazed with debauchery. He stroked his index finger beneath Toussaint's chin, as the cursed serpent lashed his tail back and forth like the pendulum on a clock before settling into a coil of scales by Bastien's feet.

Jae considered standing to deliver yet another lecture, but a tawny young woman with pointed ears and a nose turned upward at the tip—likely the offspring of a mortal and some kind of dokkaebi—frolicked past him, plump grapes falling from her slender fingers to stain the priceless carpet by her bare feet. A gaunt warlock followed in her shadow, stooping to retrieve the trampled fruit, licking his fingers with a dangerous gleam in his purple eyes.

Jae's nostrils flared. He'd had just about his fill of these unwanted guests. True, the Saint Germain family often provided refuge for the magical folk in the city. The exiles, the half bloods, the warlocks and their hollow-eyed acolytes. Better they all gather beneath the auspices of the Fallen than seek succor with the Brotherhood.

But this unending display of depravity was beyond the pale. A single month ago, it had been nothing more than subdued nights of gaming and gambling. A few drinks passed among friends. Magical business negotiated amid hushed laughter and the occasional clink of glasses.

At present, the scene before Jae rivaled an event hosted by Dionysus himself. Discarded decanters and broken crystal littered the floor, alongside articles of rumpled clothing and the occasional apple core or orange peel. Red wine dripped from a narrow sideboard, the dark liquid staining the cool Carrara marble like dried blood. Hot air collected near the coffered mahogany ceiling, mixing with the blue-grey smoke of opium and the suspiciously sweet tinge of absinthe.

Droplets of champagne showered Jae's shoulders as a dark-skinned young man Jae had never seen before uncorked another bottle. Half its contents sprayed around the room, staining the paneled walls and trickling from the corner of a priceless painting Nicodemus had acquired in Madrid two months ago.

Jae leaned back in the chamber's most uncomfortable chair

and continued to glare at Bastien, who lounged along the far wall on a chaise covered in navy silk, champagne dripping from his short black hair, a goblet of warmed blood and absinthe dangling from his fingertips.

A half-dressed kobold, banished from the Wyld for selling empty wishes to unsuspecting mortals, and a giggling spriggan wearing a laurel crown were sprawled on the floor beside Toussaint's pile of coiled scales, inebriated past the point of reason. At Bastien's back, a passel of admirers—two half sprites, a boy with the white hair of a phouka, and a girl with the telltale fox eyes of a gumiho—loitered in a semicircle around the chaise, exchanging expressions of open hunger.

Little fools. They knew what Bastien was. What a vampire could do. All guests of La Cour des Lions were required to know the truth, per Bastien's orders. What happened to their memories afterward was not his concern. Only that they enter the space aware of the danger present. They knew what a newborn vampire was capable of doing. And still they clambered for Bastien's notice.

The carved wood at Jae's back creaked as he shifted forward, his gaze murderous. This chair was indeed exceedingly uncomfortable, but he favored it because it did not match its appearance. Its curved backing and plush silk cushions—dyed a deep rose—looked inviting. But beneath the surface, it was lumpy and misshapen. If Jae sat on it long enough, the chestnut frame would dig into his lower back and behind his knees. Still he refused to give it up or replace it. He thought it a fitting perch for a killer like him. One who did not match his appearance.

"Have y'all started this evening's festivities without me? How uncharitable." Boone came to rest on the padded arm of Jae's chair, his cravat undone, his cherubic blond curls in disarray. "Who are we drinking tonight?" He leered, and the smudge of blood beside his mouth made it appear even more sadistic.

Jae said nothing. He merely looked up at Boone. Then back down to where Boone sat. Boone stood at once, his wicked grin spreading even wider. "Eleven *billion* apologies," he drawled in his thick Charlestonian accent. "Sometimes I forget how much you love this shitty old chair."

Jae remained silent. Boone lifted a shoulder and turned toward Arjun, who was seated on a nearby divan, a crystal tumbler swirling in his right hand. The half fey took a practiced swig of the amber liquor.

"So"—Boone clapped his hands—"what do we have planned for this evening?"

"Bourbon." Arjun tilted his glass, studying its cut facets through the lens of his monocle. "The good, strong kind. Full proof."

"From where?"

"Kentucky, of course."

"A foolproof way to my heart." Boone stretched an empty glass Arjun's way.

With a cultured laugh, the ethereal poured Boone a splash of liquor. He knew better than to offer any to Jae.

Some vampires enjoyed the taste of spirits. It did nothing to satiate their thirst for blood, but many immortals relished the sensation of the burning liquid sliding down their throats. If they consumed enough, sometimes a pleasantly disorienting feeling would settle on their limbs for a short period of time.

Jae could not afford to be less than sharp at all hours of the day and night. He glanced down at the countless scars on the back of his right hand, gleaming white in the lamplight. A memory rose to the forefront of his thoughts. Of that terrible night a warlock in Hunan province had trapped Jae and tortured him with a silver blade in an attempt to gain information about Nicodemus. That night, Jae had almost succumbed to the Death of a Thousand Cuts. Once he managed to escape, it took him a full year to regain his strength.

An evil light entered his gaze. The following year, Jae enacted his own particular brand of revenge on the warlock. He still relished the memory of Mo Gwai's blood smearing his face and dripping down the walls of the cave. The way the warlock's screams echoed around Jae like a twisted symphony.

Alcohol dulled Jae's senses. And he would never again fall prey to even a moment of weakness.

Odette sidled toward the center of the room. She rested a gloved hand beneath her chin and examined the two vampires and the ethereal seated around the filigreed tea table. "Would you look at this pickle party . . ." Her eyes flicked left and right. "Where are Hortense and Madeleine?"

"Madeleine is with Nicodemus," Arjun replied, studying the way the light from the oil lamp caramelized the liquor in his cut-crystal glass.

"Hortense is probably on the roof, singing to the moon," Boone said.

Odette's attention drifted toward the back of the chamber. Lines of consternation settled on her brow. Jae did not need to guess what troubled her. In the month since Bastien had been turned, she'd spent more time than even Jae trying to temper the worst of the newborn vampire's proclivities. His fervent desire to drown all trace of his humanity in vice and sin.

No matter how much Jae and Odette attempted to sway Bastien from this path, the young vampire refused to heed their advice. Nothing would change tonight, of that Jae could be certain. At present, there was too much magic—too many unpredictable elements—in this room. It made Jae more uncomfortable than he cared to admit. Set his fangs on edge.

A loud cough emanated from behind him. "Is any esteemed gentleman interested in making some extra coin for barely an hour's worth of work?" a shockingly tall young man asked, his long arms open wide, like a hawker of stolen wares.

Jae's hands turned into fists.

Nathaniel Villiers.

"What is that greasy machaar doing here?" Arjun swore before tossing back the rest of his drink.

Villiers had been forbidden entry to La Cour des Lions six months ago. A half giant with a penchant for half-baked schemes, he'd tried to bribe Boone into selling him vampire blood, which supposedly granted its consumers lucid dreams when mixed with a precise amount of peyote. The concoction had become an increasingly valuable commodity in European circles, and Villiers had obvious designs on the American market.

"His mother was an honorable woman. The best giantess of my limited acquaintance," Boone said with a disdainful sniff. "She'd unleash every ice bolt in the Sylvan Wyld on him if she knew what he's become."

Her eyes glittering with malice, Odette rested her arms akimbo. "Who allowed the overgrown scamp entry tonight?"

"Two guesses." Boone tipped his head toward Bastien's makeshift throne.

With a groan, Odette tossed up her hands in despair.

Jae sat back, his cheeks hollowing.

What could possess Bastien to grant Villiers admittance? Worse than that, it looked like the overgrown scamp in question arrived with a familiar trio of warlocks from Atlanta. Ones who routinely bamboozled the young scions of wealthy Southern families into "donating" a goodly sum of their inheritances to nonexistent charitable organizations.

Jae couldn't decide what he hated more. Warlocks. Or Atlanta.

"Since when did we start letting their kind in here?" Boone said as he stared at the scheming warlocks, a muscle jumping beside the cleft in his chin.

"Two guesses," Jae retorted before the door near the back of the room blew open as if a storm had entered the building. The next second, Hortense de Morny glided across the threshold, her arms wrapped in a cloud of cream-colored voile and her ivory skirts swirling about her. She stopped short when she saw Villiers. Inclined her head to one side.

"Non," she said with a toss of her curls. "Je n'ai pas assez faim pour ça." Then she plopped down on the other end of the couch and reached for Arjun's glass. After a sniff of its contents, she wrinkled her nose and looked about, her gaze settling on a carafe of blood and absinthe warming above a tea candle, positioned to Jae's right.

"Pour me a glass, mon chaton," Hortense chimed, extending an empty tumbler Jae's way. "It's the least you can do, after all." Her aura seemed to simmer, like steam rising from a kettle.

Jae almost did as he was told. His arm stretched of its own volition before he caught himself and sent Hortense a frown.

She grinned like a lynx, her brows arching, the empty glass still dangling from her hand.

Jae hated how much Hortense resembled Madeleine in appearance, though the two sisters could not in truth be more different. Hortense had taken advantage of these physical similarities on countless occasions, cajoling Jae into doing her bidding with a simple bat of her eyelashes and an imploring expression.

Guilt was a powerful motivator, after all.

Odette rapped the back of Hortense's hand like a schoolmarm. "That's not for you."

"Strike me again at your own peril, sorcière blanche," Hortense said. With a glance toward the back of the room, she snorted once, a finger winding through a dark curl. "Anyway, you have enough problems maintenant." She indicated Bastien with her chin. "Keep feeding him like a god at a banquet, and he'll never learn how to fend for himself. It's time he learned our ways. A whole month has passed."

"Everything is still new to him," Odette protested. "I want

Bastien to learn how to survive on his own just as much as any of us, but—"

"You want the ne'er-do-well to learn how to survive?" Boone said, his voice low. "Then stop pampering him like a babe in swaddling."

Outrage cut lines across Odette's forehead. "I don't pamper him!"

Jae braced his elbows on his knees and peered at her through his long black hair.

Odette's features flushed, the blood she'd recently consumed warming her cheeks. "Your opinion was not wanted, chat grincheux."

"I said nothing." Jae sniffed.

"And you cut nonetheless."

Boone snorted. "Perhaps he meant only to scratch."

Odette stood in a flurry of pastel silk. "Go back to glowering at nothing, grumpy cat," she said to Jae. "And spare us your pithy retorts, Lord Hellhound." She aimed a withering glance at Boone.

Hortense's laughter bounded into the smoke-filled ceiling. Another breeze coiled through the room, accompanied by the scent of French lavender and iron gall ink. Jae breathed in the familiar perfume—steeling himself—before acknowledging the Court's newest arrival. When he turned, his eyes met the unmatched stare of Madeleine de Morny. The warmth he found there vanished the next instant. Jae cleared his throat. Looked away.

Some things could not be changed, even after more than a century.

Jae searched around him for a distraction. Fool that he was.

Sébastien Saint Germain had descended lower in his make-shift throne, a single booted foot resting on one of the chaise's arms, his wrinkled white shirt slowly being unbuttoned by a girl whose grandmother had been a celebrated nymph of the Sylvan Vale before she was banished by its ruler, the infamous Lady of the Vale, for reasons still unknown.

Just last week, the girl—Jessamine was her name—had set her sights on the nephew of Nicodemus Saint Germain, a target unattainable to her a month prior. Nicodemus would not have permitted his only living heir to dally in the open with any young woman unless she hailed from the uppermost echelons of New Orleans society. But times—and circumstances—had changed. Bastien was no longer mortal, so the chance of siring a son to carry on the Saint Germain line was gone, along with most of their maker's most cherished dreams.

In short, Bastien was no longer bound by anyone's expectations. Even his own.

Distaste curled in the back of Jae's throat as Jessamine straddled Bastien, hitching her skirts in one pale hand and resting the slender fingers of the other on his bronze chest, over the place his heart used to beat.

Bastien said nothing. Did nothing. Only watched her, his eyes narrowed, his pupils black.

Jessamine loosened the ties on the front of her blue linen dress and lowered her bodice, her features sly. Then she drew a finger from the top of one exposed breast to the side of her slender neck, her head canting to one side, as if to offer him a taste. Bastien pushed her chin upward with his thumb, his fingers twining through her auburn hair. Then he leaned forward, the tip of his nose trailing along her collarbone.

Without a second thought, Jae crossed the room in three strides and grabbed Jessamine by the wrist. She shrieked in feigned protest when Jae hauled her to her feet as if she weighed no more than a feather. "Be gone from here," he demanded, anger sharpening his accent. "While you still breathe."

"I think not, vampire," Jessamine replied primly. "Do you have any idea who I am? My grandmother was among the gentry of the Sylvan Vale's Summer Court, my mother an ethereal of the highest order. Sébastien invited me as his special guest. If he wishes for me to remain at his side, then—"

"Stay at your own peril, you silly little bloodsac." He pulled her closer. "But I promise you this: if he doesn't kill you, *I will*. To a vampire, there is nothing sweeter than the blood of the Vale."

The color drained from Jessamine's pretty face, her grandmother's aquamarine eyes blinking like those of a cornered rabbit. Without a word, she straightened her bodice and fled down the curved staircase toward the bustling restaurant below.

"Get up."

Jae turned in place at the sound of this voice. The voice of their maker. The voice they were bound by blood to obey. Nicodemus stood before Bastien, who continued to sprawl on his chaise and sip from his macabre goblet as if nothing of import had transpired.

"Get up," Nicodemus repeated, his voice going softer. Dangerously so.

Jae worried Bastien would continue defying Nicodemus, as he had everyone else for the past month. Instead, Bastien raised his goblet in salute and drained it before setting it down, his movements like a drop of honey on a cold December's eve. Then he stood to his full height, his unbuttoned shirt hanging off one shoulder, the signet ring on his right hand glinting in the lamplight.

"As my maker commands," Bastien said with an icy grin.

Nicodemus studied him in silence for the span of a breath. "Collect your coat and hat."

Bastien pursed his lips, his jaw rippling.

Nicodemus matched him, toe to toe. "Tonight you will learn who you are meant to be."

Bastien

Beyond the city lies a swamp that stretches as far as the eye can see.

It is almost impossible for a horse or carriage to travel freely here. The mud is too high, the road too unpredictable. For centuries, this natural barrier has protected New Orleans from intruders, much like the waters of the Mississippi.

I have not wandered into the swamp since I was a boy. The last time I remember trudging through the muck and mire was the day my best friend, Michael Grimaldi, and I hatched a plan to lay traps for bullfrogs. Later that afternoon, I was forced to race back to his cousin Luca's house in the Marigny, so we could save Michael from a mudslide. At eleven years old, I was too small and wiry to pull him out by myself, and I knew I couldn't ask Boone or Odette for help, since I'd lied to them about where I was going and what I was doing.

Madeleine would have refused to save Michael simply because he was a cursed Grimaldi. Hortense would have laughed at me for even asking. And Jae? I couldn't stomach another curt lecture from the ghoul-eyed demon. So I decided to eat crow and ask Luca for help. By the time we returned, Michael was buried waist-deep in mud, scared out of his wits that a gator would find him and make a feast of his bones.

Once we freed Michael, Luca forbade us from being friends. His words should have frightened me. After all, Luca was in line to lead the Brotherhood one day. At eighteen, he was almost six and a half feet tall, his arms like tree trunks and his voice like thunder.

I decided I would show fear if Michael showed fear first. Since he didn't look the least bit worried, we continued to defy both our families. Until another fall evening four years later, when Michael found me kissing the girl he'd admired for months at our cotillion ball.

Not my finest moment, I'll admit.

My foot slides through a pile of leaves and sludge as I continue following my uncle through the dark swamp, listening to the groaning, muttering creatures gather around me, trying to decide whether I am food or foe.

I should have apologized to Michael that night. Instead I argued with him. Portrayed myself as a *victim*, of all things.

She kissed me first.

It doesn't matter! Where do your loyalties lie, Bastien? I should have known better than to trust a thieving Saint Germain.

It isn't my fault she prefers me to you, Grimaldi. Who wouldn't?

I wince, recalling the way the blood drained from Michael's face when I said that. How my fingers tugged through my hair, the only indication of the guilt roiling in my gut. I remember how he never again confided in me. How we both retreated into ourselves. The following morning, I cut my hair short and have worn it that way ever since.

I lost more than a friend that night. I lost a brother. It doesn't matter how Michael retaliated in the years to come, attempting to undermine me. How he rose to the top of our class as I won every award for marksmanship and horseback riding, each trying to best the other.

One day, they will all see through you, Sébastien. And no amount of money or influence will stand in the way of them knowing what it's taken me too many years to realize. You are nothing without your uncle. Nothing.

Even now, Michael's words scratch open wounds that will never heal.

I should have told him that kiss at cotillion was my fault and mine alone. I knew better. I thought he would forgive my rapscallion ways, as he always had before. I was wrong.

But I will burn in Hell before I ever admit it now, especially to a sanctimonious Grimaldi.

"Do you know why we are called the Fallen?" Nicodemus comes to a sudden stop in the middle of the watery wasteland, tearing me from my reverie.

When I was mortal, I would have weighed my response before making it. Since I have nothing to lose now, I say the first thing that comes to mind. "I've never known a modest vampire, so I can only assume it has to do with Lucifer being a fallen angel."

Nicodemus turns in place. It rankles me how he still manages to look regal, even though his dark trousers and his walking stick are covered in mud. "That would be the prevailing thought, yes." His lips form a thin line. "But it is not the sole reason."

I wait.

He resumes his walk, his strides purposeful. "A thousand years ago, the Sylvan Vale and the Sylvan Wyld were not separate," he begins, the words barely audible to the human ear. Like the susurration of an insect. "They were part of a whole. A place with a name we no longer speak out of anguish, ruled by a king and a queen, who sat on a horned throne. An otherworld mortals sang about in nursery rhymes and poets wrote about in sonnets. Tír na nÓg, Fairyland, Asgard, the Valley of the Moon—all sorts of whimsical names were bestowed on it over the centuries." I hear the smile in his voice. "But for those who lived there, it is simply called home." Unmistakable melancholy softens his tone.

I say nothing, though I desperately wish to hear more. My uncle has never spoken of his past in anything more than generalities. I recall a time when my sister, Émilie, begged Nicodemus to tell her what the mysterious Otherworld was like before vampires and wolves were exiled during the Banishment. To describe the castles carved from ice and the forests of never-ending night. He denied her request, his laughter distant. Almost cruel.

It is in her memory that I refuse to beg my uncle to continue.

Nicodemus trudges surefooted through the darkness, toward a band of warm light flickering in the distance. We pass a grove of twisted tupelo trees, and a turkey vulture cocks his head at me from his perch on a skeletal branch, his beady eyes unblinking. To my right, gators nestle in the marshes and bullfrogs croak a dissonant melody.

Everywhere I look, I see the watchful eyes of predators. The sting of insects, the flurry of tongues lashing through the air like bolts of lightning, followed by the crunch of wings or the snapping of jaws. Strangely I feel at home here. As if I, too, am a predator of this age-old swamp.

Perhaps I am. Perhaps this wasteland seeks to swallow me whole.

I welcome it.

The scent of mortal blood curls into my nostrils, causing me to halt midstride. Distant human shouts bleed through the cacophony of sound. As I step closer, they sharpen into curse words and barks of encouragement.

I remain silent, though the smell of warm, coppery salt grips my throat, the hunger pounding in my veins. My eyes narrow. Something about the scent is . . . different. Like warm honey instead of melting sugar.

Nicodemus pauses again. Turns toward me. "Is something wrong?"

Another unspoken challenge.

I think for no more than an instant. "No." My shoulders roll back. "Please continue." I indicate with an outstretched hand.

A knowing smile curves up Nicodemus' face. "When the last ruler of the Otherworld perished without an heir to the Horned Throne, two prominent families began vying for the crown. One was a family of blood drinkers, the other a family of enchantresses."

I listen and wait, though the cries and the blood in the distance beckon me forward like a bee drawn to nectar.

"The vampires were shrewd." Nicodemus looks through me, lost in thought. "They had managed to acquire immense wealth over the centuries. Land and crops, as well as the most desirable source of wealth in both the mortal world and the Otherworld: gemstones, buried deep within a mountain of ice." He inhales, taking in the scents around him. "The vampires believed themselves to be invincible, for they were almost impossible to kill or catch unawares. They blurred through space and time, and the dark magic in their blood healed their injuries with the speed of quicksilver. Indeed only a perfectly aimed blow to the chest or to the throat with a blade fashioned of solid silver could render them completely defenseless."

The tumult along the horizon turns feral, the air filling with bloodlust. Nicodemus treks toward it once more, the light from crude torches dancing through the dripping Spanish moss. "By contrast," he says over his shoulder, "the enchantresses controlled all forms of elemental magic, which was no mean feat in itself. Wielders of such gifts had become scarcer with each passing generation. Nowadays the birth of an elemental enchantress warrants a celebration. Some channel fire. Others manipulate water or air or make the earth tremble beneath their feet. The enchantresses believed this rare magic made them powerful, for it inured them to the creatures of the Otherworld. Water fed crops. Fire forged metal. But more than anything, this magic gave these enchantresses knowledge. The magical folk throughout the land turned to these women, for their wisdom enabled them to create weapons and fashion armor from solid pieces of silver. Gave them the ability to conquer instead of be conquered."

I shift closer to my uncle as I listen, like a street urchin following a food cart along Rue Bourbon.

"A war was fought between the vampires and the enchantresses for control of the Horned Throne," Nicodemus says. "The wolves and the goblins and most of the night-dwelling creatures sided with the vampires, while those who basked in sunlight fought alongside the enchantresses." His expression turned contemplative. "Many lives were lost. After half a century of bloodshed, a victor had yet to emerge. Wearied by all the death and destruction, the heads of these two families agreed to a stalemate. The land was split in two halves, the wintry Sylvan Wyld to be ruled by the vampires, and the summery Sylvan Vale by the enchantresses.

"For a time, they lived in peace. Until the blood drinkers began carving a foothold for themselves in the mortal world." A gleam enters his eye. "They began with small things. Silly wishes. Simple fortune-telling. Gemstones too trifling to be of any real value, but worth their weight in gold to the foolish humans who vied for them. The wolves—shifters who had risen in the ranks to become the guardians of the Wyld—built businesses throughout the mortal world, creating a wider market for magical wares in cities like New Orleans, Jaipur, Dublin, Luxor, Hanseong, and Angkor—cities where the veil between worlds has always been its thinnest. Cities our kind is destined to rule." His gaze sharpens. "It was during this time that my maker shared the dark gift with me. Impressed by my business acumen, he made me a vampire and took me with him to the Wyld, where I lived for fifty mortal years . . . until the Banishment."

He says nothing more as we weave through the trees. The howls grow louder, the scent of violence lengthening my fangs, my blood turning hotter with each step. We stride closer to the circle of torch fire, around which is gathered an assortment of creatures I have never before seen in my life. In the center of this odd assembly is a rudimentary boxing ring, the mud tamped with clumps of filthy sawdust.

I take in a long breath.

"Gut him like a fish," a one-eyed goblin shouts, his clawed fists punching through the air.

The strange fragrance mixed with the blood and the sweat makes sense as I peruse the two men in the ring. One is inhumanly tall, his dark face stretched thin. The other is stocky and barrel-chested, his stance like that of a goat, his legs bowing outward at the thighs. The stumps of two malformed horns protrude from his mass of scarlet hair.

I scan the crowd further, and what I see confirms my suspicions.

Most of the creatures who have gathered in the swamp for a night of spectacle are half bloods. The children or grandchildren of mortal-and-immortal couplings. Ones who lack the magic to maintain a glamour, which would help conceal their true natures from mankind. This must be the reason they are forced to gather in darkness, far from the lights of civilization.

The fighting turns fierce as the half giant picks up the half puck and shoves him through the mud. Bare-chested, he slides into a group of men along the sidelines who topple over like chess pieces, vulgar invectives hurled into the night sky. The puck swipes away the tufts of bloodied sawdust from his bearded face before charging at the giant, his hands like clubs as they pummel his opponent's thin face.

"Rip his horns off, you useless sack of bones!" an elderly man with the grizzled jaw of a shifter growls through the crowd. "I won't lose my hard-earned coin again, goddamn you."

My uncle's eyes shine like gold as he watches the half giant spit a mouthful of teeth into the muck.

I want to ask him why we are here. But I know all too well.

The fighting continues as a rusted dagger is tossed into the ring. Both the half giant and the half puck lunge for it, the fighting descending into chaos.

"When the enchantresses discovered what the blood drinkers were doing—the wealth and influence the vampires were amassing—they bided their time," Nicodemus continues, his tone conversational, despite the calls for violence rising around us.

I listen, my eyes glazed, my lips pursed.

He tilts his head toward me. "Instead of instigating an outright rebellion, the enchantresses began spreading lies about the blood drinkers. How the vampires had turned their backs on our world, favoring that of the mortals. Eventually they claimed we preferred mortals outright because humans were easier to control, for they treated us like royalty. Revered us like gods." His sneer is laced with bitterness. "And everyone knows that is what a vampire craves most . . . to be loved above all." He turns toward me, his expression fierce. "Tell me, Sébastien, what is the most elegant weapon in the world?"

I answer without thinking, my eyes locked on his. "Love."

"A wise guess." He nods. "But no. It is fear. With it, you can send armies to their deaths and rule a kingdom on high." A smile coils up his face. "With enough fear, you can stoke hatred until it becomes a wildfire, burning everything that stands in your way."

Shouts of triumph echo in my periphery. I turn just as the half giant yanks the rusty dagger from between the ribs of the half puck, who bellows, blood gushing from the wound.

My uncle's fangs shine in the torchlight, his irises blackening. "Wielding this most elegant of weapons, the enchantresses declared that the blood drinkers belonged in the mortal world, if they yearned for the love of such wretched creatures so desperately." He stops to applaud when the puck collapses into the sawdust, chest heaving. Money changes hands around the ring, the shouts turning even more feral. A brawl erupts to our right, sweaty bodies squelching through the mire.

Nicodemus ignores the tumult, flicking mud from his shoulders. "Then the leader of the enchantresses—the Lady of the Vale—uncovered information she knew could ruin us. A vampire had offered to *sell* a powerful human the gift of immortality, for an exorbitant price. For the chance to rule the kingdom he desired more than anything," he whispers, his eyes leached of all light. "A most grievous offense. Immortality is a gift to be granted to the most deserving, not bartered about like chattel. It didn't take long before the whole of the Otherworld united to exile vampires from the Sylvan Wyld, along with the traitorous wolves who'd protected us for centuries. Our guardian dogs," he says, hurling the words through the air like an epithet.

A squat man with a belly round as the moon marches into the center of the sawdust ring, stamping the ground flat as he walks. He raises his arms, spreading them wide, beseeching the crowd to fall silent. "And now"—he pauses for dramatic effect, his oiled mustache twitching—"we come to the match you've all been waiting for."

My fists curl at my sides. I am no fool.

"For the glory of his kind and a hefty stake in the winnings, our very own *undefeated* Cambion of the Swamp has been challenged by an outsider," the portly man continues, "in a match for the ages!"

The crowd parts behind him as a tall young man with arms like cannon barrels makes his way into the center of the ring. His eyes are black with lines of yellow through their centers, his hair flame red, his skin the color of sour milk. Instead of fingers, his hands end in sharpened claws that gleam like polished jet in the torch fire.

I eye my uncle, rage scalding my throat, fear gripping at my insides.

"And his challenger?" the announcer continues with a flourish. "An elegant blood drinker from the very heart of the *Vieux Carré*!" he crows. Jeers of disdain echo in the wake of his cry.

Nicodemus turns to me, a look of supreme pleasure on his face.

I glare at him sidelong. "I refuse to—"

"This is your first lesson," he interrupts with a dismissive wave. "My maker was Mehmed, Lord of the Sylvan Wyld. It is *your family* who was forced to cede their territory. It is *your royal blood* that was declared fallen. Exiled from its home, despite having ruled the Wyld for almost five hundred years. We lost everything. We are the only immortals cursed to kill in order to create more of our kind. Damned to darkness for all eternity."

The cheers grow louder around us, the taunts like the swipe of talons against my skin.

My uncle takes me by the shoulders, his fangs curling snake-like from his mouth. "I did not want to believe there might be a purpose to your mortal death. To the end of my line in the world of mankind. But now I know the truth. *You* will take everything back for us, Sébastien. *You* will return us to our rightful place on the Horned Throne. This is only the beginning. Show them how powerful you are. *Make them fear you.*"

Then he pushes me into the ring.

BASTIEN

There is no time for me to think or argue.

The instant I set foot in the ring, Cambion charges at me, his yellow pupils like vertical slits. I blur to one side before his claws slice through the air a hairsbreadth from where I once stood. My mind is a jumble of thoughts, none of them coherent, all of them cloaked in fury.

He is much larger than I am, but I have the advantage of speed. I try to lunge for his back, thinking to bring him to his knees, but my coat constricts my movements. I tear it off as I evade another attack. Rage colors my sight red, my white shirt and waistcoat falling to the mud in tattered strips of linen and wool.

Thoughts are for the foolish. If I wish to win, I must become fear. I must become Death.

Cambion aims a punch at my stomach. I manage to twist away, my motions like those of a coiled asp. I do not recognize his feint until it is too late. Before I can redirect myself, Cambion's right hook lands against my jaw with a crack of thunder, the reverberations ringing in my skull. I blur backward to buy myself a moment to clear my head, pretending to stumble and overcorrect in the process. Then I charge at him, my fangs bared.

He is a foot taller than I am. As wide as an ox, his blood mixed with that of a demon I do not recognize.

But I am a Saint Germain. Running through my veins is the blood of the oldest immortal in the American South. The blood of vampire royalty.

And I have never run from a fight, in either of my lives.

Fury seething beneath my skin, I launch a series of punches at his stomach, doubling him over with the intention of sinking my teeth into his throat and ripping his windpipe from his body. As I pull him close, instead, he grabs me by the waist and lifts me above his head. The night sky and all its twinkling stars flash across my sight as I pry back the fingers of his left hand, a dark satisfaction winding through my limbs as his bones break in my grasp. He howls, the sound causing the cypress branches around us to shake. Cambion spins in place, hurling me through the warm mid-March air. The moment he lets go, I drag my clawed hand across his meaty shoulder, drawing blood as I fly above the mud-filled ring. I land upright in a pile of sawdust, my feet sliding through the muck, my arms raised at my sides.

He glares in disbelief at the gashes on his upper arm. At the ribbons of torn flesh dangling from his shoulder. At the shattered fingers of his left hand.

Then the wounds on his shoulder begin to darken. Begin turning into stripes, which grow and multiply across his back and down his arms. The lines in his eyes become starbursts of black and gold. Both rows of his teeth begin to lengthen and form fangs. His skull widens. His scarlet hair lightens to burnished copper, whiskers bursting from beside his lips. When he howls again, it is no longer the howl of a man.

It is the roar of a tiger.

Incredulous, I take a step back.

Concentrate, Sébastien.

A voice blares through my mind as if it were my erstwhile conscience, though I know that to be far from the truth. It is a voice I know all too well. I blink again in shock.

Concentrate! the voice demands once more.

My uncle. As my maker, we are able to communicate without words. I've witnessed him issue orders to Odette and Jae and Madeleine in such a fashion, though he has never attempted to do so with me in the month since I was turned into a vampire.

I don't know why he would choose now—of all times—to make use of it.

What in hellfire is this thing? I shout back without words. For I have never seen a half man, half beast like this. The shifters I know—the Grimaldi wolves—take full form when they change, resembling the earthbound creatures that hunt the forests in fleet-footed packs. It is why they are able to blend into the night and move about without anyone the wiser.

But Cambion is not a tiger. Nor is he human. He is a creature of both worlds, one with the face and fangs of a jungle cat and the body of a man.

A thing of the swamp.

It does not matter what he is, my uncle replies. *You must destroy him or be destroyed.*

One of these days, I will give my uncle the sound walloping he is due.

Cambion roars again. His claws—longer and sharper than they were before—gleam as if they have been dipped in molten glass, a liquid as dark as ink dripping from their razor-sharp tips. He charges at me again, and I am frozen still for half a beat.

Move, damn you! my uncle yells into my head. *Not as a man, but as a* vampire.

I remember how Jae dodged me the night I first woke to my second life. How he spiraled through the air, defying gravity. I close my eyes and leap. For a second I am suspended in darkness, the branches of the swamp flashing around me, the night sky twinkling beyond. Then I arc my body through the damp heat, landing in a crouched position, my fangs bared, an inhuman hiss ripping from my throat.

Cambion snarls and attacks, his fangs dripping with saliva. We clash in the middle of the ring, the crowd around us in a frenzy. He growls and snaps his jaws at me. My fingers wrap around his thick wrists, preventing him from slashing through my skin with his inky claws.

It is exhilarating, allowing the fury to control me. Granting leave for the monster in my blood to take hold. I want nothing more than to rip Cambion limb from limb. To crush his bones in my hands and drain him dry. To destroy before I am destroyed.

I can hear my uncle's laugh in my skull.

My blood sings as the demon caged within is fully unleashed. The veins in my arms bulge, and another bestial howl punctuates the night.

It is me.

Then I snap to one side and hear Cambion's left wrist break in my grasp. His cry of pain brings a smile to my face. Before he can recoil, I leap onto his striped back and bury my fangs in his neck, ready to make good on all my promises. He swipes at me with his uninjured hand, and when his claws break through the skin of my forearm, I relish the pain. Laugh as I take in a hot draft of his blood.

Good, my uncle says. *Drink, my son. Drink. Lose yourself in this creature's memories. Let his life become yours.*

I close my eyes, ready to drown in thoughts of blood and fury.

But it is not images of violence I see in Cambion's memories.

It is a woman with tiger eyes and a kind smile. One who brings him food and sings him songs in a language I do not recognize. It is the memory of his mother, who hid her son from his angry, drunken father. Of a tired woman who bore the scars of her husband's rage so that her child would not be subjected to it. I watch as she teaches a younger, smaller Cambion to control his shifts. To fight only when it is necessary. To protect.

Through his eyes, I see her succumb to a wasting disease. I listen as she tells him, with her dying breath, how much she loves him. How he should seek out his great-aunt Alia or her friend Sunan the Immortal Unmaker, if ever he has need of guidance.

I watch her funeral in Cambion's memories, his sight dampened by tears and despair. The way the flames licked at his mother's body from atop the pyre, deep in the swamp. I witness him search and search for another family. Another place to call home. I take note of all the people who shunned him, both in the mortal world and among the half bloods. For he is not one of them, and he never will be. These worlds that turned their backs on Cambion for being half of one thing and not enough of the other.

Through the eyes of the beast, I see the humanity.

I blink, a tremor running down my spine, the heat of his blood boiling beneath my skin.

Stop when his heartbeat slows, my uncle says. *Only then can you ensure his death without losing yourself to it. If your mind is lost in the wasteland of death, it is difficult to return.*

Struggling to subdue Cambion's thoughts, I take another draft. A trail of something wet glides down one of my cheeks. When I avert my gaze, I catch sight of the coquí inked above my left wrist, the design symbolizing my father's Taíno heritage. My arms shake, my fingers turning white as they clutch Cambion's shoulders in a twisted approximation of an embrace.

He loved his mother as I loved mine.

He searched for another family as I searched for mine.

Neither of our parents wanted this life for us.

My body trembles. I stop drinking, letting Cambion fall to the ground. His chest heaves as he struggles to breathe, the stripes fading from his skin, his hair turning flame red once more. Black ichor stains his fingertips when his claws retract.

I know he will live.

"What are you doing?" my uncle demands aloud.

I whirl toward him, my vision blurring along the edges, blood tears trickling down my cheeks. The cuts on my forearm ooze, the smell strange. Noxious.

"I don't want this," I rasp.

"What?" He steps toward me, anger sharpening the angles of his profile. His gaze flicks to my open wounds, his golden eyes widening. My injuries should have healed by now.

I sway unsteady on my feet and blink hard.

"This life you wish for me to lead," I say through the cries for blood swelling through the crowd around us. "Take it back. I don't want it. Take all of it back," I yell to the heavens. "I want no part of this."

Then I fall to the ground, wrapped in a warm blanket of darkness.

CELINE

———— ≈ ————

It was too soon for Celine to be wandering the streets of New Orleans on this late March evening. Every corner she turned—every footfall she heard over her shoulder—caused a tremor to unfurl down her spine.

Celine stopped midstride. Lifted her chin. Straightened her back.

She was tired of letting fear rule her every waking moment. It was Good Friday. Almost six weeks had passed since she'd been kidnapped by the now-infamous Crescent City killer. Forty days and nights since the evening she'd sustained multiple injuries, tied atop the altar in Saint Louis Cathedral. Contusions to the head, a nasty gash in the side of her neck, three broken ribs, and a dislocated shoulder.

Everyone said it was a miracle she'd survived. A blessing that her head injuries prevented her from recalling anything in the way of details. How the entire night seemed shrouded in shadows, candlelight and incense wavering through her mind.

"Celine?" a patient voice inquired from beside her.

Michael Grimaldi. The youngest detective of the New Orleans Metropolitan Police, he was also the one who'd rescued Celine from the clutches of a murdering madman. In the ensuing tumult, Michael had shot Celine's unknown attacker in the face. For these actions, he'd been crowned the Crescent City's newest hero. Wherever Michael went, glances of appreciation followed. Men shook his hand. Women gazed at him covetously. Twice this evening, Celine had been sent murderous glares by some of the young ladies strolling past them. A fact that had not gone unnoticed by Celine's attractive escort, though he appeared to pay them no mind.

"Are you all right?" Michael asked, concern lacing his tone.

Celine tossed her ebony curls and aimed a smile his way. "I'm fine. I was just momentarily . . . disoriented. But the feeling has passed," she finished in a hurry, looping her arm through his, angry young ladies be damned.

Michael studied her for a beat. She could see him considering whether or not to press the matter. Truth be told, there had been several instances in the last few weeks when spells of dizziness had overcome Celine. Twice she'd stumbled over nothing or found herself lost in a flash of feeling, caught up in a strange memory. The last time, Michael had been there to catch her, as if Celine were some fainthearted milquetoast. A character from a penny dreadful, destined to die.

Infuriating. What kind of silly little fool couldn't stay on her own two feet?

Just this afternoon, her friend Antonia had remarked on how romantic it was—to be caught mid-faint by the dashing young detective. The girl from Portugal hummed a love song to herself while arranging boxes of grosgrain ribbon in Celine's new dress shop. Antonia's behavior had irritated Celine beyond measure. But not nearly as much as her own inability to recall even the most insignificant detail from that night.

As if Michael could sense Celine's mounting agitation, he nodded, and they resumed their evening stroll down Rue Royale.

Celine looked about, letting the hustle and bustle of the busy thoroughfare calm the tempest in her mind. Though it was past dusk, families still milled about, stopping to peruse the offerings in the shop windows, chat with acquaintances, or dip into bakeries to snag a box of warm pralines or a paper sack of hot beignets. The early spring air carried the scent of melting butter and magnolia blossoms. A carriage trundled past, its canopy trimmed in delicate white fringe.

"It's my favorite street in all of the Vieux Carré," Michael remarked, his pale, almost colorless eyes sliding down the lane, pausing to note every detail, as Celine had come to expect from him.

"It *is* a beautiful sight to behold," Celine agreed. "Everywhere I look, I see something lovely." *Along with the suggestion of something sinister,* she thought.

"Yes." He nodded. "Lovely is precisely the right word." The tenor of his voice dropped, turning almost husky.

Dread coursed through Celine's body. She glanced in Michael's direction and realized he was still studying her intently. Her pulse thudded in her veins, more from trepidation than excitement. It wasn't the first time he'd gazed at her like that. With a spark of hope alighting his handsome face.

"Thank you for being so persistent," Celine blurted.

A furrow formed above his brow. "You're welcome?"

"You know what I mean." She waved her gloved hand about like a ninny. "I appreciate you inviting me on a stroll every night, especially after I refused you all those times." Celine realized what she was saying as she said it. "I mean . . . well, putain de merde," she swore. "Never mind."

Michael laughed. The way the sound rumbled off his lips was . . . pleasant. Even though her memory was worse than that of a mayfly, she seemed to recall he didn't laugh that often.

And it was nice when he did.

Warmth flooded Celine's cheeks. "I shouldn't have said that," she muttered.

"The swearing or the bit about repeatedly refusing my invitations?"

"Both?"

His laughter continued. "I like that you're no longer careful about what you say to me or how you say it."

Celine frowned. She knew Michael meant it as a compliment, but it nonetheless reminded her how much she'd lost that night at Saint Louis Cathedral. Indeed there were times she felt she'd misplaced intrinsic pieces of herself.

Exasperation clung to her like a rain-soaked cloak.

Enough of this nonsense. She was here tonight, safe, in the company of a fine young gentleman who'd saved her life, at great peril to his own. Celine should be thankful to have forgotten the ordeal, thereby escaping the horrors that would have darkened her days and haunted her nights for Lord knows how long.

It was just . . . she *should* recall something of what happened to her, should she not?

The sorts of injuries she'd sustained were not commonplace. The scars on her neck were still pink and puckered. Her chest smarted anytime she took a deep breath, as if a slender blade had been shoved between her ribs.

When Celine was twelve, she'd burned herself pulling a loaf of bread from the iron stove in her family's flat. She bore the scar of that awful morning to this day: a thin red line on the back of her left hand, near her wrist. It served as a constant reminder to proceed with caution around fire of any sort.

She would not have learned that lesson, save for that scar.

"How was your first full week working at the new shop?" Michael asked in a conversational tone.

Celine brightened, thankful for the change in subject. "I have to admit it's been a welcome distraction. And it's wonderful to see everything come together so brilliantly."

"Well, it was an excellent idea to bring Parisian fashion to New Orleans, especially for the everyday woman." Michael grinned, admiration warming his expression. "You are to be commended in all respects."

"I appreciate your praise, but the truth is, I could not have managed it without Pippa's and Antonia's help. What they've accomplished in the last few weeks is nothing short of a miracle." As Celine spoke, she and Michael passed a millinery, the shopkeeper tipping his hat at them. "And of course none of this would be possible without Mademoiselle Valmont's generous patronage."

A frown shaded Michael's face, there and gone in an instant. "Have you spoken at all with your mysterious benefactress?"

"She has corresponded with me via letters, and promises to visit as soon as she returns from Charleston."

They strolled half a block farther before Michael replied, his tawny features lost in thought. Celine could see him weighing his words in the same manner with which he adjusted his stride to match hers. Calculated, yet concerned.

"Do you have any . . . recollections of Miss Valmont, prior to the ordeal?" His question was careful. Far too careful to be posed out of mere curiosity.

Celine contemplated asking him why. Michael never seemed pleased whenever anyone mentioned the dress shop's silent investor. "I know I designed a masquerade costume for Mademoiselle Valmont, but I'm still unable to recall most of our interactions. And nothing worthy of note, beyond her being fashionable and funny and richer than King Midas." She tamped down a wave of frustration. "Nevertheless, I'm glad she liked my work enough to support our venture. She was also the one who put me in contact last week with my newest employee, Eloise Henri, who has been a godsend when it comes to managing the finances." She forced herself to grin. "I balance books as well as I bake cakes, which is to say not at all."

"Eloise . . . *Henri*?" Michael quirked his mouth to one side.

"Yes, do you know her?"

He paused, then shook his head.

He's lying, Celine thought, taken aback by the realization. It

was unlike Michael to be anything less than forthright. Sometimes he offered his unsolicited opinion to his own detriment.

She considered him sidelong. "Why are you—"

"Do you trust Miss Valmont, Celine?" Michael interrupted.

"Should I not?"

"I just think it would be better if you didn't rely on someone
so . . . mysterious."

"Michael, do you know something about her that should give
me pause?"

Another hesitation. "No." He brushed his free hand over his
wavy dark hair, mussing it.

He was lying again, and it irked Celine enough to respond
uncharitably. "Don't worry yourself over it. I won't be *relying* on
anyone for long. With Mademoiselle Valmont's vouching for us
and Eloise's head for numbers, the bank has extended the shop
an excellent line of credit, despite Pippa's concerns they would
not wish to support a business helmed solely by women." Her
laughter was bitter. "Perish the thought of lending money to
any member of the fairer sex!"

Michael cleared his throat. "I suppose it *is* unusual."

"But as a *man*, how would you know?"

He blinked, but not before Celine saw the hurt in his eyes.
A wave of regret spread through her chest. What was she
doing? Of all people, Michael did not deserve her spite. From
the minute Celine had woken in the hospital bed, he'd been
there, attending to her every need, reading to her to keep her
company, and bringing her bowls of his grandmother's delicious soup.

Celine halted beneath a shop awning. Michael paused alongside her, ever patient. Steady, like the mast of a ship in a storm. "That was unkind of me. I'm sorry, Michael. You are the last person who should be subjected to the worst of my moods."

"You know I don't mind." His tone was gentle. "You've been through an awful ordeal. I count myself lucky that you're here with me tonight, hale and hearty."

Celine swallowed. Nodded. "Maybe a guardian angel is watching over me, which would be a nice change of pace," she said, attempting to joke, her free hand fidgeting with the folds of her ruby-red skirts. It was odd. She'd never had a penchant for fiddling with things before, but she'd noticed herself doing it more and more in the last few weeks. As if her fingers searched for something to hold. Something to anchor her, like she was a boat unmoored, set adrift.

Again, Michael seemed to sense her mood without Celine having to say a word. He gripped the hand she had wound around his arm as they resumed their stroll. "At the risk of sounding ridiculous, please know I am here if ever you have need of me. No matter the hour or the circumstance."

"I know, Michael. I know." Celine should say more. She should tell him she would not be alive if he hadn't come to save her. That her gratitude knew no bounds. That she wished she were ready to return his feelings, in all ways.

But it would be wrong to let Michael believe she wanted what he wanted. At least at this time. It was just too soon after . . . everything.

So instead Celine offered him a smile. His arm brushed

against hers as he drew even closer, heat flooding his gaze. A tingling sensation raced down her spine, followed by a flare of surprise. Perhaps this was the attraction she had been waiting to feel. That thrill of being desired by the one she desired. Of seeing and being seen.

The tingling sensation unfolded in her stomach. It warmed and spread. And then something gripped her heart, stealing the breath from her body.

An image flashed before her eyes. A pool of blood stretching around the hem of her black taffeta skirts. Her fingers stained crimson, gripping a lifeless hand, a signet ring glistening on a gentleman's finger, blood marring its etched gold surface.

Save him. Please. Save him.

Celine could hear herself screaming. She stopped short in the middle of the sidewalk, causing the people at her back to mutter beneath their breaths as they skirted around her. She closed her eyes. A shudder drew the blades of her shoulders together.

"Celine?" Michael held a steadying arm about her waist. Celine stumbled, her pulse racing in her temples. The smell of incense and melting candlewax wound through her nostrils. Fear raked its icy hand across her skin.

Save him. Please. Do we have a deal?

"Celine." Michael pulled her close.

Her eyes fluttered open, her chin tilting up. Michael wrapped both arms around her, his touch—his warmth—unfaltering. Lines marred his forehead, his eyes glittering with worry.

"Are you all right?" he whispered.

"I think . . ." She hardened her voice to ward away the tremble. "I think I should return home now."

Michael nodded without question, tucking her protectively beneath his arm before leading them away.

Celine's head pounded, her fingers pressed to her temple. Her vision blurred along the edges, then caught on the wheels of a carriage as it splashed through a nearby puddle. The water silvered, then darkened, and for a beat of time, Celine saw a pair of steel-grey eyes rippling across its surface. Then they vanished like smoke in the wind.

Michael steadied her. Grounded her. With his help, Celine hurried down the lane.

What was happening? To whom was she begging?

And who was the faceless boy with the bloody ring?

A soothing voice warmed through her mind, its accent foreign. Deep. It bid her to relax. Lulled her, like a song sung from a mother's lips. She allowed it to settle around her thoughts, her pulse starting to unwind.

She welcomed it. Anything was better than these sharp stabs of agonizing fear.

Wasn't it?

BASTIEN

---≈---

There is a moment that forever marks your life as before and after.

For a vampire, I suppose this moment is obvious. But I do not wish to be defined by the loss of my humanity, any more than I wish to be defined by the countless faces I am forced to wear each day. The face of the obedient son. The benevolent brother. The cool-headed leader. The vengeful vampire. The lost soul. The forgotten lover.

The trouble with wearing so many faces is that you forget which one is real.

I'd rather my life be defined by the things I should have done. The words I should have spoken. The moments I should have savored. The lives I should have protected.

I should have walked away from the ring that night in the swamp two weeks ago, just like I should have turned away the instant I saw Celine walking along the opposite side of Rue Royale.

But I hungered for more of her, even from a distance.

I knew it was Celine the moment before I noticed the flash of her brilliant red dress. The night I first saw her months ago,

I was struck by a line from a poem Boone often recites in the glow of a full moon:

She walks in beauty, like the night . . .

At the time, I found it ridiculous. Idiotic to think of poetry when confronted with a pretty face. Poetry was the stuff of foolish fancy. And I was not a fool.

I think of that poem often now. In my delirium after the fight with Cambion in the swamp, the last two lines ran through my head in an endless refrain:

A mind at peace with all below, / A heart whose love is innocent!

I am neither at peace nor innocent, no matter how much I may wish it. Such things are the demesne of mortals, not of demons. In moments to myself, I still feel the inky poison from Cambion's claws burn beneath my skin. It would have killed a human within seconds. Perhaps I should feel gratitude that it did no more than incapacitate me for a single evening.

Jae takes hold of my left arm in an ironlike grip. "Bastien." It is a low warning.

I know he has seen Celine strolling toward us on the opposite side of the street, her arm looped through that of my childhood friend Michael Grimaldi.

Boone draws closer, grinning like a shark, his eyes bright. "Let's visit Jackson Square and ogle the silly tourists playing the Minister's Cat." He jostles my shoulder with his. "We can save those murderous looks for fairer game."

I shake them both off, my eyes locked on the pair striding ever closer.

Jae stands before me, blocking my view. "If you don't leave, I will have to remove you by force."

"Try," I whisper, stepping closer. "Since I feel I'm owed at least this moment of grace." I echo Odette's words from the night I was first turned.

Another moment. And another. My life is reduced to nothing but these stolen moments.

Boone crowds us. "If Bastien stays to the shadows, I don't think there's anything wrong with him seeing her from a distance."

Jae glowers at him. I use the distraction to slip into a nearby space between two narrow buildings. When Jae and Boone shift into position behind me, I tilt my Panama hat lower on my brow and continue watching Celine and Michael walk down Royale.

At first, it is not anger I feel. Rather it is a singular kind of pain. One lanced by amusement. I stole a kiss from the girl Michael fancied, those many years ago at cotillion. Fitting that I should stand by and watch as he steals the heart of the only girl I've ever loved.

Michael speaks to Celine as if they share a secret. In return, she offers him a smile, and even from a distance, I can see how much it lightens his soul. He leans closer, and the demon inside me wants to take him apart like a clock, piece by piece, cog by cog. It is the same demon that almost killed Cambion in the swamp. The one my uncle wants to take control, no matter how much I might wish to be rid of it once and for all.

Michael's fingers flex at his sides as they struggle to overcome an unspoken emotion.

Only a fool would deny the obvious.

Michael Grimaldi is in love with Celine Rousseau. It is in every word he speaks, every glance he spares, every tilt of his head toward hers.

I swallow the anger, the tendons in my knuckles pulled tight. Though I have been forged in fury, I have no right to dwell in it.

I need to unmake this anger. To unmake who I have become. To seek out Sunan the Immortal Unmaker, whose name has haunted me since I first heard it in Cambion's thoughts.

An immortal unmaker. One who could return me to my mortal form. The idea of such power taunts me, as it did my mother. The irony of this is not lost on me.

Michael and Celine walk past us on the opposite side of the street. The instant she steps into my direct sight line, Celine stops. Appears to sway as if she might faint. I realize I have moved into the lamplight like a moth drawn to a killing flame when Jae takes hold of my shoulder, returning me to darkness.

"Sébastien." Though Jae's voice is firm, there is sympathy in the way he says my name.

I don't care. I tug at his grasp until he is forced to restrain me.

Something is wrong with Celine. I can see it in Michael's eyes. In the way he has to hold her upright, as if she were some kind of delicate flower. A feeling I know Celine would despise.

I breathe in through my nose. Out through my mouth, the muscles in my chest straining against Jae's iron grasp. Celine tells Michael she wishes to return home. I turn to follow them, unconcerned with everything around me.

Boone takes hold of my other shoulder. "I'll make sure she is safely ensconced in her home." His grip hardens. "You should remain here with Jae."

I know he is right. Instead I spin about, my nostrils flaring. "I'll be damned if—"

"This is not a suggestion, Sébastien," Boone interrupts. "Under no circumstances are you to learn where Celine lives. This is not about what you need. This is about her protection." Lines etch across his forehead. "For God's sake, think with your head and not your heart, brother. Her memories of you are lost. You are no longer of her world. What could you hope to bring her now but pain and misery?"

The rage turns bitter in my throat. I say nothing, only glare at him, my anguish a yoke around my neck.

"It isn't your place to protect her, Bastien," Boone continues. "If you care about Celine, let her live and love among her own kind."

The pain is so sharp that I cannot speak. The tendons in my fists stretch until my fingers turn bloodless. No matter how much I wish it were a lie, I know Boone speaks the truth. I have no right to feel anything when it comes to Celine Rousseau. She asked to be forgotten, just as she asked to forget. It is selfish of me to desire anything more. She gave up her memories to save me. I owe it to her to respect that decision.

But that feeling—that feeling of wanting to unmake the world—rips through my chest. If this Sunan character is real, I would find him. I would have him unmake me. No matter the cost.

"I hate the Brotherhood even more than you do," Jae says, his eyes like obsidian. "But Michael Grimaldi will keep her safe. And we will always watch over her. Make no mistake."

Even as I nod, biting back the taste of bile, I want to defy them. I want to stand before Celine and tell her all that I feel. I want to take Michael apart with my bare hands.

I want. I want. I want.

ÉMILIE

―――≈―――

The wolf spoke in a low growl, a hairsbreadth from Émilie's ear.

His words reverberated through her mind like the clang of a bell, but she took care not to react. She was beyond a place of anger. Beyond a place of retribution. Hers was a fire of blue flame. Pure and uncompromising.

When Émilie's spy left the small, darkened garden, she stood straight and began to pace.

Her brother lived. Sébastien Saint Germain was alive.

The wolf who spied for her—the one who listened and reported on the mutterings of the magical folk throughout the city—had just informed her that Bastien had been seen last night, walking along Rue Royale as if nothing were amiss. As if he had not been attacked by a vampire and had his throat torn out a mere six weeks ago.

Incredulous, she paused and looked toward a night sky spangled with stars. To her right stood a towering bald cypress, its uppermost branches cloaked in strands of Spanish moss.

Though many people loved the haunted look of the moss, it had irked Émilie since childhood. Spanish moss was a weed. If left untended, it could weigh down the branches of even the healthiest tree, choking the life from it over time.

Émilie laughed to herself and continued pacing.

Sébastien was like this weed. No matter how many times fate tried to rip him out by his roots, poison him, or starve him of sunlight, he continued to flourish. To choke the life out of everything around him, even members of his own family and his first true love.

Émilie touched the raised scar of the burn along her collarbone. A burn from the fire her brother had inadvertently started twelve years ago, the day her human life had come to an abrupt end. Heaven knew how it had happened. She supposed such a thing did not matter. Little boys played with fire, and when they did, other people burned.

When Émilie realized her younger brother was still trapped on the top floor of the burning building, she had been the one to break through the line of men and women struggling to extinguish the blaze. A boy in the fire brigade had tried to stop her, but fifteen-year-old Émilie had not cared about the danger. Had not given it a second thought.

Her little brother might die. She could not allow that to happen.

After an agonizing search, she found six-year-old Bastien cowering in a third-floor closet. She raced for the stairs with him in her arms, only to realize the wooden landing and banisters were engulfed in flames. As a last resort, she'd thrown her brother out the window, smoke choking the breath from her body. He'd landed in a sheet a group of men had splayed in the courtyard below. It was a miracle Bastien had not been injured, though the smoke had rendered him unconscious. A moment later, the eave above the window collapsed, preventing Émilie from escaping the same way. But not before she saw her uncle Nicodemus staring grimly at her from the world below, his walking stick gripped in one hand.

Émilie had found herself in a tomb of fire. She'd backed into a corner, her eyes burning, her hair beginning to smolder. When a lick of flame touched the sleeve of her dress, it had ignited before she could muster a scream. The fire had singed her skin, the blaze roaring in her head, her heart raging, begging to be set free.

Fear had overcome her. She'd breathed deeply of the fiery air, letting it burn through her lungs, praying for a reprieve.

She had not seen the figures moving through the flames until the last instant. Until she'd believed them to be angels sent from above. No human could move like that. With such grace and speed, even when threatened by the fires of Hell itself.

When she'd awoken, she'd been on the cusp of death, her body wracked with pain.

"Émilie," a gruff voice had said. "You don't have much time."

She'd struggled to open her eyes.

"You're dying, but I can stop it," he'd continued. "I can give you the power to cheat death."

"U-Uncle?"

"No. I am not the coward who stood by and watched you die a fiery death. But I am here to give you what you wanted from him. What he refused to give to you." The man leaned in until his mouth was beside her ear. "The power to overcome your weaknesses. All you have to do is nod."

Émilie did not have to think twice. The burns on her skin were raw. Every motion she made was excruciating, but she managed a single nod. The man bit her arm, and the pain that spread through her limbs caused her to lose consciousness. When next she woke, she was a werewolf. Meant to cast aside her worldly desires along with all her earthly loyalties.

From that moment onward, Émilie was no longer a Saint Germain. The very utterance of the name caused hot anguish to race through her veins. The Saint Germains had brought her nothing but death and suffering, just as they had with the wolves, who'd lost everything for casting their lot with the vampires. In the end, her uncle—the one who was supposed to protect them all—had stood by and watched her die.

The sight of Nicodemus' golden gaze staring up at her through the smoke had been etched onto each of Émilie's memories for more than a decade. It fed her. Sustained her hatred.

In the end, it was Luca and his family—especially his father, who had turned her—who gave her what she'd desired for so long. A place to call her own. They answered any and all of her questions. All the things Nicodemus had denied her, they gave without reservations.

And Émilie had become one of them.

From Luca, she'd learned how vampires and werewolves had once lived in the Otherworld, in a land of perpetual night known as the Sylvan Wyld. He told her how the vampires and werewolves had consorted with one another to lord over the mortal domain. How the vampires had attempted to sell immortality to the highest bidder. How they'd all been banished from the Sylvan Wyld for the vampires' actions.

How the vampires had eventually forsaken the wolves in their quest to achieve dominance in the mortal realm.

Over time, Luca professed his love. And Émilie returned it, in her own way. She loved him for being her family. For always putting her first. But Luca wanted to marry her, and a woman like Émilie was not meant to be contained. When she gave love, it was without restraint, to men and women alike. And whatever she offered was hers to give, to whomever she chose, whenever she chose to give it. Something men like Luca or her uncle or even her younger brother would never understand.

Wrath took hold of Émilie, all but strangling the breath from her body. What was it about young men like Sébastien Saint Germain that blessed them with the nine lives of a cat? No mortal could have survived his wounds. Émilie had been specific when she ordered Nigel Fitzroy to murder her brother that night in Saint Louis Cathedral. For everything their uncle Nicodemus had done to Émilie in life—for all Bastien had taken from her—her little brother was not to breathe in the free light of day ever again.

If you must, separate his head from his body. But make sure he does not survive.

Those had been her very words.

She stopped short again.

If Bastien's wounds were intended to kill a mortal man, that could only mean one thing. Nicodemus had turned the last living member of his bloodline into a vampire.

Which meant he'd broken his treaty with the Brotherhood.

A slow smile unfurled across Émilie's face. She should tell Luca at once. Let her erstwhile lover know that their decade of peace with the Fallen had come to an ignominious end. What followed would ensure at least several years of war between the vampires and the werewolves. And war was a time for great strides to be made, especially for the industrious.

Of which Émilie was and always would be.

Since no one in life had drawn attention to her myriad talents, she would be the one to do it now. If a mediocre young man could crow to the world about his mediocrity, then why should a superior young woman not do the same?

Yes. Émilie should tell Luca. It was past time.

But she wouldn't. Not now. Not when she still had a winning hand to play.

Her grin widened. Her wolf spy had told her something else. Luca's younger cousin Michael was falling in love with Celine Rousseau, the girl Bastien had died trying to protect.

Fortune truly did smile upon the bold.

A simple mind might think it sufficient to upset the balance between these immortal foes by telling Luca what she had learned. But Émilie wished to wreak more than temporary havoc. She wished to destroy the very foundation. A foundation that put her in second place, no matter how much more gifted or worthy she might be to those lauded above her.

It would be a victory to savor when Michael was drawn into their world. A world from which Luca endeavored to spare his cousin for the whole of the young detective's life. Though the blood of the wolf ran through Michael's veins, he managed to evade the curse bestowed on his kind by the Banishment. He had not yet turned, nor was there much chance of him turning. If things continued in this fashion, Michael could live his entire life removed from this world of dark magic.

Émilie had no intention of keeping Michael removed, especially after what she'd learned. True, it was unfair to the boy. But boys like him played with fire, and when they did, other people burned.

Now that the tables were turned, should it be any different?

Delicious to think Nicodemus Saint Germain's heir and the youngest cousin of Luca Grimaldi could be set on a path of mutual destruction. The events that were sure to follow would be delightful to witness and exploit.

But first . . . but first . . . Émilie had much to consider.

Unlike vampires, there were three ways for a wolf to be made.

The first was to be the immediate heir to the legacy. The eldest remaining male of the bloodline, which was how Luca had inherited the role, following the death of his father during the last war with the Fallen. Indeed, Luca's father had only earned the position a handful of years prior, after Michael's father had perished in battle.

The second way to be turned was to be bitten by a wolf. This was the way Émilie had become a member of the pack. It was risky and painful, for the mortal in question had to forfeit their human life in order to undergo the change. Many succumbed to their wounds or died during the agony of their first full moon.

It was a risk Émilie had gladly undertaken. Fire was necessary to forge a weapon of steel.

The last and most heinous of all ways to become a wolf was to kill a member of your own family within the bloodline. Often the wolves who were turned in such a manner were shunned. Hunted by the rest of the pack for daring to murder one of their own.

Émilie tilted her head toward the sky.

How . . . thrilling a prospect.

And in the ensuing chaos, if a star were to rise from behind the shadow of a waning moon, who would hesitate to gaze upon its light?

Émilie la Loup had plans. Plans upon plans. And it was time for her to execute, in more ways than one.

Perhaps she would start with a wedding.

Bastien

I cannot sleep, so I do not dream.

Perhaps it is impossible for a vampire as troubled as I am to dream. Perhaps such a thing is the purview of the living: to envision a life apart from reality. To hope for something better and richer than the wretched now.

I lie awake in my four-poster bed, the velvet curtains drawn. I stare at the golden lion medallion situated in the tufted canopy above me, my thoughts taking shape in the darkness like shadows coming to life.

Without warning, I sit up.

Sunan the Immortal Unmaker.

If I returned to the swamp and asked to speak with Cambion, what might happen?

Dark laughter rumbles from my chest.

I bested the tiger-beast in the ring using nothing more than sheer luck. I shamed him in front of his peers. In front of those he considered family. Cambion of the Swamp would not look kindly upon me, despite my sparing his life. It was clear the moment the portly master of ceremonies announced our bout that those who dwelled in the depths of the swamp had nothing but disdain for the vampires who ruled from their gilded thrones in the city.

But the wanting inside me continues to grow each day.

I want to learn more about this Sunan. Does magic like this even exist? Would it truly be possible for me to return the dark gift that made me a vampire? What would be the cost?

Is it possible to be human again?

These things plague me. Gnaw at my insides. Or maybe they are only distractions.

Maybe these are the kinds of dreams permitted me now. A chance to once again walk unencumbered in the sun. To go to Celine. To win her heart once more. To find a way to return her stolen memories. Or work to earn her love a second, a third, a thousandth time.

Love is a strange beast. It is not so different from fear. Both make us feel uncertain and on edge. Uncomfortable in our own skins. Hot and cold at the same time.

But only one of them is drawn from hope.

I think about what drew me to Celine in the first place. It would be a lie to say I wasn't struck by her beauty. But the Crescent City has the loveliest young débutantes in the whole of the South. Belles of every proverbial ball. The last few years, my uncle has made several pointed introductions to daughters of important men throughout Louisiana. Each young woman was accomplished and articulate, spoke several languages, and understood her supposed place. Perhaps that is why I found none of them appealing.

I don't want someone who understands and accepts the world she is given. I want someone who expects more. Who fights for it and isn't afraid to dirty her sleeves in the process.

I want a girl like Celine Rousseau. No, not *like* her. I want *her*. The want consumes me.

Again I laugh into the darkness.

Such selfish thoughts. Even in my waking dreams, I think only of what I want.

My thoughts return to Sunan. If an unmaker such as he—or she—exists, there might be something about it in the written lore. The old library in the heart of the Vieux Carré contains many of the best-known accounts of fey creatures this side of the Mississippi. Additionally there is a bokor on Dumaine with a famous collection of mystical tomes. Alas, this particular voodoo priest would be unlikely to lend them to a vampire, as he is known to serve good mystères rather than evil.

Perhaps it is time for me to have my fétiche made so that I can walk about in the daylight and plead my case in person. Or maybe I should ask one of the mortal servants in my uncle's household if they would mind borrowing a few books from the library for me.

I could also simply continue wearing the mask I have worn for the last six weeks, one of dissolution and debauchery. That is the easiest, most expected course of action for a newborn vampire.

If I wear this mask long enough, perhaps I'll forget that I ever wanted anything else.

CELINE

───────────❧───────────

The puppy bounded through the shop, her short legs causing her to tumble every third step. Nonetheless she righted herself each time, her stubby tail wagging with joy, her cheerful barks filling the space with the sound of happiness.

Then the little corgi squatted right in the center of the new rug, lolled her tongue at Celine, and began to urinate.

"Pippa," Celine wailed toward the back room. "Collect your tiny terror or else she's liable to ruin the entire establishment before we've even opened our doors."

"Queen Elizabeth!" Pippa scolded as she rushed into the shop in a flurry of pale green linen, her white silk sash trailing behind her. The second the corgi saw Pippa, she rolled over and yipped once, her four little feet in the air. "Elizabeth"—Pippa pointed a finger down at the grinning dog—"we've discussed this. Your behavior is unbecoming of a monarch of England." With an apologetic glance at Celine, Pippa swiped the protesting royal off the floor and passed the puppy to Antonia, who'd only just finished taking stock of loose merchandise to be sorted tomorrow.

"Such a naughty little cadela," Antonia cooed, the Portuguese word rolling from her tongue. "Come sit beside me in the store-room, minha filha. If you behave, I promise you a piece of ham and maybe a bit of bread and cheese."

"No ham," Pippa implored. "She'll be a beast later."

Laughter rumbled from the storeroom. "Quelle surprise, for she's a beast now." Eloise Henri emerged from the doorway, wiping her hands on an otherwise pristine apron. The smell of honey and lavender filled the room with every step the lovely Créole girl took. Her dark skin shone beneath the length of colorful fabric wrapped around her head, its ends folded in an intricate fashion resembling the points of a crown.

"Antonia?" Eloise asked. "Would you mind coming to test the latest batch of cold cream, tout de suite? I added more lavender oil, and I think it's quite an improvement, especially with your suggestion of a rosehip infusion."

"Of course," Antonia said, placing Queen Elizabeth on the floor beside the till.

"I can't wait to try it," Pippa chimed in. "Would you like me to offer my opinion?"

Eloise's smile was warm. "Of course. I'd like everyone here to try it once it's ready. I just haven't quite mastered my mother's recipe, and Antonia's advice on medicinal herbs has been une révélation. Would you mind waiting until the next batch?"

Pippa nodded just as the mischievous corgi made an attempt to flee. A brief spate of chaos rang throughout the shop as the three young women attempted to corner the puppy, who decided the entire enterprise was a most amus-ing kind of game. Soon Antonia managed to capture the little queen, holding the corgi tightly as she followed Eloise into the storeroom with Pippa in tow. A moment later, the dog yipped in outrage. Likely she'd been returned to her little box in the corner to contemplate her actions. Antonia began to sing a Portuguese lullaby, her rich alto swirling through the air in tandem with the puppy's cries.

Celine bit back a smile as she adjusted the chintz drapes around the front of the shop window until they hung just so. She stepped back, pleased with the overall effect. Soft fabric and jewel tones surrounded her. A tufted chaise covered in ivory damask lined the back wall, along with four matching stools, one for each corner. Framing three of the shop's walls were freshly painted shelves lined with bolts of fabric, rolls of ribbon, and stacks of the newest fashion plates from Paris, bound like books by the ever-industrious Eloise. Oiled ladders glided along brass casters, reminding Celine of her favorite library on Rue de Richelieu in Paris.

Their shop was almost perfect.

To be sure, a few lingering issues remained. The sign in front of the shop had yet to be hung. Two of the covers for the gas lamps had cracked in transit, their replacements scheduled to arrive by the end of the week. But even before their doors were officially open, six orders had been placed. Two seamstresses in the Marigny had been hired to begin the work, based on Celine's designs. Every so often, a potential customer would ring the bell outside or knock on the narrow double doors to make an inquiry.

Toting a rag and a bucket of sudsy water, Pippa emerged from the storeroom to begin cleaning Queen Elizabeth's mess from the carpet.

"It's nice to see you smile," Pippa remarked as she rolled up her sleeves.

Celine turned in place. "Today has been a rather good day."

Pippa beamed. "I agree." She dipped the rag in the water and wrung it out. "And how did you fare last night? Did you sleep well?"

Celine's smile faltered. "Of course."

"Don't lie to me, dearest. I heard you tossing and turning through the walls of our flat," Pippa replied, her Yorkshire accent winding through the words. "Was it the same dream?"

Unease brought color to Celine's cheeks. "I think so. But it's . . . difficult to recall. Like trying to hold on to a handful of water."

"Dreams often are." Pippa's expression turned pensive. She gnawed at her lower lip while she scrubbed the carpet. "And the doctor did say you would have trouble with your memory for the next few months because of your head injury."

Celine pressed her fingers to her temple, irritation drawing her dark brows together.

Pippa stood at once, bubbles dripping down her hands. "Does your head hurt?"

"No. I'm just . . . frustrated."

"Of course you are. Who wouldn't be, given the situation?" She gnawed at her lip again.

"There's no need to look so guilty, Pippa," Celine joked. "*You* didn't strike me in the skull or break my ribs."

Pippa toyed with the chain of the golden cross around her neck. "You're right. But perhaps . . . I could have done more to protect you. And I wish—I wish I could restore your memories. At least fill in some of the holes."

"It would make it easier," Celine agreed. "But the doctor says it is better for me to find them on my own, so that my mind might seek order for itself in its own time . . . or whatever that's supposed to mean." Her sigh was rueful. "Michael's grandmother agreed. She told me when Luca returned from fighting for the Union forces in the war, she didn't push him to tell her all that he'd seen or suffered. She waited for him to come to her when he was ready. Perhaps I should do the same and wait until my mind is ready."

Pippa nodded. "It makes a great deal of sense. In any case, it's best to heed the doctor's advice." She took in a deep breath. Then forced an even brighter smile on her face before stooping to finish her work. "Did I tell you Phoebus has invited me to dinner tonight?"

Celine sat on the carpet beside Pippa, her amethyst skirts pooling around her. "You did not. Where is he taking you?"

"All he said was that it would be to the most celebrated dining establishment in the Vieux Carré."

Celine's eyes went wide. "You don't think he might—"

"Propose?" Nervous laughter flew from Pippa's lips. "Goodness, no. He only promised a dinner with cut crystal and sparkling chandeliers and centerpieces of glorious hothouse flowers. Perhaps that famous dessert they set on fire. Nothing more."

A sudden image—of champagne being poured into a brass basin filled with rose petals, of meringue islands floating in a sea of sweetened cream, of caramel and bourbon bursting into blue flame—flashed through Celine's mind. She squeezed her eyes shut. When she opened them once more, a name flickered along her periphery, a sign written in elegant script with a blurred symbol beneath it. "Are you talking about Jacques'?"

Pippa paled. "I—how would—I mean, yes, I am."

"Have I been there before for a meal?"

"No, no. Not for a meal." Pippa waved a dismissive hand. "We went there once, for a short amount of time, to take measurements for Miss Valmont's masquerade costume." Another smile bloomed across her face. "It's wonderful that you remember it, though. That's progress."

"Strange," Celine said softly. "I could have sworn I've eaten there. I can almost taste the food on my tongue."

"Or perhaps you heard someone speak of it?" Pippa gathered the bucket and the rag. "Jacques' is famous even outside the city. If the food is as wonderful as it is touted to be, we should go sometime. Perhaps even to celebrate the opening of the shop?"

Pippa's babbling struck Celine as unusual, for it was so uncharacteristic. Coupled with the strange way Pippa kept chewing at her lip, Celine became convinced her friend was hiding something from her, in the same way she felt Michael had been lying three nights ago along Rue Royale.

Hell and damnation.

Why was everyone acting as if Celine were too frail to handle the truth?

Her annoyance spiked hot in her stomach. She was about to corner Pippa and demand honesty when the bell in the front of the shop chimed. Celine turned to answer it, but Pippa raced past her, clearly thankful for the distraction.

The gentleman who stepped across the threshold possessed a bearing reminiscent of a painting. One depicting a victor surveying a field of battle. Though he was not tall, something about him struck Celine as regal. Even the way he strode into the shop demanded respect.

He seemed . . . familiar.

The young man studied her without speaking. Celine met his gaze, certain she would recall him if she stared at him long enough.

He appeared to be from the Far East. When the light of the setting sun touched his brow, Celine had the strangest feeling he didn't like it. As if the rays of sunlight caused him pain. He looked to be in his early twenties, though his features retained a suggestion of youth. His eyes—a deep, dark brown—shone with a bright light, almost as if he were feverish. He turned his back to the window and gave her a curt bow, his top hat in hand.

"Good evening," Celine said with a smile. "How may we help you?"

"I would like to order a gift, please."

"Is there something in particular you are looking for, sir?" Pippa's words were clipped. Tinged with an odd sort of irritation. As if she did not wish to welcome the young man into their establishment.

He ignored Pippa, choosing instead to offer Celine a stiff kind of smile. "Perhaps some gloves, a hat, or a set of lace handkerchiefs?"

"Of course," Celine replied. She turned to find Pippa hovering beside her, an anxious expression lining her brow. Celine shooed her away.

"You'll have to forgive my colleague," Celine said to their customer. "It's unusual for a gentleman to come into our shop alone. Is there a certain color or type of fabric you prefer? We can assist you with the gloves and the handkerchiefs, but the milliner two streets over would better suit your needs if you're interested in a hat or a bonnet."

The unusually laconic customer made his way toward a small white table with a neat arrangement of embroidered gloves. When he reached for them, Celine noticed a set of vicious scars on the back of his hand. A gasp flew from her lips.

He pivoted at once, his eyes narrowing. "Is something wrong?"

When Celine looked back down at his hands, the skin there appeared unblemished once more. As if she'd imagined the scars in the first place. "I'm sorry," she said. "I thought I saw something."

"May I ask what it was?" His lips formed a thin line.

"Please excuse my strange behavior. It's clear I'm in need of rest."

The gentleman continued watching her. He cocked his head to one side, like a bird. Then the edges of his face began to shimmer like the surface of a stone baking under the summer sun.

Celine blinked. Took a startled step back.

For an instant, the gentleman before her looked entirely different. As if the whole of his body was marred by the same smattering of crosshatched scars she'd seen on his hands. Even his face was marked in the same fashion. His features became more angular, the tips of his ears tapering to points. When one side of his mouth rose in the suggestion of a smile, Celine could swear he had fangs, like those of a demon.

She shook her head. Squeezed her eyes shut. When she opened them again, he appeared to be a normal man once more. Fear ricocheted through her blood.

Celine blinked again. "I apologize. Please—excuse me," she stammered. "Pippa, would you mind assisting the gentleman at the till?" Then she fled to the storeroom, feeling the unsettling young gentleman's gaze follow her with every step.

I

———≈———

U nbeknownst to those inside, a stranger in a bowler hat studied the scene unfolding within the dress shop. He cracked his gloved knuckles once, then removed a graphite pencil and a pad of paper from his left breast pocket.

No more than a minute was spent jotting down today's observations. Then the stranger smoothed his handlebar mustache and vanished around the nearest street corner.

Jae

―――≈―――

"Here he is, that strange Chinaman."

Jae was so lost in his thoughts, he almost missed the hatred aimed at him like the barrel of a gun. He paused just before the entrance to his building, listening to the elderly woman speak from the gallery above.

He knew it was her. It was always her.

"I still have trouble believing they allowed those boys to take up residence here," the woman continued, her words soaked in spite.

Her friend beside her clucked in agreement. "It couldn't be helped. Le Comte de Saint Germain owns this building. He gave them leave to reside here, for Lord knows what reason."

"The count should care what the neighbors think. To let a Chinaman and that peculiar dark-skinned boy from the East Indies live among us . . ." She tsked. "They aren't Christian, I tell you," she whispered. "I'm almost certain I saw one of those profane statues in their hallway."

"That Indian boy grows strange herbs on his balcony. They smell wretched and attract flies."

"He's nowhere near as bad as the Chinaman. He's like a ghost, the way he walks without making a sound. Why, this one time . . ."

Jae listened to their continuing conversation, a variation on a theme from three days ago. He focused on it. Let their ignorance flow through him and around him, bathing in the heat of their hate.

Then he let it go. Released it, like the petals of a flower on a passing breeze.

It had been the same wherever he went. The lesson he had learned the moment he set foot on Western soil. If he fought against these falsities—if he tried to reason with the unreasonable—matters would only escalate, to no one's satisfaction.

One time in Dubrovnik, he murdered a man for proudly wearing the badge of his prejudice. In the moment, Jae relished the feeling of crushing the man's windpipe in his fist after draining him dry. But the next night he discovered another putrid sack of hate in his place.

It wasn't about the individual. It was about the collective.

Until hate was untaught as it had been taught, this would be Jae's lot in life. Arjun's lot in life. Hortense's and Madeleine's lots in life. Indeed, even Odette—with her pale skin and radiant smile—was subjected to hatred for loving as she did, against someone else's beliefs.

Strangely this thought was comforting to Jae. The only place he'd ever lived where he'd not had to explain himself was in New Orleans, among his brethren in the Court of the Lions.

And he was thankful for every member of his chosen family. For the bonds they formed together as outsiders, in more ways than one.

Jae took the stairs three at a time. He paused on the landing beside the elderly woman's flat. Nodded once in mocking salute before resuming his climb to the top floor of the four-storied building. Using an ornate key, he unlocked the door to the two-bedroom flat he shared with Arjun. The wards spelled into the floor beside his feet glowed in welcome as he crossed the threshold. One of only two individuals permitted solo entry.

Then Jae removed his cap and checked to make sure the small blades concealed in the cuffs of his shirt were accessible. That the revolver in his shoulder holster was still loaded with silver bullets. It was his ritual. Had been for years. The first thing he did before letting down his guard at home was to check and make sure each of his weapons was ready and close at hand.

Jae strode past Arjun's statue of Ganesha—the deva's elephant head tilted to one side—toward the full-length mirror leaning against the far wall. A strange thing for two young men of seemingly modest means to possess in this day and age. Framed in tarnished brass, the mirror's surface appeared aged, the silver dotted with dark speckles.

He stared at his reflection. Pondered what had happened earlier this evening with Celine Rousseau. She'd pierced through his glamour. Of that Jae could be certain. The question was how.

As he stared at the scars on his right cheek—tracing them with his eyes, as he always did—his reflection shimmered. The surface of the mirror turned to liquid mercury, like a lake disturbed by a sudden breeze.

Jae was not alarmed to see this. Rather he expected it. It was time for him to answer for his most recent transgressions. He waited until the surface of the mirror settled. Until it no longer reflected an image of his own face. Instead a large rowan tree bloomed to life, flanked by a copse of emerald ash, their trunks covered in tiny blossoms. Pale green, pink, purple, and blue peonies covered the base of the gnarled rowan tree. The edges of each petal appeared to be dusted with flakes of gold. When a breeze coiled through the branches above, a powder made of crushed diamonds trailed in its wake. The feathers of the lone bird that flitted by glowed from within, its beak gleaming of sharpened iron and its eyes the sinister red of rubies.

A single glance was all it took to realize this was not the kind of forest that existed on the mortal plane.

From behind the rowan tree emerged a stunning woman, the layers of her thin organza gown rustling around her bare feet. She said nothing as she floated into view, her slender shoulders draped with a white silk cape trimmed in fox fur. A silver coronet rested across her pale brow, her face highlighted by crushed pearls, her lips lacquered black. Her long ebony hair hung past her waist, her sloe-shaped eyes alert. Focused.

"You've been avoiding me," she said in the language of Jae's childhood, the Korean words soothing to his ears. "I find it unforgivable. Were you a lesser creature, I would have fed you to my mole rats. They do enjoy a disappointing meal."

Jae bowed low. "Deepest apologies, my lady. There is no

excuse for my behavior. Please do not hesitate to summon me whenever you desire, for whatever punishment you deem appropriate."

She blinked once. Perused his face, her chin tilting to the right. A gentle smile softened her expression, the pearl powder along her cheekbones glowing. "Our last interaction left much to be desired. Perhaps I have been avoiding you, too." Her smile grew, causing her jet-black eyes to crinkle at the edges. "Forgive my rash words, Jaehyuk-*ah*. There was little you could have done to keep Celine safe. It was wrong of me to blame you."

"I did fail in my task to protect her, my lady. Your anger is warranted."

A furrow formed across her regal forehead. "My anger should not be with you. The Fallen have crossed me one too many times. For Nicodemus to take liberties with a daughter of the Vale's memory is something I cannot allow to stand." Her voice rose as she spoke, its dulcet tones weaving through the branches above, shaking free a cascade of leaves. Then all at once her features returned to serene. "But that is a matter for another time. I wish to accelerate our plans. You must bring Celine to me at once."

Alarm flickered across Jae's face. "My lady, respectfully, I do not think that would be wise. The mist will be lifted from her sight soon. Her eighteenth birthday is less than three months away. Would it not be better to wait and—"

The beautiful woman's anger caused all the petals by her feet to scatter. They threaded through her fingers and around her wrists before vanishing into nothingness. "Celine is no mere mortal. I will not allow her memories to be stolen from her again by a cursed blood drinker. Bring her to me at once, Shin Jaehyuk."

Jae steeled himself. There were few creatures in either world that truly scared him. The powerful Lady of the Vale was one of them. "My concern for Celine's well-being is not unfounded, my lady. Tonight I received proof that the sway over her memories is starting to fracture. Nicodemus' control over her is waning. I fear what might happen if we press her too far. She has endured much in the last few months. If her mind is pushed beyond the brink, she may turn her back on our world entirely." He paused. "And she will never willingly return to the Summer Court of the Sylvan Vale."

Worry etched a path across the fey woman's countenance. "It was folly for me to make that promise to her father. I regretted it the moment I made it." She lifted her chin. "But a promise is a promise, no matter how much I might wish it otherwise."

"You did what had to be done to keep Celine safe from the monsters of our world."

"And instead I surrendered her to the monsters of the earth. Would she not have fared better in our world, after all? For it appears she was destined to be surrounded by monsters from the day of her birth. Perhaps in my attempt to protect her, I have made her more vulnerable."

"She only suspects there might be such a thing as monsters, my lady." Jae's tone was sympathetic.

"And would it not have been better to know that in truth?"

Jae bowed once more. "Apologies, my lady, but suspecting

monsters might exist is not the same as meeting them in the flesh. Celine is a fearless young woman. Much of the strength she possesses is because she was allowed to flourish with her father in the mortal world." His frown deepened. "Ethereals do not fare well in our world, as you know. Arjun Desai is proof of that fact. He suffered a great deal of torment as a child growing up in the Vale."

After a time, the woman in the mirror nodded. "Very well, Jaehyuk-*ah*. We will wait until Celine's eighteenth birthday. Then you will bring my daughter to me. It is time for her to learn who she truly is."

"Yes, Lady Silla." Jae bowed deeply. "As ever, I am in your debt."

CELINE

⚊≋⚊

It was the sort of night made for enchantment.

The sky was filled with winking stars. A rare blue moon silvered the wet streets of New Orleans. Along Royale, gas lamps danced in their iron cages, and the sound of laughter and the clattering of horse hooves rang out in the early April air.

Celine had read about nights made for enchantment in the books she devoured as a child. Mostly fairy tales by the Brothers Grimm or Hans Christian Andersen. Her father had preferred Andersen's lighter, moralistic tales, but Celine had found the darker Grimm stories ever so much more appealing. Something about them spoke to her. Drew her into a deep, dark well of delicious secrets.

From there, she'd collected romantic tomes about enchanted evenings in forbidden forests. Many of them had been prohibited by her scholarly father. But Celine had borrowed them in secret from her friend Josephine. The ones she'd enjoyed most had been about sworn enemies who fell in love. About mysterious princes and princesses. Masked balls and fey creatures. Tales filled with blood and murder and retribution.

Among them were the novels written by Alexandre Dumas

père. Celine's fascination with the Man in the Iron Mask had been so great, she'd reread *Le Vicomte de Bragelonne* enough that the seams of the book had begun to fray. Her love had only grown following Dumas' death two years ago, when Celine learned he was a writer of mixed heritage. A man with a French nobleman for a father and a Haitian slave for a grandmother. Someone with lineage from two different worlds, like her. She wondered whether Dumas had known much about his grandmother's story, or if his father had cloistered him from it as Celine's father had with her. In moments of whimsy, she'd wondered whether they could have been friends.

It had been an age since Celine read a book. A year ago, her father discovered her cache of forbidden novels and destroyed them, claiming that she was rotting her brain with such nonsense. The only tome that had survived was Celine's frail copy of *Le Vicomte de Bragelonne*. She'd left it behind when she fled Paris in January, after murdering a wealthy boy who tried to assault her on a night she still had trouble recollecting in full.

Celine had lost so much. Her own mother. Her own memories.

Darkness hovered above her like a specter threatening to descend.

She swallowed. Stared up at the flickering stars, determined not to let these worries dampen her spirits any more than they already had. A warm feeling—akin to the sensation of settling in a hot bath—spread across her skin. Perhaps it was better for her to forget the circumstances that caused her pain. Celine did not feel remorse for what she had done in protecting herself from the boy who'd assaulted her, but she wasn't foolish enough to ignore the consequences that might come to pass one day. Likely, she'd spend the rest of her life looking over her shoulder.

When Celine turned the corner and saw the ornate sign hanging above, she made a promise to herself that she would ignore the descending darkness for tonight and worry about such things tomorrow. Then she sent a smile to the young man beside her.

"Isn't this the right place?" she asked Michael, staring up at the three-storied building of red brick, its narrow double doors and lacquered shutters glistening like polished pewter.

Michael's lips pursed, his pale eyes shifting across her face in slow deliberation. He nodded.

Celine reached for his arm. "Don't worry about the cost. I invited you as my guest, which is a pittance when compared with everything you've done for me these past seven weeks."

"It has nothing to do with the cost." Michael bristled. "And there is no need for you to repay me."

"You and Nonna and Luca have treated me like family. No, *better* than family. I only wish they would have accepted my invitation to join us tonight."

Michael snorted. "Nonna refuses to pay for prepared food, even from the finest dining establishments. She doesn't believe anyone can cook better than she can."

Laughter bubbled from Celine's lips. "She is probably correct."

"And they treat you like family because that is how they feel." Michael's words were soft. Careful.

Celine smiled with equal care, though something gripped inside her chest. She tugged on Michael's arm, but still he remained rooted to the flagstone pavers just beyond the threshold. "I feel the same way," she said. "So will you not let me treat you to the finest cuisine in New Orleans?"

"As I said before, it's unnecessary."

"Pippa told me it was the most beautiful meal she's ever had in her life."

"I've heard the same." Despite Michael's reticence, a grin ghosted across his lips. "And I've never known someone more passionate about food than you."

Her green eyes danced. "Food is life, after all."

"Food *permits* life," he amended. "We should eat to live, not live to eat."

Celine's expression turned grave. "I've never been so disappointed in someone. It's time we changed your perspective for the better, Detective Grimaldi." She pulled him toward the opened doors.

Michael held back a moment more. Took a deep breath. Then followed her into the warm, well-lit space.

The instant they crossed the threshold, another odd sensation warmed through Celine's stomach. A feeling of being pushed back and pulled forward, all at once. As if half of her wished to flee and the other wished to sink its teeth into this world of cut crystal, fine china, and intoxicating decadence.

Celine inhaled the rich scent of bloodred wine, warm spices, and melting butter. "Isn't this marvelous?" she said, her eyes flitting about the glowing chamber.

"It is indeed," Michael replied, though his frown deepened.

"You worry too much." She wrapped her arm around his in a

reassuring fashion, the sleeve of her French linen dress fluttering with the movement. "Our shop's benefactress, Mademoiselle Valmont, told me she would make sure to save the best table in the house for us. She's well acquainted with the purveyor, and said he owes her a favor."

The corners of Michael's eyes tightened. "I didn't know you told Miss Valmont about our plans to come to dinner here."

"It was at her suggestion that I come to Jacques' tonight."

"Of course it was," Michael muttered under his breath.

Celine shot him a withering look just as a white-gloved gentleman in an ivory dinner jacket offered them a bow.

"Mademoiselle Rousseau?" he said, his brown eyes warm. "I've been directed to escort you to your table." He led Celine and Michael toward the far-left corner of the expansive room. It was obvious to anyone in the establishment that this was a place of honor, situated for guests to see and be seen. In the table's damasked center was a beautiful bouquet of hothouse roses, their petals like crimson velvet, their scent reminding Celine of a famous parfumerie on the Avenue des Champs-Élysées. A crystal-and-brass chandelier glittered above them, its refracted light catching fire on the Wedgwood china and the solid silver utensils.

Delight rippled through Celine. She'd never experienced something so luxurious in all her life.

Nearby, another server removed a domed lid from a tray of steaming food. The smell wafting their way startled Celine, for it brought a flurry of thoughts into sharp focus. Of the same flowers with the same scintillating perfume. Of another table in a shadowy room. Of muted feminine laughter. Of sparkling champagne and roasted quail.

Of feeling safe and warm and loved.

Celine shook her head and squeezed her eyes shut as if to banish the false memory. She'd never eaten at Jacques' before. Pippa had said so, and it made no sense for her friend to lie about this. Celine would not allow her mind to betray her tonight.

Another elegant server set two fluted glasses before Michael and Celine, pausing to pour each of them a measure of bubbling champagne. Then, with a flourish, he placed napkins of fine ivory linen across both their laps.

An awkward smile curved up one side of Michael's face. He reached for his glass and held it aloft. "To all you have achieved. And to all you *will* achieve."

Celine's smile was bright and easy. Filled with unfettered gratitude. She liked Michael Grimaldi more than she could ever remember liking any other young man. He was kind and thoughtful. Conscientious and attentive. All the things a desirable gentleman should be.

So why was she still equivocating about her feelings?

She should fall in love with him. It would be easy to fall in love with him.

As Celine studied Michael from across the table, a searing intensity honed his features, sending a riot of emotions through her veins. She hadn't meant to linger in her sentiments as she had. It would only serve to encourage him, and she wasn't ready to make that kind of commitment. Not yet.

Clearing her throat, Celine said, "Isn't this lovely? I've never eaten at any establishment quite so extravagant."

"Not even in Paris?"

She shook her head. "My father loves fine cuisine as much as I do, but we never could have afforded something like this. He's always been a pragmatic man. A scholar of language and linguistics." Celine grinned. "But that didn't stop him from bringing me my favorite pastry every year for my birthday."

A fond light entered Michael's gaze. "It's good to hear you speak of your father. You rarely say anything about your past."

"I suppose"—Celine weighed her response before making it—"it's because I did not leave Paris under the best of circumstances. I miss my father a great deal, and the thought of him brings me pain." She said no more, hoping Michael would not press her for more information. Almost six months after the fact, it was likely her father had been apprised of what happened that fateful night in Paris this past winter. Which meant Guillaume Rousseau would think his only child a murderess.

Would he believe her story? Would *any* man?

It wasn't a topic Celine wished to ponder at length. So instead she propped her elbows along the table's edge and settled her chin atop her folded hands. "We will have to tell Luca to bring his new wife to Jacques' once they return from Europe."

Michael groaned. "Don't remind me of that travesty. It still galls me how my heretofore-responsible cousin could do such a reckless thing."

"He's in love." Celine smiled. "I don't know why Nonna is in such a snit over it."

"Luca knows how much Nonna wished to attend his wedding. In a proper church. With a proper priest."

"But an elopement to London is so romantic, don't you think?"

"I don't favor the idea of elopement. It seems rather selfish. But . . . I suppose if it's what my future wife wanted." Michael settled his piercing eyes on hers. "I might entertain the notion."

Celine drained her glass of champagne. They were both treading on dangerous ground. Was it too much for her to hope for one more night without the weight of the future pressing down on their shoulders? She would face the inevitable tomorrow, she swore she would. Michael had been patient with her. It was time she told him in no uncertain terms whether or not she returned his feelings.

"Have you ever indulged in rash behavior of any kind?" Celine asked.

Michael toyed with the scalloped handle of his butter knife. "When I was a boy. My childhood friend and I made quite a few errors in judgment. One afternoon we devised a rather ingenious way to snare bullfrogs in the swamp beyond the city, and I was caught in a mudslide." He flinched at the memory. "It smelled like sulfur and wood rot. My friend ran to get Luca so they could pull me out. For a harrowing hour or so, I was certain the gators would pluck the skin off my bones." He paused, his expression morose. "In fact, most of the worst things I did when I was boy were in the company of this particular friend, a selfish young man from a prominent family. I'm grateful we had a falling-out some years ago, before he went away to West Point. Perhaps I would not have set my sights on the police force if I hadn't had the clarity of that distance." His tone was clipped. Precise. A trait Celine had come to expect from the young detective.

"What was the reason you had a falling-out, if I may ask?" she pressed.

"There was a streak of wickedness in him I could no longer afford to ignore."

"Not to mention the selfishness, a characteristic you despise."

"I think there are times to be selfish and times to be selfless. It is the measure of a man which path he chooses in any given moment."

"So wise, Detective Grimaldi." Celine grinned. "But maybe there are times when you could be a little wicked, if you wanted?" She leaned forward as if she were chatting with a friend.

Which she was, wasn't she? No matter what happened, they would remain friends.

It was a mistake for her to edge closer. For the briefest of instants, Michael's gaze dipped to Celine's chest. He flushed crimson when she pulled back, his embarrassment plain. "I suppose I could." Michael glanced right, and his attention caught on a figure approaching from behind Celine. "That stout fellow striding our way is the police commissioner. He'll want to speak with me." He groaned.

"Of course he will," Celine said, thankful for the distraction. "You're the hero who caught the Crescent City killer." Though she smiled as she spoke, a twinge of discomfort knifed through her stomach. She stood in a lithe motion, her tufted chair sliding across the wooden floor beside her satin slippers.

"I'll beg him off." Michael reached for her hand as he rose to his feet.

"Nonsense," Celine said as she slipped from his grasp. She dabbed at the corners of her mouth with the edge of her linen napkin. "I'll freshen up in the powder room and return in a few minutes."

Michael straightened his navy waistcoat. "Celine, please—"

"Don't worry yourself on my account." Without a second glance, she wove back through the crowd, looking every which way for the entrance to the ladies' powder room. To her left—in the opposite corner—was a winding staircase cordoned off by brass posts and a black velvet rope. A gentleman with skin the color of stained mahogany and a gold ring through his right ear watched her closely, his head tilted to one side, his eyes lost in thought.

Celine returned his measured stare, but he did not look away. Instead he lifted his chin as if in challenge. She drew closer, her curiosity spiking. In response, the gentleman inclined his head upward, his pristine satin lapels lustrous.

Her breath caught when something called to her from the darkness above. A dull roar above the cheerful din. That same feeling of being pushed back and pulled forward beckoned Celine ever closer. She ignored it. Moved away from the stairwell. Then a cool breeze floated by, caressing the bare skin of her throat and forearms.

She . . . recognized the scent it carried, though she did not know from where.

Celine took a tentative step toward the stairs. The stately gentleman standing before the simple barricade continued watching. A grin touched his lips when she reached for the velvet rope. Without a word, he unlatched it from its post and stepped aside, as if he knew exactly who she was. As if she belonged in this exact place at this exact moment.

Celine's lips hung between silence and speech for the span of a breath. She considered asking him if he knew her. Or worse, if she should know him. But that same something hooked around her spine, summoning her toward the shadows above.

It called out to her again, without words.

At first Celine's footsteps were hesitant. As she climbed, she glanced over her shoulder more than once, to find the gentleman with the earring standing there, his gaze expectant. The noise around her began to die down to a murmur, the air cooling as if the walls were lined with frosted glass. The path ahead was dark, the light waning around her. It should have been discomfiting, but a delicious shudder rolled down her spine. When Celine neared the top of the rounded staircase, she noticed that the banisters were embellished with the same symbol that hung on the sign outside the establishment: a fleur-de-lis in the mouth of a roaring lion.

Dim gas lamps burned on either side of the railing. It took Celine a moment to acclimate to the darkness. When she stepped forward, her slippered foot sank into plush carpeting.

She looked up. And gasped.

The shadowy room before her was a den of pure iniquity. A world completely apart from the one below.

Stunning young men and women lounged in various stages of undress on silk-covered chaises and velvet settees, holding glasses of champagne and tumblers of deep red wine. On a divan set against a darkly paneled wall sat a trio of pale figures sipping from snifters of glowing green liquor. Faint silver smoke tinged with a floral scent collected near the coffered ceiling. In the center of the chamber, a girl around Celine's age was sprawled atop a boy, the ties of her ivory lawn gown loose, a smudge of rouge in the hollow of her throat, her brown eyes feverish.

At first Celine's gaze was caught on the girl. She'd never seen another young woman in such a state of dishabille. Nor had she ever seen a girl quite so lovely, her limbs long and lithe, her bare feet swaying lazily above the Aubusson carpet.

Then the boy lying beneath the girl turned his head toward Celine.

She almost stumbled where she stood. A stabbing pain radiated from the center of her chest.

In all her nearly eighteen years, Celine had never beheld a more beautiful young man.

His face was sculpted bronze, his cheekbones cut from glass. Half-lidded eyes trailed after tendrils of smoke above, framed by sooty black lashes. A hint of stubble shadowed his jawline, his brows heavy and low across his forehead. But it was his perfect mouth that arrested Celine. Made her breath catch and her heart pound.

Everything about him suggested sin. Hinted at a complete disregard for propriety. He wore no cravat or waistcoat, and he'd shorn his hair close to his scalp in defiance of the current fashion. A crystal tumbler filled with red wine dangled from his fingers, his right hand tracing slow circles on the girl's back. When she saw Celine staring, the girl aimed a pointed grin at her, then took hold of the boy's chin and pressed her mouth to his.

Rage spiked in Celine's throat. An odd, possessive kind of rage, her skin tingling with awareness. When the boy's gaze slid her way, the rage melted into despair.

He broke away from the girl and stood at once, his perfect lips pursed, his expression strange. Almost wild.

"What are you doing here?" he demanded.

Celine remained frozen to one spot, her fingers trembling in the folds of her blue linen skirt. A mad part of her wanted to run to him. His voice seemed to beckon her closer, the sound filled with a lulling music.

"I—I'm . . ." She thought to apologize, but stopped herself. Straightened, her hands clenched at her sides.

He glided toward her, his movements liquid. His eyes were the oddest color, the grey of molten gunmetal. Another unreadable emotion crossed his face, causing his pupils to flash as if he were a panther.

"You don't belong here," he said, his whisper like ice against her skin. He reached for her, then pulled back, his fingers twisting into a fist. "Who sent you?"

Though her knees shook and her voice trembled, Celine did not falter or look away. "The gentleman downstairs."

"Rest assured, I'll have words with him later."

"You will not." Celine took a step forward. "If you are cross with anyone, be cross with me. I chose to come upstairs. No one forced me to do anything."

A woman with dark skin and jeweled rings the size of walnuts tilted her head back and laughed throatily; a young, tanned-skinned gentleman with cherubic curls grinned like a fox.

Frustration crossed the beautiful boy's face. The muscles in his forearms pulled taut. Celine had the distinct feeling he wanted to reach for her just as much as she wanted to reach for him. Wanted to touch her as much as she wanted to touch him. The longer she looked at the boy, the more she simply wanted, the desire taking on a life of its own.

Over his shoulder, the disheveled girl on the chaise scowled at Celine.

"Why does it hurt me to see you kissing her?" Celine asked without thought. As soon as the question left her lips, something cracked behind her heart.

He flinched as if she'd slapped him. Then his expression hardened. "Why should I give a damn if something hurts you?"

His rudeness should have shocked Celine. But it didn't. "Do you love her?"

"That's none of your business."

"You're right. It shouldn't be. But still I would like to know," she said, another pang knifing between her ribs. Why was she so captivated by him? By the line of his jaw, the bronze skin of his bare chest, and that cursed, cursed mouth.

"Leave. Now." He strode toward her, bringing them within an arm's length of each other.

"You're trying to frighten me. It won't work." Celine lifted a hand to his face. Then stopped herself, stricken by the breadth of her desire. "Who are you?"

He swallowed, his eyes unblinking. Then all at once, the intensity in his gaze dampened. He let his voice fade to a hypnotic drone. "You will go downstairs at once, Celine Rousseau. You will have no memory of coming here, nor will you repeat this intrusion."

Her bones seemed to vibrate inside her body as her limbs began to move of their own volition. Celine turned in place, a cloud settling over her mind. She fought for her bearings, gritting her teeth. Then she spun around, forcing the haze around her thoughts to clear. "I do not have to listen to you." Her jaw locked in defiance. Anger threaded through her veins. "And how the devil do you know my name?"

All motion halted in the space. Countless pairs of eyes settled on her, all unmoving and unblinking. It was as if Celine had stepped into a painting by a Dutch master, one of light and shadow, every stroke bewitched.

"Well, I'll be hog-tied," the young man with the foxlike smile murmured, his angelic blond curls falling across his forehead. "She's bested you, Bastien."

Bastien?

She . . . knew that name. Didn't she? Flickers of desiccated fruit peelings in a darkened alley, of being chased down a shadowy street, of feeling relief at the scent of leather and bergamot raced through her mind.

With a glower that would have melted stone, the beautiful

boy twisted his head around, his wrinkled shirt shifting over his trim torso, exposing more of the bronze skin across his chest. "Go to the devil, Boone. And take her with you."

Footsteps pounded up the stairs at Celine's back. She turned just as Michael snared her by the arm, his features frantic. Even in her periphery, she noticed the boy named Bastien lower his chin dangerously, a muscle ticking in his jaw.

Concern had blanched Michael's tawny face of color. "What are you . . ." His voice trailed off, his eyes widening at the sight before him. As if he were shocked to his core. He recovered the next instant and said, "Pardon the intrusion. Please excuse us." Then he laced Celine's hand through his and led her down the winding staircase.

As they made their way into the light and sound of the world below, Celine could not stop herself from glancing over her shoulder one last time.

The boy named Bastien watched them from over the railing, his eyes glinting like a pair of honed daggers.

BASTIEN

———— ≈ ————

Time freezes for a second. Then thaws all at once.

Blame begins to fly around the room like a flock of starlings.

"This is Kassamir's doing," Odette accuses, invective heating each of her words. "He's the world's worst romantic."

Hortense points a finger at Odette. "Ne t'avise pas de le blâmer. You were the one who invited the chit and her lapdog to dinner. Nous savons que c'était toi!"

Odette whirls in place, the tails of her baroque frock coat swirling about her. "I did *not* tell her to bring that hairless mongrel into our home."

I say nothing, the words knotting in my throat. Still the air in front of me is filled with Celine's scent. Still I cannot shake the irrepressible desire to race after her. To hold her, if just for an instant. To send her away. Compel her never to return.

Revulsion courses through my chest, tasting bitter on my tongue. I tried to glamour Celine. I tried to force her to leave against her will.

I am the selfish monster my uncle hoped I would become.

Madeleine steps between Odette and Hortense just as

Kassamir reaches the top of the stairs, his expression subdued. Unapologetic.

"Pourquoi voudriez-vous faire une telle chose, Kassamir?" Odette demands.

"Because I don't wish to perpetuate a lie," he retorts, his Créole accent harsh. "The girl knew she belonged here. She realized it the instant she crossed the threshold. Who am I to tell her otherwise?"

Boone's laughter is dry. "Well, perhaps you didn't have to make it quite so easy. A warning would have been nice." He pitches his voice louder. "Beware, fair folk, I'm sending the goddess of madness and mayhem your way!"

Kassamir frowns. "I am under no obligation to any of you on this account. Nor do I wish to maintain the wall of ignorance you and your kind have built around this poor girl. I am not one of you. As such I will not bow to the demands of any immortal, even Nicodemus, who should know better by now." His nostrils flare. "If you'll excuse me, I have an establishment to run."

Odette puts up both her hands, as if to placate him. "We know you were well intentioned, Kassamir."

"I was not," he says. "But I am right, nevertheless, and that is what matters."

Madeleine sighs. "Do you know the danger you inflict on Celine Rousseau by interfering in these affairs?"

"I am not a seer of the future. For that you would have to ask Odette."

Odette wrings her gloved hands. "As I've said time and again, I can no longer see the future as it pertains to Celine. When we meddled with her memories, we changed the course of her fate. It will take time for the new path to become clear."

Lines of irritation gather across Kassamir's brow. "What you've allowed Nicodemus to do to Mademoiselle Rousseau's mind is criminal. It is the cruelest form of punishment to allow Sébastien to bear witness to it." He is angrier than I've ever seen him. My face grows hot as he speaks. The revulsion in my chest continues to spread. To fill the emptiness around my heart like water poured over ice.

"Maybe you have forgotten," Kassamir continues, "but I have worked alongside Nicodemus for decades. I was here when he first brought Bastien to us. I remember what a sad, lonely child he was. How much he wished to love and be loved. In him, I saw myself. A boy taken from all he knows. From everything he loves. He has lost everyone dear to him. Must he lose this young woman as well? I will not be—"

"Mademoiselle Rousseau asked me to take away memories that might cause her pain, my friend," a voice chimes in from the back of the chamber.

Kassamir stands taller. Refuses to avert his gaze, even when confronted by my uncle's unflinching countenance. "She was given an impossible choice," he says. "A decision made with a proverbial revolver pointed at her head. You took advantage of her pain, Nicodemus. It was wrong of you."

I watch as my uncle crosses the room, our guests parting around him like Moses through the Red Sea. The words remain lodged in my throat, though I know I should defend my brothers and sisters—my uncle—against Kassamir's accusations.

But I cannot. I cannot think beyond the echo of Celine's question.

Why does it hurt me to see you kissing her?

She shouldn't be asking that. To her, it shouldn't matter who or what I do with my life. Nicodemus is the most powerful vampire I know. If he glamoured away Celine's memories, it should be impossible for her to care about anything to do with me.

How has this mortal girl defied the will of such dark magic?

Though I am lost in my thoughts, I am aware of how my brothers and sisters eye me, even from a distance, like a powder keg about to explode. Every once in a while, Arjun or Hortense glance my way. Odette hovers near me like an elegantly attired wasp, Jae a step behind her. Madeleine watches in silence, the pity in her gaze only fueling the pain inside me.

I know what they are doing. They are waiting for me to react. Waiting for me to rage. To attack, hurling venom at anyone in my vicinity.

A few weeks ago, I did just that. But I refuse to let rage be my master.

I will not succumb to the demon inside me.

It is not anger I feel. It is cold, unforgiving anguish. The kind of anguish I experienced as a boy, when I realized my mother would not be there to greet me the next morning or sing me to sleep that night. When I understood my father chose immortal power, risking madness, over a single human lifetime with his son. When I knew my sister was never coming back, her body burned to ashes in a fire I inadvertently started.

It is that feeling of being utterly alone. Of being nothing to no one, except a nuisance.

I know I matter to those around me. But it isn't the same. It will never be the same. Everyone here serves my uncle from a place of responsibility. Of loyalty to their maker. Perhaps they have learned to love me in their own way, but the choice has never been theirs to make.

Celine loved me because she wanted to love me. Because she saw something more than Nicodemus Saint Germain's heir apparent. Something beyond the money, the power, or the mystery.

She saw *me*.

The revulsion in me dissolves into grief. It was that same courage of conviction that gave Celine the strength to walk away. To choose a life apart from this world of dark magic and dangerous creatures.

No. I do not feel rage. My despair is too great for rage.

I wish that I could walk away from this life. But it is too late for me.

"I've always respected you, Kassamir," Nicodemus says, his voice going soft. An unspoken warning. "You have been a great friend to me for many years. You were the one who made all this"—he raises one of his hands, indicating the entirety of the building—"possible. Without your guidance in the complexities of the modern man, my businesses here would not have flourished as they did." He paces forward another step. "I know you suffered as a boy, as a result of this country's greatest sin. How I wish I could bring your parents back or return your lost childhood to you. But the affairs of the Fallen are not your concern. Take care not to interfere." His golden eyes glint with fury.

"I don't give a damn about the affairs of the Fallen or the Brotherhood, Nicodemus. I never have." Kassamir does not waver. "But I do care about Bastien. And as long as there is breath left in my mortal body, I will fight for him to retain his humanity. No matter how much you may wish to deny it, he needs that young woman. He must learn what it means to *live*."

"Sébastien is immortal." Nicodemus draws himself up to his full height. "Life is a given to a creature with such a gift."

A long sigh escapes Kassamir's lips. "Life is not a given to any of us. Neither is love. A hundred thousand years will not teach you that truth. You must accept it for yourself." He turns to me. "What you are has no bearing on who you become, Sébastien. Man or demon, that is entirely up to you. It is *never* too late to chase the better version of yourself." Without waiting for a reply, Kassamir makes his way down the stairs.

Though my uncle remains still, I can sense his fury. His teeth are clenched, not unlike mine. The whorls of his dark hair gleam as he glances my way, the handle of his walking stick gripped in his fist.

Nicodemus faces all those present, his attention fixed on the immortals who have formed a protective ring around me. Still I have not managed to say a word. I am too haunted by the things Celine said. The harsh truths Kassamir revealed.

What I am has no bearing on who I become. It is the kind of thing Celine would have enjoyed debating.

I almost smile at this thought.

Without warning, Nicodemus heaves a nearby tea table into the air, knocking everything from its surface. Muted screams follow the sound of breaking glass and smashed china.

"Do you think this is a game?" my uncle says, his eyes black, his fangs extending from his mouth. With another flick of an arm, he slams a priceless Ming vase from its pedestal, watching as mortals and immortals alike shrink away from his fury. "How long do you intend to waste the gift given to you, Sébastien? How long do you plan to languish about like a spoiled child?"

Because he expects a reply, I remain silent.

All at once, Nicodemus straightens. Smiles. Rounds out the rich tone of his voice. When he speaks, it is layered with the weight of his magic. "All our guests will forget what has transpired here in the last twenty minutes. Not a word of it will be breathed beyond these walls."

The hum of his directive passes through my bones. I see the faces of the ethereals and the goblins and the witches and the halflings present smooth into looks of supreme ease. The next instant, low laughter and conversation resumes as if nothing of import has occurred.

It is powerful magic. The kind a mortal girl like Celine should not be able to thwart.

Nicodemus looks at me. "This?" He glances about the room, glowering at the absinthe and the opium, the bare flesh writhing in the shadows. "This ends tonight," he whispers. "Your time of rebellion has ended. I forbid you from burying yourself in such base amusements. From tomorrow, you will work with me to make the future I envision for you a reality." He grabs me by the lapel, pulling me closer. "Ever since you were a boy, I hoped to grant you a position of power in the mortal world. A senator perhaps. At the very least a statesman of repute. I had dreams for you. You were to be the culmination of my work on the mortal plane. A respectable man of wealth and influence. Through you, I would establish a dynasty worthy of its name." His fingers twist through the linen fabric of my shirt. "I thought I had lost that chance when you became a vampire. It will not be taken from me again. You will do as your maker commands and return our family to its rightful place on the Horned Throne."

I consider refusing, for no other reason than the pleasure it brings me to defy him. For the chance to retain control of something in my life. A life that is not a given, even for an immortal. A love that was never anyone's to take.

What I am now should have no bearing on what I become.

Conviction rises in my blood as I stare at my uncle. For the first time since I woke as a vampire, purpose flows through my veins. I do not have to be the demon I was made to be. I can choose my own path. Build my own future.

A future that would be easier to construct if I no longer waste energy defying Nicodemus.

It is never too late to chase the better version of myself.

I will do as my uncle asks, in name only. I will play the game he wishes me to play. I will become a master at it. And in the meantime, I will work to make the life I want a reality. If I have to move heaven and earth—if I have to find my lost soul buried in a treacherous underworld—I will undo what has been done to me. What has been done to Celine.

I will find a way to unmake my future.

And once Celine learns the truth, I will do whatever she asks, even if she tells me to walk away and never lay eyes on her again.

This is what it means to live. To choose a path and face the consequences.

"I'm sorry, Uncle," I say, letting my posture fall to one of resignation. "I have taken the gift you gave me for granted. My ingratitude is shameful. Tell me what must be done, and I will do it."

Surprise flashes across Nicodemus' face. He releases me. Settles back on his heels and nods. He is about to reply, but then his eyes swirl to black, a vicious hiss emanating from his mouth.

I turn, a familiar scent curling into my nostrils. Acrid, like overripe fruit.

Michael Grimaldi stands at the top of the stairs. Though he is not a wolf, the smell of his blood is tainted with magic. He glares at me, an unfathomable expression on his face. "I had to see it again for myself," he says. "I . . . thought you had died, Sébastien. Everyone said you had died."

I smile without showing my teeth. "And were you gladdened to hear it?"

"No." His lips form a tight line. "But I was not surprised."

"If I had died, Michael," I drawl, "I would expect nothing less than the most overblown funeral parade this city has ever seen."

"No one has heard from you in weeks." Michael shakes his head, still in disbelief.

"And it would have remained that way, had you not been foolish enough to bring Celine Rousseau to this establishment," Nicodemus interjects.

"You clearly do not understand the first thing about Celine," Michael says to my uncle in a cool tone. "Once she settles her mind on something, there is little anyone can do to dissuade her." He looks back at me, his eyes narrowing. "Did you honestly think becoming a vampire was a solution?"

I raise a flippant shoulder. "It wasn't my solution."

"Then allow me to propose another one," Michael says. "Stay away from Celine. She wanted nothing to do with this world. She asked to forget. For once in your life, be selfless and listen."

My laughter is brittle. "You mistake me for someone who gives a shit what you think."

"It's not a request, *leech*."

Jae blurs before him. "Flee, little cub. While you still have legs to carry you." Menace radiates from his every syllable.

"If you lay a finger on me, the Brotherhood will return the insult, tenfold." To his credit, Michael Grimaldi does not shrink away from Jae's threat.

"Not if there's nothing left of you to avenge." Jae's response is more breath than sound.

Michael turns to Nicodemus. "You realize what this means, don't you?"

My uncle says nothing.

"You promised the Brotherhood you would not break faith," Michael says. "Ten years ago, you swore never to bring another vampire into New Orleans."

Nicodemus whirls away without a word and vanishes into the darkness.

"Perhaps your uncle doesn't care about keeping his promises,"

Michael says to me. "But there is no reason for me to hide the truth of what you've become from my family. You shattered this peace, Bastien." His hands fist at his sides. "What happens next is on you."

"And what happens if we choose to share your secrets with the girl you love?" Odette says softly. "What happens if Celine discovers you are not the hero you've cast yourself to be? That you, too, are part of this world she wishes to forget?"

Michael does not blink, though his jaw clenches. "I lay the consequences at your feet, Miss Valmont." His lip curls. "But if you cause Celine any pain, you will answer to me."

Hisses ripple around me. I hold up a hand, staying my brothers and sisters before they take it upon themselves to attack. No one threatens Odette in our presence. No one.

"Celine is yours to protect, then," I say with a malicious smile. He nods.

"Then have at it," I continue in a mild tone. "It's sure to be an easy task." I lean forward, my hands in my pockets. "Tell her Bastien says hello."

Anger descends on his face like a storm cloud. He opens his mouth to issue a reply. Reconsiders it. Then races down the stairs.

Madeleine comes to stand beside me. Every muscle in my body is stretched like the surface of a drum. I do not move. I do not speak.

"Her memories are returning," she murmurs. "How is this possible?"

I say nothing. For I am wondering the same thing.

BASTIEN

———— ❧ ————

The following evening, Arjun waits until the precise moment the last rays of the sun dip below the horizon to knock on my chamber door.

I do not respond, but the ethereal turns the brass handle and steps inside, uninvited. "You're to come with me." It is not a request. His poncy British accent makes that quite clear.

I sit up. Make a show of swinging my legs to the floor beside my bed, the velvet drapes swaying around me. Then I place my open book beside the single candle on my bedside table and quirk a brow at him.

"Valeria Henri is waiting for you in her shop," Arjun says, dropping onto an ornate chair positioned in the corner of the room. He lights a cheroot, the blue smoke unwinding above his head. "Nicodemus says it's time for you to have your fétiche made so that you may move about freely in the sun."

I rub my left hand across the back of my neck. "Bold of me to walk about in broad daylight after Michael Grimaldi levies such threats. If he did indeed tell the wolves I am no longer mortal, Luca Grimaldi will have my head."

"Which will happen whether you wander around in the

middle of the day or the middle of the night. And it's all the more reason to give yourself every advantage. You don't want to be one of those foolish immortals left to die in the sun. It's too droll, even for you."

"Do you know what you're talking about, or did you read about it in a book?"

Arjun snorts. "I heard some stories in the Sylvan Vale."

"Wishful thinking, perhaps. I'll bet those in the Vale love to envision creative ways of bringing about a blood drinker's demise."

He inclines his head toward the book on my bedside table. "Speaking of wishful thinking, is that more research on the elusive Sunan the Immortal Unmaker?"

Surprise flares through me, though I'm careful not to show it. "The subject merely piqued my interest."

Laughter rumbles through his chest. He exhales twin plumes of smoke from his nostrils. "You really are a terrible vampire. If you're going to lie, at least make it believable. We all know what you're reading. Odette and Madeleine have been keeping watch over any requests you make, including those as mundane as books from the library."

I swear beneath my breath, the Spanish words rolling from my tongue.

"Don't be too fussed about it," Arjun continues. "Mother and Auntie are trying to make sure you're not drowning in literature about the futility of life. Death is not the only outcome, old chap."

"As a point of fact, it is."

More low laughter. "And this Sunan character can help you along your merry way?" He stands. Adjusts the monocle clipped to his jacquard waistcoat. "Stop reading fairy tales and collect your things. Let's spend a night among the living."

∽

I keep my head down as we make our way through the Vieux Carré, my Panama hat pulled low on my brow. My eyes flit from side to side. Ever since we encountered Celine and Michael walking along Royale last week, I've become aware of my own recklessness.

At any given time, we could be confronted by a member of the Brotherhood.

If we were, what would I do?

Run like the wind, I suppose. If I were to stay, it would be in defense of someone else. After what happened in the swamps with Cambion, I have no interest in an altercation of any kind. Violence seems to bring out the worst of my inclinations.

"Do you know how to fight?" I ask Arjun as we make the final turn onto Rue Dauphine.

"I boxed at university," he says. "And I'm fairly proficient with a bagh nakh."

"Which is what?"

"If it ever comes down to it, you'll see."

I glance at his tailored, immaculate ensemble. "You're carry-ing a weapon on you now?" My brows rise in disbelief.

"That's what the ladies say, anyway."

"Fucking hell," I mutter as he laughs.

A pair of young women stroll beside us arm in arm. Once they pass, we pause before a nondescript blue door to our right, the sign above it swaying in a soft breeze. Lettered in gold across its surface is the single word PARFUM.

An intoxicating array of scents surrounds the slender building: rose water, oud, peonies, tonka bean, sandalwood, and vanilla. Another layer of fragrance lies deeper beneath it, something headier, spicier. Herbs and burning incense. Melting wax and a trace of blood.

The bell above the blue door rings when Arjun pushes it open.

The shop itself is long and narrow, like many of the small apothecaries in the heart of the French Quarter. Along the wall to our left are endless rows of shelves, many of them covered by tiny bottles of perfume, followed by stacks of scented soap and sachets of dried flowers. On a small stool to the left sits a young lady with skin the color of porcelain, a matching parasol artfully arranged beside her flowered skirts. Her inner forearm is exposed so that a shopgirl can test the sillage of different fragrances. The veins in her wrists pulse in time with the beat of her heart.

If only she knew that, to a vampire like me, this is the most delectable perfume of all.

I look away and swallow. After nearly two months, the desire for blood still trumps almost everything else. It's made me wary of hunting without the buffer of one of my siblings.

"Bonne nuit, gentlemen." The shopgirl conducting the fragrance test stands. "How may I help you?"

When I step into the gaslight, recognition flares in her burnished face, a scowl forming around her mouth. "Sébastien Saint Germain," she says, a groove etched between her delicately arched brows.

My eyes go wide. "Eloise?"

She moves toward us, her patterned skirts in hand. The intricate scarf around her head is styled in the same fashion as her mother's, the points folded into triangles.

Eloise gestures with her chin, beckoning us toward the back of the shop. We slip through the curtains into darkness, and she pivots in place, her irritation plain. "So it's true, then?" she asks. "You've become the very thing that killed your mother."

Something glitters in Arjun's hazel eyes. "Is that really necess—"

"Cállate, fey boy," Eloise interrupts. "You're in *my* home now."

Irritation filters through my chest, but I force amusement to settle in its place. "I can see not much has changed since we were children, Ellie."

"Don't call me that." She whirls back toward me. "You lost the chance to call me that when your family stopped associating with us ten years ago, despite all we've done for your kind throughout the decades."

I take a step back, unsettled by her hostility. "I was under the impression my kind would be welcomed here tonight. If that is not the case, then—"

"I have no issues with your kind. My quarrel is with you alone. Just because my mother welcomes you does not mean

I am pleased to see your ridiculous face." Disgust curls Eloise's upper lip.

"You despise the sight of me that much?"

"Claro, though you're even more beautiful now than you were as a child. It's frankly disgusting. No man should have eyelashes like that. It's obscene."

Arjun laughs, and Eloise aims her ire at him. "You should be ashamed," she says, crossing her arms. "Are you not of the Sylvan Vale? What are you doing working in service to a Saint Germain?"

The ethereal blanches at her accusation. It is rare to see unchecked emotion on Arjun's face. "I like his style," he says.

"Meaning he pays well. And I suppose—"

"Eloise," another voice emanates from the staircase near the far corner of the poorly lit space. "Es suficiente."

"Sí, mamá," Eloise replies without turning around.

Valeria Henri glides closer, her right hand brushing across her daughter's shoulder in a soothing gesture. She smells of fresh-cut herbs and vegetables, her dark skin luminous in the dim light. "After so many years, it's good to see you, Sébas."

Only Valeria and my mother ever called me Sébas. It's like a blow to the chest to hear it.

With a smirk, Valeria glances at her daughter. "And rest assured that a part of Eloise is pleased to see you, too."

Eloise harrumphs.

"You have the look of your father even more than you did when you were a boy," Valeria says. Then she glances toward

Arjun. "And who is your friend?" Her chestnut eyes narrow in consideration. "A halfling of the Vale? Muy interesante."

Arjun straightens. "Well, I would characterize our association as more of a—"

"Yes," I interrupt. "He is my friend."

Valeria nods. "Hold your friends close," she says, "for you never know when they might be taken from you, as your mother was from me." Her voice trails off, lost in memory. "Sígueme." She turns toward the stairs and gestures for us to follow her. With a scalding glare, Eloise marches to the front of the shop to finish helping her customer select a fragrance.

On the second floor of the building is a room I have not seen in ten years. The kitchen in the center of the open space has not changed much since then. Sprigs of thyme, rosemary, lavender, and oregano hang above a long wooden table marred by nicks and deep scratches. Pots and pans are stacked on oak shelving along the far wall, beneath a row of ancient books, their spines all but crumbling to dust. The air here feels cooler and freer, much like the second floor of Jacques'. Imbued with unseen magic.

"Your uncle informs me you have need of a fétiche," Valeria says as she steps behind the long wooden table and begins clearing its surface.

I nod.

Her lips purse. "It's been over seven weeks since you were turned. Why have you waited so long to see me?"

The blunt way she speaks reminds me of my mother. It's part of the reason I avoided her after I lost my family. It unsettled me to be around an approximation of my mother, as if I were seeking a substitute for the real thing.

Valeria Henri and Philomène Saint Germain grew up together in the heart of the Vieux Carré. When they were children, they learned to practice Santería from Valeria's aunt and attended Mass together every Wednesday and Sunday. It was Valeria who introduced my mother to my father. Given what happened, I wonder if she regrets it.

After my sister, Émilie, perished in a fire, my uncle found a set of paw prints in the ashes behind the charred structure. Though I confessed to being the cause of the inadvertent blaze, no one listened to me. Nicodemus and the rest of my family were eager to blame the wolves for my sister's death. From a desire for vengeance, my mother demanded that my uncle turn her into a vampire so that she could fight in the war to come. The change drove her to madness. Soon she became obsessed with finding a cure. Of being unmade. She met the sun less than six months later.

My father's grief consumed him not long after that. When Nicodemus refused to turn him, my father took me to Haiti in search of another vampire. Overcome with loss and drunk on the blood of innocents, he met the same fate as my mother the following year.

"Lost in your thoughts again, are you, Sébas? Just like when you were a child." Valeria laughs. "Ruminate a while longer, but I expect an answer to my earlier question. It wounds my soul that you have not come to visit me once in ten years. Your mother would be ashamed."

I want to say something poignant. Something Odette would say. A poetic turn of phrase that would excuse a decade of cowardice. But I'm certain Valeria would see through it, just as my mother always did. "I wasn't ready," I say simply.

"Claro." She nods. "There will always be pain for what you have lost, and it is a weight, becoming what you have become." Valeria holds out her right hand. "What do you plan to use as a talisman?"

Without a word, I remove the signet ring from the smallest finger of my left hand. Embossed on its surface is the symbol of La Cour des Lions: a fleur-de-lis in the mouth of a roaring lion.

Valeria takes it from me. Inspects it. Closes her eyes. "This object holds a great deal of emotion," she says, her thumb brushing across the markings. "Fondness, loyalty . . . rage." Her eyes flash open. "I sense your uncle in this ring." For the first time, annoyance tinges her words. "The item you choose as your fétiche will follow you for the rest of time. It will be the only way you can stand in the light of the sun. Should you lose or misplace it, another can never be made."

"I understand," I say.

"And still you would not like to choose something else? Something . . . un poco menos maldito?"

"I think a cursed ring is an appropriate choice, given its purpose."

"Very well." A small sigh escapes Valeria's lips. One of resignation. Then she reaches into her sleeve and withdraws a thin blade of solid silver.

I react as any vampire would in the presence of that kind of weapon. The kind that can cause us bodily harm. I flash backward with a low hiss.

Valeria snorts. "When you let fear rule your actions, you remind me so much of your father. What was it Rafa used to say? Act first and apologize later." She rolls her eyes heavenward.

I grit my teeth, fighting the urge to prove her point. The desire to let the worst of my nature rule my actions. Arjun was right. Fear and anger are indeed two sides of the same coin.

"No?" Valeria shakes her head and tsks. "Perhaps you are less like Rafael Ferrer than I thought." She turns the handle of the blade to me at the same time she slides an empty ceramic bowl across the nicked wooden table. "I need nine drops of fresh blood. No more. No less."

My skin burns as I slice open the tip of my index finger. Because the dagger is solid silver, the cut does not heal right away, the blood flowing past the wound, carried by the same dark magic that moves it through my body. I count out nine drops, letting them collect in the center of the glazed bowl. Valeria promptly whisks it away and turns her back on us while she works. "Bite your tongue and press it to the wound," she directs from over her shoulder. "It will heal faster."

Arjun watches in fascination as the cut seals shut on my finger, the sound like a paintbrush across canvas. Though he assumes a posture of nonchalance, it is obvious how captivated he is to witness Valeria work. An enchantress like her—one with old fey blood in her veins—is a rarity in the mortal world. Valeria's ancestor in the Sylvan Vale practiced elemental magic, her gifts granted to her by the earth itself.

"I lament that this has been your fate, Sébas," Valeria says as she pours another tincture into the ceramic bowl. Black smoke coils from inside it, sparks flying as she crushes dried leaves into the mixture with a granite pestle. "Your mother—"

"I'm aware she would have been displeased," I interrupt. "Given the situation, I'm not sure she would have chosen my death, however." Irony lances through me. Only a few weeks ago, I told Odette I would have preferred dying the final death to becoming a vampire.

Valeria sniffs. "She would have wanted you to be happy."

"Is that all?" I joke morosely.

Her eyes closed, Valeria inhales with care. When she exhales, a slew of unintelligible words trails through the cool night air. Then she drops my signet ring into the bowl and rests it along the windowsill, a beam of moonlight shining down on the feather of black smoke coiling from its center.

Arjun shifts closer, his interest plain. "I've never seen an earth enchantress work magic."

"This is not the magic of the Sylvan Vale," Valeria says as she pours water from a pitcher into a basin and washes her hands. "This is the magic of my mother's people. We are not simply born into it. It must be taught, and one must have faith in order to control it." She brings a covered platter toward the middle of the long table and rests it beside a pile of chopped vegetables.

Then Valeria begins dredging raw meat in a bowl of flour.

Despite his curiosity, Arjun recoils from the slabs of pink flesh.

"The key to a perfect gumbo," Valeria says, "is that you must first season and lightly brown the gator. If you don't season it well, you'll be like a Puritan serving up a plate of sand." She laughs to herself. "Now, the Huguenots . . . at least they knew how to make a sauce." With deft motions, she continues dredging thin slices of gator meat. "Sébas' friend . . . do you have a name?"

"Arjun." He clears his throat. "Arjun Desai."

"And does your name have a meaning?" Valeria asks.

A sheepish expression flares across his face. "It means 'shining lord.'"

"Your mother must have expected great things of you."

"My father named me."

Valeria grunts in amusement. "Claro." She laughs. "And does our Shining Lord know what the Trinity is?"

"The Father, the Son, and the Holy Spirit," Arjun replies.

"Wrong," Valeria says. "Our trinity is onions, celery, and bell pepper." With a flourish, she lights the flame on the nearby iron stove and proceeds to melt a mound of churned butter into a pan. "I know this food doesn't appeal to your kind, Sébas, but I'm hoping you and your friend will share a meal with us. Food is one of the celebrations of life. The farther we dwell from the living, the more the darkness takes root." She looks to Arjun as she sprinkles spoonfuls of flour on the melted butter to create a roux. "I'm told ethereals of the Vale enjoy food, even in the mortal world."

"Food is indeed a great passion in my life," Arjun says.

"Good. You will have some of my gumbo."

"Eh . . ." Arjun clears his throat again. "I don't, erm, I don't eat meat."

Valeria stops stirring. Blinks once. Twice. "Then what do you eat?"

"Vegetables. Beans. Pulses. Lots of rice. Cheese."

"Interesting. And how do you prepare these dishes?"

He smiles. "Not unlike gumbo, actually. My father cooked with at least eight different spices in any given dish."

"And you know how to do this?" Valeria's brows arch with approval.

Arjun's head tilts from side to side as if in consideration. "More or less," he says.

"Then you will teach me." Valeria nods with satisfaction. "In return, I will show you how to do a simple earth spell of your choosing."

"Done," Arjun agrees with a grin.

She smiles back at him. "Now, Sébas, it is time for you to apologize for not coming to see me once in ten years."

I almost laugh. Then I realize she is serious. Her stare is dead-eyed and unflinching.

I clear my throat. "Lo siento, Tía Valeria."

"I visit your mother's crypt every year for her birthday. I leave flowers and tell her about my life. Sometimes Eloise accompanies me." Valeria stirs the roux, waiting for it to darken to a rich brown color. "I've never seen you there. Not once."

"It's because I never go." There is no purpose in lying to her. Any discomfort I may feel is my own fault.

"Why?"

I do not answer.

"Philomène's forty-seventh birthday is in a few months. You will go with me this year." She pauses. "Your mother liked gardenias. Bring them with you."

I nod. "I promise I will."

"Good. Promises mean something to his kind." She nods to Arjun. "I expect the halfling to hold you to it. Now that is done, and we won't speak of it again."

The nutty smell of browned butter and flour suffuses the air. Though mortal food holds little appeal for me, I cannot help but appreciate the fragrance. The memories it brings. As I look around, my gaze falls on the row of ancient books stacked above the pans along the wall.

A thought takes shape in my mind. "Tía Valeria?" I ask.

"Yes?"

"Have you ever read about a warlock or a witch named Sunan?" Beside me, I hear Arjun groan.

She pauses in her stirring, her expression wary. "Why do you ask?"

I push my lips forward, mulling my response while I glare at Arjun. "It's a name I've come across in my reading recently."

"Ay, you're an awful mentiroso." Valeria snorts. "You need to learn to lie better."

"I said the same thing," Arjun says. "The damned snake is a better liar than he is."

They share a laugh while I scowl at them.

"What do you really wish to know, Sébas?" Valeria asks. "Are you asking about who Sunan is or what he can do?"

He. Sunan is a man. That is a detail I did not have prior to this evening.

"Does he even exist?" I press.

Valeria mixes the trinity into the roux and continues stirring. "As far as I know, he lives deep in the ice forests of the Sylvan Wyld, where he has resided for eight hundred years."

"And"—I struggle to contain my eagerness—"what kind of magic can Sunan perform?"

Sympathy ripples across Valeria's face. "You are asking if he can unmake you."

It's useless for me to deny it. I nod once.

"Why do you wish to be unmade?" she asks. "Is it for your benefit, or for the benefit of someone else? And don't lie to me, boy. I will know."

I want to lie, nonetheless. But I want to know the truth more. "It's both," I admit. "I lost someone I loved when I became a vampire."

"Do you fear being alone?"

"No." I think of the things Kassamir said to me that night at Jacques'. "I fear a life without meaning."

"You think this Sunan will help you find it?"

"I . . . don't know," I answer truthfully. "But if there is even a chance to regain a piece of my humanity, I believe I have to try."

She hums in understanding. "I do not know if Sunan of the Wyld still exists or if the tales about his power to unmake immortals are true. Alas, you must take your request to him in person. He has not crossed a portal into the human world for more than half a century."

My excitement vanishes like the flame of a doused candle. "Vampires are forbidden from using a tare like that to enter the Winter Court of the Sylvan Wyld."

"They are," Valeria agrees. "But there is no such law against traveling to the Summer Court of the Vale." She pauses for effect. "And what you do once you've entered the fey realm is up to you. Enough power and influence—enough sway with those in control—can get a vampire far, I'm told."

"And how would you suggest I go about such an endeavor?"

Valeria looks at Arjun. "That is a better question for your friend, the Shining Lord of the Vale."

Arjun's hazel eyes are as round as those of an owl. "You're both daft. I can't bring a bloody vampire into the Summer Court."

"You've traveled between the worlds, haven't you?" Valeria asks. "You know which tares will take you to the Sylvan Vale?"

"Yes." He hesitates. "But it would be the height of foolishness for me to accompany a vampire."

"I am not their enemy," I say. "I have no desire to cause those in the Vale any trouble."

Arjun's laughter is dark and dry. "You are Nicodemus Saint Germain's direct descendant. It was your family who led the charge against the enchantresses of the Vale. They'll smell you the second you cross through the tare."

My mind sifts through other possibilities. "What if I made them a promise? Offered them something of value?"

"You sound like your uncle." Arjun's cheeks hollow. "And not one of you has the first understanding of the Sylvan Vale. You think vampires are cruel? That wolves are quick to start a fight? At least you know who your enemies are, old chap. My mother is a huntress. One of the chosen few in the gentry who serves the Lady of the Vale directly. The Sylvan Vale is the kind of place where a smiling water nymph will offer you a fistful of gold with one hand and slice open your throat with the other. Where a hob will feed you a crust of bread that turns you into dust at their feet . . . upon which they will then delightedly dance."

"Are you not welcomed there, as one of their own?" Valeria asks.

Arjun frowns before responding. "I can't pretend I was ever welcomed among my mother's kind. They . . . tolerate ethereals because we are the only mixed bloods that retain immortality, as a result of being the offspring of pureblooded fey gentry and human pairings. In the Vale, many of us become playthings of the court. It is a life not unlike that of halflings in the mortal realm, who often seek out the protection of a vampire or a wolf or a warlock in order to stay alive." He takes a deep breath. "It is not the kind of life I would wish on anyone I loved. Which is why I will never have children of my own."

Valeria tsks. "At least you have the choice to sire children. At least your heart still beats in your chest." She sighs. "To me, these are the cruelest punishments placed on blood drinkers. That the heart of a vampire no longer beats. That the only way they can create more of their kind is to take the life of another." Her words fade to silence as she ladles stock over the wilting vegetables.

These are matters I have never considered. There was never a time in my mortal life where I pondered having children of my own. Such concerns are not pressing to most eighteen-year-old boys of my acquaintance. Now that it is no longer an option . . . I don't know whether it is something I would have wanted.

I say nothing while Arjun studies me sidelong. I can sense his apprehension. His worry that I will be angry with him for refusing to take me to the Vale. Perhaps he thinks I will continue behaving like my uncle, tossing threats at any perceived problem.

He is right about one thing. I *am* angry. I am always angry. But my anger is not with him.

And Arjun is not the only ethereal in existence.

Valeria turns toward us, her hands on her hips. "Our Shining Lord will not help his friend make his way to the Vale, then?"

"No." Arjun pauses. "I will not."

Valeria nods. "That is your choice. And we must accept our friends' choices, Sébas," she says to me. "A friend in truth is not there to serve you, despite what your uncle might have to say on the matter."

"I never knew how much you disliked Nicodemus," I say.

"What is there to like?" She sneers. "He is the worst kind of man and an even worse immortal."

I press my lips together.

"Despite all his power, Nicodemus is small and petty. Not once have I seen him apologize for anything," she clarifies. "A man who will not take responsibility for his actions is no man I wish to know." Her gaze pierces into mine. "Have a care that you don't follow in his footsteps."

I say nothing. I simply listen. It is the second night that I've witnessed someone worthy of respect take my uncle to task. First Kassamir. Now Valeria. For so many years I wanted nothing more than to be like him. To have that kind of power and influence.

For the first time in my life, I wonder if I have valued the wrong thing. Maybe my uncle's brand of power is not real power at all. And if that is true, then what should I have prized in those around me?

What is the measure of a good man?

Valeria reaches for the ceramic bowl along the windowsill. The ring she retrieves from inside glows softly, as if it has taken in the light of the moon itself. Before she hands it to me, she turns it over in her palm, her expression somber. "Your fétiche will work from tomorrow. It will protect you and you alone. Keep it safe." When I reach for it, she pulls back. "I expect you to honor the wishes of those who care about you, Sébas. Avoiding the past will no longer be tolerated. Your mother understood the difference between loyalty and love. The next time you see me, I want you to tell me if you have learned what that is." With a sly smile, she leans closer. "And your next apology will be better than the last one."

I nod as I take the fétiche from her. The gold feels cool to the touch.

"Protect and be protected," Valeria says.

"Thank you, Tía Valeria." I wrap her hands in mine. "I will try to do better."

"Yes, Sébas. I believe you will."

BASTIEN

―――― ≈ ――――

It is long past midnight when we leave Valeria's shop. Late enough that most of the streets of the Vieux Carré are deserted, the sky above casting the world below in tones of indigo and ebony.

We cross the cobblestoned streets in silence. Despite his many protests, Arjun carries a linen-wrapped parcel of bread and gumbo.

He brandishes it with exasperation. "I'm flabbergasted by why it's so difficult for you Yanks to understand that I don't eat meat. It's like you think I'm committing a cardinal sin. Let me ask you this: Did those slabs of alligator flesh actually appeal to you at one point?" He shudders. "It's a dead animal, for God's sake."

I laugh. "If Valeria heard you call her a Yank, she would unhinge her jaw and swallow you whole."

His mouth hangs ajar. "She didn't support the rebel cause, did she?"

"Of course not. But it's not as if any Yank would care about granting a woman like her the rights afforded to men."

Arjun grunts in agreement. "God save the queen," he says, his tone sarcastic.

I look upward. A fleece of clouds wraps around the moon, darkening the path before us. Still I feel like I'm seeing things clearly for the first time. My entire life, I thought everyone revered my uncle. He moved about in all kinds of circles as if he were born to rule. Whenever there was a problem, he appeared to have a solution. He offered me the guidance of a father and the wisdom of an elder all while presiding over a court of powerful immortals. Nicodemus was everything I wanted to be.

It is unsettling to realize the image I have of his greatness is not shared with those around me. My dead heart feels strange in the face of this revelation. I suspect it has something to do with Valeria Henri. Her nearness has kindled memories within me. Ones I have not contemplated for many years. The sound of my mother's laughter. Of watching someone prepare a meal for me. Of listening to my father sing. Of squabbling with my stubborn sister.

Of being loved without demand or design.

I sense Arjun watching me. "What is it?" I ask.

"I confess I've been living in fear for the last two hours."

"Because?"

"I can't believe you haven't accosted me for refusing to take you to the Sylvan Vale."

It is sobering to hear this from a supposed friend. "What did you think I would do? Cut out your heart and feed it to Toussaint?"

"The usual." Arjun wipes his monocle and places it in a small pocket of his waistcoat. "Offer me immeasurable riches.

Cajole me. And then begin the process of browbeating me into submission."

I frown. "That sounds rather uncharitable."

"It's what your uncle would have done."

"It's what I would have done, too," I admit.

"And what has changed?"

"I don't know." I sigh. "But for my own edification, would it make a difference if I offered you money?"

"It might." He grins.

"Really?"

"Not on your life. My mother would kill me if I brought a vampire to the Summer Court. There's not much a dead man can do with a pile of money."

"Have you always been so afraid of your mother?"

"Weren't you afraid of yours?"

I push my lips forward in thought. "I don't remember being afraid of her. I remember wanting to make her smile. Wanting to hear her praise me. But I wasn't afraid."

"Whom did you fear?"

"My sister and my uncle."

He laughs. "Right."

"It's telling that you chose to work for the sworn enemy of your mother's court."

"As I said before, I prefer your kind to mine. At least there isn't a dispute about who or what you hate. At least I know where I stand among vampires." Arjun pauses. "Not to mention that I made your uncle a promise to work for La Cour des Lions for a period of no less than five years, with a handsome financial incentive both during and after my tenure. Promises mean something to us in the Vale. They are not to be made lightly. If we fail to honor one, we can no longer set foot on fey land."

We walk for half a city block before I reply. "Have you promised never to bring a vampire into the Vale?"

"No."

"So then it's not technically forbidden."

"I'm not taking you to the Summer Court, Bastien." Arjun halts and turns toward me. "Why do you want so badly to become a human again? Isn't it better when you don't have to worry about dying? You're stronger and faster now than you ever were before. Virtually indestructible. Why do you wish to forgo these advantages?"

"Are *you* afraid of dying?" I ask.

"I've never thought about it. I'm young, and it would take a lot to kill someone like me."

"I think a brave man fears death. It's what makes him brave."

"So you're looking for glory on the battlefield?" He crooks a brow at me. "A chance to be a hero?"

"No." I rub the back of my neck. "Honestly, I don't have a good answer to your question. Not yet."

"Let me know when you do."

I laugh. "That will be the first thing—" I stop short, a strange scent assailing my nostrils.

Arjun draws up beside me. "What—"

My immortal blood rushes to my limbs, energy coursing through my veins. "Run," I mutter. "And don't look back."

A low growl resonates from behind us. Another from our

right. Even though I cannot see them, I sense several wolves loitering in the darkness around the corner. A few more gathering to the left. They smell of overripe fruit and musty fur. The scent is cloying.

Arjun drops his parcel of food and removes a set of silver claws from inside his breast pocket. He grips the weapons in either fist and assumes a fighting stance.

"I told you to run, damn you," I say through gritted teeth, my revolver at my side. My fangs lengthen, a low hiss emanating from my throat.

"I'll run when you do, Saint Germain," Arjun replies. "And don't fire that tiny cannon. You'll wake the entire city."

"Hang the entire city." I cock the hammer.

From the shadows emerges an immense wolf, at least twice the size of any I've seen before. It crouches like a predator about to spring, moving with calculated slowness. An awareness of who I am and what it is.

Of why we are here at all.

More members of the pack materialize from the shadows. Saliva drips from their mouths, their long teeth glistening in the blue moonlight. At least eight of them surround us in a shrinking semicircle, their intentions plain.

Arjun and I are outmatched. If we fight—as I am inclined to do—one of us could be injured. I may manage to escape unscathed, but Arjun is half mortal. He will not fare as well. It is not a risk I am willing to take.

I grab Arjun by the shoulder and whirl us in the opposite direction. He does not waver as we race through the deserted streets of the French Quarter. Snarling wolves nip at our heels, their fury splitting through the night air. A howl echoes to my right, and three more sets of paws join the first eight, racing toward us from a side street.

They intend to box us into a corner.

I veer left onto Rue Rampart, Arjun following close behind. I scan the eerily silent buildings around us, searching for a way to escape. There is no place to hide unless we smash open a locked door. I consider scaling a wall of brick toward an open rooftop. At least that would give us the advantage of higher ground.

But any misstep could see us worse off. And I will not save myself at Arjun's expense. He is here because of me. Even if he is not a vampire, he is one of us. I will not leave my brother behind.

I leap across a set of streetcar tracks and blur toward the high walled entrance of the old cemetery on the outskirts of the Quarter. In a burst of speed, I kick through the iron gate, shouting for Arjun to join me. The second he crosses onto con-secrated ground, I slam the gate shut and twist the iron bars around themselves so the wolves cannot follow.

My chest heaves from the wrath mounting in my blood. I am not designed to run from a fight. The muscles in my arms shake as my fists search for something to destroy. I turn toward the wall as the largest wolf crashes against the gate.

It holds, though its hinges whine.

In this moment I feel more like an animal than I do a man. The nauseating smell of the wolves spreads as they mass just outside the iron gate, pacing back and forth, their eyes glowing yellow in the darkness.

I want to tear them apart. Hear their bones break. Relish their dying whimpers.

Another howl punctures the night air. The next instant, the largest wolf—undoubtedly the leader of their pack—leaps onto the top of the whitewashed stone wall. He glares down at us.

I swear he is smiling.

Like a strike of lightning, I shove Arjun forward and bolt for the center of the cemetery, aiming for one of the largest tombs. One replete with intricate carvings and towering pillars difficult for four-legged creatures to climb.

"That one," Arjun shouts, angling toward a recently completed marble monolith. A final resting place for forty of the city's wealthiest Italian families.

We are less than ten feet away from the tomb's base when the wolf attacks. It leaps from the shadows, knocking us both to the ground. I roll to my feet, my fangs bared. Arjun brandishes his silver claws and rakes one set of blades across the wolf's immense jaw.

Three gashes appear, the blood like salted metal as it drips from beneath the wolf's ear. Incensed, it takes only a second to decide which of us to attack first.

Arjun shouts when the wolf snaps its jaw around his forearm and hauls him backward, shaking him about like a rag doll until the claws fall from his hands.

I fire my revolver. The silver bullet grazes one of the wolf's hind legs, but all it does is enrage the creature further. I ram the full force of my weight into the wolf's injured side just as another member of its pack snaps at my feet. Before I have a chance to turn around, the second wolf yelps and vanishes from sight. The crunch of breaking bones resounds from between a row of crypts.

My smile is one of menace.

My brothers and sisters have arrived.

The hiss of stalking vampires blends with the growling of the wolves. In a burst of fluid motion, my vampire siblings flash between the granite and marble monuments, attacking and defending in equal measure. The wolves manage to hold their own. They are well organized. Well trained. Well led.

From my periphery, I watch Jae throw a grey-backed wolf into the air. It cries out when its spine shatters a stone obelisk. Another wolf tries to impale Hortense on the tines of a low iron fence, but she manages to twist away, a delighted gleam in her gaze. Another blur of movement, and the wolf in question is missing an eye.

Boone rasps through the darkness as he draws away two wolves from the pack.

I do not see Jae, but I hear the damage he wreaks. The snap of lupine limbs and the howls of pain. The deathly silence that follows.

I smell the wolf that attacks me before I see it. It moves faster than any of the others. It must be the leader of this pack, the one who first appeared from the shadows. If I had to hazard a guess, I would say I am facing a member of the Grimaldi family itself. I cannot be sure if it is Luca, but I do not have the luxury of worrying about what that might mean.

I smash my fist against the side of the wolf's face, right where Arjun raked his silver claws. Unmitigated wrath blazes in the wolf's bloodshot eyes. It thrashes, then closes its powerful jaws around my wrist and bites down hard enough to nearly sever my hand from my body.

Arjun jumps onto the wolf's back and wraps his arms around the creature's neck until it relinquishes hold of me. It does not miss a beat before it rolls across the stones and pins Arjun beneath its heavy body.

Then the wolf sinks its teeth into Arjun's throat.

Without a second thought, I grip the wolf's skull with my uninjured hand, then take my bloodied fingers to its muzzle and tear in the opposite direction. The animal's jaw separates from its head with a sickening snap. Like the sound of a plate being smashed against stone.

The wolf collapses to the ground, lifeless.

Growls ripple through the pack. Teeth gnash together in fury. The sight of their vanquished leader has left them all the more crazed.

Boone, Jae, and Hortense surround Arjun and me in a protective circle, their backs to one another. I stand, blood dripping from one arm, my vision swirling into focus. Power threads through my veins. It is unlike anything I have ever experienced in life or in death. As if everything around me has narrowed, converging on a single point.

Destroy or be destroyed.

I am a Saint Germain. I choose to destroy. Maybe it is not a choice at all.

By my count, the wolves have lost a third of their number. At least four more are severely injured, one of them partially blinded. They come to the same conclusion I do the next instant. Snarling while they collect their dead, they vow wordless retribution as they slink back into the darkness.

We stand in silence for at least a minute, waiting to see if they will return.

Gruff laughter rolls from Hortense's throat, her beautiful face filled with delight as she gulps in the night air. She is in her element, her face covered in blood, her fangs coated with crimson.

Boone laughs with her, his arms stained up to the elbows like a butcher's.

Jae has not moved in the last two minutes. He stands like a statue, his gaze focused on the path before him in morbid meditation.

With my good arm, I reach down to help Arjun to his feet. When the ethereal struggles to stand, I remove the torn jacket from my shoulders and press the fabric against the dripping wounds on his neck to stanch the flow.

His smile is weak, his stance unsteady. "I slowed your escape. You should have left me behind. I would have left you behind."

"Fucking liar," I mutter as I hold him upright.

"It's not a lie," Arjun says, his expression grave. "Ethereals are taught from an early age to fend for themselves."

"As I said to Valeria, you're my friend. A part of our family. I would never leave you behind."

He says nothing in response, but falters as he tries to take a step forward on his own.

"Arjun is badly injured," I say to Hortense, Jae, and Boone. "Where is Madeleine?" She is the best healer among us.

"In the past, Le Pacte liked to set traps," Hortense says, using the French name for the Brotherhood. "So my sister and Odette stayed behind to guard Nicodemus." She licks blood from her fingertips as she turns toward me.

"I'll carry Arjun home," Boone says, taking hold of the ethereal's uninjured arm.

"Like hell you will," Arjun croaks, his face pale. "I'll carry myself, thank you very much."

"Don't be a damned fool, little fey brother." Boone grins. "Besides, I don't mind spilling a little blood of the Vale." They begin leaving the cemetery, Arjun's protests fading with each step.

When he looks at me over his shoulder, his smile is one of gratitude. One of promise.

I linger in their lengthening shadows, pausing to gaze at my hands. The puncture marks around my wrist have healed, though the skin there is lighter than normal. All around me are signs of a vicious struggle, blood splashed across the stones beneath my feet and the slabs of marble at my back.

The thrill of battle begins to wane, and my features turn bleak. Hortense stands beside me. She rests a palm on my shoulder.

"Are you ready for this war, Sébastien?" she asks.

I shake my head. "I would avoid it if I could."

She frowns. "You would?"

"Blood begets more blood. I don't relish the thought of harm coming to anyone I love."

Her lips thin into a line, her displeasure evident.

I take her hand, realizing she seeks reassurance, not resignation. "But if these wolves want a war, they shall have it. That is my promise to them. And to you."

A smile ghosts across Hortense's face. "Précisément."

Celine

———— ≈ ————

The Devereux mansion stood stalwart on Saint Charles
Avenue, one of the most moneyed addresses in New
Orleans' Garden District. Last week—a mere day after Philippa
Montrose had accepted Phoebus Devereux's proposal of marriage—the brick exterior had been whitewashed, the shutters
painted a fashionable shade of dark green. Porches enclosed all
three of the home's elegant stories, offset by white latticework
and intricate wrought iron. Vines of powdery blue wisteria
snaked up one side of the impressive edifice. Flames danced in
rows of small iron torches, winding around the lane leading up
to the home's entrance.

It was a perfect spring evening for an engagement party.

Pippa was radiant, dressed in a beautiful gown of wispy
organza, her blue sash a match for the blue fire in her eyes.
Her blond hair was piled on her head, demure curls framing her heart-shaped face like a golden halo. She lingered on
the arm of a rather bookish-looking young man, his smudged
spectacles sliding down his nose, his flashy cravat overpowering his otherwise unremarkable face.

"She looks happy," Celine said to Michael as they made their way up the lane into the mansion's immense back garden, where two long tables were set with Limoges porcelain and pressed linen, sparkling crystal and glowing candles in brass holders.

"It's a happy time in life," he replied, pulling her arm through his. "She's found her match."

Celine quirked her lips.

"You disagree?" Michael lowered his voice.

She shook her head. "Pippa always said how important it was for her to find a husband."

"Are you displeased with her choice?"

Celine mused a moment before responding. "Phoebus is a kind man who will provide well for her. I just—I wish she thought more of herself. She could be so much more than a rich man's wife. She is smart, capable, and resourceful. I hate that she thinks the only suitable aspiration for a girl like her is that of a bride."

"It's important to see the merit in her dreams, even if you disagree with them. Isn't that what a friend does?" Michael led Celine to one of the long tables and pushed in her seat before taking his own.

"I don't disagree with her dreams," Celine said. "They simply . . . frustrate me in their simplicity. A wife is always second to her husband, and I don't see the merit in settling for second place."

Michael leaned forward, an amused light in his pale gaze. "I agree. But perhaps an engagement party isn't the best place to have this discussion."

Celine's ears went hot. She wasn't sure if it was because of what Michael said or his proximity. A hint of apple tinged his breath, the scent rather pleasant.

"I've overstepped, haven't I?" Michael said in a flat tone. "Nonna told me I shouldn't be so forward with my opinions. It makes people less apt to like me."

"No." Celine shook her head. "I prefer it when you're forward with your opinions. And I like you as you are."

Michael took her hand in his, his touch fervent. Unmistakable in its affection. Something fluttered in Celine's stomach. Was it the butterflies she'd read about in books or overheard young women whisper about in private? It felt . . . strange, but not unwelcome. His smallest finger curled around hers. She smiled, and was rewarded with a grin that crinkled the corners of his eyes and softened the severe set to his lips.

Celine was all at once struck by the thought that she should kiss Michael. That this kiss would offer her the clarity she desperately sought. In fairy tales, a kiss was a powerful thing. If she kissed him, it would be like magic. The haze in her mind would clear. Her memory would be restored. She would wake as if from a dreamless sleep.

And she would just . . . know.

Just as suddenly, another image flared into sharp relief. Of another young man's lips a hairsbreadth from hers. Of how she'd lain awake at night and imagined them brushing across her skin, his touch soft and hard all at once. Asking and offering in equal measure.

Bastien. That damnably beautiful boy who had haunted her dreams since that evening at Jacques' less than a week ago.

It had taken a great deal of restraint to weather the effects of that altercation. Celine had spoken with her doctor at length about it. He'd reassured her that moments like those were not unusual for people who'd suffered head injuries. In fact, he'd recently read about a French philosopher with a developing theory on the matter. He'd called them "la sensation de déjà-vu." A feeling of experiencing something a second time. This phenomenon would explain why Celine had felt the way she did in the boy named Bastien's presence. As if she'd known him from a different life, even though the very idea was absurd.

Perhaps it could all be attributed to her injuries, as everyone kept insisting.

Or perhaps they were all lying to her.

It was a discomfiting thought. Would Michael lie to her? Would Mademoiselle Valmont—who'd returned from Charleston last week—agree to perpetuate such lies? Would Pippa, her dearest friend in the world?

A server bustled toward their end of the table, carrying a basket of pillowy brioche. He offered a bun to Celine, and she reached for the butter, the tips of her fingers grazing the large silver dinner knife to her right. A jarring sensation rippled through her bones. One of recognition and awareness. She tilted her head and picked up the dinner knife. Wrapped her hand around the embellished handle, its blade flashing in the light of a nearby candle flame.

When Celine caught sight of her startled face in its reflection, her fingers started to shake. Michael was being introduced to the elderly gentleman sitting beside him and had not yet noticed her distress.

Celine grasped the handle tightly in an attempt to conceal her trembling. She became overwhelmed by the sudden urge to pocket the knife. Not for the purpose of stealing it, but rather to protect herself.

Protect herself from whom? What was wrong with her?

Celine glanced about, fighting a wave of nonsensical panic. The gentleman beside Michael clapped a hand against the young detective's back, offering effulgent praise for his recent accomplishments. Michael grimaced, but accepted the kind words with a murmured response of his own.

Her eyes flitting to and fro, Celine brought the knife into her lap. When she looked up once more, it appeared that no one had noticed her odd behavior. Less than ten seconds had passed since she'd first touched the dinner knife.

Smiling as if nothing were amiss, Celine tucked the knife into her skirt pocket with a deft motion.

Immediately her trembling ceased. Her body relaxed, her shoulders dropped. She reached for the brioche bun and locked gazes with Odette Valmont, her shop's generous benefactress. Though the elegant young woman was seated much farther down the table, it was clear from her expression that she'd seen everything Celine had done.

Panic once more swirled in Celine's chest. Of course Pippa would have asked Mademoiselle Valmont to attend her engagement party. Three days ago, their benefactress had come to the shop to order a custom gown complete with the newest style of Parisian bustle. Likely Pippa extended the invitation then.

And now here Mademoiselle Valmont sat, studying Celine in surreptitious silence, her sable eyes knowing, her bow-shaped lips pinched.

Celine stood the next instant.

Michael started, concern lining his brow. "Celine?"

She forced herself to smile. "I'm just going to take a turn about the garden."

"I believe dinner will be served shortly."

"I'll return in a moment."

"Would you like me to accompany you?"

Celine shook her head. "I need a moment to myself." She discarded her linen napkin and stepped away from the table, taking in deep gulps of rose-scented air. Energy pulsing through her veins, she wandered closer to a trellis laced with grapevines, trying in vain to calm herself.

"Is everything all right, mon amie?" a soft voice said from behind her.

Celine turned around. Odette Valmont stood there, her brown hair lustrous, her silk batiste like a jeweled raiment around her neck. A familiar cameo surrounded by a halo of bloodred rubies flickered near the base of her throat.

"I'm fine." Celine swallowed before smiling brightly.

One side of Odette's lips kicked up. She stepped closer. "Don't bother lying. I watched you filch some of the Devereux family's silver."

Horror took hold of Celine, an icy wave spreading down her back. "I—I didn't filch it. I meant only to borrow it."

"Pour quelle raison?" Odette canted her head. "Et pourquoi?"

"I don't know," Celine admitted in defeat. "I just felt . . . safer with it."

Odette's eyes became slits. "Is someone threatening you, mon amie?"

"No. Not at all." Celine took a step back. "You must think I'm mad."

A thoughtful expression settled on Odette's face. "I don't think you're mad at all. I—" She stopped midsentence, tension banding across her forehead.

"Celine?" a male voice said from behind her, tugging at her already frayed composure.

She reacted on instinct. Celine whipped the knife from her pocket and held it aloft, her heart pounding in her chest. A horrible recollection stormed through her mind. The fleeting image of being stalked. Of having a man attack her unawares.

Of possessing nothing but a silver knife with which to defend herself.

Shock rounded Michael's gaze. He raised his hands to either side of his face and took a step backward. "I'm sorry," he said. "I didn't mean to frighten you."

"It's all right, Celine," a familiar voice said. "You're safe here. I promise. Nothing and no one will hurt you." A small hand reached for hers, its touch tender. Celine blinked, and Pippa's lovely face came into focus. Pippa threaded their fingers together and led Celine toward the house and into a small parlor of paneled ash, its shelves lined with leather-clad books.

"I'm so sorry," Celine began in a hoarse whisper. "I've caused a scene at your party. I should leave before more people take notice."

"Of course you haven't caused a scene," Pippa said with a kind smile. "Besides that, I want you to stay. It wouldn't be a celebration without you." She gestured toward a damask chaise positioned near the black marble fireplace. "Please have a seat, dearest."

Celine settled into the chair, her marigold silk skirts rustling, the silver knife still clenched in her right hand.

Pippa looked around the well-appointed room. "I still find it a bit strange that one day I will call a place this grand my home. It's more than I could have hoped to have."

"It *is* lovely," Celine agreed. "And you deserve a life of love and comfort."

"Don't we all?" Pippa said.

"Some are more deserving than others."

"I'm not sure about that." Pippa took a seat in the chaise opposite Celine. "To be honest, I keep waiting for something to go awry." Soft laughter bubbled from her lips. "Perhaps Phoebus is concealing some kind of terrible secret. Maybe he tortures bees or turns into a goat beneath the harvest moon." She grinned.

"But none of that would matter if you were happy."

"None of it?" Pippa's eyes sparkled. "Not even the bees?

Only a monster would torture an innocent little bee! Can you imagine?"

It was so absurd, Celine could not help but laugh.

Pippa's grin widened. "I *am* happy, Celine. I'm marrying a good man. Phoebus is gentle and kind. His mother has been very gracious. His father"—she wavered—"is well intentioned, if a bit overbearing."

Celine's grasp on the knife loosened. "Is his father unfair to you?"

"Not outwardly." Pippa shook her head. "But the deepest cuts can come from the smallest blade." She sighed. "Phoebus isn't what his father wanted him to be. But—in my opinion—he's a much better sort of man. He doesn't long for those around him to cower in fear. He doesn't prize loyalty above all else."

Celine nodded, the knife dropping into her lap. Already she'd begun to breathe easier. Already she felt more relaxed. How did Pippa always seem to know what to do?

"It worked," Celine said in a wry tone.

"What did?"

"Your distraction."

"If it worked, then why do you still look so troubled?"

Celine met Pippa's worried blue eyes. "I hate being like this. It's not . . . me. I feel like I've lost myself."

"You've been through such an ordeal."

"*I know.*" Celine bit back a spike of irritation. "I know."

"Do you want to tell me what happened tonight?"

"I wish I could," Celine said as she stared at the knife in her lap. "I just felt . . . threatened. As if I needed something to defend myself."

"Has this happened before?" Pippa asked. "Since your recovery in the hospital?"

"No. But you've known for some time that I have these"—Celine searched for the words—"vivid dreams. Often I don't remember what happened in them, but I always remember how I felt."

"Frightened?"

Celine shook her head. "Powerful. As if I could destroy anything and everything in my path." She hesitated. "These kinds of dreams have become more frequent since Michael and I went to dinner at Jacques' last week."

Alarm gathered at the bridge of Pippa's nose. "Heavens, why would he take you there, of all places?" she blurted. Her hand flew to her mouth, as if to catch the words before they could spill.

Further proof that Pippa was hiding something. That those around Celine were keeping an important truth from her. "Was I not supposed to go to Jacques'?"

Pippa exhaled slowly. Bit her lower lip.

"There was a boy on the second floor," Celine pressed, her gaze intense. "He knew me. I'm certain of it. And I knew him, though I cannot recall from where or from when."

Pippa remained silent.

"Please tell me, Pippa. If you know something, please share it with me. I feel like I'm going mad. Like the world around me is conspiring to conceal the truth. I need to know the truth."

She moved to the edge of her seat. "Do I know that boy named Bastien? Tell me, once and for all."

Pippa hooked a stray blond curl around an ear, her expression torn. "Yes. You know him."

"Is he someone I should remember? Is he important?"

Another hesitation. "No. You shouldn't remember him. He isn't . . . good for you, dearest."

"Does he know what happened to me?" Celine said. "If I ask him, can he tell me—"

Pippa stood in a rush. "No. He's the reason you almost died, Celine. Please. I'm begging you. Stay away from him. He isn't right for you. Knowing him brought you nothing but pain. There are so many suitable young gentlemen out there. Take your pick! Detective Grimaldi has moved heaven and earth to make sure you are safe. If you would only give—"

"'Suitable young gentlemen'?" Celine scoffed. "You mean men like Phoebus."

Pippa recoiled. "Do you find fault with him?"

"No. I simply don't understand why you're marrying someone you don't love."

It was a cruel thing to say. Celine knew it the instant she saw the blood drain from Pippa's face. But Celine was angry. So very angry. As she suspected, everyone had lied to her.

Pippa had been lying to her this entire time.

"Real love isn't like a fairy tale, Celine," Pippa said, her tone clipped. "It isn't this all-consuming force that blinds you to reason. Real love is a choice. And I choose to love Phoebus, even if he isn't a knight in shining armor or a dark prince in a shadowy underworld. I don't need such childish dreams to be happy. I'm not a little girl anymore."

It was like a slap in Celine's face. Pippa had never passed such judgment on her before. Celine stood, the pilfered knife falling to the carpeted floor. "I refuse to believe that *Phoebus Devereux* is your match. I think you're terrified of being alone and have said yes to the first rich boy who asked. Like a coward, you've let fear make your decisions, Philippa Montrose," she seethed. "And real love may be a choice, but I plan to choose someone who steals the breath from my body and haunts my very dreams. That is the only kind of love worth having."

Splotches blossomed on Pippa's cheeks, her shoulders starting to shake. "It doesn't matter what you think," she snapped. "Phoebus would never put me in danger. I can't say the same for Sébastien Saint Germain. You almost *died*, Celine. If Michael hadn't been there, Lord knows what would have happened. How can you be so foolish, even now? Have you learned nothing?"

"How can I learn anything when everyone keeps lying to me!" Celine raged. "And I'd rather be foolish than settle for a fool."

Pippa's eyes began to shimmer. Her lower lip trembled. The next second, tears started to slide down her cheeks, a sob escaping her lips.

The knot in Celine's throat tightened like a garrote. She swallowed, but her sight began to water in response. She and Pippa were *fighting*. She'd caused her dearest friend to cry at her own engagement party. What kind of person was she?

In two long strides, Celine enveloped her friend in an embrace. "I'm so sorry. So very sorry. I spoke out of turn. There is no excuse for my behavior. Please forgive me."

Pippa sobbed louder, but wrapped her arms around Celine's waist.

"I'm sorry, Pippa," Celine whispered. "I don't know what's come over me. I don't know who I am anymore."

"I—I wish I could help," Pippa said through her tears. "I almost lost you once. I can't do it again."

"I know," Celine whispered. "But I have to find a way to make sense of all this chaos."

Pippa nodded. "I understand. But please, Celine"—she looked up, her face flushed and her voice quavering—"please don't put yourself in any more danger. Stay away from Bastien. Away from Jacques'. Away from that cursed world."

Celine said nothing.

"Promise me," Pippa pleaded.

"I promise." Celine wiped the tears from Pippa's cheeks as she lied to her closest friend.

And she planned to keep lying, until she learned the truth.

CELINE

———— ≈ ————

This was the height of foolishness. She deserved whatever ill fortune came her way.

Less than three hours after promising Pippa she would stay away from Sébastien Saint Germain, Celine stood outside Jacques', searching for an opportune moment to stomp onto the premises and demand an audience. It didn't matter how long it took. Celine had no intention of leaving until she'd obtained answers.

Who was Bastien to her? What did he know of her lost memories? Would he help her?

At first she considered making a request of the same imposing gentleman with the earring who'd allowed her upstairs at dinner that night last week. But something told her he would not be so accommodating this time.

After Celine wasted half an hour hemming and hawing about the best way to proceed, she shored up her resolve and marched through the narrow double doors, her chin in the air.

The establishment had begun its preparations for the evening's close. Servers polished silver trays and wiped crystal glasses, stacking them in preparation for the next day. A young girl swept the shining wooden floors while two other boys set chairs atop the empty tables.

"Mademoiselle, may I help you?" the girl with the broom asked, her Créole accent lilting.

"I wish to speak to Sébastien Saint Germain," Celine said.

The girl stepped back in surprise. Then dipped into a curtsy. "Un moment, s'il vous plaît."

A minute passed before the dark-skinned gentleman with the earring approached from behind a swinging door. "Mademoiselle Rousseau," he said without preamble. "It is not right for you to be here at such a late hour." He glanced about. "Have you come alone?" His thick eyebrows shot into his forehead.

"Yes," she said, defiant. "I am tired of allowing society to dictate my behavior."

He almost smiled. "Be that as it may, I—"

"Pardon the interruption, monsieur, but I have no intention of leaving until I've spoken with Sébastien."

"Alas, Bastien is not here."

"I think you're lying to me, monsieur. And I've had enough of that to last a lifetime." Celine grabbed a chair and sat, taking a moment to arrange her marigold skirts. "I'll wait here until Bastien comes to speak with me."

That time, the gentleman offered her a fond smile. "I apologize, mademoiselle, but we are closing our doors soon. What you ask is simply impossible."

"Improbable perhaps. But not impossible. I will wait outside all night if need be. It is a sad state of affairs when a girl must resort to threats in order to be given the attention she is due."

She folded her ungloved hands in her lap. "If I'm outside all night, I hope it weighs on your conscience."

"Rather uncompromising of you, mademoiselle," he said.

"Hmmm. Rather like looking in the mirror, I'd wager."

His laughter was rich. Unexpected. Familiar.

Celine blinked. Took to her feet. "Do I know who you are, monsieur?"

"You do." He nodded. "I am Kassamir."

Her teeth clenched in frustration. How much had she lost? How much would she give to have these missing pieces returned to her? "I apologize for not recognizing you, Kassamir. I've recently—"

"I know, mademoiselle." His sympathy was unmistakable. "I know of your troubles."

"Kassamir," she repeated, her features twisting in the wake of his kindness. "I . . . can't continue like this, with such glaring holes in my memory. You helped me before. Please help me again."

He took a deep breath. "You wish for my help even though it may not gain you the peace you seek?"

"It doesn't matter. I . . . need to know the truth."

Kassamir nodded again. "Wait here a moment."

Five minutes passed. The girl with the broom motioned for Celine to make herself comfortable. Celine accepted the offer and returned to her seat. After another fifteen minutes passed, the remaining workers had all but completed their evening chores. Celine watched them dim the gas lanterns and draw the drapes closed, her annoyance on the rise, her foot tapping against the newly mopped floors.

Soon she was left alone in the large room, shrouded in near darkness. Celine considered leaving, but if she failed to wait a mere hour after making threats to loiter all night, she would never be able to show her face at Jacques' again.

"What are you doing here?" a deep and sonorous voice asked, its echo trailing from the ceiling. Celine's vision strained until she could almost see a figure resembling a living shadow gliding down the stairs.

"I—I was hoping you would tell me." Celine hated that she'd stammered. Hated that she'd betrayed herself in such a simple manner. She stood, her silk skirts swishing with the movement.

"And what if I told you this was the wrong place to have hope?" he continued.

"I would tell you to go to the devil."

He paused in his slow descent, his silhouette coming into focus. "What if—"

"I swear to God, if you say you're the devil, I will scream."

"What will you do after that?"

"Start breaking things."

Laughter rumbled from his chest. Even from a distance, it caused a shiver to pass between Celine's shoulder blades. "Of course you would," he murmured, his voice like silken sin.

Bastien came to stand in front of her, moving like smoke from a candle flame, a giant serpent slithering in his shadow. He wore no cravat or jacket. His waistcoat was fashioned of simple charcoal silk, his white shirt unbuttoned at the throat, the sleeves rolled to his elbows. When he placed his hands in the pockets of his trousers, it was like watching a statue come to life. An ache spread through Celine's chest. Even in low lighting, he was striking. Beautiful enough to cause her pain.

Celine took a step back when the snake at his heels hissed before vanishing into the darkness beneath the winding staircase.

"What do you want, Mademoiselle Rousseau?" Bastien asked.

She cleared her throat. "I came here because everyone is lying to me, and I'm tired of it."

He lowered his head. Peered at her through his sooty eyelashes. "And you expect me to tell you the truth?"

"You may not tell me the truth, but I shall know it regardless."

"Despite my better judgment, I'm intrigued. How will you know?"

"Because your eyes don't match your words."

Bastien leaned back on his heels. "And what do my eyes tell you, Mademoiselle Rousseau?"

Celine swallowed. It was like peering down the barrel of a gun. "You may say you want me to leave. But your eyes are begging me to stay."

She could swear on her soul that a flicker of dismay passed across his face. Then his expression hardened into one of ice. "Go home, mademoiselle. Fall asleep in your warm bed. Dream your ridiculous dreams." He turned to leave.

Desperation drew Celine closer. "You won't like my dreams."

He paused, glancing at her over one shoulder. "Why is that?"

"You haunt them." She took another step. "You haunt me."

"Fitting. My family used to call me the Ghost." He bowed. "If you'll excuse me."

"Bastien." Celine's voice shook. "Please. Don't walk away from me."

He stopped short, his back to her, his fingers flexing at his sides.

"Please," she said again in a broken whisper. "Help me."

"I can't help you, mademoiselle."

"You can. You can tell me what happened."

Bastien turned around, his gaze hooded, his expression detached. "You don't need someone to tell you what happened. You already know. You were attacked by a madman. You almost died. The most I can offer you beyond that is this: the man who attacked you did so because he hated me." He spoke as if he were delivering a medical diagnosis, completely devoid of emotion. "It is my fault you almost died. Learn from your past mistakes so that you don't make them again." He began to leave.

"No." Desperation clutched Celine's heart. Bastien wasn't going to help her. He wasn't going to offer her a way to regain what she had lost. Despite what she'd suspected, her pain did not seem to matter to him. "If you're the reason I almost died, then you owe me an explanation," she demanded.

"I owe you nothing."

"I want my memories back."

His lips pushed forward as if to taunt her. "Your memories are not mine to give."

"At least answer my questions. That much you can do for me."

Bastien waited in cold silence.

"Did I . . . love you?" Celine asked.

He said nothing in response. The beat of her heart thundered in her ears.

"Did you love me?" she pressed, hating how much she craved his answer.

"You're asking the wrong questions."

Her treacherous fingers ached to reach for him. "It doesn't matter what I ask, since you refuse to answer me." She twisted her hands in the folds of her skirts.

"If you want an answer, ask a better question."

"I don't want to play these games with you." It was a risk, but Celine closed the distance between them without warning, moving far too close for polite company. In response, Bastien took half a step back before he stopped himself.

"If you don't want to play games, then what is this?" he asked, looking down.

She stood tall. Unwavering. "A test."

"I hate tests." He matched her, toe to toe.

Some part of Celine knew they'd done this dance before. Knew how much Bastien despised ceding ground to anyone.

When he gazed at her like that, Celine thought she might catch flame. Bastien leaned closer, as if he might kiss her. Stopped a hairsbreadth from her face. "Go home, Celine," he whispered, his words a cool brush across her ear. "Don't come back here again."

Celine snared his forearm before he could leave. The touch of her bare skin to his sent a jolt of awareness through her body. Bastien wrenched free as if he'd been scalded. Nearly stumbled before he caught himself. As if he were the one who should be afraid of her.

As if she had been haunting him this entire time, too.

Celine's mouth fell open in amazement. She'd been wrong before. She *did* matter to him. Mattered more than he would dare to admit.

"It's guilt, isn't it?" she asked. "You are *racked* with guilt."

He said nothing. Only stared at her, his chest rising and falling in time with her pulse.

"I'll absolve you of your guilt," she said. "I'll do as you ask and never come here again."

"What do you want in return?"

"Just one thing."

Bastien kept silent.

"It won't cost you a penny, nor will it involve anyone but you," Celine continued. "And it can be granted in a moment."

He pursed his lips in consideration. "You won't say what it is?"

"Not before you agree to do as I ask."

"You swear never to seek me out again."

She nodded. "Do you agree?"

Another beat passed in weighted silence. Then he nodded.

Celine did not waste time. "I want you to kiss me."

She expected him to be angry. To refuse outright. Instead he took a careful breath, as if he were making a study of the air around her. An emotion Celine could not identify rippled across his face. Then Bastien took her chin in his hand and leaned forward.

The closer he came, the faster her pulse raced. He smelled of leather and bergamot, mixed with something strange. Something cold and bracing, like a winter frost. The stillness around them grew, the silence becoming a low hum. She closed her eyes and angled her face toward his.

Bastien pressed a chaste kiss to her forehead.

When he pulled away, Celine threw her arms around his neck and slanted her lips to his.

It wasn't what she'd expected. Her memories weren't returned to her in a flash, as if she'd woken from a dreamless sleep. This was not that kind of fairy tale.

But Celine *knew*, the instant they kissed.

She'd wanted to free the chains around her mind.

Instead this kiss unlocked her, body and soul.

Bastien surrendered as Celine melted against him. The next instant his hands framed either side of her face. He couldn't break away from this any more than she could.

This was as inevitable as death.

"Celine," Bastien whispered into her skin, sending a delicious thrill down her spine. His fingers threaded through her hair, her curls loosening at his touch. Celine brushed her tongue across his lower lip, and Bastien deepened the kiss, one of his hands sliding to the small of her back. Celine didn't realize they'd moved until they ran into the edge of a table.

Bastien lifted her onto the polished oak, trailing kisses down the side of her neck. Celine knew he could feel the way her pulse raced through her veins. The way she bowed into his touch. He shuddered when she pulled him even closer, her fingers shifting to the buttons of his shirt.

Celine turned her head and arched into Bastien. His grip tightened on her hips as he stepped between her thighs.

Then he stopped moving, his face buried along her collarbone, ragged breaths flying from his mouth.

"Bastien?" Celine asked.

He did not move.

"What's wrong?" she asked, the words breathless.

He pulled away from her in a blur, faster than she could blink. It took Celine a moment to regain her bearings. To realize how close they'd come to complete indecency. Her bodice was askew, her breasts spilling over the top of her silk dress. Once her feet touched the floor, Celine stood on unsteady legs.

"Bastien?" she repeated. "What's wrong?"

He did not turn around. "I gave you what you wanted," he said. "Never come here again."

Then he made his way up the stairs, never once looking back.

PIPPA

This was a ghastly mistake. The kind of mistake worthy of a cautionary tale.

Here lies Philippa Montrose, a girl who knew better.

It was certainly poor form for an engaged woman to be standing in a deserted back alley behind a dining establishment. But it wasn't just the where of things that mattered. It was the why. The who. And the how.

Hours after attending her own engagement party, Pippa stood in the darkness outside of Jacques', hoping to speak to a young man. A young man who was not her intended.

As far as Pippa was concerned, she had no choice in the matter. Her friend was in danger. When Pippa had returned less than half an hour ago to the pied-à-terre she shared with Celine, her friend was nowhere to be found.

So Pippa had made her way to Jacques', hoping to speak with Sébastien Saint Germain. To beg him to do something so that Celine would stay safe. Would stay far away from these . . . odd creatures. For if Pippa could be certain of one thing, it was that they were not human.

She'd discovered this truth in the days following Celine's

attack. Not once had Pippa pressed for answers, but she'd seen enough to know they were not what they appeared to be. Human beings did not move as they did, as if they were shrouded in smoke. Nor had she ever encountered so many faultlessly beautiful men and women in her entire life. Lastly, they never seemed to eat or need rest or appear the slightest bit tired. Often they blinked as if it were an afterthought.

Pippa fretted to herself, wringing her hands as if they'd been soaked by a rain shower.

If Sébastien Saint Germain refused to speak to her tonight, she would have to seek out his uncle, and she dreaded the thought. His uncle frightened Pippa greatly. Whatever dark magic he wielded—whatever powers he used to shield Celine from the worst of her memories—none of it was working. Not anymore.

Even more pressing was the fact that Pippa could no longer maintain this charade. It had been taxing enough concealing the truth from her best friend, but the entire time, Pippa had believed it was for the best. No one should be forced to relive the details of such an ordeal. Pippa should know. It had taken her years to find a measure of peace after all she'd suffered as a child in Yorkshire.

These last few weeks, many worries kept Pippa up at night. She'd listened to Celine cry out in her sleep, and she'd tossed and turned in her own bed, thinking she might have made a mistake. Was it right to take someone's memories from them, even if it spared that person pain?

Pippa had experienced a great deal of pain in her past. One

could argue that pain had taught her valuable lessons. Her expression hardened. She didn't want Celine to suffer pain in order to learn about life. No one who loved someone as she loved Celine would ever wish such memories upon another.

The door at Pippa's back creaked open. She spun in place, the words already forming on her tongue, only to die the next instant.

"Why are you here?" she said at once, aware of how peevish she sounded.

Arjun Desai—the Court of the Lions' smarmy solicitor—smiled at her without showing his teeth. "You're not even the slightest bit pleased to see me?"

Pippa crossed her arms. "I asked to speak with Bastien."

"Bastien is . . . indisposed at the moment. I was sent here in his stead." Arjun crossed his arms as well, mocking her with every movement. "How may I help you tonight, Miss Montrose?" His head tilted to one side. "Was this not the evening of your engagement party?" He made a show of searching his pockets, then brushed his fingers through his unruly black hair. "Dash it all, I forgot my hat. Otherwise I would tip it in salute to your lifetime of happiness."

"You're coarse and conceited, sir," Pippa said in a cool tone. "And this conversation has gone on long enough. If Bastien is unavailable, then I'd like to speak with"—she grimaced—"his uncle."

Arjun laughed. "You really are serious, aren't you, pet?"

"I am not now nor have I ever been your pet, Mr. Desai. If you refuse to help me, then—"

He held up his arm to keep her from leaving. "Nicodemus is not going to speak with you. Your best bet is to tell me what you want."

Pippa harrumphed. Then began toying with the golden cross around her neck. "I came to tell you that Celine is starting to remember. And that I can no longer keep your secrets."

"I haven't the foggiest idea what you're talking about." Arjun removed his monocle and began cleaning the lens with a silk handkerchief.

"Then why am I speaking with you, sir?" Pippa placed her fists on her hips. "I never should have agreed to keep the truth from Celine that night in the hospital, even if we all thought it was the best way to protect her. I have lied repeatedly to someone I love, and it was wrong of me—wrong of us all—to be complicit in what happened to her memories."

"She asked to have those memories taken from her, Philippa," Arjun interjected gently.

"Nonetheless, it was wrong of Count Saint Germain to take them from her." She sniffed. "And don't ever call me Philippa."

"Why?"

"It's what my mother called me."

"You'll have to tell me that story sometime."

"Not on your life, Mr. Desai." Pippa gathered her skirts in hand. "I've said what I came to say. Please deliver my message to whoever needs to hear it."

Arjun offered her a curt bow. "As you wish."

Pippa hesitated. "I wish I believed you would do as I asked."

"If wishes were fairies."

"Then at the very least they'd keep their promises." Pippa bit her lower lip. "We're . . . toying with people's lives, you know. It was a mistake to think a lie—however well intentioned—was better than the truth."

"Sometimes a lie is all we have," Arjun said. "And I promise to deliver your message to Bastien."

"Can I take you at your word?"

"Mademoiselle, I am the only man on these premises who can be taken precisely at his word." He grinned. "Congratulations on your engagement."

"You sound as if you're offering condolences for my dead cat."

"You have a *cat*?" Amusement tugged at his features. "And marriage is a death, is it not? Death of freedom, death of dreams, death of—"

"You're insufferable. Good evening, Mr. Desai."

"Good evening, Miss Montrose."

BASTIEN

———≈———

I pause, my right foot hovering above the staircase landing. For the first time since I committed to this course of action, trepidation settles onto my skin.

"In case I forget to tell you later, or something . . . unfortunate happens, thank you for changing your mind and agreeing to take me to the Vale," I say under my breath. Then I follow Arjun up the flight of steps.

"I owe you a life debt. And I despise being indebted to anyone," he throws over his shoulder. "But don't thank me yet. You still haven't met my mother."

I almost laugh. The ethereal's sense of humor is razor sharp, as usual. We pass the second landing of the building toward the next staircase. Behind the nearest door, I overhear the angry mutterings of an elderly woman.

"Don't mind the honorable Madam Buncombe," Arjun says. "She and her one friend are hampered in life by rather large chips on their shoulders when it comes to"—he drops his voice to a whisper—"foreigners and their blasphemous ways." He waves at the bolted door. "Afternoon, Mrs. Buncombe!" he shouts as he continues marching up the stairs.

I grin to myself at the sound of her outraged spluttering.

We pause before the entrance to the fourth-floor pied-à-terre, a space Arjun has shared with Jae since the former's arrival to New Orleans a little more than a year ago. When I lean against the doorjamb, the faint glow of the wards spelled into the wooden frame flashes twice, and a burning sensation spreads across my skin. I pull away before the protective magic has a chance to take root in my bones. These wards are almost as intricate as the ones around my uncle's private chamber in the penthouse of the Hotel Dumaine. Likely the work of Nicodemus' favorite warlock in Baton Rouge.

"Are you certain you want to do this?" Arjun asks for the fifth time this afternoon. "It could end quite badly."

Again trepidation ripples through me. "I appreciate the concern for my welfare." I set my jaw. "But I have no intention of changing my mind."

"The concern is for *myself*, as I am in fact a bit more . . . breakable than you." Arjun sends a caustic glance my way while he unlocks the door, but there's a note of humor in his expression. "I still don't understand why you feel a compulsion to make this journey. This Sunan character may not even exist. Truth be told, I don't mind you as a vampire. You were a disaster those first few weeks, but now that you've seemed to calm down a bit, you're not so terrible."

"I thank you for that vote of confidence."

"You're quite welcome. As they say, a broken clock is right twice a day."

I follow him into the small, neatly appointed space. Along

one plaster wall hang tapestries and scrolls of black-and-white calligraphy, paying homage to Arjun's Maharashtrian heritage and Jae's childhood in Hanseong. A simple wooden table with two chairs sits in the center of the main room, a bookshelf situated close by. The only thing that seems amiss is the large mirror positioned against the far wall, near the back of the flat. It's old and tarnished, its frame fashioned of ornate brass.

Arjun pauses beside me, his gaze settled on the strange mirror in question. "A stroke of luck that Jae's profession necessitated one of these spelled silvers. They're quite uncommon and extraordinarily expensive. They're also the best way to travel through the earthly realm."

I recall our conversation several nights ago with Valeria Henri. "Is this not a tare?" I should have asked this question then, but pride is a difficult beast to conquer. Especially the pride of a Saint Germain.

Arjun shakes his head. "A tare is a portal directly to the Otherworld. This is merely a stepping-stone." He turns to me. "Have you told your uncle what you intend to do?"

I make my way to the mirror to buy myself some time. "For most of my life, I've admired my uncle, even when I disagreed with him. But I've always known this life—the life of an immortal—isn't what my mother wanted for me. It's the reason my uncle refused to turn my sister, even after she begged him to do it. Before my mother succumbed to the bloodthirst, she used to say we are given one lifetime. In that one lifetime, we have countless chances to become the best version of ourselves.

Each day presents another chance." I stare at my reflection in the mottled surface.

Arjun crosses his arms, his monocle flickering with the movement. "I guess that means no."

"I did not tell Nicodemus what I intend to do." I raise a shoulder. "I'm sorry."

He sighs. "No, you're not." His right hand rakes through his hair.

"Nicodemus has lived many lifetimes. I wonder if he's ever felt like he's become a better version of himself. Or if it's even possible when time isn't a consideration." I pivot toward Arjun. "You asked me not long ago why I wanted to do this. I have part of an answer. I want to find Sunan because I wish to become a better version of myself, and I believe that returning to my mortal form will make this possible. Is that a good enough answer?"

"No," Arjun says, his voice weary. "But I suppose it will have to do." He comes to stand beside me. "I should warn you—this silver is not meant to transport your kind. I don't know how it will react to you or how you will react to it."

"Haven't you heard?" I hold up my left hand. My fétiche flashes from the smallest finger. "Not even the sun can hurt me anymore."

Arjun shakes his head. "If you're not fussed about it, then I won't be." He closes his eyes and presses his right palm to the silver surface. Ripples pulse around his fingertips, like small waves spreading across a pond. Once they reach the brass frame, the entire mirror shudders, the ripples reverberating back on themselves. For a moment, Arjun keeps his eyes closed, his lips moving soundlessly as if in prayer.

The mirror stills all at once.

"Off we go," Arjun says, and he walks through the liquid surface without a glance back.

Another twinge of apprehension cuts through me with the sharpness of a newly honed blade. But I fix my shoulders and push my left foot through. The sensation that follows is curious. Surprisingly cold, especially since I am no longer affected by such things. The cold is absorbed through my clothing to my skin before it starts to burn like acid. Quickly—before I can talk myself out of it—I press through. The mirror resists me for a moment, though it drew Arjun in like a pool of warm water. Almost as quickly, it spits me out the other side as if it were disgusted by the taste of me.

When I land, it is against a rise of hot sand. Silken grains sift across my skin, leaving a trace of glittering residue wherever they touch. Hot air blasts around me, followed by a rush of scent and sound. To my vampire sensibilities, it is almost too much. As if I've stepped from the bliss of utter silence into a world of total chaos.

"Graceful, as always," Arjun jokes from where he stands over me, his amusement plain.

I straighten and begin looking around.

The mirror has transported us to an umber desert. A brilliant blue sky stretches above us, the horizon at my back wavering in the heat like a mirage. We stand in the middle of a bustling thoroughfare. Shrieking children, bartering townspeople, and the occasional clang of a cowbell reverberate around me. To my right, a man dressed in a long tunic stokes a small fire beneath an immense domed pot. He splashes oil into its center and begins calling out to those around him, who gather like bees drawn to honey.

I dust the sand from my frock coat before shrugging out of it entirely. Arjun has already begun rolling his shirtsleeves. Bedlam erupts around us in bursts, but it does not seem to bother the masses of people milling nearby. A cacophony of sound—clips of a language I've never heard—mixes with the bleating of goats and the rumbling of rickshaws, along with the shouts of other street vendors and the warnings of those nearby.

Bright colors flit across my periphery. Women with burnished skin, bearing immense parcels atop their heads, balance their burdens like magic as they weave through the crowd, the ends of their thin shawls trailing behind them. The smell of spiced tea wafts from a trio of elderly men seated on wooden boxes around a makeshift table.

When a young boy darts past Arjun, trips in his haste, and nearly sprawls to the ground, Arjun catches him. The boy yells with outrage, to which Arjun replies in the same tongue. They exchange words, the syllables clipped and rapid. The boy begins to smile halfway through the spat, his expression turning sheepish.

Realization dawns on me, though I should know better than to be surprised by anything in life or in death.

"Are we in the East Indies?" I shout over the din, my English blaring through the crowd like a foghorn.

Arjun laughs. "Welcome to Rajasthan. Specifically an area just on the outskirts of Jaipur."

"And you speak this language?"

"I speak Hindi and a bit of Marwari. It's enough for me to get by while I'm here. In the major cities, it's easier to find people who speak English. You have the British Crown to thank for that," he gibes in a humorless tone. He begins weaving through the crowd with purpose, threading between tight spaces at a leisurely pace.

My senses are inundated. It takes a great deal of effort for me to subdue my need to react, to stop myself from moving too quickly or gazing every which way. The smell of the food and the spices catches my attention more than anything else. It's perhaps even more intricate and layered than the cuisine of New Orleans.

Arjun pauses beside a burnished street vendor, who hands him a paper cone filled with a thick liquid tinged a pale orange hue. I move closer to avoid being struck by a donkey hauling a cart as Arjun takes a long sip.

He breathes in deeply. "It's been too long since I was last here." The distinct smell of saffron suffuses the air around him.

"And why is that, especially if it's as easy as stepping through a mirror?"

"It isn't easy, old chap," he muses. "It's never easy for me to make this journey." He takes another long swallow of his drink. "Would you like to try some?"

"What is it?"

"It's a saffron lassi. Made with cool yogurt and honey. The best thing on a hot day."

"I wish such things still appealed to me." I stare at his drink wistfully.

"I've heard it does for some vampires. Occasionally Odette will ask for some fruit. Her favorite things are pomegranates and mangoes. Is there something you still crave?"

"The blood dripping from a rare steak."

He laughs. "I can't help you with that. Especially not here. Cows are sacred in this part of the world. If you so much as insult one or step in its path, beware." Though his tone is light-hearted, his attention flits behind me for an instant, the corners of his eyes tightening.

Someone—or something—is making him uncomfortable. It would be foolish for me to press the matter out in the open. "Why isn't it easy for you to be here?" I ask, my words equally lighthearted, my senses alert.

He drops his voice to below a whisper, his smile easygoing. "The last three times I traveled to Rajasthan, I was stalked less than an hour after passing through the mirror. It will be only a matter of time before they try to stop me."

"They?" I step closer.

He waves his right hand as if bored. Then takes a final swallow of his drink, crushing the paper cone in his fist. "Not a moment to waste, then." With a clap of both hands, he begins strolling at a rapid pace in the opposite direction.

I follow him, my gait uneasy. "Are we running away?" I ask through gritted teeth.

"Is that in conflict with your Saint Germain sensibilities?" He grins.

"If someone here has been threatening you, I wish to put an end to it."

His strides lengthen. "I don't like to engage with these jacka-napeses, if I can avoid it. Fey circles are small, especially in the Vale. You never know when you might be fighting someone in your own family. And with my family, you'd *then* be accused of striking a member of the gentry. It's more trouble than it's worth." His pace quickens as he cuts through a small square with a well in its center, a queue wrapping around it, each person waiting a turn to refill a pitcher or a drum or a skein of waxed fabric. To my right, I catch a glimpse of a figure in a hooded grey cloak.

We continue moving at a brisk pace for several more blocks until we reach a section of town less traversed. Behind stacked stone walls lie larger, more intricate structures several stories high. Signs of wealth are evident in the manicured gardens and the decorated walls with their carved bricks and imposing scrollwork.

Arjun's steps falter as we round a bend alongside an embel-lished fountain, a wrought-iron gate wrapped around it.

"Impressive," I say.

Arjun mutters, "It's not being guarded. The gate is wide-open."

"Does that present a problem?"

"It's usually guarded." He glides closer. In the same instant, blurs of motion gather along either side of us. "Can you believe this fountain is actually powered by the flow of the nearby river?" he remarks.

I arch a brow. "Fascinating." The fine hairs on my arms stand on end, the muscles working in my jaw.

We are being followed. Surrounded. Cornered.

"It is, isn't it?" Arjun grins in a lighthearted fashion, then flicks his gaze toward the fountain with unmistakable intent.

I blink. Does he expect us to—

"Now!" Arjun breaks into a run, aiming straight for the open gate, toward the center of the fountain. Around me, hooded shapes converge. I blur toward the water, balking for an instant when I see Arjun dive beneath its surface without the slightest hesitation. Since I have no idea what might happen if I linger, I take a deep breath on instinct and jump in headfirst.

The water is warm. As warm as the air around us. It's the first time since I've become a vampire that I've had a chance to swim. My lungs are tight, clinging to the vestiges of their humanity, but I no longer need air. I open my eyes and realize the fountain is much deeper than it appeared at first glance. Perhaps twenty feet. Arjun is halfway down, swimming like a shark toward the bottom. I follow, marveling at how well my instincts adjust to an airless environment. I claw toward Arjun, who waits for me before reaching his right hand toward the silty floor. The second he does, the sand seems to draw him in. He does not appear the least bit bothered, so I reach for the silt with my own fingers.

The second they touch the sand, my fétiche begins to slide off my finger. I ball my hand into a fist, panic gripping through to my spine. It's broad daylight outside. Even with the deep water, the rays of sun manage to filter through unimpeded. If my ring is taken from me, there is no chance for me to find shelter before being set aflame.

Both my mother and father burned in the light of the sun, my father as payment for his sins, my mother because she believed there was no other choice. When she met the sun, my uncle did not let me watch. He pulled me to him, refusing to let go, though I screamed into his waistcoat, demanding to be set free.

I have no desire to die as my parents did.

The quicksand pulls me through to my shoulder. On instinct, I resist when it closes around my chest and throat. But I watch Arjun let the sand take him, swallowing him whole. A flare of doubt catches in my throat. What if he's been leading me to my inevitable demise all along? What if I follow him and my fétiche is ripped from my hand entirely, my death a veritable certainty once I fall to the other side?

What will I find on this other side?

I close my eyes and let the magic take hold. Darkness surrounds me the second the quicksand surrounds my face. It's like being drawn into an endless void.

The next instant I spill into a patch of sunlight brighter than any I've ever witnessed before. I'm blinded for the span of a breath, my arm coming up to shield my face.

We land on a glittering shore, waves lapping at our feet. I take a deep breath of the strange air. It smells warm and thick.

Like hot tea mixed with molasses and anise. My wet hands rake through packed sand. When I stand, my skin shines as if it's been brushed with diamond dust.

Arjun waits for me, his wavy hair dripping, his features serene.

"Don't take another step, you filthy leech," a voice barks from behind us.

When I wipe the salty water from my eyes, fury sets in.

A beautiful woman waits along the pristine beach, her long white gown offset by the grove of swaying palm trees at her back, the fronds an unnatural shade of dark blue, the bark resembling shards of sharpened copper. Around her brow is a coronet of pearls. In the distance behind her, the sun hangs high, its white rays glowing with angelic menace.

"Assemble," she says softly.

A semicircle of grey-cloaked warriors, bearing spears of gleaming alabaster, step forward, brandishing their weapons, aiming their blades straight at my heart.

BASTIEN

I t is the same as always.

Whenever unmitigated fury takes root in me, my blood turns to ice. If these bastards think to strike me down, it will not be without a fight. I advance, my fingers clawed at my sides, my fangs lengthening. Though I am outmatched by more than ten of these grey-cloaked soldiers, I will not wait for them to make the first move.

Melodic laughter chimes through the air.

"Stand down, Sébastien," she says. "No one is here to harm you."

I halt, but I do not let down my guard. "Forgive me for misunderstanding." Sarcasm drips from each of my words. "But I've never been cornered by twelve fey warriors wearing solid silver cuirasses and brandishing alabaster spears."

"Oh, you didn't misunderstand." Her lovely eyes twinkle. "I wanted you to be afraid. Those weapons are not merely made of alabaster."

"I am not afraid." I glance at the blades. They are also tipped in silver. Intended to strike a lethal blow.

Her smile resembles a scythe. "Then you're a fool."

I say nothing for a moment. Without warning, I blur forward in a rush, snagging the smallest of the grey-cloaked warriors and hauling her backward, my fangs bared above the skin along her neck. Her wrist rotates in my grasp until the spear falls from her fingers into the glittering sand.

"Let us pass, or I'll tear out her throat," I say in a calm manner.

Arjun sputters. "Good God, man, what are you—"

More bell-like laughter emanates from the woman dressed in layers of white spider-silk. "I doubt that. You are not made of that kind of mettle, Sébastien Saint Germain."

Anger threads through my veins. If she knows who I am, then she should also know better than that. Staring at her, I bend the warrior's neck to one side and sink the tips of my fangs just beneath the skin of her ear. She tenses on instinct, the other grey-cloaked warriors stepping forward in outrage.

I taste the warrior's blood on my tongue. It is sweet. Sweeter than any blood I've ever known. Filled with longing and flickers of sun-swept memory. For a breath of time, I want nothing more than to drink her dry. To prove my mettle. My worth as a Saint Germain.

A slender black brow curving into her forehead, the woman in white raises a staying hand to her warriors. She is no longer smiling.

Like my uncle, she is testing me.

I know what Nicodemus would do. He would kill the warrior. Make a show of her death, damn the consequences.

Instead I draw back, taking only a taste. "Stand down," I say softly, echoing the woman in white's earlier directive. Perhaps it is rash what I have done. But she wanted to establish control. I've learned in my short time as an immortal that it is best for control to be met with chaos.

Now she will know better than to test me.

The fey woman steps forward, and the air around her shimmers. It's impossible to guess her age, just as it is with Ifan, the full-blooded fey warrior who guards the entrance to my uncle's chambers at the Hotel Dumaine. She could be twenty. She could be two thousand years old. Her features are similar to those of Jae, her skin pale, her hair hanging past her waist in ripples of darkest black. All her fingers and toes are festooned with thin chains of silver set with pearls. Her lips are stained the color of dried blood. The way she walks—the way the remaining cloaked warriors move around her, their gazes watchful—tells me she is important.

Her gaze is trained on me. "Release my guard, and you have my word no harm will come to either of you. For the time being."

I linger for a beat. Then shove the fey warrior forward. She spins in place, her fists clenched at her sides, her nostrils flaring. Quicker than lightning, she takes hold of her spear and spins it through the air with the grace of a master, before leveling its tip at my face.

A declaration and a promise. This warrior *chose* not to fight back.

"Why have you brought this blood drinker to our shores, Arjun Desai?" the woman in white asks, her face expressionless.

"Because he asked me to bring him, in full knowledge of the

risk to himself." I can hear Arjun's heart thrashing in his chest, but he does not falter in his response.

She cants her head his way. "Are you in the habit of taking orders from a member of the Fallen?" She tsks. "Riya would be loath to hear it. Our kind does not choose a position of subservience when it comes to nightdwellers."

"Yes, but the nightdwellers possess a vast trove of wealth." Arjun grins, but it does not touch his eyes. "And perhaps my mother would be less inclined to render judgment if she knew I was taking more than my fair share of it."

That same scythelike smile curves up her face. It's unsettling to behold, for it is a smile that belies a threat. "Nevertheless." She extends her fingers, and the air around her undulates. An unseen hand takes Arjun by the chin, directing him closer, his feet floating above the sand. When I move to intercede, Arjun stops me with a single glance. "You know as well as any, son of Riya, how . . . displeased I am to discover you in the company of a leech." She takes his jaw between her thumb and forefinger as she sets him on his feet. "And a blood drinker like him has no business in the Vale."

Arjun swallows, the knot in his throat bobbing. I am struck again by the weight of my selfishness. He has put himself in great peril by bringing me here, just as he said. And not once did I consider the gravity of his actions. I thought only of what I wanted. To triumph at all costs.

If this is the better version of myself, what kind of young man was I before?

I take another step forward, my fangs retracting. Four of

the hooded guards step between me and Arjun, their spears pointed at my chest. "I can explain, if you would—"

"Bastien." Arjun scowls at me. "Hold your tongue, for once." He offers the woman in white a sheepish smile. "My lady," he says, "we are here because my business associate wishes to travel through the Vale to the borders of the Wyld. As you well know, there are no tares from the mortal realm into the Wyld to which a blood drinker may avail himself. I thought to bring him here and entreat upon your unfailing generosity." He bows. "We humbly ask permission to cross the edges of the Vale in order to reach our desired destination in the winter wasteland of the Wyld."

The woman's slender eyebrows arch high into her forehead, her onyx eyes widening. She begins to laugh. Its melody resonates with a familiar note.

Its sound cuts through to my core.

I know this laugh. It is one I often heard in my mortal dreams. A sound I longed to hear even in death. I take another step closer, heedless of the weapons aimed in my direction. My eyes rake across the ageless woman in white. She catches me studying her. Tilts her head just so, a knowing glint in her gaze.

It is there, in that moment, that I see the truth. It steals the words from my tongue.

She is the Lady of the Vale. She is also Celine's mother.

Celine is an ethereal. The daughter of fey royalty.

Her smile widens. "I am Lady Silla of the Vale," she says to me, "and you have entered my domain, which puts you at my mercy. If I wish for you to cut off your nose and present it to me as a gift, you will do so without question. And if you desire to traverse my borders freely, there will be a cost."

"Name your price, my lady." Arjun executes another crisp bow, and I hear the blood thunder in his veins. "And rest assured that our noses are yours to take, if you should but ask. Though I will say my associate's is quite elegant. Rather aquiline. Definitely preferable to mine."

One of the guards coughs to conceal her amusement. Lady Silla arches a brow her way.

I do as Arjun asked and keep silent. The only full-blooded fey I have ever encountered prior to this is Ifan, who served as a warrior in the Sylvan Vale's Summer Court before he was exiled for falling in love with a blood drinker. From Ifan, I learned never to enter into a binding agreement with any creature of the Otherworld in which the terms are not articulated in advance.

Shouldn't an ethereal like Arjun be more than aware of this fact? Where is the shrewd attorney I've known for the last year? The one who skillfully negotiated so many deals with magical and non-magical folk alike? A knot of doubt in my stomach pulls tight.

Is Arjun trying to betray me?

A disturbing feeling settles on my limbs. Nigel betrayed us all less than three months ago. And he was a member of my family for far longer than Arjun has been. Would the ethereal turn on us, after everything?

Lady Silla directs her guards to stand down. In a single fluid motion, they point their spears toward the sky and step back. "Do not fear, Sébastien Saint Germain. I will allow you to travel through the summer splendor of the Vale toward the frozen wastelands of the Wyld. I have but one condition. A simple one, which need not cost you a great deal of discomfort."

I almost laugh. I was tricked in this exact way five days ago, by this woman's daughter. The girl I loved when I was alive. The girl whose laughter haunted my dreams. Celine desired answers from me that night she asked me to kiss her. And now I possess the answer to a question that must have plagued her since childhood.

I know who her mother is. I know why Nicodemus' glamour is waning on her mind.

Celine has always been part of this cursed world, from the day of her birth.

"Bring the girl to me here in the Vale, Sébastien. Of her own free will." Lady Silla's black eyes bore through me. "Bring her here, and you may travel through my lands unimpeded. Though I cannot speak to the dangers you will find in the lawless Wyld."

Arjun looks to me, then back at the Lady of the Vale. "Girl? Which girl? Jessamine? What did she do now?"

"Do we have a deal?" she asks me, disregarding Arjun entirely.

I press my lips together, my thoughts whirring through my mind like the cogs of a clock. I want to ask the Lady of the Vale if she will harm Celine. But something tells me the question alone would be an insult. I cannot fathom why she would want to see her daughter now, after staying away from her for all these years. "I will not allow her to be placed in harm's way."

"Who, goddamn it?" Arjun demands.

"Nor will I," Lady Silla says, a furrow forming between her brows. "And you well know why. She is most precious to me." The Lady of the Vale glides closer, past a protesting Arjun. "If you refuse, it is of little consequence. I will have what I want in due time. Soon I will send others to the mortal realm to retrieve her. But I prefer it to be you, for her sake above all. She will believe you. She will trust you. You will keep her safe. Where you go, she will go without question." A smile blooms across her face. "Just like where she goes, you will undoubtedly follow." Her fingers weave through a zephyr of wind, which bows to her touch. "And would it not be preferable for all involved if you accompanied her, rather than members of my guard, whom she does not know or trust?"

Anger floods my veins. It catches in my throat, the taste as bitter as bile. I despise her logic. But not as much as I hate myself for setting the wheels of this train in motion.

The Lady of the Vale wants me to bring her daughter here. Of her own free will. The option before me now is the best of the worst.

"Yes," I say, hatred buzzing across my skin. "I would prefer it to be me."

"I thought you would see things my way, Sébastien," Lady Silla responds with a satisfied nod.

"Blast it all, what are you talking about?" Arjun shouts. "Which girl? To whom are you preferable?"

Behind us, the salt water starts to rise, the waves lapping at the glittering beach. The enchanted sea wraps around our ankles, taking hold of us as if it intends to pull us under. When it reaches waist level, we can no longer fight the magical current. It is impossible to remain upright.

"Ask the owner of the silver, Arjun Desai," Lady Silla says over the crashing waves, her expression one of delight. "Tell him his lady offers him salutations. And wishes he would come to see her sometime soon, as promised."

Her last word drifts through the air like a feather on a passing breeze. It lands on my chest like an anvil, its weight crushing me from within and without.

Promised. The owner of the silver made a promise to the Lady of the Vale.

Before I have a chance to speak, Arjun and I are swallowed by the water and promptly spat back through the fountain, landing unceremoniously on the blazing sand of an elegant street on the outskirts of Jaipur.

I sit on the ground, water dripping from my garments, my mind awash in treachery.

It is not Arjun whose betrayal I should have feared.

It is Jae.

CELINE

———— ≈ ————

C eline glanced at Michael as they walked through Jackson Square not long after sundown. Loss had never been an easy topic for her. It was like picking at a wound that refused to heal. She searched for the right words to offer condolences, and then decided it was best to say what was in her heart. "Is there anything I can do for your family? Anything that might help with their grief, even in the smallest measure?"

Michael shook his head. "I wish there were. Antonio's death has struck them like a battering ram." He inhaled, then linked his hands behind his back. "I haven't seen Nonna so upset since Luca's father, my uncle, died ten years ago."

"I'm sure they're all in shock. How old was your cousin Antonio?"

"Twenty-four."

"So young," Celine remarked.

A bitter smile settled on his lips. "Did I tell you he fought in one of the last battles of the war?"

"No, you did not."

Michael nodded. "It was the very day Lee surrendered at Appomattox seven years ago. The battle for Fort Blakeley, just outside of Mobile. Antonio was only seventeen, but he defied the wishes of his parents and went to fight against the rebel forces anyway."

"He sounds like a courageous young man."

"He was." Michael smiled in remembrance. "He was also loud and brash and obnoxious. He and Luca got along swimmingly as children."

They continued traversing over the pavestones at a leisurely pace. Saw palmettos swayed in the warm April breeze. The scent of rain hung in the air, smelling of metal and earth. "Have you managed to apprehend the person responsible for his death?" Celine chewed at the inside of her cheek. "Were there any clues regarding the identity of the perpetrator?"

"We haven't caught him yet." Something dark flashed in Michael's icy gaze. "But we will."

"I'm so sorry, Michael."

"Thank you, Celine."

She waited a breath. "I asked about your family, but . . . is there anything I might do for you?"

He looked at her sidelong. Wavered a moment. Then reached for her hand. "It is enough that you are here with me. Antonio was closer to Luca in age and experience. As such, I didn't know him well, but I did feel a sense of kinship because he served on the police force in Baton Rouge. I remember when I told Antonio I wanted to be a police detective. He wrote to the academy on my behalf, and he was there the day I received my commission." A wave of sorrow rippled across his face.

Celine squeezed his hand. "If you need anything, don't

hesitate to let me know, even if it's simply to lessen the burden for a moment. Sadness can be such an unbearable weight."

"I'm not sad. I'm furious."

Celine nodded. Michael's fingers threaded through hers as he drew her to his side. For a second, she hesitated before wrapping his hand in both of hers.

It was time for her to make a decision.

Though it pained Celine to admit it, Pippa had been right about many things. Michael Grimaldi was a good man who obviously cared a great deal for her. It would be foolish of Celine to ignore that fact. Pippa said love was a choice. A wise young woman would choose to love a young man like Michael.

But Celine could not shake the memory of that kiss she'd shared with Bastien. For long days and long nights, she'd tried to forget it. Tried to ignore the way her hands had trembled. The warmth that had pooled in her belly. The touch of his lips against her skin.

An onslaught of emotions had roiled through Celine in the five days that had passed. She was angry at all the lies. Frustrated by the realization that everyone refused to help her retrieve her memories.

But more than anything, Celine felt the weight of her sadness most keenly.

She'd lost so much. More than she could begin to fathom. Two nights ago, she'd toyed with the idea of breaking her promise to Bastien. She'd gone as far as to don a simple frock and walking boots, intent on going to Jacques' once more and demanding . . . something from him. Anything from him but this icy distance.

Thankfully Celine had come to her senses before leaving her flat. She needed to forget about Sébastien Saint Germain. He'd made it clear he did not want anything to do with her. She would not debase herself by begging for attention from any man, much less one like him.

Bastien was the kind of young man who cared about himself, first and foremost. True, he felt remorse. But never enough to take responsibility for the pain he caused or to choose a different path. Michael Grimaldi was steadfast and direct. Celine never had to doubt his affections or his intentions. A young man like this deserved to be loved.

Michael deserved Celine's love.

Never mind the voice in the back of her head, the one she could not seem to silence, the one telling her it wasn't quite right.

Michael and Celine continued their stroll, past the tines of black wrought-iron fences onto the paved walkway before Saint Louis Cathedral. Over the course of the last few months, Jackson Square had become one of Celine's favorite places in New Orleans. It was strange, therefore, that she didn't care for the structure at its heart: the tri-spired church with its famed clock tower. The last time she'd attended Mass there, she'd become dizzy and light-headed, an unsettling sensation spreading through her stomach. Pippa had escorted her from the nave the very next second, vowing that they could simply attend Mass elsewhere in the future.

"Violence has taken so much from us both," Celine mused to Michael.

"I wish I could have spared you such suffering."

"Everyone keeps saying how lucky I am that I do not remember most of it." Her lips quirked to one side. "Sometimes I'm inclined to agree."

"Only sometimes?" Concern flared on Michael's face. "Are there moments you wish you could remember it, even if it meant reliving the horror?"

Celine toyed with telling him how much she despised being sheltered from the truth, no matter how dark it might be. But she didn't know if Michael would understand. He did not seem like the kind of young man who found beauty in darkness, as Celine often did. He seemed like the type who always looked to the light. "I feel as if I'm missing so much of myself," she said. "It makes me feel . . . broken. As if I will never be whole again, no matter what I do."

Michael stopped walking. Turned toward her and took both her palms in his. Slowly, carefully, he brought her right hand to his lips and pressed a gentle kiss to it. "You are not broken, Celine. Not at all." He paused. "And if it is important for you to remember everything that happened, perhaps we should speak to someone about it."

"Another doctor?"

"I will make inquiries." A determined look formed on Michael's brow, as if he already had in mind the right person to ask.

Though she doubted it would make a difference, his conviction settled some of the turmoil lingering in Celine. Michael had done that for her from the day she woke up in the hospital over two months ago. Her sense of misgiving was ever present, but at least when Michael was with her, she didn't feel quite as lost.

A part of her wanted to recoil from the sentiment. She hadn't always been this way. Hadn't always needed someone beside her to feel safe. After losing her mother at an early age, Celine had learned the value of self-reliance. Now she resented its loss.

"I wish we both had answers," Celine murmured over their joined hands. "I wish I could uncover the truth of what happened to your cousin."

"And I wish what happened to you had not happened," Michael said. "I wish I could erase its truth."

When Celine looked up, he was watching her with a new kind of tenderness. He'd been so careful the last few weeks. Never once had Michael pushed her to return his obvious affections or caused her to feel uncomfortable.

But something had changed tonight. Celine could tell in the way he looked at her. The spark of something she'd never seen in his pale eyes.

His gaze steady on hers, Michael leaned forward. "I hope I might always be there to keep you safe. That is . . . if you'll have me."

Celine swallowed. Any young woman should be thrilled to have Michael Grimaldi vying for her affections. If lasting love was a choice, maybe Celine could choose to love him as Pippa had chosen to love Phoebus.

Perhaps she *should* keep her fairy tales where they belonged, in books.

Michael brushed a kiss across her forehead. Then on the tip of her nose. Then—ever the gentleman—he took his time as he drew closer, giving Celine every opportunity to stop him from doing what she knew he'd been wanting to do for a long while.

She didn't say no. There was no reason to say no.

Michael kissed her, his eyes closed. His lips were soft. Warm. Gentle. Celine leaned into his kiss. Waited for her eyes to fall shut. They didn't. She could feel her brain continuing to work, even as Michael wrapped his arms around her, pulling her into an embrace.

The kiss seemed to go on for a long while.

An image rose to the forefront of Celine's mind, unbidden. Of another kiss. One in which time seemed to stand still, only to speed forward in a sudden rush. As if a single kiss were both a moment and a lifetime. Forever, in the blink of an eye.

She forced her eyes closed just before Michael pulled away. He left a final lingering kiss on her lips before stepping back. Celine smiled at him, her thoughts in turmoil.

As if the holes in her memory were mirrored by the holes in her heart.

BASTIEN

O n a typical evening, I sink my teeth into the neck of my
victim, and nothing else matters. For a breath of time, it's
as if the rest of the world fades into oblivion. I am no longer a
creature of darkness, longing for my lost humanity. There is no
Brotherhood. There is no Nigel.

There is no Jae.

But this is not a typical evening. The plans I've set in motion
since meeting the Lady of the Vale two days ago are far from
ordinary. Our trap has been laid. The mark is one of our own.

This will not be a welcome victory.

I drink deeper, and my victim's thoughts invade my mind
like a stack of lithographs flipped into motion. As I suspected,
this man lived a sordid life. I chose him for this exact reason
when I spotted him yesterday, just after nightfall. I followed
him for hours, waiting to see if he could redeem himself in
my eyes.

The faster his memories flit through my mind, the more convinced I am that I have chosen well.

For years my victim has been leading orphan boys and home-
less street urchins to their twisted fates. The sailors along the

dock call it being shanghaied. He offers his victims food and drink laced with laudanum. Waits until they are lulled into a drug-addled sleep. When the boys wake, they are already out to sea. Forced to work the rigging and swab the decks until they are no longer of any use, all while he pockets the proceeds of their indentured servitude.

Many argue this is another form of slavery. I cannot speak to that. I have lived a life of favored fortune, despite the color of my skin. The conversations I've shared with Kassamir—who was taken from his parents as a child thirty years ago and sold to another plantation outside New Orleans—merely scratch the surface of his pain.

Kassamir never saw his parents again, even after the war ended.

I think of that fact as I drink deeper, gripping my victim by the shoulders. I think of all those boys and girls who will likely never see their homes or their families again. It doesn't matter if some of them were orphans. Every child deserves a place of refuge. A place to feel safe.

The more I drink, the more distorted the images become. They darken as if they've fallen into the path of a shadow. As I watch the man's vicious life unfold, my grasp tightens. My hands move from his shoulders to either side of his head. I feel his heartbeat begin to slow.

"Bastien," Boone says from behind me, a warning note in his voice. "He's dying."

I ignore him. I drink more. The man's hands—which have hung limply at his sides for the last few minutes—begin to flail.

He tries to strike me, but I am drowning. Drowning in all the violence he has committed. Drowning in his salvation.

"Sébastien." This admonishment comes from Jae, who blurs to my side and takes hold of my shoulder. "That is enough." His fingers dig into my arm.

I draw back. Then, at the exact moment Jae relaxes his grasp, I twist my hands in opposite directions, snapping my victim's neck.

Blood drips down my chin. I meet Jae's gaze. My expression is mirrored in his. I look murderous. Demonic. The whites of my eyes are gone. My ears have sharpened into points. My fangs are stained and gleaming.

A dark part of me—the soulless part—relishes it.

Without a word, Jae directs me to follow him. I carry the body of my victim across the rooftops of my city until we reach a pauper's cemetery, where I leave him to bake for several months in an empty chamber in the stifling Louisiana sun.

The water table in our city is high. Too high to bury our dead in the ground. It was a lesson the first imperialists learned when the coffins of the dead rose from the earth following a heavy storm, the rotting corpses clogging the city streets. After the Catholic Church took hold of New Orleans, something had to be done. The Holy See did not permit the burning of its dead.

But they granted a special dispensation for the Crescent City. The coffins of our dead are placed in brick mausoleums aboveground. In the tropical heat, these spaces turn into ovens. Over the span of a year, the bodies are slowly burned, until nothing remains but ash. One year and a day later, the bricks around the entrance are removed, and the ashes of its former occupants are swept aside into a caveau at the base of the crypt. In this way, entire generations of families share the same burial space.

Never was there a better place for a murderer to hide a body.

Never was there a better place to set the stage for a trap.

∽

"I still don't know why you hold this place so dear in your heart," I say to Boone.

He, Jae, and I stand side by side on the walkway outside one of New Orleans' most infamous bawdy houses. Its stucco façade is simple. Unadorned. Even its exterior is painted an uninspiring shade of grey. Unusual on a street peppered by structures in light pink and cheerful green and pale blue.

Jae frowns as Boone knocks on the door in a specific pattern. "I have no intention of accompanying you inside this sort of establishment."

"Ever the monk," Boone teases, his tone flippant.

He is playing his role well. But I expected nothing less. It is why he was chosen.

"Nor do I see reason in paying for any woman's favor," Jae continues.

"Isn't that what happens all the time, though?" Boone arches a brow. "A boy needs a wife. His mama and papa want his marriage to bring the family more wealth and clout. So they find a girl with a hefty dowry or an inheritance." He snaps his fingers. "Or do you only object when a woman is the one to decide the terms?"

"If you think all the women in this establishment had a say when it came to their lot in life, I'll eat my hat," I interject. "A choice under the barrel of a gun is not a choice at all."

"Perhaps you're right," Boone agrees. His grin is wide. Tooth-less. "But far be it from me to deprive them of their living." He winks. "Join me for a drink, gentlemen. I promise to behave . . . for at least an hour."

Jae's frown deepens. I appreciate Boone in this moment more than words. It's as if he'd been given a playwright's script. A necessary ruse when dealing with an immortal like Shin Jaehyuk. One likely to smell our trap from several miles away.

It cannot be helped. Such intrigues are necessary. We need to catch Jae unawares while on the town, far from the familiarity of Jacques' or the sanctuary of his heavily warded abode.

"No. As usual, I will not be partaking in your evening festivi-ties." Jae looks to me. "If you wish to stay with Boone, I will not object."

I shake my head, my expression subdued. "I took a life tonight, despite my best efforts. My evening has been eventful enough." I tip my Panama hat at Boone. "Give the ladies my regards, Casanova."

"I certainly shall." Boone nods with a devilish wink.

As intended, Jae and I are left alone.

We take our leave, strolling along Rampart toward the water-front, closer to both Jacques' and the flat Jae shares with Arjun. As we near the turn onto Royale, I pause as if I've suddenly remembered something.

Jae stops beside me and glances my way.

"Damn it all," I mutter.

He waits for me to explain before he reacts, in typical Jae fashion.

I sigh. "It doesn't concern you. Nor have I any wish to place my troubles on your shoulders." Jae is both a simple man and a complicated vampire. His curiosity will be sure to get the better of him.

Most battles are won or lost before they are ever fought.

"What is it?" he says.

"Nothing of import." I take a step as if I plan to resume our prior path. "I'll handle it tomorrow, if there's still time."

Jae stands firm. "Sébastien."

I turn in place. "Nicodemus wanted me to check on a ship-ment of malted barley bound for a Kentucky distillery. I prom-ised I would bring proof of its arrival to him before sunrise." I shrug. "I can attend to it later, just before dawn."

"It's not safe for you to travel anywhere in this city alone. Not with the Brotherhood on the prowl." Jae pivots toward the docks. "I'll go there with you."

I snort. "I doubt any of our furry friends will be lying in wait on the off chance I decide to take an evening stroll beside the sugar shed. Don't trouble yourself. I can take Odette with me tomorrow. You know how much she loves to watch the sun rise."

"It isn't a trouble." When Jae proceeds in the direction of the sugar sheds, I take a measured breath and follow in his footsteps.

Checkmate.

Four blocks later we arrive at the long wooden building that houses many different types of refined sugar and molasses before they make their way up the Mississippi into the heartland.

"Which berth?" Jae asks.

I place my hands in my trouser pockets. "Forty-seven."

We wander down the yard and stop at a series of sliding wooden doors, not unlike those of an immense barn. A cat screeches as I yank one of them open.

Jae does not enter. He pauses at the doorstep, his black hair falling into his face.

Though I understand his reticence, I feign ignorance. "Jae?"

"No one is guarding the stores."

Dark laughter emanates from beside burlap sacks of sugar. "You are the best among us for a reason," Madeleine says as she steps from the shadows.

It is no accident that I've asked for Madeleine to be the one to spring this trap. She unmoors Jae, as she has for decades. Whatever past they share makes Jae doubt his present.

And preying on doubt is the key to ensnaring a predator.

"What are you doing here?" Jae rasps, the tendons in his neck straining with awareness.

"It's time we had a discussion, Jaehyuk-*ah*," Madeleine says softly.

He whirls in place. But her distraction has served its purpose.

Before Jae has a chance to flee, Arjun grabs him by the wrist, freezing the assassin where he stands.

Exactly as we planned.

Jae

---≈---

The instant Arjun's hand touched Jae's wrist, Jae knew all was lost.

The last time he'd been bested like this was long ago in Hunan Province, when the warlock Mo Gwai had tortured him for a month in a cavern deep beneath the earth. Jae would bear the scars of that ordeal for the rest of his immortal life. In a way, he was grateful for them. They served as a constant reminder of his greatest failure.

That time in the cavern had been the beginning of the end for Jae. The darkest nights of his memory. A time when revenge had consumed him like tinder in a blaze. It wasn't until the smoke cleared that Jae had realized the depths of his failure.

The true price of his retribution.

To make his revenge possible, Jae had struck a bargain with the Lady of the Vale. The consequences mattered not to him. Only the outcome. And now these consequences had come home to rear their heads.

A fitting end to a chain of events set in motion so long ago.

Jae stared at his found family. The ones he'd come to value more than life itself. Even though Arjun's touch froze Jae where he stood, it still left him in possession of his faculties. He could see, hear, taste, and smell with the heightened senses of a vampire. Humans were usually rendered completely unconscious by Arjun's gift. Perhaps, given the circumstances, Jae would have preferred that.

No. He deserved their anger. Their heartbreak. Their judgment.

"Hurry," Arjun said, his hazel eyes wide, his jaw clenched. "Jae is strong. He won't remain immobile for long. And I'd rather not be here if and when he breaks free."

Despair choked like bile in Jae's throat. As soon as the magic wore off, his brothers and sisters expected to meet the full breadth of his fury. They were no doubt counting on that. Emotions made even the best warrior weak. Made them unable to see past their own desires.

Jae knew this truth better than most. Revenge had blinded him to all else. Even after he exacted punishment on Mo Gwai—even after he relished his enemy's final screams—it had been a hollow victory. The peace Jae fought to achieve was nothing more than an illusion, gone with the fruit of his dark purpose.

Madeleine stepped into his sight line, her brown eyes haunted, her cheeks hollow. More than anything, Jae wished he could turn away from this face. He could not look at her. He did not want to look at her. The pain in his chest was too great, like the weight of a thousand worlds pressing down upon him.

A century ago, Jae would have given anything to see the light in her eyes. The way her smile turned up the rest of her features, tilting them toward the sky. Jae willed Madeleine to avert her gaze. But she was Madeleine. She would never do what he wanted. Only what he needed.

Bastien moved beside her, his expression detached. "Did you think we wouldn't find out you were in league with the Lady of the Vale?" His voice was like ice cleaving off a mountain. "Did you think we would not discover the breadth of your duplicity? I suppose I should no longer be surprised by such a betrayal, especially after Nigel."

"You will answer for this, Shin Jaehyuk." Madeleine stumbled over the words, her lower lip quavering. So uncharacteristic of her. "Comment as-tu pu faire cela?"

How could you do this?

For years, Jae had nursed the belief Madeleine might understand. After all, she'd surrendered everything for the sake of Hortense, who would have died of disease if Nicodemus had refused to turn her. For the sake of her family, Madeleine renounced her affections for Jae. Nicodemus had not wanted his best assassin to form an earthly attachment.

So she relinquished her love. Jae had not protested. He should have fought for her. Should have argued with Nicodemus. But revenge so consumed him that even Madeleine did not matter. When he realized the error of his ways, it was too late.

Sensation returned to the tips of Jae's fingers and toes, yet he did not move. Not yet.

His brothers and sisters were not the only ones capable of setting a trap.

Arjun stood behind him, ready to freeze Jae once more,

should he attack. They expected Jae to strike with his usual swiftness. Even Jae had to admit it was the best way for him to escape. Strike hard and fast and true. If he injured one of them enough to distract the others, he could buy himself the chance to flee into the night and make his way back to the mirror in his flat. From there, he could travel to Lady Silla and inform her of the recent happenings.

The rational side of Jae knew this was the best course of action. In fact, he'd already chosen which of them he would injure. Not enough to cause permanent harm, but enough to provoke a necessary response. To send a ripple of confusion through their ranks.

But Jae couldn't do it. He wouldn't strike out at them. Instead he would flee. Disappear into the misted night. He'd done it before. He could do it again. He would not have it on his head if he hurt any member of his family.

It would all come down to an instant. Less than an instant.

The moment sensation returned to Jae's knees, he blurred into the darkness of the sugar shed and knelt in the shadows, intent on taking up the least amount of space. Cries of frustration trailed in his wake. All around him, the smell of sugar permeated the air, its dust coiling through the moonlight filtering from the wooden slats.

Jae took in a single breath, taking in the collection of scents around him. Letting his trained ears absorb all signs of movement, tracking his brothers and sisters as if they were his next targets. Bastien was the one to worry about the most. He was young. Strong. Unpredictable. Jae had not forgotten how Bastien had cracked Boone's skull like an egg the night he first woke as a vampire.

Once Jae took stock of his surroundings, he ducked into an alcove, then blurred toward the ceiling, angling for higher ground. Grasping an exposed beam, he watched the scene unfold below him, splinters fraying under his grasp.

"Jae," Bastien said.

The single syllable reverberated to all four corners of the cavernous warehouse.

Bastien continued. "Don't fight us."

Figures blurred between the piled sugar sacks, causing more sweet dust to curl through the night air. Jae remained silent. Unmoving. Waiting for a path to clear toward the exit. Scanning the ceiling for a possible egress.

"I only wish to know what Lady Silla wants with Celine," Bastien said. "Please, brother. Help me."

Tension banded across Jae's arms. Lady Silla must have revealed more than Jae's treachery. She must have confessed that Celine was her daughter. Jae could not fathom why she would do that. It was clear his brothers and sisters knew he worked in service to the Lady of the Vale. But did they know the terms of their arrangement? Had she told them how Jae struck a bargain with her to obtain the location of Mo Gwai's hidden lair?

Jae waited. Listened, every muscle in his body taut.

He'd given up so much in his life. But he'd received much in return. Perhaps it was enough that he surrender now and accept his fate. He'd known this day would come eventually.

Motion stirred in Jae's periphery.

"He's on the ceiling," Madeleine said. "That's where I would go first." She stepped into a beam of waning moonlight. "The corners. Preferably the darkest one."

Jae's fangs began to lengthen. She knew him too well.

Two vampires and one ethereal began closing in on Jae.

His options were narrowing with each passing moment. Though he loathed the thought of harming any member of his family, he could not allow them to capture him. He doubted they would ever resort to such a thing as torture to wreak their revenge. But Nicodemus would.

And Jae had sworn years ago never to suffer the agony of torture again.

He locked in on Arjun as the half fey moved closer. It was unfair, but Arjun's mortal father put him at a distinct disadvantage. He was not as strong. Not as quick. And the half-breed was, after all, the one with the power to immobilize him. Better to eliminate that possibility.

Jae caught himself. It had been an age since he used that particular epithet, even in his head. It took him back to the time he'd spent in the Vale, vying for Lady Silla's attention. The fey of the Summer Court had always been obsessed with pure bloodlines. Jae himself had seen the kind of torment they inflicted on the ethereals who dwelled among them. The way they jeered at the so-called half-breeds, making sport of their pain. Mocking their inability to heal as quickly or run as swiftly.

Nevertheless, Arjun was the one Jae would attack first.

Moving soundlessly, Jae extracted one of the small silver daggers from inside his shirtsleeve. Set his sights on Arjun Desai. And slid from the shadows, moving quicker than a bolt of lightning across the sky.

Vampires do not see the world with the encumbered eyes of a human. They see it in minute detail, as if they were afforded a small eternity to examine it. A focused vampire is the deadliest creature known to man or beast.

Even then, Jae almost missed what happened next.

Madeleine glided into his path, anticipating his motions as always. Jae changed tactic, but Madeleine was there, attempting to disarm him. They struggled, her hands wrapping around his wrists. He tried to pull back, but Arjun leapt toward them, a hand outstretched to freeze Jae where he stood.

Jae twisted away, the knife in his hand pointed at an odd angle. Bastien shouted but it was too late. The solid silver blade embedded in Madeleine's body like a hot knife through butter. Time stopped. Something lurched in Jae's chest. Something that had been silenced for nearly a century.

It was the sound of his dead heart breaking.

Madeleine pulled the blade from her skin with a wince. Blood dripped from the dagger's silver edge, down toward its ivory handle. It stained the front of her dress before the wound attempted to knit itself together. It failed, and the blood began spurting from her chest in a torrent, buoyed by the dark magic that had set it on its immortal course so many years ago.

She offered him a weak smile, a trickle of crimson dripping from her mouth.

Then Madeleine collapsed in Jae's arms.

BASTIEN

J ae surrenders without protest. All his weapons are turned over at once. He does not attempt a struggle. Nor does he say a word in his own defense.

Because Boone is the most fleet-footed of us all, he bears Madeleine through the streets of the Vieux Carré, moving faster than sound. When Jae, Arjun, and I arrive at Jacques', the second floor is bedlam.

The moment Hortense sees Jae, she attacks. "Fils de pute," she screams, her fingers tearing at his face, her nails drawing blood. "I will rip out your dead heart and feed it to the pigs! I will make a meal of you," she cries. "I will drink you dry until you shrivel into a husk at my feet." It takes the strength of three vampires to keep her from ripping Jae to pieces. Still Jae does not try to defend himself.

I steel my spine for the ordeal to come. Despite my best efforts, there is no way Nicodemus will not learn of the events that have transpired tonight. For the last two days, I tried to conceal Jae's treachery from my uncle. It's why I sought to avoid a confrontation at Jacques' at all cost. Our maker would not wait to ask questions. He would destroy before he could be destroyed, as he'd done with Nigel.

Despite what Jae has done, I feel we owe him more than that.

Since Nicodemus is sure to discover the truth now, Ifan is summoned. The fey warrior arrives soon thereafter, bearing a small leather-bound case. The fey in the Summer Court of the Vale are not weakened by silver as those in the wintry Wyld are; instead they are at the mercy of pure iron. As a warrior of the Vale, Ifan learned how to exploit his enemy's greatest weakness. How to cause a blood drinker pain using silver weapons, only to heal the wound and begin again. After Ifan was exiled from the Vale for the crime of falling in love with a vampire, he came to my uncle for sanctuary in the mortal world. For nearly half a century, Ifan has bound himself in promise to Nicodemus.

Madeleine is lying supine on the longest table in the room. The same table upon which I was placed while undergoing the change. Odette holds a compress to her chest. Blood pools around them, dripping from the edges of the mahogany table onto the priceless carpet.

Ifan opens up his case and comes to peer at Madeleine's injury. "She is lucky," he muses, brushing back strands of hair from the long auburn queue trailing down his back.

"Lucky?" Hortense sputters from the corner, where Boone and I continue to restrain her.

"Yes, vampire," Ifan retorts. "Your sister is lucky the blade missed the center of her chest. If solid silver splits the breastbone or severs the head from the neck, the wound is impossible to heal." He grunts. "The blade missed her breastbone by no more than a hairsbreadth."

"How do you know it missed?" I ask.

"Because she still bleeds. If it had struck true, the magic in her veins would cease to move her blood, and she would become a withered husk." As he speaks, Ifan removes a poultice from a pouch concealed in his trunk, along with a small vial of dark green liquid.

"I can heal her, but it will cost you," he says.

Boone snorts, his face incredulous. "You work in service to Nicodemus, warrior of the Vale. Do as his progeny commands."

"Nicodemus has not summoned me," Ifan says in a smooth tone. "And I doubt he has knowledge of what occurred here tonight, or he would be the one directing me, not you." His smile is vicious, as if he relishes our discomfort. "I do not serve *you*, leech." He looks to me.

"I'll pay whatever the cost," I say. "Heal her now."

"There is a fey blade in the Saint Germain vault," Ifan says, his affect flat. "The silver is laced with diamonds. It was made a millennium ago by one of the most celebrated metalsmiths in the Vale. I want it."

"It is yours."

"Then we have a bargain." Ifan nods.

"Is everything a bloody bargain with your kind?" Odette says, her fingers crimson.

"Yes," Arjun replies. "It is."

Ifan removes a handful of dried herbs from inside the pouch.

"You'll have to hold her down," he says to us. "This will not be pleasant." The smile has not faded from his face.

"If you hurt my sister," Hortense says, "I swear I will—"

Arjun freezes her in place without a word.

I sigh. "Boone, please take Hortense onto the roof and keep her there for the next hour."

⁓

An hour later, the bleeding in Madeleine's chest has lessened to a trickle. Though she remains unconscious, Ifan assures us she will be fully healed once she has fed. Odette leaves to find blood, and I sit with Arjun, Boone, and Hortense in the darkness, our clothes stiffened by rust-colored stains, our expressions set in stone.

Jae has been tied to a chair with silver chains. He says nothing, but his face tells a different story. Everything about the way he watches Madeleine is haunted.

Lines bracket Boone's mouth. He sits down and buries his face in his hands. "I can't do this again," he says. "I can't suffer through another betrayal." He takes to his feet and blurs toward Jae, his movements erratic. "Why have you lied to us this entire time?" he whispers. "In you, I saw a brother. How—how could you betray us like this?" His voice breaks.

"I did betray you," Jae says. "But I never lied. Everything I've ever said or done, I meant. This family"—he pauses—"is my life."

I listen to him. Before Lady Silla's revelation, I believed Jae incapable of subterfuge or deception. He was always the most honest of us all. Not once did he shy away from painful truths. But now everything I've ever believed is being called into question.

Nigel betrayed us. After years of laughing, smiling, and living among us, it was the work of a moment for him to stab us in the back. It would be foolish of me to believe this could not happen again.

When you care about someone, they are able to hurt you and betray you.

I watch Hortense enfold her elder sister in her arms, crooning to her in French. It is unusual to see Hortense offering comfort to Madeleine. Usually it is the other way around.

Jae finds my gaze. "What do you intend to do with me?"

For a breath of time, I think about my uncle. Nicodemus would deal with Jae without mercy, just as he did with Nigel. He would not give Jae a chance to speak for himself.

If I could have been the one to decide, would I have listened to what Nigel had to say?

My heart is heavy when I realize I would not have cared. Nigel's actions cost me everything. If you had asked me at the time, I would have agreed to everything that transpired. Maybe I myself would have been the one to tear Nigel limb from limb.

I was raised to believe a traitor deserves a traitor's death.

It's possible I might have agreed to even more violence. Perhaps to torture. I think of Ifan and the set of skills he possesses. To hurt and heal in equal measure. I wonder how often my uncle used them to his advantage. As I look at Jae and the countless scars along his face and neck, I think of what that means.

I would have supported causing pain to someone in a defenseless position. I would have relished this pain, believing it to be the righteous path. But I know what I should do, despite my desire for the twisted kind of justice my Saint Germain blood demands.

When you care about someone, they are able to hurt you.

But it is your choice whether you return the favor.

"Why did you betray us?" I ask. "Tell me everything. I swear I will listen."

Jae's shoulders roll forward, his long hair falling into his face. "Why do you care what I have to say? Just do what you plan to do, Sébastien."

I consider sniping back at him. Letting the desire for pettiness win out. But that would be weak. I think of the strength it must have taken for Celine to fight for my life when no one else would. "Because I love you. You have been my brother for years. I owe us this much."

Jae blinks once. "I was disloyal. Why not do as your God tells you? An eye for an eye. All the gods of the world would agree I deserve it."

"That would make sense, wouldn't it?" I say. "It would be easy. But life, even for an immortal, is not easy." I think about what Valeria said to me. "Love and loyalty are not always the same thing. Loyalty is easy. Love is doing what is right, even when it is difficult."

He peers at me, a strange light in his gaze. Then he leans back in his chair, wincing as the silver chains brush across his bare skin. "Even as a mortal child, I knew something about me was different. I first saw a dokkaebi the spring of my sixth year. It was nighttime in Busan. The smell of the sea was strong. The sprite came to me from the water. It looked like a child my age, with hair the color of the moon and skin the color of a summer sky. It smiled at me. I followed it into the water and nearly drowned in the waves.

"When I told my mother what happened, she did not believe me. She said I should never speak of such things again, or people would think me possessed by a demon. From that night on, the fey never left me alone. They continued beckoning me closer. I became obsessed with following one to its home, so that I might catch it and make it do my bidding. I'd read somewhere that there were certain kinds of fairy creatures who could grant wishes." His eyes still on the carpeted floor. Even Hortense listens, her expression rapt. "But they would always vanish into the mist, through tears in the world I could never see.

"One day on the eve of my eleventh year," Jae continues, "I was walking along the beach alone when a chollima galloped toward me, its wings whiter than a cloud and its hooves kicking up gold dust. I said nothing, but I knew to grab hold of its mane and hoist myself onto its back. It took me to the land of the Sylvan Vale. You can only imagine what I saw and experienced. Fruit with nectar sweeter than honey, collected from a forest of nettles and thorns. A world that shimmered on the edges. Flowers that blossomed to life before my eyes, their centers cut from yellow sapphires, ready to slice open your skin at the first touch.

"This was the first day I met Lady Silla. From then on, the chollima would come for me once a year on my birthday, and

I would spend an afternoon with the fey. It was in the Sylvan Vale that I first learned of my skill with weapons. It was there that I began training to become an assassin. Time passed, and I saw myself growing older each year, while those among the fey remained the same. When I turned sixteen, I begged Lady Silla to give me the power to stay young always. She refused. I swore fealty to her. I asked her what it was she wanted. She said there was nothing she could desire from a mere mortal. But I continued asking, again and again. Two years later, she said she wished to bring an end to the enmity between those of the Sylvan Vale and those of the Sylvan Wyld. I asked what the Wyld was, and she said it was the Vale's counterpoint. The darkness held against the light. The shadow cast by the sun. I recalled my mother explaining the difference between yin and yang—the necessary balance between the two—and I thought I understood. Though I'd never been there, I thought the Wyld to be a world littered with bloodthirsty monsters, poisonous glasswing butterflies, and giants carved from ice who would tear out the trees by their roots."

Jae pauses as if mulling over his next words. "I believed everything I was told by those in the Vale. Everything Lady Silla said. I did not waver when I said I would do whatever I could to bring about peace between the Summer Court of the Vale and the Winter Court of the Wyld. She informed me where I might find Nicodemus, who was the direct descendant of the last Lord of the Wyld. I was told to become useful to him. To make myself invaluable, in the hope he would one day trust me." A bitter smile curls up his face. "I did even better than that. After several years of proving myself indispensable, I convinced him to make me one of his children. Finally I had what I wanted: the chance to be immortal." His expression sobers. "Fool that I was, I did not understand the price."

He averts his gaze. "Nicodemus was the one who sent me to find Mo Gwai, a powerful warlock in Hunan who'd been his enemy for more than three decades. I traveled there, searching in vain for his hidden refuge. But Mo Gwai was the one to find me first. He took my fétiche and tortured me for information on how to best Nicodemus. To rid the world of vampires once and for all. Not once did I capitulate. Soon Mo Gwai began hurting me simply for sport. Because it pleased him to watch me burn beneath his silver blades. When I finally managed to escape, I collapsed in the mountains less than a league away from his lair. If Lady Silla's Grey Cloaks had not found me, I would have burned to death in the light of the sun."

"Une punition appropriée," Hortense mutters through her teeth.

"Lady Silla saved my life," Jae says. "In my delirium while I healed in the Vale, I asked for a way to seek revenge on Mo Gwai. She told me the time would soon come for my vengeance. Once I could move about, Lady Silla sent me back to Nicodemus. She promised she would tell me where to find both Mo Gwai and my fétiche, when the moment was right." He inhales. "I did as I was told. I returned to New Orleans, revenge ever present in my mind." His words become halting. "This obsession so consumed me that I did not protest when my love was taken from me. I did not fight for it. I did not fight for her, as I should have." Jae swallows, his eyes squeezed shut, his hands forming fists. "But through it all, I will never forget how my vampire brothers and sisters stood at my side. How all of them—even my former love—swore to help me seek my revenge. Swore to burn down the world to regain my honor." Jae stops talking. I look around at the rest of our family. Hortense is staring at a point of nothingness. Silent tears stream down Odette's face. Boone's eyes are closed, his lips pressed together.

They are all lost in the memories of a time long past.

"Lady Silla came to me less than a year later," Jae says quietly. "She promised to tell me what I wished to know in exchange for a binding promise of my own. One I had already offered her numerous times." He stares at me. "She asked me to swear fealty to her until the end of my days."

"And you did it," I say.

He nods. "Without hesitation. She was the one to save me when Nicodemus sent me into Mo Gwai's cavern alone." Jae braces his elbows on his knees. "Like a fool, I did not consider what this would mean. For years I thought she would order me to strike out at Nicodemus. But she did not. In recent times, our communication has been so infrequent, there are moments I trick myself into believing she has forgotten about my promise."

I brace myself for the answer to my next question. For the dread I know will inevitably follow. "Why does Lady Silla want us to bring Celine to the Vale of her own free will?"

Odette stands straight, her sable eyes wide with alarm. Hortense hisses in fury.

"You know the answer to that already, Sébastien," Jae says in a hoarse tone.

"I want you to say it regardless."

"Celine Rousseau is an ethereal. She is—"

"Lady Silla's daughter," I finish.

Jae nods once. All around us, everything stills.

Odette speaks first. "Celine's mother . . . is fey?"

"Not just fey," Jae says. "Celine is the daughter of the most powerful lady of the Summer Court. A member of its gentry."

Odette's arms cross. She begins pacing, her brow set with incredulity. "Why has Celine been kept apart from her mother for all these years?"

"Lady Silla made a promise to Celine's mortal father that none of her kind would approach their daughter until Celine's eighteenth birthday," Jae says.

I frown. "If that is the case, why has Lady Silla breached this agreement? I thought bargains in the Vale were sacrosanct."

Soft laughter falls from Arjun's lips as he sends me a rueful smile.

Jae looks at Arjun and then returns his attention to me. "This is the true magic of the Sylvan Vale. Once they find a way to manipulate the language of a promise, they are able to do as they please. It is why Lady Silla wishes for you to bring Celine to the Vale of her own free will. If Celine crosses into the Otherworld by choice, then Lady Silla has not violated the promise she made to Celine's father."

Clever. I almost laugh as Arjun did.

"I told you," Arjun says. "Those in the Vale are far more

duplicitous than those in the Wyld. Do not be fooled by the sunny skies and the fragrant food and delectable drinks. Death lurks in every corner."

I push off the paneled wall and walk toward Jae, my mind humming with questions. When I nearly collide with Odette—who has not stopped pacing since she discovered the truth of Celine's parentage—a thought occurs to me. "Odette."

She halts midstep and turns. The instant she sees my face, she understands what I want to ask.

"I know you dislike telling those closest to you about their futures," I begin, "but—"

"I do hate it," Odette interjects, though her words are not unkind. "But after what happened with Nigel, I haven't been able to shake the notion that I might have prevented it, if only I hadn't been so afraid."

"Afraid?" Hortense asks. "When have you ever been afraid of anything, sorcière blanche?"

"I've always been afraid of this power," Odette says simply. "The thing I feared most was that I would bear witness to the death of someone I love and be unable to prevent it. That is the real reason I don't bother to look. I . . . couldn't bear it."

"I know you gazed into Celine's future the night you first met," I say. "Will you not tell me what you saw?"

"Even though you asked that I not divulge your future?"

"This is not about my future," I say. "This is about Celine's."

Dark laughter flies from Hortense's lips. "You silly fool. If you cannot see how your fates are linked, then all that money spent on your fancy education was a complete waste."

"Never mind that. What did you see?" I press Odette.

Odette sighs. "I saw Celine sitting on a throne in this very room. On either side of her feet lay a tamed lion and a tamed wolf."

"The tamer of beasts," I say in remembrance.

She nods.

"What kind of throne was it?" Jae asks.

Blinking, Odette closes her eyes as if to reconstruct the memory. "Golden, but strange. As if it were covered in vines that twist into something sinister near the top."

Arjun moves toward her. "Do you remember what the top looked like?"

"As if it had . . . horns. Not ones like the devil, but more like antlers."

Jae grunts. "Then it is exactly as Lady Silla wishes it to be."

"What do you mean?" Lines form across Odette's forehead.

"The Lady of the Vale has long wished to reunite the Winter and Summer Court under one banner, and it appears she wishes for her daughter to rule over both," Jae says.

Laughter flies from Odette's lips. "Are you making jokes? I suggest you try again."

"It is not a joke," Jae replies. "It is merely a logical conclusion."

"Well . . . that's . . . absurd," Odette sputters. She points at Arjun. "He always says how much the Summer Court despises ethereals. And their lady wishes to install one on their throne?"

"Does Lady Silla not have other offspring?" I ask.

Arjun shakes his head. "The bloodlines of elemental enchantresses have struggled to reproduce for almost half a century. It is why many of them take mortal lovers. Human blood seems to strengthen the chances of a child surviving. This was the reason my own mother sought out my father. A child is a precious thing to any member of the gentry."

"Si les enfants sont précieux, then why are they so cruel to ethereals?" Hortense asks.

Arjun lifts a shoulder. "That is the way of the Vale. I suspect they resent ethereals for thriving. For possessing the gift of immortality without having earned it. Perhaps they wish to lord over us with their last remaining advantage: their pure bloodline."

Hortense spits at nothing. "This is the same disease that exists in mortals. An obsession with purity. Mark me, it will be their end."

I listen as they speak. Even though the news of Celine's parentage is not a surprise to me, I still don't know what to make of it. Perhaps I should simply tell Celine the truth and leave the decision to her. But another, more visceral part of me wishes to protect her from all of it. To keep her away from this world and its perils. "Celine's eighteenth birthday is less than seven weeks from now," I say to no one, my attention settled on the far wall.

"Which means nothing you might have done or said could have prevented this exact outcome," Odette replies. She reaches for me, her fingers coming to rest on my hand. "Stop blaming yourself for every bad thing that has happened to Celine in her life."

I gaze at her sidelong. "Is it so wrong to want to keep those you love safe?"

"It is if you are lying to them," Jae says from his chair across the room. "Don't spare Celine the truth to appease your own ego, Sébastien."

Hortense glares at him, then turns toward me. "Listen to the traitorous chaton. He may be cannon fodder in my eyes, but there are times he speaks true. Tell Celine what you know. Leave the decision to her. It is what a good man would do. One who trusts the heart and mind of the woman he loves." Intensity sparks in her rich brown eyes. "Do not make her story about you."

Her last words are like a punch to the stomach. If Nicodemus were here, he would do just that. His anger at being betrayed by Jae would eclipse all else. He would make these stories about himself.

I will not be my uncle.

I look around at each of my brothers and sisters. I think of the measure of them. What makes them who they are. What makes me who I am.

And I know what I must do.

CELINE

———— ≈ ————

All day at the shop, Celine had warred with herself.
       She'd promised never to seek out Bastien again. She'd
sworn to leave behind his world and all the troubles that came
with it. The questions remained: Did she owe it to him to keep
that promise? Did she owe him her loyalty? Or was it more
about honor?

Honor had not done Celine much in the way of favors. An
honorable young woman would not have fled Paris after committing a murder, no matter the circumstances. She would have
faced justice and hoped it prevailed.

Laughable. When had justice ever prevailed when it came
to a richly entitled young man and a young woman of modest
means?

Celine did not owe any man anything. By midafternoon, she'd
decided that honor and loyalty were nonsense if they prevented
her from living the life she wished to live. As soon as she closed
up shop for the evening, she resolved to return to Jacques' and
demand to speak with Bastien again.

An hour later, she changed her mind. As much as she hated
to admit it, Bastien was right. She already possessed all the

information she needed. The madman responsible for her injuries was dead. She was safe. Barring a miracle, there was little chance of her memories being restored. It was time for her to resume her life. To live in the present, rather than in the past.

To choose Michael Grimaldi and build a future with him in the light.

For the rest of the afternoon, Celine behaved like an absolute boor. Just before sundown—when Antonia asked her to repeat herself—Celine scowled at her with all the vim of an outraged schoolboy.

"I would like to know," Eloise commented in a contemplative tone, "how we might kill that bee in your bonnet."

Celine's scowl deepened. "What bee?"

"There is a . . . bee?" Antonia shrank into herself, her long brunette plait swaying like a pendulum as her eyes darted to all four corners of the shop.

Eloise pursed her lips. "If you want me to ask what is troubling you, then simply say so. I don't have the patience or the inclination to tease it out of you, Celine." Her grin was tight. "I'm not Pippa, after all."

The way Eloise peered down at her made Celine want to disappear or lash out. The crown of intricately folded fabric atop Eloise's head did not help. It was like being judged by the queen herself.

"Where is the bee?" Antonia demanded, her lovely accent turning high-pitched.

"There's no bee, dear one," Eloise answered. "But there will definitely be a swarm of some kind if Mademoiselle Rousseau doesn't stop snapping at everyone who asks her a simple question."

Appropriately chastised, Celine chose to sequester herself in the back room until closing, where she passed the time sorting a new shipment of decorative buttons and lace trimming. Only once did she leave, to wish both Antonia and Eloise a good evening. Then she bustled about tidying the space, the war within her continuing to wreak unseen havoc. Half an hour later, she still had yet to decide whether she would ignore all good sense and make her way to Jacques'.

After dimming the gas lamps and securing the inside of the shop, Celine stepped out the front door, withdrawing the key to lock it from the side pocket of her navy-striped frock.

As Chaucer would say, why was it so hard for her to let sleeping dogs lie?

I'll never understand the fascination with the infinite. There is an end to everything, to good things as well.

Chaucer was an ass. And the infinite captivates us because it allows us to believe all things are possible. That true love can last beyond time.

Celine stopped short, the brass key dangling from her fingertips.

The memory that washed over her was rich in detail. She could see the moonlight reflected in Bastien's gunmetal gaze. Hear the rich baritone of his voice. Feel the way he looked at her through the darkness, the heat in his eyes unmistakable. Smell his nearness, the spicy bergamot wrapping around her like warm silk.

She'd wanted to kiss him that night. He'd wanted to kiss her. She was certain of it.

Like a string of unraveling thread, the memory began to fall apart, as if it had never existed in the first place.

Frustration barreled up Celine's throat, making her want to shout into a void. She whirled in place and caught the last traces of the sun as it began to vanish along the horizon. She stood still for a moment and watched the colors melt across the sky.

It was beautiful. Something Celine could trust. Whenever she would lose hope as a child, her father would tell her to remember that every setting sun brought the promise of a rising dawn. A tomorrow that could change the course of today.

Maybe Celine didn't know what tomorrow would bring.

But she knew what she could do today.

Celine spun on her heel and nearly collided with the broad-shouldered young man standing on the sidewalk behind her.

"Putain de merde," she muttered as two strong hands shot out to steady her. As the familiar scent of leather and bergamot assailed her nostrils.

"I didn't mean to startle you," Bastien said, his hands falling from her arms.

"Then why are you standing there like a panther ready to pounce?" she demanded as she straightened the front of her bodice and tried her best to ignore the traitorous flush creeping up her neck. "Do I look like your next meal?"

A half smile curved up one side of his face. "You always could make me laugh."

The way Bastien looked at her made Celine want to throttle him. "You're welcome," she said. "One day I hope you return the favor. For I have yet to find you the slightest bit amusing."

His expression sobered. He shifted back, his hands in his trouser pockets. "May we speak in private?"

"Why?"

"There are some things I wish to say."

"Am I going to like what I hear?" Celine knew she was acting like a child. But if everyone insisted on treating her like one, she was happy to oblige them.

A brow crooked into his forehead. "Do you usually like what you hear?"

"No, I don't usually like what I hear. Especially when you're the one speaking."

"That's unlikely to change anytime soon," Bastien admitted. "But I was informed—by those much wiser than I—that you deserve to hear these things and make your own decisions."

Suspicion fluttered through Celine's stomach, causing her body to tense. "May I ask to what it pertains? Does it have anything to do with my lost memories?"

"Not exactly," Bastien said. "But I do possess answers about your past." He took a single step closer, his stance wide. Almost protective. "And I believe you desire the truth, even though it may cause you pain. Am I wrong?"

Celine swallowed. Shook her head. And unlocked the door to her shop.

☙

For the next hour, Celine mostly held her tongue. Mostly listened.

But some things were too ridiculous for her to ignore. Twice she almost threw Bastien out of the shop, her hands trembling, her pulse trilling in her skull.

A world of . . . fey creatures? Enchantresses? *Blood drinkers?*

Perhaps she truly had gone mad. Perhaps the injuries to her head had done her irreparable harm.

For the fourth time since Bastien had begun speaking, Celine pinched her arm, feeling certain it would rouse her from the most bizarre dream of her life. Actually it wasn't a dream. It was more like a nightmare. With each sentence Bastien spoke, Celine found herself struggling to marshal her disbelief.

Bastien paused, his features subdued. Waiting for Celine to react to his most recent revelation.

"So . . . ," Celine began, "you and all the members of La Cour des Lions are"—she swallowed—"not human."

He shook his head.

"What are you, then?" she breathed, her fingers twisting around the brass key she still held in her hand.

"Arjun is half fey and half human. A kind of immortal known as an ethereal." He watched Celine as he said this. "The rest of us drink blood to live."

Celine grasped the key tightly. "Are you . . . dangerous to me?"

"This entire world is dangerous to you, Celine. But I can make you this promise: my vampire nature is the last thing that should cause you concern."

Chewing the inside of her cheek, Celine pondered his words. Every so often she stared at Bastien as if he were a puzzle she had yet to solve. Twice she began to speak and stopped herself. If she possessed a modicum of self-preservation, she would throw him out like the lunatic he obviously was. Nothing he said made a whit of sense. None of this was possible.

And yet she found herself . . . wanting to believe. As if the girl who'd loved the tales of the Brothers Grimm had finally found the answers to her most ridiculous questions.

"Strangely," Celine said, "it's a comfort to know these things. You've—"

"There's more," he interrupted softly.

Her eyes went wide. "More than an enchanted world of deadly fairy-tale creatures?"

For the first time this evening, Celine saw Bastien waver. He nodded once. "You . . . are a part of this world, as well. An ethereal, by birth."

Celine almost laughed. It was too ridiculous.

He leaned forward, his movements liquid. Inhuman. "Your mother is an enchantress named Silla. The Lady of the Vale."

Incredulous laughter barreled from Celine's lips. "That's the most—" The color drained from her face as understanding gripped her chest. *Is.* Not *was.* Her mother *is* an enchantress.

Bastien was too careful to make this kind of mistake.

Celine shot to her feet, the brass key clattering to the carpeted floor. "My mother is *alive*?" Her knees shook beneath her skirts, awareness pricking at her skin.

Bastien looked up at her. Nodded.

"Have you . . . have you . . . ," she stammered. "Have you seen her?"

Again he nodded.

Her right hand wrapped around the base of her neck. Her pulse raced through her veins like a spooked horse. "And does she"—Celine cleared her throat—"does she wish to see me?"

Bastien stood. "It doesn't matter if she wishes to see you. What matters to me is whether you wish to see *her*."

Celine nearly stumbled as she took a step back. Bastien moved to help her, but she raised a hand to stay his motions. Then sank into the plush chair behind her.

"Why are you telling me this now?" she whispered, her fingers still closed around her throat, her palm brushing the lace along her collarbone.

"Because I respect you. And I should not be the one making decisions for you, despite my feelings on the matter." The intensity in his gaze made Celine want to avert her eyes. But she didn't.

"Your feelings on the matter?" she asked. "Do you wish you could make this decision for me?"

His lips pushed forward. "I do. More than I care to admit."

"Then why have you given me the choice, against this inclination?"

"Because I should not make your story about me." The heat of his intensity unmoored her. Bastien seemed to come to life in the darkness, the lines of his body limned in smoke.

There were many things Celine wished to say. Many questions she longed to have answered. It was the oddest thing, to feel so many opposing emotions at once. Sadness, joy, anger, uncertainty.

If Celine's mother was alive and wished to see her now, it meant she'd deliberately kept away for fourteen long years. When Celine was still a little girl, she'd often dreamed about her mother returning to their family, only to have her father insist that she resign herself to the truth. Her mother was lost to them. Forever.

It appeared that both her mother and her father had lied to Celine. How long had so much of her life been hidden from her? Would she ever know the full extent of the truth?

Her fingers dropped from her throat. "If my mother is an enchantress, do you think she could help restore my memory?"

Grooves appeared between Bastien's black brows. "Is that what most concerns you?"

"It is." She nodded, the motion cold. Almost detached. For the time being, perhaps it was better not to feel. Or else she would have to feel everything at once. "Pieces of my life have been stolen from me. And I want them back. I want them all back."

"I understand. I regret that loss more than you can know."

"Why would *you* regret it?"

"Those memories were taken from you at your request."

Celine froze where she sat, her breath catching. "Why would I ask to have my memories taken from me?"

"Because of love," Bastien replied. "You offered your memories in exchange for the life of someone you loved."

"And . . . did this person return my love?"

Bastien exhaled. "He did."

"But he doesn't anymore?" Her voice went soft, the last word almost brittle.

"It would be wrong of him to continue loving you. You deserve better than a demon of the night like him. You deserve to live a life in the sunlight, safe and warm and loved."

Celine swallowed, her thoughts drifting toward Michael. That was precisely what life would be like with him. Sunlight. Warmth. Safety. But . . .

"Is there any chance this person might change his mind?" she whispered.

"No. There isn't."

A knot gathered in Celine's throat. She worked around it, refusing to allow Bastien to see how much his answers wounded her soul.

"Celine," Bastien said in a kind tone, "you asked me for the truth, even though I told you it would hurt you."

"I know." She brushed her fingers beneath her eyes, trying to swipe away the hint of tears. It was ridiculous. Bastien had just told Celine her mother was alive. That should be a cause for happiness that far outweighed the pain of his gentle rejection.

But Bastien . . . seemed so much more real to Celine. He was someone she could believe had loved her at one point in time. Her mother had left when she was a little girl, of her own volition. That particular rejection was not new. It was one she'd relived every day for the last fourteen years. Perhaps she was inured to it by now.

Why would anyone desert their own child? What kind of person was Celine's mother?

"I want to meet her," she said. "Will you take me to see my mother?"

Bastien's cheeks hollowed, his displeasure obvious. "It will be dangerous."

"I understand. You've already told me this world is dangerous. But if it is to be my world, then it is past time for me to face it. Will you take me?" she repeated.

He inhaled through his nose. Leaned forward in his chair, the low flame in the gas lamp beside him flickering with the movement. "I'll take you. If you make me a promise."

Celine waited to see what he wanted.

Bastien continued. "Promise me that if I say we are in danger, you won't put yourself at risk for anyone. That you will care first and foremost about your own safety."

"I'm not a complete idiot," she snapped, her arms crossed. "Why would I protect you anyway? It appears I tried that once, and it didn't exactly work out in my favor. Or yours, for that matter."

His grey eyes went wide. Then Bastien laughed. Its melody took Celine off guard. Warmed something around her heart.

Celine coughed. Then stood. "I appreciate your candor, Monsieur Saint Germain. If you will make all the arrangements, I will inform those who might be concerned that I will be making a short journey to visit a distant relative in Atlanta."

He took to his feet in a ripple of grace. "As you wish, mademoiselle."

CELINE

———≈———

Her heart had not stopped pounding for the last hour. The thundering in her blood made her hands shake and her breaths shallow. Nevertheless Celine held her head high, refusing to balk in the face of *actual magic*. Magic she had not believed existed only three days prior.

This morning, she, Arjun, and Bastien had traveled through a *mirror* to a land halfway around the world. To a place Celine had never once thought she would see. Strange that this wasn't the most interesting journey of the day. After winding through the streets of Jaipur, they dived into a fountain to be transported *to another realm*.

At any moment, Celine expected to succumb to total madness. That was the only explanation for any of this. The only one that made a semblance of sense.

Now they stood on a glittering beach, dripping wet, salt water lapping at their feet. All the colors around them appeared enhanced, as if they'd been painted by an overly imaginative child. The thing that struck Celine most—beyond the vivid hues and the unnatural glare of the sun—was the scent. It was what she'd imagined honey to smell like before she first tasted it as a child. Like drops of melted sunlight. A hint of citrus, along with the tang of hot metal.

Celine's fingers balled into fists at her sides. More than anything, she wanted to look to Bastien for reassurance. But it would be a mistake, for more than one reason. That night at her shop three evenings ago, Bastien had made it abundantly clear that, while he'd once cared for her, she was to have no expectations of him. There could be no future between the daughter of a fairy enchantress and a demon of the night. Beings at odds with each other for millennia.

It was why Celine had gone to Michael yesterday. Why she told him she wanted to build a future together once she returned from Atlanta. Still she could feel the warmth of his arms enveloping her. The way his breath had washed across her forehead just before they kissed.

Celine had made her decision. The safety of love over the thrill of the unknown.

Inhaling with care, Celine stole a glance in Bastien's direction. His eyes found hers in less than an instant. Heat washed across her skin. Not the warmth of safety but the flash of utter awareness. A spark threatening to burst into flame. She shuttered her gaze, her nails digging into her palms.

A mistake. One she could no longer afford to make.

It mattered too much. To both of them.

From behind the grove of palm trees with blue fronds and copper bark, several cloaked figures approached, their alabaster spears glinting in the over-bright sun. Celine took a step back, her green eyes wide. Almost wild. Even from a distance, she could tell they were not entirely human. Their ears were pointed, their features angular. Sharp. Similar to a rendering of elves she'd once seen in a book. All but one of them stood taller than most men and women. Though they remained expressionless, an air of danger lurked about them. A suggestion of menace.

The smallest of their ranks stepped forward, her grey cloak falling from her head onto her shoulders, revealing a slight young woman who appeared similar in age to Celine, with eyes and hair the color of ebony and skin a sun-kissed bronze.

To Celine's right, Arjun breathed a sigh of relief. As if he had been expecting someone else and was grateful to see this young woman instead.

"Marceline Rousseau," the grey-cloaked warrior said, her voice like a wind chime.

Celine took a tentative step forward.

"You will come with us," the girl in grey continued.

Again Celine looked toward Bastien. "Do you trust them?"

"No," he replied without turning her way, his eyes glittering.

The fey warrior snorted. "If you don't trust me, Marceline Rousseau, then trust that the blood drinker will die the final death before he allows any harm to befall you."

"Beyond my trust in others, I trust myself." Celine moved closer to the leader of the assembled warriors. "And I will not take kindly to anyone who attempts to deceive me."

Something shifted in the warrior's cold gaze. A glint of approval. She nodded and pivoted in place, those at her back waiting for her to pass.

Celine steeled herself before she followed, Arjun and Bastien flanking her. She almost stumbled when a vine wrapped around one of the long copper tree trunks burst into bloom, the centers of the flowers beaming a warm light, casting hazy shadows around them. As if rays of sun had been dipped in molten gold.

They trudged through the first grove of tall palm trees. The sand before them soon gave way to moss, which muffled their footsteps and brought the sounds of the burgeoning forest to life. Notes of fresh-tilled earth mixed with the citrus and metal in the air.

A member of the grey-cloaked warriors turned to ensure their progress, the tip of his alabaster spear brushing against a low-hanging branch. The leaves rustled, the sound crisp and clear. High above, the drone of winged insects hummed in Celine's ears. When one of the creatures flew lower, Celine gasped. It was larger than her head, its wings like hammered silver, its eyes iridescent green. Startled by the wasplike thing, Celine's foot slid in a pile of loam, the hem of her salmon-colored skirts kicking up pearlescent dust.

They arrived before a curtain of shimmering vines, which parted as the leader of the grey-cloaked warriors drew near. While they made their way through a long tunnel of curling leaves, Celine glanced to either side and saw branches ripple and pulse as if they were part of a beating heart. Once, she could swear she saw a satyr caught in their embrace, a muffled scream on its lips. But before she could blink, the image was swallowed once more by the burrow of shifting vines.

Celine coughed to ward away a fresh wave of panic. She could not seem to clear the sudden tightness from her throat. The feeling intensified with each step. She attempted to take a deep breath. Failed. Terror took hold of her heart when she realized she was struggling for air.

Bastien reached for her from behind, his fingers closing on her forearm. For a moment, Celine resisted the urge to lean back against him, her chest rising and falling at a rapid pace.

Arjun stepped closer. "She can't breathe." He yelled for the grey-cloaked leader.

"What are you doing to her?" Bastien demanded in a low voice, his tone resonating with menace.

"The feeling shall pass soon," the leader of the fey warriors said. "The air here is much thinner than it is in the mortal realm. It will improve once we emerge in Lady Silla's court. Not to worry; this is simply a deterrent. If an unwanted mortal wished to sneak into the court of the Vale, such a thing would stop them from crossing our borders."

Celine almost choked. It appeared the summer fey were rather inhospitable.

A minute later, the sensation began to fade. Once they reached the end of the tunnel, Arjun bent toward her ear as if he wished to tell her a secret. He said nothing. He placed one hand on Bastien's shoulder and the other on Celine's. Though the wordless exchange lasted no more than the blink of an eye, Celine understood his warning.

They were treading into a world of danger. The world of Celine's mother.

They could not afford to be separated.

As they emerged from the tunnel of leaves, the blaring white sun sliced down on Celine's skin. Beside her, Bastien recoiled on instinct, his left hand—the one with the gold signet ring—clenched tightly.

The grove of trees before them formed an immense circle, the branches above like a bower of knitted leaves, creating a vaulted canopy a hundred feet high. It reminded Celine of a cathedral, both in appearance and in feeling. Colorful songbirds flitted to and fro. A narrow carpet of emerald clovers paved the path, leading to a throne made of bleached birch wood. A sunburst rested in its center, carved from a block of solid gold.

Celine's steps faltered when the slender woman seated upon the throne stood in a lithe motion. Even from a distance, Celine felt her immense power. She reached for Bastien's hand. He threaded his fingers through hers.

A soft murmur began to ripple through the gathered crowd. Celine glanced about, uncertainty tripping in her chest. Everywhere she looked, she was confronted by sights that challenged her sense of reason. Tall, willowy figures dressed in gossamer silk, with sashes of hammered gold and hair in an array of colorful hues flowing down their backs. Pointed ears. Cold affects. Cutting cheekbones. Bejeweled fingers and immense goblets. Occasionally she noticed creatures with horns or green skin or transparent wings.

When one of the horned creatures growled at Bastien, its fangs bared in warning, Bastien loosened his grip on Celine's hand. She realized then that most of this courtly assemblage disliked the sight of her linked with the tall blood drinker at her side.

For that reason alone, Celine tightened her grip on Bastien's fingers. Lifted her chin.

The slim figure standing before the throne took a single step down from her marble dais. Then she smiled at Celine, her expression one of unabashed warmth. The beauty radiating from her face caused Celine to stop short.

The woman's hair was black and long, not unlike her own. It had been arranged in a loose braid over one shoulder, wound with thin vines of tiny glowing leaves. Atop her brow was a pearl coronet. Her gown was liquid silver, her shoulders trimmed in white fox fur. An artist had enhanced her pale skin with gleaming powder and stained her lips a vibrant red, similar to the color of fresh blood.

When the woman stepped closer, her arms outstretched, Celine gasped, distant memories sharpening in her mind.

This was the Lady of the Vale. Celine's mother.

"Welcome, my daughter," the woman said, her voice like a lilting melody. The birds overhead warbled in response, the sunlight glittering brightly. "You don't know how much I've longed to see you."

Celine stood rigid on the carpet of emerald clovers, Bastien at her side. A low hum of awareness began to gather in the air about her. Her vision started to distort. She struggled to find a point of reason. Something that made sense in this world of searing sunlight.

What she found was . . . anger. A raw, seething kind of anger, masking a hollow pain.

Celine's body shook. "Is it true, then?" she demanded, shocked by the unchecked wrath in her own tone.

Murmurs rippled through the throng of fey gathered beneath the lacy canopy. Celine's disrespect did not sit well with them. The immense wasps hovering above began to settle on lower branches, their iridescent eyes gleaming.

"Is what true?" The Lady of the Vale's smile grew, her expression serene.

"Did you choose to leave your daughter behind in the mortal world?" Celine continued without flinching. "Did you let her think you were dead for fourteen years?"

The regal woman took the last step down from the marble dais, its veins shot through with flecks of gold. They shimmered with the weight of her bare footsteps. She glided closer, all the while studying Celine, her gaze flitting from her head to her toes.

Then, instead of replying, she began to sing. From the first note, the trembling in Celine's limbs intensified. Her fingers fell from Bastien's. Tears trailed down her cheeks. It was a melody that had haunted her for years. One sung in a language she could never seem to place.

Familiar. Filled with unmistakable love.

The last note echoed through the air, unfolding into the treetops above. "I did not want to leave you," the Lady of the Vale said softly. "I regretted it every day." She came closer, her arms extended once more. "Please . . . forgive me."

"Mother?" Celine sobbed, her heart cracking in her chest like a dam about to burst.

"Aga," her mother replied, her hands outstretched. "My child."

Before Celine could stop herself, she raced into the Lady of the Vale's arms.

It was like waking from a nightmare. The anguish remained, but beyond it lay hope. The promise of a rising dawn. Celine knew this hope would not erase her anger, nor would it silence the questions burning within her. But the fact that she could hold her mother now—that her mother could return her embrace—was a gift in its own right.

Her mother brushed her long, slender fingers across Celine's cheek, wiping away her tears. As Celine considered her mother's inhuman features—the pointed ears, the sharp cheekbones, the eyes that glittered like onyx—she became aware of an obvious fact. One she had failed to consider at first blush.

If Celine's mother sat on the throne, it meant the Lady of the Vale ruled this court of elegant fey. Which meant Celine was not merely the daughter of an enchantress. She was the daughter of fey royalty.

Was this . . . was this the reason for Bastien's rejection?

Were they more than simple rivals from opposing realms?

"Now that you are here," her mother said quietly, "we can spend as much time as we wish becoming acquainted with each other. I can answer all your questions." She stroked her fingers through Celine's hair. "Why I made that misguided promise to your father, to keep away until your eighteenth birthday. Why I believed a childhood in the mortal realm was preferable to one here." A kind smile curved up her face. She gazed out at the gathered crowd, the timbre of her voice growing louder. "Perhaps we can all make amends for the past." Something glinted in her dark eyes. "And hope for a better future for fey and ethereals alike."

It was everything Celine had never known she needed to hear. "I'd like that," she murmured. "Very much."

Then her mother extended her right hand toward one of the two figures standing silently behind Celine. Celine turned and saw Bastien waiting there, his hands in his pockets, his expression aloof. Arjun said nothing, an easy smile on his face, his brow hooded.

"Sébastien Saint Germain," Celine's mother began. In a swirl of ivory skirts, she shifted forward and wrapped Celine's hand in one of her own. The hand Bastien had been holding not long ago. "I thank you for honoring your word and bringing my daughter to me of her own volition."

His . . . word?

Celine's brow furrowed. He'd agreed to bring her here? Why?

Bastien did not react, though Arjun's eyes widened with dismay. The half fey said, "Celine, what my lady means is—"

"In accordance with our earlier agreement," Celine's mother interrupted, a knowing smile on her face, "Sébastien Saint Germain and Arjun Desai have my permission to travel through the summer lands of the Sylvan Vale toward the winter wasteland of the Sylvan Wyld. My daughter will remain here with me."

Had Bastien . . . used Celine to get something he wanted from the Lady of the Vale?

It certainly seemed to be the case.

Celine stared at Bastien, her lips thinning into a line. Tension banded across her features, betrayal taking shape in her stomach. Her mother's fingers laced through hers, and Celine responded without thought. Easily. All too easily.

It struck her all at once, as if she'd been doused by a bucket of cold water. Was it a simple coincidence that Celine's mother had done and said everything Celine needed to hear? Where had Celine's wrath gone? She'd been so angry at first. For a short time, it had been all she'd known.

Suspicion twisted through her chest. Her mother was an enchantress. Both Bastien and Arjun had said this world was dangerous. Just before they'd entered this court, Arjun made a specific point: the three of them were not to be separated.

And one of the very first things the Lady of the Vale wished to do was just that.

Celine stared down at Bastien from where she stood, before her mother's throne.

Would he use Celine for his own personal gain?

He remained silent, his gaze locked on hers. No. He would not use her. Nor would he tell her how to feel or what to do. He trusted she would know the right thing. That she would tell her own story.

For far too long, Celine had looked to others for answers. It was time for her to look within herself.

She studied the gathered crowd. Despite her mother's reassurances, Celine did not sense welcome among them. She sensed tolerance. As if this court of immortal fey were merely enduring her presence. They would not care what she wanted or how she felt. Bastien would respect her choices. Arjun would trust her to know the best course of action for herself. Not once had her mother asked what Celine wanted to do.

Her eyes found Bastien's once more. His expression softened.

"If Celine wishes to remain in the Vale, of course she will stay," Bastien said, his words clear. Unfaltering. "But if she wishes to go with us, that is her decision and hers alone."

The Lady of the Vale tightened her grip on Celine's hand. "I'm afraid I cannot allow my daughter to travel outside the safety of the Vale."

For the first time since their reunion, Celine's mother said the wrong thing.

"No." Celine did not falter in her reply. "I will go wherever Arjun and Bastien go."

"It is far too dangerous, my child," her mother protested, pulling Celine even closer. "The Ice Clans run rampant in the Wyld. That lawless land has not had proper leadership for nearly four hundred human years. It is a world of perpetual darkness, filled with all manner of bloodthirsty beasts."

"I understand," Celine said. "But I do not wish to be separated from my friends."

Hurt crossed the Lady of the Vale's lovely face. "Do you not wish to spend time in my company after all these years? I was hoping to show you around my home and learn about the things that bring you joy."

"Of course I do," Celine said softly. "But I need some time to acclimate myself to this world. I will not be able to do that freely if I am worried about the safety of my friends."

Her mother's nostrils flared, highlighting the inhuman sharpness of her face. "And what of your safety, daughter?"

"I can promise that Celine's safety will be my foremost concern, my lady," Arjun interjected.

The Lady of the Vale turned to Arjun, her expression culled from ice. "You would make that promise to me, son of Riya?" She paused, the silence laden with meaning. "You would swear *on your life* to keep her from harm?" Her dark eyes glittered. "A word of caution: another member of your found family once made a promise to me. I fear it cost Shin Jaehyuk his immortal life."

Arjun swallowed, then nodded once. The rest of the gentry began to mutter, the winged creatures flitting about in chaotic patterns. The weight of Arjun's promise was heavy. Not at all like promises in the mortal world. Celine did not need anyone to explain this obvious fact.

Arjun Desai had promised his life would be forfeit if something happened to Celine.

She could not remain idle in the face of that.

"I'm afraid I must insist," Celine said through the mounting din. "Once my friends have completed their journey, I will return to the Vale." She offered her mother a guileless smile, her fingers falling from the Lady of the Vale's grasp.

Celine expected to encounter further protests. Perhaps her mother would forbid her from leaving outright. After all, it appeared the Lady of the Vale held dominion over these lands and all those who dwelled upon them. For an instant, Celine thought her mother would call her grey-cloaked warriors to her.

It was impossible to know what the Lady of the Vale was thinking. But Celine saw the silent war raging within her.

Then her mother relaxed. Smiled. "I must admit to my disappointment," she said to Celine. "I had hoped we might spend time with each other, after all these years. You can't imagine how much I longed for this chance."

A trace of wistfulness crossed Celine's face. "Please believe me when I tell you I understand. You can't imagine how much I longed for you as a child. How much I wanted to know you." Determination lined her brow. "But I have made a promise of my own to my friends, and I cannot break it. I swore to help Sébastien Saint Germain and Arjun Desai in their journey to the wintry Wyld, and I will not let one of the first things I do as your daughter in the Vale be to disregard a promise I made in good faith."

If promises carried the weight Celine suspected they did in her mother's court, then it would be difficult for the Lady of the Vale to overlook Celine's admission.

An inexplicable emotion flitted over her mother's face. "Of course." There was steel in her reply. Celine could not tell if it was fury or resolve. "Several of my Grey Cloaks will accompany you to the border," her mother continued, "but once you cross into the Wyld, I can no longer afford you my protection." She lifted her right hand and twisted it through the empty air, as if she were turning the handle of an invisible door. Sparks of light collected, spinning toward her fingers, gathering with her every motion, until a ball of gilded light formed in her palm. Celine's mother murmured toward it in an unintelligible tongue, and the ball condensed into a sphere of solid gold.

The Lady of the Vale handed the golden bauble to Celine. "In moments of unrelenting gloom, let this be your light. It is the best I can offer you for protection in a world of perpetual darkness. A drop of pure sun." When Celine reached to take it, her mother wrapped both hands around Celine's palm, the bauble pulsating between them. "Be warned that its power will wane the longer you dawdle in the Wyld and the more you use it. Save this magic for when you need it most, daughter. And return to me." She shifted her right hand to Celine's cheek.

"Thank you, Mother," Celine replied, something shimmering in her eyes.

"One day, I hope you again call me Umma, as you did as a child."

Celine nodded. "I hope for that, too. One day soon."

"A word of caution, Sébastien Saint Germain," the Lady of the Vale said to Bastien, her smile turning sweeter. "Avoid the Frozen Wastes at all cost. You'll know what they are the moment you step too close to them. They are a world without color or sound, where those who have betrayed my court are sent to serve out their sentences. Many who remain there lose their minds. The instant your senses start to muddle, run." Celine swallowed at the way her mother's voice dropped to a whisper. "And if something happens to my daughter, you will answer to me, heir of Nicodemus."

BASTIEN

———❦———

It is a strange sensation, crossing from the Sylvan Vale into the Sylvan Wyld. From a court of perpetual sun to one of perpetual night.

The border is not an imaginary line through the dirt, but a river. One side is bathed in ochre warmth. The other bank is shadowed, the rocks along its shore crusted with blue ice.

A lone bridge connects the two lands, spanning the width of the rapidly flowing water. This scene is a fitting representation of this world. From a distance, it appears tranquil. Up close, the water hurtles over the stones at breakneck speed, the center of the river blacker than pitch.

Even though we stand on the sunlit shore, I am grateful for the darkness across the way. There is honesty in it. Unlike the court of the Vale, the dark does not pretend to be something it isn't. And I've had my fill of the light.

The leader of the assembled fey—the small warrior I trapped along the beach—introduces herself as Yuri just before she and ten of the Grey Cloaks in her command leave us at the entrance to the bridge.

She turns to me, her face stern and unforgiving. Carved from granite. "I would ask one last time that our lady's daughter accompany us back to the Summer Court of the Vale. If you care at all about her safety"—she glowers at me and at Arjun— "tell her to heed this advice." The entire time she speaks, she avoids looking at Celine.

I'm certain Celine is well aware of this.

Laughter flies from Arjun's lips. "You've truly mastered that expression," he says to Yuri. "You could burn the feathers off a nighthawk with nothing more than the force of your glare. My mother would be proud."

Yuri frowns. "At least one of us can say we've made the general proud." Her waist-length braid of straight black hair swings over one shoulder. "If General Riya were here to see you working in service to blood drinkers . . ." There is no malice in her tone. Simply cold truth.

"Thankfully I forswore the desire to make my mother proud years ago," Arjun says with a grin. "Would you believe I chose to work for Nicodemus Saint Germain just to see if her head would explode?" He pauses, his words dripping with sarcasm. "Or perhaps for nothing more than the sheer joy I knew it would bring her."

"Nicodemus Saint Germain's assassin murdered your mother's best friend," Yuri says.

"Don't fret," Arjun retorts. "Shin Jaehyuk isn't exactly my favorite vampire at present."

Yuri sucks in her cheeks as if she's swallowed a lemon. Then she angles her unyielding gaze at me. "I hope you're not as foolish as he is, *leech*." Her lips twitch, her disgust plain. "Our lady's daughter turns to you for more than guidance. She trusts what you have to say. Tell her to remain in the Vale, where it is safe."

Celine steps between us, her brows gathered low on her forehead. "I'm still here, Yuri."

"I know," Yuri says without blinking. "I also know I will not succeed in persuading you; therefore, it is not a worthwhile use of my time." She shifts back toward me. "What say you, *leech*?"

I say nothing in response. Instead I look at Celine. "What do you want to do?"

"I don't know how decisions are made in the Vale, Yuri," Celine says, "but I gather it was not easy for you to attain such a lofty position. And I believe neither you nor my mother appreciate being told what to do by any man, friend or foe."

Yuri's lips twitch again.

"I will do as I please, and neither you nor these gentlemen will make such decisions for me," Celine finishes.

Yuri harrumphs. Stabs the staff of her spear through the fragrant soil at her feet.

"At least in the Wyld," I say, "I will see the monsters that come our way and *know* they are monsters." A part of me thinks such a pointed statement will kindle Yuri's ire.

But she seems to appreciate candor.

"You have no idea of what you speak." Yuri's tone is grim. "The monsters of the Wyld attack without provocation. They do not need a reason or a purpose to rip you to shreds."

Unease radiates down my spine. I want more than anything to do as Yuri asks and demand that Celine remain in the Sylvan Vale, under the protection of her mother.

I am still not the man I want to be. I can only hope I am better today than I was yesterday.

"Thank you for the warning," I say to Yuri.

"Be it on your head, then, vampire," Yuri replies. She reaches into her cloak and removes two longer daggers and a short dirk. All three blades are clearly fashioned of solid silver, their matching sheaths bejeweled with rubies. She turns to her second in command, who produces a weapon much like a crossbow, but shorter, its quarrels blunt, their tips gleaming silver as well.

"We were told you are a bit of a marksman," Yuri says to me. "A revolver will draw too much attention in the Wyld. Such a bombastic, uncivilized sort of weapon. It reveals your position after the first shot. The lack of subtlety is so like a vampire." She sneers. "This crossbow will fire ten quarrels in succession before it needs to be reloaded. I suppose your much-lauded aim will be of use with at least one of them." She snaps her fingers, and three of the Grey Cloaks nearest to her remove their hooded garments and pass one to Arjun, one to Celine, and one to me.

"Since you clearly lack all sense of reason, you might as well take these, though they won't save you from your own stupidity," Yuri says. "Also you'll need gloves, leech. These weapons were designed to work against you, not for you." She pitches a pair of soft leather gloves my way. "A final word of warning," she finishes. "Tread lightly wherever you go. Speak only when necessary, and never stay too long in one place. If you find yourself ambushed, protect Celine. If you don't, your lives will be forfeit." She sniffs. "And the Lady of the Vale likes to take her time when she exacts punishment."

I almost smile. In another time and place, I would like Yuri. She reminds me of Odette.

A grin ghosts across my lips. They would hate each other.

Yuri gestures toward the other Grey Cloaks, who form a line on their side of the bridge and watch as Celine, Arjun, and I cross.

The cold descends on us slowly, just like the darkness of an encroaching dusk. Halfway across the bridge, clouds of air form around Celine's and Arjun's mouths with each exhale. There is a shift in the wind, like the changing of the seasons. Even the smell turns to one of frost and mint and something else, unlike anything I've ever encountered on the mortal plane. Light sprinkles of snow begin to fall, our boots crunching through the frozen stillness. The only other sound is that of the skeletal trees, icicles tinkling together like wintry wind chimes.

We complete the crossing and step into the drifts of powdery snow along the riverbank. When I glance over my shoulder, I see the Grey Cloaks watching us on the opposite shore, their spears pointed toward the bright blue sky. One last time, I consider asking Celine to return with them. There is no need for her to risk herself in this land of perpetual night, chasing after a fool's dream.

But I glance her way, and I keep silent.

"The borderlands of the Wyld are known for their labyrinthine forests," Arjun says. His voice startles us, for it sounds different in this place. As if it has been sent down a long tunnel. "I've heard there are trees here who have a taste for mortal blood." He quirks his lips. "Perhaps they're your ancestors, Bastien."

"Charming," Celine replies, drawing her cloak closer about her. A gust of wind blows, scattering a flurry of snow in our faces. The next instant, fox fur appears on the hood around her head. It spreads until it forms an inner lining on the entire cloak. Celine hums in appreciation. "I suppose not everything about this place is dreadful."

"Cling to that," Arjun continues in a droll tone. "It's bound to worsen from here."

We trek through the edge of the wood and beneath its twisted canopy in complete silence. This forest is a stark contrast to the one in the Summer Court. Where gold and silver dust shimmered, flecks of iron dot the landscape, glittering in the moonlight like black diamonds. A pair of emaciated birds caw to our right as they flap slowly through the bare branches before landing together to stare down at us. Their eyes are tarnished pewter, their beaks made of solid ice. I stop to look at the smaller one, who turns its head, then cackles before taking flight once more, its mate quick to follow in its shadow.

My nerves spark, the fine hairs on the back of my neck standing on end. It's as if I can feel eyes upon me, though I hear nothing. My senses flash as I throw them wide.

It is disorienting to be surrounded by such silence. As if I've become accustomed to the constant drone of life all around me.

But I know in the marrow of my bones that we are not alone.

We are being watched. I would bet my immortal life on it. I

want to tell Arjun and Celine, but it would be of no benefit to inform the creature lurking nearby of my awareness. So instead of saying anything, I gesture toward both of them, my eyes roving around us, speaking without words.

They do not move or nod or say anything in return. But I know they understand.

For a harrowing instant, all the light fades around us. I am still able to see, but I feel Celine's apprehension in the race of her pulse and the sharpness of her gasp. The dark lingers as the moon has passed behind the shadow of a cloud. Then the sky begins to clear, and a sliver of moonlight emerges from between the skeletal treetops.

Celine stops to stare at the moon just as the last of the clouds shifts to unveil its cool light in all its glory. The snow-covered forest comes to life, the soft blue of the rime resembling that of a pale dawn, the trees silhouetted in white.

"It's . . . beautiful," she says.

"I don't disagree," Arjun replies.

"Beauty often masks the decay beneath," she murmurs.

It's something my uncle has said many times before. A memory Celine should have lost. "A fitting sentiment for such a place," I remark in a casual voice, my eyes scanning our surroundings. "Where have you heard that saying?"

Celine frowns. "I . . . don't know." She shakes her head, the fur-lined hood falling to her shoulders.

"You know, if not for those horrific birds a few paces back, I would not be unnerved by this," Arjun says. He shudders. "They looked like demonic ravens ready to feast on our bones."

"Perhaps I'll catch one and gift it to you as a pet." Celine grins.

Arjun snorts. I watch as his hands, ever so casually, disappear in the folds of his cloak, where I know he hid two of the blades Yuri left with us.

In response, Celine places a hand in her skirt pocket, her fingers wrapping around the golden bauble of sunlight gifted by her mother. Arjun continues smiling as we weave between the trees. Then he pauses a moment, his head tilted to one side.

Nothing happens.

"Shall we carry on?" Celine asks, her green eyes bright and alert.

I nod.

She screams just as the creature lands on my back.

BASTIEN

―――◇―――

I reach behind me, and my gloved fingers grasp at nothing but air. A sound hisses past my ear, something sharp grazing the side of my neck. It sears my skin like fire.

"To your right," Celine shouts, brandishing her silver dirk in one hand and the golden bauble in the other.

I spin in place, and the thing on my back is flung across the snow. When it rolls to standing, I see that it is a collection of twigs in the shape of a man. Its face is nothing but two holes where its eyes should be. The creature draws back a rudimentary bow and aims an arrow my way, which I dodge.

"Cut off their heads or their hands!" Arjun yells, both his silver blades arcing in graceful sweeps.

Now at least a dozen of these twig men surround us. All I can think of is Celine. I blur to her side. She holds the bauble in her palm, her fingers turning white. It begins to pulse with warmth.

"Don't use it now." I dodge another arrow. "Save it for when circumstances are direr."

"Worry about yourself," she says.

With a gloved hand, I crush the outstretched arm of a tree creature who lunges our way. When I turn to see how Celine is faring, I miss the attack over my shoulder. The arrow embeds in my arm, and the burning sensation flows through my blood, causing me to grunt and fall to one knee.

Though the injury sets my entire right side on fire, I press the trigger on my crossbow, and a single quarrel flies toward the twig man closest to me. The thin creature is a poor mark for such a weapon. Like trying to shoot a moving post. I attempt to yank the arrow from my arm, but only succeed in breaking off the shaft.

Cursing, I stand again. Arjun shouts and tosses one of his short swords toward me. I catch it by the handle, thankful for my heightened reflexes.

Putain de merde. I never spent a great deal of time learning how to fence. It didn't make any sense, given how much more civilized and efficient a revolver seemed to be.

Perhaps Yuri was right about our reliance on such weapons.

I begin swinging the blade in my left hand, my right side aching from the arrowhead, which continues to burrow into my skin, the silver poisoning me from within. Arjun is faring much better than I. Celine holds the pulsing bauble in silent threat, and it seems to be enough to keep the twig creatures at bay for the time being. The hem of her cloak is in tatters, and a smattering of ripped fox fur surrounds her feet.

I slash again and manage to lop off one of the twig creatures' heads. When I do, the whole thing falls to the ground, breaking into a pile of splintered wood.

The fighting lulls as both sides take stock of their injuries. Half the creatures have fallen to pieces around us. The other half parley in silence before making a decision. I brace myself for the next bout, and then the twig men scurry back up into the trees without so much as a whisper.

The pain in my arm is nearly blinding me.

"Well, that wasn't so bad," Arjun comments.

Celine frowns. "It felt like they were toying with us. Their attack was halfhearted. Disorganized."

"Testing the waters, perhaps?" Arjun nods. "Which means they'll return soon."

I fall to my knees, the silver blade in my gloved hand dropping to the snow.

"Bastien!" Celine scrambles closer, crouching beside me.

"There's an arrow in my arm," I say through my teeth. "It's solid silver, and every time I move"—I grimace—"it digs in deeper."

"Of all the ridiculous things," she says. "Why weren't you paying attention? What is the use of all these abilities if you can't dodge a simple arrow?"

I stare at her and say nothing.

"He wasn't paying attention because the only thing that mattered to him was keeping you safe, princess." Arjun kneels beside me and begins pressing around the wound to see how to remove the arrowhead.

I wince again but not from the pain.

Dismay blanches across Celine's face, but she is quick to conceal it. "You should heed your own advice and protect yourself, Bastien," she says in a matter-of-fact tone. "If you are hurt, you become a target. You're no good to any of us then."

I know she is scolding me because she wants to offer me comfort and cannot. I have made it clear that there can be no future between us. That vampires are the natural enemies of her mother's court.

In truth Celine has yet to realize how deep the enmity lies. How the blood of vampire royalty runs through my veins just as the blood of a Vale enchantress runs through hers. She saw how displeased the gentry in her mother's court were to see us standing together, hand in hand. It is not a matter of simple disapproval.

We are more than just enemies. We are blood foes.

I pull away from her, and she grips my arm, refusing to let go. "Are you really not going to let me help you?" Celine says, her eyes glittering with frustration.

Behind the mask of her irritation, I see how much she cares.

"I don't need your help," I grumble like a schoolboy.

I, too, wear a mask. I want to tell her nothing in the world matters more than she does. That I would suffer a wound like this every day of my immortal life if it meant she would be there to scold me.

"This is all quite touching," Arjun interjects, "but we need to find a way to remove the arrow from Bastien's arm so we can bloody well get out of here before the twig men decide to return with a battalion of branches." He drops his voice to a whisper. "It's foolish for us to stay in one place for so long." His fingers dig around my wound as he tries to determine the angle of entry, causing me to flinch. "The silver doesn't appear to be against the bone," he murmurs. "But I don't think prying it out is the answer. Perhaps it would be easier if we simply push it through."

"Easier for whom?" I say in an acerbic tone.

"Don't be a child," Arjun says, and tsks at me. "It's unbecoming of an immortal prince. Once the silver is out, your body will heal on its own, though not as quickly as usual." He raises a brow. "Now you know what it feels like to be me. Not as strong. Not as fast. But mad as hell." He rips off the rest of my shirt-sleeve. "Do you find that you heal rather quickly from injuries?" he asks Celine. "Because I've never truly been sick or horribly injured in my entire life."

"Oh," Celine realizes with a start. "You're an ethereal, like me. Forgive me for not making the connection sooner."

He snorts. "Alas, I am not like you, princess. I am not the direct descendant of the Lady of the Vale, nor can I claim to possess a drop of fey royalty in my blood."

She frowns, then takes hold of my wounded arm as Arjun prepares to shove the arrowhead through to the other side. "I haven't really been injured before the events of several months ago." Her frown deepens as she looks at me. "And I can't remember feeling horribly ill as a child."

Arjun grins. "I'd wager that makes you feel even guiltier," he says to me.

"Were you always such a prick, or—" My insult is swallowed by a howl of pain as Arjun pushes the silver arrowhead through my biceps.

"Relax, beta," he croons in an accent I've never heard him use before. "Or it will leave a scar." A moment later, the entire arrowhead plinks to the ground, drops of bright blood trickling in its wake. Celine sets to work wrapping the wound in remnants of my shirtsleeve.

"Why doesn't silver seem to bother us as it does Bastien?" Celine asks Arjun while she works.

"Silver is the Vale's weapon against the creatures of the night," Arjun explains. "Those of the Wyld use iron to fend off attacks from the Vale, though neither silver nor iron will cause an ethereal harm, on account of our mortal blood."

Celine nods, her expression pensive. "And what would happen if fey royalty of the Vale were to . . . fall in love with fey royalty of the Wyld?"

Though Arjun is taken aback by her question, he takes pains not to show it. "It doesn't happen," he replies gently. "It would never be allowed. Ordinary gentry are exiled forever for such a crime. Branded blood traitors."

With a curt nod, Celine finishes tying the last of the bandages. Not once has she looked at me during this exchange. It is a bitter comfort to know she understands the full weight of the situation. The daughter of Lady Silla of the Vale would never be permitted to form an attachment to the immortal heir of Nicodemus Saint Germain.

I brace myself before I take to my feet. Then I reach for Celine's palm to help her stand.

"We should keep moving before the twig creatures return," I say.

"Yes," Celine agrees, her voice soft. Tinged with sadness.

Arjun rolls his eyes as he washes the blood off his fingers with a handful of snow. "I said that ten minutes ago."

Celine quirks a brow at him. "No wonder Pippa dislikes you so. You really are an insufferable know-it-all, Arjun Desai."

"Who will die happy with the knowledge that Philippa Montrose talks about me behind my back," Arjun teases.

She laughs. "Bite your tongue and lead the way."

ARJUN

———≈———

T hey were close. Arjun knew it. He'd heard tell of this part
of the Wyld. It was how he knew to direct them toward
the silent, ice-capped mountain at the heart of the wintry land.
The same mountain that, years ago, had provided those of the
Wyld with such untold wealth.

Still Arjun was unprepared for the sight.

The Ice Palace rose from a large clearing deep in the forest
of skeletal trees. Its blue turrets reflected the moonlight, causing the entire structure to glow. Ghostly fey roamed beneath
its parapets in tattered rags, many of them hoping to beg for
scraps from whatever warlord currently ruled the roost.

As the trio neared the edifice, details began to emerge. Many
of the castle's crenellated walls were chipped near the top from
where birds with beaks of solid ice had pecked at them. No one
stood guard outside the lowered drawbridge, positioned over
a river of solid ice, its surface frozen into sharpened crags that
would impale any creature unlucky enough to plunge toward it.

From a distance, the castle looked grand. Up close, it was
anything but. The neglect was obvious. A stark contrast to the
polished warmth of the Summer Court of the Sylvan Vale.

All three of them kept their hands on the weapons concealed in their cloaks as they crossed the drawbridge.

Celine stifled a scream when they strode into the courtyard. To the right was a pack of ice jackals feasting on the carcass of a black horse with wings like those of a giant bat. Her scream was not merely because of the sight of blood and carnage or the smell of salt and iron and shredded entrails.

It was clear the horse was still alive. Its red eyes blinked slowly, the breath wheezing from its throat.

For an instant, Arjun's thoughts drifted to Jae, who'd been locked in a silver cage on Nicodemus' orders two nights ago. True to form, Nicodemus had been quick to pronounce his sentence: the final death. Jae's siblings had protested, Hortense most vehemently. As a result, Nicodemus had agreed to stay Jae's execution for a few days to give them time.

Though Arjun did not delude himself to think that mercy was in the cards for the Court of the Lions' erstwhile assassin.

Without a word, Celine glided forward and offered the dark horse much-needed mercy, using the short dirk in her hand. The ice jackals reared back and began yipping at her in fury. Their eyes glowed white, their maws covered in bright red blood.

Bastien pulled her close as Arjun brandished the silver blade in his hand. "Easy, now. No one wants to wind up a puddle in the castle courtyard." He took a step back, directing Bastien and Celine to move in his shadow. His foot nudged something as he moved. Arjun reached for a discarded bone and threw it over the horse's carcass. The jackals leapt for it and were soon distracted by the ensuing frenzy.

"Don't do that again," Arjun said under his breath to Celine. "Even if you are a princess of the Vale, don't interfere with anything you see happening here. Your mother holds no sway in the Sylvan Wyld. Anything in this place will kill you with the same effort it takes to look at you. And chollima like that one"—he gestured toward the dead horse—"love to feast on mortal flesh. Don't be deceived by their beauty."

She winced. "I'm sorry. I just—I couldn't let it suffer."

"I know," Arjun said. "We'll say a prayer for it later. After we escape in one piece." He looked over his shoulder and saw Bastien standing to one side, his lips pressed together, his expression troubled.

"No," Arjun said. "We don't have time for one of your crises of conscience."

Celine pulled her cloak around her. "And I still don't know why we're here in the first place."

Arjun canted his head like his father always did when Arjun said something ridiculous. "Because you failed to ask."

"We're here because I wanted to meet Sunan of the Wyld," Bastien said in a subdued tone.

"Why?" Celine pressed.

"Because he thinks this Sunan character can cure him of his vampiric ailment," Arjun finished. Then he clapped Bastien on the back. "Couldn't wait all night for you to spit it out, old chap."

Celine blinked. "Is that possible?"

Only a fool could ignore the hope in her words. *Poor little princess,* Arjun mused. She had the rest of her overlong life to learn of disappointment in this world. Arjun was still learning, and he'd been disappointed from childhood.

"Is Sunan here?" Celine asked, her head tilting back to gaze up at the palace of ice that had once been home to the Sylvan Wyld's gentry. A castle built to house the wealthiest blood drinkers.

Arjun raised a shoulder. "Those who dwell in this place would be the ones most likely to know where he is." He crossed toward the largest alcove, searching for the entrance to the main hall. "Let's find someone and get out of here before any other misfortune befalls us. Come rain or shine, I intend to return Celine to Lady Silla hale and hearty. Because even if I can't stand many creatures in the Vale, it's my home, for better or for worse. I don't intend to forfeit it *or* my life for failing to honor a promise."

Bastien nodded.

"Yes," Celine agreed. "Tell us what to do, and we will do it."

Arjun rolled his eyes. "If only I believed that to be true."

❧

Half an hour later, the trio passed beneath a set of smashed double doors bound in iron. The interior sconces were lit by cerulean flames. Three long tables framed three walls of the cavernous chamber. Surrounding each table were feasting creatures of all shapes and sizes. The beasties of the Sylvan Wyld. So engrossed were they in their meal that most of them did not pause to notice the three strangers standing at the destroyed entrance to what had undoubtedly been the castle's Great Hall.

"Don't look at what they are eating," Arjun said softly.

Celine groaned. Above them, small winged sprites and pixies made of shattered ice danced throughout the space, chittering and waiting to steal scraps of food. Glasswing butterflies gathered on iron torches, their translucent bodies dipped in shining black ink.

"Those are poisonous," Arjun warned. "Don't touch them or let them land on you. The ichor on their bodies burns like the devil." His attention caught on the figure seated at the head of the center table, a horned goblet in one hand, an iron crown atop his head, his red beard coated in small icicles.

"He looks as knowledgeable as any," Arjun said over his shoulder to Bastien and Celine.

Celine chewed at the inside of her cheek. "Do you think he might wish us harm?"

"Without a doubt." Bastien began walking toward the bearded man in the iron crown.

Arjun pressed a hand to his chest to stop him. "The presence of a blood drinker will likely provoke his wrath. Let me speak to him first."

As they moved between the tables lining the chamber, whispers and growls trailed in their wake. A slithering, snakelike beast with wet hair and two voids for eyes glided into their path, pausing to glare up at them and lick its fangs. Many of the creatures slowed their feasting in order to peruse the newest arrivals.

If Arjun had to guess, they were deciding which of them to eat first. Dread coursed down his spine. If he could smell the frost and mint and magic of the Wyld on their skin, he would bet a barrelful of gold that they could smell the sunlight of the Vale on him and on Celine.

A beast with hairy ears and a mouthful of cracked teeth smacked its lips with gusto when Celine passed by. Another green-skinned hob and the white-haired phouka beside it glared at Bastien without blinking.

The man in the iron crown gestured for a horde of bat-eared goblins to fill his goblet and replenish the food on his plate, his black eyes fixed on Arjun. A blue goblin bearing an immense carafe of blood-colored wine hobbled toward him last, a pained expression on its face.

"What have you brought as a sacrifice?" he asked Arjun before Arjun could even open his mouth.

A fist clenched in Arjun's stomach. He should have realized those in the Wyld still adhered to the old ways. Nevertheless he bowed low, his arms outstretched in a flourish. "What does the good lord desire?"

The bearded man sat up straight, the icicles along his chin chiming with the movement. It was then that Arjun realized he was addressing one of the fabled dwarfs of the mountain. His small stature and grizzled countenance gave him away.

Then the bearded dwarf king peered over his plate at the trio and began to laugh as if he'd been told a fantastic joke.

"You brought me nothing?" he barked, spittle flying from his lips. "You brought the King of Kur *nothing*?" He thrust his goblet into the face of the tiny blue goblin holding the carafe, who startled before refilling it at once. After draining its contents dry, the dwarf swiped his sleeve across his mouth, his amusement plain. "What about the girl?" he said after belching. "She looks fresh."

"The girl is here as a guest, not as a gift," Bastien said. When he spoke, the sound of his voice seemed to carry to the rafters, causing the glasswing butterflies to cease with their fluttering. A sudden hush descended on the crowd.

"And what have we here?" the king in the iron crown said. "Is that a . . ." He paused to take in a deep breath. "Is that a *blood drinker* on our doorstep?"

All the goblins beside him began to titter, the hob with the mouthful of jagged teeth cackling.

"Do you not know the rules, vampire?" the king said, and yanked a silver blade with an iron handle from the sheath at his belt. "Don't you know your kind were banished from here more than four hundred human years ago?" He leaned forward, pointing the end of his sword at Bastien's chest. "Go back to your beloved mortals, traitor of the Wyld."

Arjun's soul cringed as Bastien stepped forward. "I know what my ancestors did," Bastien said.

"Your ancestors?" the bearded dwarf king drawled. "You know the rules, vampire, so why would you risk coming here?"

"What is the punishment for a vampire who crosses into the Wyld?" Bastien asked. "At no time did anyone tell me what the punishment was."

"I suppose it's . . . whatever . . . whatever I choose it to be," the king stammered, clearly unwilling to acknowledge his ignorance. Arjun knew the punishment, but he had no intention of divulging it to this bearded tyrant. The dwarf king slammed down his horned goblet, causing the little blue goblin beside him to shriek in terror.

Laughter rasped from all corners of the room.

"I'll admit I'm intrigued by your brashness. It isn't every night a vampire and two ethereals with the blood of the Vale visit our illustrious court," the dwarf king said. "What brought you to the doors of the famed Ice Palace of Kur?"

"I wish to speak with Sunan the Unmaker," Bastien said.

All motion ceased in the room. Even the chittering creatures roosting in the eaves fell silent.

"That is a name I have not heard for an age," the dwarf king replied. "It's a shame he is no longer with us. Sunan would have enjoyed your story, no doubt. The wise old fool was always fond of stories."

"Where is he?" Celine asked. "Is there any way we might find him?"

"He does not exist anymore," the dwarf king said. "Sunan left the Winter Court long ago, even after the iron crown was offered to him." A snigger flew from his lips, spittle freezing on his beard. "The damned fool objected to the idea of a king so much, he turned down the chance to become one!"

Again the room filled with coarse laughter. Unsurprisingly Bastien kept silent. Not that Arjun blamed him. The vampire's entire reason for journeying to the Wyld—for taking on such a risk—had been lost in this moment.

"Curse the kings, he used to say. For they never bring anything but bloodshed and misery to their people." The dwarf barked once more. "I would have to disagree with that." He shoved his horned goblet into the face of the terrorized blue goblin once more, barely waiting long enough for it to be refilled.

Still Bastien said nothing. He had not taken a breath since the king's revelation.

The dwarf stopped drinking when his attention fell once more on Celine. "This girl looks familiar. Tell me, child, which member of the summer gentry granted you your immortality?"

Celine frowned. Took the smallest step back. And curtsied. "I'm afraid I don't know, Your . . . Majesty."

"Majesty!" the dwarf king crowed with delight. "You must be an earthbound ethereal?"

"Yes, Your Majesty."

"I love it." He chortled. "From now on, everyone here will call me 'Your Majesty.' Humans are so amusing. Sunan would have liked you, girl. He used to speak of a prophecy in which a creature with mortal blood would be the one to tame the beasts and save our world." He laughed into his goblet, wine dribbling down his frozen chin. "I miss him sometimes, if for no other reason than his amusing ways." After he drained the dregs of his drink, he thumped his other hand on the table before him. "Now then, for the matter of tribute. You've come to my court without anything of value to offer me. My ice jackals are waiting in the wings to exact the blood price for this insult." His beady black eyes sparkled. "Unless you can offer me something worthwhile."

Arjun paled at this, recalling the dying chollima in the courtyard. It was his fault for not remembering that the Wyld was a place where such tribute was necessary. If he did not offer the dwarf king a worthy tribute, it was likely his bloodthirsty minions would take an arm or a leg from each of them, at the very least.

And if something happened to Celine, Lady Silla would not be forgiving, even if Arjun was the son of her friend and general.

"I have something worthwhile," Arjun said. "I can offer you a month of service by a son of the Vale, to begin after the next harvest moon."

"Whose son?" the dwarf king said, his fingers steepled before him.

"The son of General Riya, leader of the Grey Cloaks." The din arose once more at the mention of the name. Arjun was not surprised. His mother was infamous throughout the land. Beloved and hated in equal measure. The best huntress in the Vale. The best killer of Wyld beasts who dared to cross into the summer lands.

Bastien grabbed Arjun's shoulder. But Arjun did not flinch.

"A year," the king bargained.

"One month," Arjun replied.

"Six months."

"Six *weeks*."

The king laughed. "Make the promise, son of General Riya. And I will hold you to it, as your kind never fail to honor a promise."

"In exchange for our safe passage from the Ice Palace of Kur and its immediate surroundings, I, Arjun Desai, son of General Riya, promise to return in service to the lord of the Ice Palace for a period of no more than six mortal weeks following the next harvest moon."

The dwarf king laughed harder than he'd ever laughed before. "Now be gone before I change my mind."

⁓

As soon as the strange trio of newcomers left the castle, the dwarf king and his court of feasting minions began to blur and shift. In a sudden gust of wind, they vanished, leaving behind two lone goblins, among them the smallest one with the blue face and the carafe of wine. The blue goblin hoisted himself onto the iron chair and contemplated the recent happenings.

"Do you think they will return?" the other goblin asked, his yellow eyes wide.

"Most assuredly. They are far from finished with the Wyld. And the son of General Riya made a promise."

The other goblin sighed. "Maybe he will be the one to save us all."

"Or maybe it will be the girl," the blue goblin replied with a knowing smile.

"Do you speak in jest, Sunan?" the goblin with the yellow eyes pressed.

"Never, Suli. I never jest about the future."

BASTIEN

―――――≈―――――

I have not spoken in almost an entire league.

Anger and disappointment swirl inside my chest. I fear that if I breathe life into them, I will lash out at those around me. My actions today have placed two people I care about in a dangerous world of perpetual night, populated by bloodthirsty monsters. And for what?

Nothing, it seems.

I should have known better than to fixate on such a far-fetched dream. But I cannot prevent the sorrow from settling inside my chest. From clenching my dead heart in an icy fist.

What if Sunan still existed? What if he could unmake me?

What would I have done then? What price would I have paid?

I think back on everything I've learned about myself since the night I woke on the table in Jacques' as an immortal. If I had not died and been made into a vampire, would I have continued to see the world as I always had, or would I have opened my eyes?

My mother once said that it was easy for a man to be kind and generous in times of plenty. The real measure of a man was what he did and said in times of difficulty.

My mortal life was a life of plenty. One in which I rarely paused to consider anything outside my immediate sphere. My sight was set on the future before me. A future my uncle had laid out since my birth.

As I walk behind Arjun and Celine, my mind drifts to the day I was expelled from West Point for attacking another cadet, who had brought about the accidental death of a friend. I was happy to leave the military academy. I thought my path righteous. I remember telling my uncle that if those in power refused to punish someone for wrongdoing, it was my responsibility to do it in their stead. I don't regret avenging my friend. But I do regret the way I did it.

Before I became a blood drinker, not once had I stopped to reflect upon that time in my life. Had I not been made into a vampire, I would never have sought out Valeria Henri. Perhaps I would have continued down the same path, toward the same future. One of power and wealth and influence in the city I loved.

I would be who I always was. Sébastien Saint Germain. Heir to New Orleans' largest fortune. A richly entitled boy who became a richly entitled man.

What you are has no bearing on who you become. Kassamir said that to me several weeks ago. I think back on that night often.

Perhaps it is not what I am that matters. Perhaps it is who I am.

I glance ahead to where Arjun and Celine walk through the darkened wood, the snow crunching beneath their feet. My ethereal brother, who has offered himself in service to a mad dwarf king to save our lives, and the girl I love, who would not be in this frozen wasteland if it weren't for me.

Why did I think Sunan would offer me salvation?

Fitting to discover that my dream was nothing more than a mirage in a desert.

I have learned much in the last few weeks. I have come far, but there is a long way to go.

Do I possess the fortitude to chase the better version of myself, even if that better version is not human?

"The silence is driving me mad," Arjun announces as we continue trekking toward the bridge along the border between the Vale and the Wyld. A faint mist has gathered on the outskirts of the forest, collecting near our feet and along the river.

Celine says nothing as she slows to walk beside me.

"Isn't his silence driving you mad?" Arjun asks her.

"A little, I suppose. But I always need a moment to reflect after I'm met with disappointment." She offers him a stern look. "And don't think I plan to ignore what you've done."

Arjun pauses to kick up a swirl of thickening mist. "Pardon?"

"I don't know if I should yell at you or kiss you for what you did at the palace," she says.

"You should always kiss me, princess." Arjun winks.

Celine frowns. "Are you not worried about what he'll make you do for the six weeks you're in service to him?"

"Eh." Arjun raises a shoulder. "It will be predictable. Most likely he'll relish the chance to enact petty revenge on my mother for—"

Celine screams as Arjun is wrenched from the footpath and swallowed into a patch of rising mist.

I yank the crossbow from my cloak just as Celine brandishes her dirk.

"Arjun!" Celine calls out.

"Stay back," Arjun yells. "They're lamiak." A sound rips through the darkness, followed by a keening wail. With a gasp, Arjun stumbles toward us, his silver blade coated with thick blood and an open gash near his collarbone.

"What are lamiak?" I demand as we all gather together, our weapons flashing white beneath the moon.

"Mindless blood drinkers," he says through gritted teeth. "As if a vampire had been reduced to its basest element. Stay alert. They are never alone."

All at once a pair of shimmering eyes, the color like the inside of a flame, glow through the darkness. Celine shrieks as a pale creature dressed in filthy grey rags lumbers toward us. His nails are long; his hair hangs down his back in a snarl. His face has been torn from the pages of a childhood nightmare, his eyes sunken and hollow, his cheeks gaunt. Chipped fangs protrude down his chin.

Another lamiak launches itself through the night sky, hissing through the air. It snatches Celine by the hood and tries to yank her away. Both Arjun and I move toward it, slashing at its throat. I am knocked to the ground by two more of the creatures. A sound like the clacking of teeth flies from one of their mouths, and four more bound from the mist toward us, their long, ragged nails curled like talons.

They tear at my cloak as I lift the crossbow and fire two quarrels at one of them.

"Aim for the center of the chest," Arjun instructs.

I fire another quarrel, and it flies wide. The lamiak nearest to me tries to snatch the crossbow from my grasp, and I shove it toward the snow. Three more land on my back. I look up as I struggle to stand, throwing one of them off my shoulder as another digs its talons into my arm, just above the arrow wound inflicted by the twig men.

Snow flies around me, obscuring my vision. My fangs have lengthened in my mouth, my vision sharpened by my fury. In my periphery I see Arjun pull Celine from an attack as she turns her blade around and sinks its point into the chest of the creature nearest to her, who draws back with an ear-piercing screech, taking the blade with it.

I cannot stop the onslaught of lamiak descending on us. They do not try to drink from me, as if they know I am one of them, but this knowledge has also identified me as their enemy. They bear down on me in force, preventing me from coming to Arjun's or Celine's aid.

Arjun falls to the snow, overcome by two lamiak, as Celine is grabbed from behind by another.

I shout and try to stand.

Something starts to glow in Celine's hand. With a cry, she brandishes the sphere of sunlight in the air above her head. It starts to burn brightly. She gasps, and I can see that her fingers have started to shine as if they've caught fire. With both hands, she lifts the bauble high. The lamiak shriek, their skin beginning to burn. The ones far enough away try to crawl toward the darkness, but many of them smolder and catch flame, their clothes turning to ash.

Celine waits until the last of the creatures is nothing but tendrils of smoke. Tears stream from her eyes, the scent of burning flesh carrying on the wintry air.

She collapses into the snow, her hands and arms blistered.

CELINE

---—≈—---

When Celine sat up, panic began to set in. The same panic she'd felt in the hospital after she'd been attacked at Saint Louis Cathedral the night of Mardi Gras.

The first thing she noticed was the light. Even though dusk appeared to have settled around her, the sun still shone from beyond the window, its light faint and warm. Tiny baubles flickered throughout the room, multiplying as they neared the high domed ceilings. Her bed was the largest bed she'd ever seen in her life. It appeared to be fashioned of twisting vines carved from a pale tree that smelled of cedar and spice. The coverlet felt as soft as a cloud to the touch. The faint scents of honeysuckle and citrus suffused the space.

Even at a glance, Celine knew this was not the sort of chamber one found in the mortal world. All at once, recent events flashed through her mind's eye. She swallowed at the memory of the lamiak coming toward her, the chittering echo of its death cry. The perfume of the frigid mist in the Wyld seemed to curl through her nostrils and ripple down her spine.

Shivering, Celine pulled the cloudlike coverlet to her chin.

A buzzing sound rang in her right ear, startling her. A tiny winged fairy zipped before her, inspecting her as it muttered in a language Celine could not understand. Then it vanished out an open window, undoubtedly to deliver a message.

She was in the Vale. The sunlight alone told her this truth. She was safe and warm. No creatures of the night would barrel from the shadows, intent on causing her harm.

Celine fell back against her mound of pillows and sighed. With a start, she recalled the way the golden bauble had burned to the touch. She sat up to examine herself. Her hands and forearms should be horribly burned. Yet she failed to find a single mark anywhere. The smell of crushed herbs lingered on her fingertips, as if some kind of tincture had been applied to her wounds. She stretched her limbs, expecting to feel a twinge of pain.

Nothing at all disturbed her. It was as if she'd woken from a healing sleep.

A knock resounded at the door.

"Come in," Celine said after tugging the coverlet higher once again.

Bastien walked in. Alone.

Celine's grasp on the coverlet tightened. He was the last person she wished to see. The only person she wished to see. Conflict warred within her. It had been the same in the Wyld, whenever Bastien drew near. She wanted to push him away or pull him close so she might breathe in the scent of bergamot on his skin.

It was infuriating.

Bastien stood at the foot of the immense bed, dressed in

loose trousers and a long, collarless tunic of raw silk. He looked . . . strange. The clothing of the Vale did not suit him. He wasn't willowy enough. Too broad in the shoulders. But it would take far more than ill-fitting garments to make a young man like Bastien look less than beautiful. Perhaps it was the hue. Perhaps the soft gold clashed with the icy grey of his eyes.

Color rose in Celine's cheeks. She'd spent the last minute staring at him like a lovesick fool. She cleared her throat and pursed her lips.

"Are you feeling well?" Bastien asked.

Celine nodded. "It's a bit shocking how . . . well I feel."

He crooked a brow. "That's the second time you risked your life to save mine."

"I couldn't very well let you die." Celine crossed her arms, letting the irritation flow through her veins. It was better to be irritated with him. Better to kindle this aggravation than be consumed by her desire. "Not again, at least. It was horrible the first time. I still hear the echo of my screams ringing in my ears. Truly I saved you for me."

Bastien stilled. He did not appear to be breathing. "You . . . remember the night I died?"

"I can't set foot in Saint Louis Cathedral anymore, thanks to you," she snapped. "It was one of the top three worst moments of my life, and I . . ." Celine's voice trailed off when she realized what she'd just said. What she'd remembered. Her hands flew to her mouth, the color draining from her face. "Oh," she breathed. "Ohhhhh."

Everything came to her in a sudden rush. All the answers she'd sought for so long. All the hopes and feelings and dreams she'd yearned to know again. Her eyes burned with unshed tears as she looked at Bastien. As he watched her take back her lost memories. The weight of it fell on her shoulders, causing her to double over, her arms wrapped around her stomach. The remembrances of what she'd seen—what she'd done, what she'd felt—flooded her mind.

And she knew. She knew. Not because her memories had been returned to her. But because Celine understood that it was never about seeking the truth from others. It was about finding it within herself.

"Bastien," she whispered.

He was beside her before she could blink. "I'm here."

Celine buried her face in his chest and let the tears fall. Bastien held her. He did not offer words of affection or promises to make the sun shine on her always. It was as if he knew what she needed. A place to feel safe. A place to call home. A place to be herself.

That's what Bastien had always offered her. It didn't matter if Celine dwelled in darkness or basked in the light, so long as she could be who she was, for better or for worse.

"This shirt," she said against his chest, her words muffled, "doesn't suit you."

His low laughter rumbled against her ear. "A shame, because it's quite comfortable."

"It would look much better on Arjun."

"Should I feel insulted?"

"Yes. You should always feel insulted. I like you best when you're slighted."

Bastien tilted her chin upward. "And you're sure you don't need me to send for that goblin with skin like the bark of a tree? He fed me a ghastly drink that helped me heal quite nicely."

Celine shook her head. "No. I don't need anyone or anything else." And in that moment, it was the truest thing she could think to say.

He pressed his lips forward. And began to pull away.

Celine held him there, her fingers twined in his silk shirt. "Stay."

"I can't. You should rest."

"How long have I been asleep?" she asked.

Bastien tucked an ebony curl behind her ear. "Two days."

"Then there's no reason for you to go." She drew him closer, her fingers tracing along his jaw.

"Are you not hungry?"

She bit her lower lip. "I am. Quite hungry," she murmured, her eyes bright.

"Celine, I don't think—"

"You love me. And I love you. Enough of this nonsense."

"It isn't nonsense," Bastien argued. "For the second time this year, I watched you endanger yourself to save me. We come from opposing worlds, Celine. My kind and your kind . . . we kill each other. After our time in the Wyld, I thought you understood. What part of us being together makes sense?" He paused, his fingers clenched around hers. "We are blood foes, Celine. My uncle and your mother . . . they've conspired to destroy each other for generations. That won't end anytime soon. Especially when your mother wants you to—"

"I don't give a damn what my mother wants when it comes to us. The only thing that matters is what we want." Celine sat up. "Everything you're saying now is an excuse. I never thought you would be such a coward, Sébastien Saint Germain. This is my world, too. If I'm going to be in danger anyway, I would rather be in danger with you."

"Your mother will never allow this," he said softly.

"My mother is not my keeper."

"Nicodemus will—"

"I'll handle Nicodemus. I promise I won't let him hurt you."

Bastien laughed, his palm coming to rest on her cheek.

"I learned something in the time I lost sight of my memories," Celine said. "I should not be looking to others to uncover my truths, no matter how dark or twisted they may be. I need only look inside myself. Everything I need is here." She placed her hand on her chest, over her heart. "There is only one question that matters now. Do you want to be with me, Bastien?"

"Yes."

"Then be with me." Celine pulled him close and pressed her lips to his with a gentle kiss. His left hand traced along her collarbone. When his fingers twined through the curls at the nape of her neck, Celine dragged him down onto the bed, luxuriating in the feel of his body against hers. In the way the cloudlike coverlet seemed to swallow them whole.

The hem of her nightshift rose as she wrapped her legs around

Bastien. Then Celine gripped his shoulders and rolled until he was beneath her, her knees on either side of his hips.

Before Celine had a chance to think, she tugged her gown over her head. She knew what she wanted, and she had no plans to be coy about it.

Celine stared down at Bastien, her fingers dragging across his chest. Slowly. Deftly. He took in a sharp breath, his grey eyes darkening into drops of black ink. His fangs began to lengthen, and he closed his eyes, as if to shield her from the truth of what he'd become.

"No," Celine said, a hand against his jaw. "Don't look away from me. Don't hide what you are. Beside the river, when we were attacked by the lamiak, I wasn't afraid to see what you are. It is *who* you are that matters most. I've seen you at your best and at your worst. And you are beautiful to me in any light."

He sat up at once, unchecked emotion in his gaze. "Thank you." His words were a whisper. When Celine kissed him, it was gentle, the tip of her tongue brushing across his fangs with the softest caress. Bastien shuddered and drew her closer, his arms enveloping her in an embrace.

"Bastien," Celine whispered in his ear. "Make love to me."

In response, he pulled his tunic over his head. The feel of his skin against hers caused a spark of delicious warmth to race through her body. That same spark she'd felt for weeks in his presence. Perhaps it wasn't safe. Fire was rarely safe. But it made her feel alive. And she was not a damsel in distress, waiting to be rescued by a knight on a shining horse.

She was Celine Rousseau. The daughter of a linguistics professor and the Lady of the Vale. The girl who had defended her own honor and fought to protect the one she loved.

Fey royalty in her own right.

Bastien's hands brushed up her bare rib cage toward her chest. "Tell me how you want me to touch you," he said. "Show me."

Celine thought she would feel bashful or embarrassed. But she didn't. Not at all. This was Bastien, after all. He'd asked her, without pride or agenda. And she loved him more for it. Celine took his hands and showed him how. Showed him where. When she gasped and threw her head back, her heart trilling in her chest like a bird longing to be set free, the whites of his eyes vanished in swirls of delicious darkness.

Her limbs wondrously heavy, Celine began to touch him as he had touched her. She pushed him back against the bed, her palms trailing across the sculpted planes of his chest and chiseled muscles of his stomach.

"Tell me what you like," she murmured.

"If I tell you, this will be over all too soon," he said with a wicked grin.

Celine shifted, conscious of where their bodies touched.

Again Bastien sat up, until their eyes were level. He lifted her by the hips and waited for her to move.

Celine brought them together in one careful slide, gasping at the twinge of pain and the sudden fullness. Then she pressed her lips to his, her hips rolling forward. The rest of the world faded away, and it was nothing but touch and sound and sensation.

Nothing but each other. This kiss that was a moment and a lifetime.

Celine fell back against the coverlet, her fingers grasping his arms. When she opened her eyes, the flickering lights above her glittered like stars. She lost herself in the rise and fall of Bastien's shoulders. In the way the rhythm of her body matched his. In the feel of his strong hands as they twined through hers.

A lush warmth took shape within her, spreading through her body until she gasped his name and gripped the carved vines along the headboard and let the starlight above them fade into oblivion.

Later, their arms and legs threaded together, Bastien's fingers trailing down her spine, he turned toward her, his gunmetal eyes soft. "I have loved you in both my lives. I will love you in all the rest to come."

And Celine slept the sleep of dreams.

❧

The next day, they strode into the Summer Court, hand in hand.

Celine expected to see disapproval on her mother's face. After all, it was clear the Lady of the Vale's daughter had fallen in love with their blood foe. A cursed vampire. And not just any vampire, but the immortal heir of Nicodemus Saint Germain.

It did not matter. Celine had already decided to defy the stars. And she would defy them again and again if it meant she could keep what she wanted close to her heart.

The gentry in her mother's court frowned and whispered behind their hands, their displeasure plain. One of them—a man with long silver hair and eyes the color of dark citrine—stepped forward as if to protest outright, but he was drawn back by a slender man standing to his left, who stared at Celine with a calculated expression.

A man whose angular face she would not soon forget.

The Lady of the Vale stood from her sunburst throne and welcomed Celine and Bastien with open arms.

"I am grateful to you for bringing my daughter back to me," Lady Silla said to Bastien. Her laughter was bright, her features kind. "Though I am a bit put out that she did not arrive in the Summer Court hale and hearty, as Arjun promised."

"Please," Celine said. "That was not his fault. Arjun nearly gave his life to spare me from harm. As it was, he made a bargain with a creature in the Wyld so that we could move through what remains of the Winter Court safely."

Celine's mother returned to her throne, her elegant fingers curling beneath her pointed chin, her long nails shining like the surface of a mirror. She smiled indulgently, her ebony eyes soft. Like the richest kind of velvet. The waves of her waist-length hair hung about her shoulders like a shining cape. "Don't worry yourself over Arjun. I am grateful for him as well."

Inhaling, Celine stepped forward, her fingers falling from Bastien's. "May I make a request?"

"Of course you may, my daughter."

"I want to stay in the Vale with you for a time. But first there are people in New Orleans to whom I owe an explanation. Affairs I wish to put in order. Will you grant us leave to travel back if I promise to return?"

Lady Silla tapped a silver nail against the curved arm of her golden throne, another serene smile settling on her face. "You know promises are not made lightly here, my child."

"I know." Celine nodded. "And I promise I will return. As you said, I would like to spend time in this world. More important, I want to know who my mother is." She offered her a smile. "I want to learn the things that bring her joy and the things that bring her sorrow."

Her mother's velvet eyes shifted over Celine, then moved toward Bastien, their sloe-shaped corners narrowing in consideration. Celine wasn't sure what her mother was thinking, but she suspected the Lady of the Vale did not hold much love in her heart when it came to the handsome blood drinker standing before her now.

With bated breath, Celine stood in silence, awaiting her mother's decision.

Then Lady Silla stood, her long ivory dress rippling as she glided toward Celine. "Of course, aga. You have a life in the mortal world. It stands to reason that you have affairs you wish to settle first. We will take our time learning from each other when you return. I want nothing more than that." She pressed her pale hand to Celine's cheek. "Do you still have the bauble I gave you?"

Celine reached into her pocket and removed the golden sphere, which no longer retained its previous luster. The Lady of the Vale wrapped her palm around it and squeezed. When she opened her hand again, a gold ring with a large yellow stone in the shape of a rectangle was all that remained of the bauble.

Her mother gave the ring to Celine. "As soon as you wish to return, twist the gem in the center of the ring three times to the right and three times to the left. A tare will form that will bring you directly to this court. After all"—she smiled with open affection—"this is where you belong."

Celine placed the ring on her finger. Then she embraced her mother. "Thank you, Umma."

Surprise flickered across the Lady of the Vale's lovely face. But she took her daughter in her arms and pulled her close. "Never forget how much your umma loves you."

"I'll return soon," Celine said. "I promise."

"I know you will."

The Lady of the Vale

———— ≈ ————

As soon as her daughter and the damned blood drinker left court, escorted by Yuri, Lady Silla called for Riya. She beckoned her general close, until her most trusted huntress was the only one to hear what she had to say.

The leader of the Grey Cloaks nodded. When she stepped back to carry out her lady's orders, a cold smile tugged at the corners of Lady Silla's mouth.

After all, she had not attained the height of power in the Summer Court by anything less than sheer cunning. And she would not lose this power to anyone. Much less to the heir of the vampire she hated most in this world. The vampire who'd taken more from her than any other enemy still in existence.

Lady Silla would know.

All her other enemies had perished by her own two hands.

BASTIEN

———— ≋ ————

We return to a world of ash and smoke. A world of fire. It is June in New Orleans. Though it is sunset, the air swelters around us, the smell of the sea sharp. Almost two months of mortal time have passed in the five days we spent in the Otherworld. Though Arjun warned us this would happen, it is still difficult for me to believe.

But not as difficult to comprehend as the sight before me now.

Jacques'—the place I have called home for ten years—has been burned to the ground, along with two other buildings along the same block. All that is left are piles of smoldering rubble. Half a chimney. Stacks of broken bricks. The occasional flash of melted brass. Remnants of my uncle's marble chess set.

I wander through the remains of my home, Celine standing silent beside me, the sun descending at her back. Passersby pause to take in the scene, their jaws agape, their tongues clicking against the roofs of their mouths.

Such a shame. Their whispers carry through the air, clear as a church bell. Sometimes I am grateful for my heightened senses. Tonight is not one of those times.

Celine sidesteps a pile of red bricks and moves alongside me.

She glances about, her green eyes brilliant. Like emerald beacons shining through the darkness.

"Do you know who might have done this?" she whispers, taking my hand.

"I have a—" I snarl as movement resonates in the darkness behind us. A pile of bricks collapses in a puff of smoke. I pull Celine behind me, a low hiss emanating from my throat.

"Bastien."

My shoulders fall at once. From behind the blackened chimney, Odette emerges, her face devoid of emotion. She is dressed like a man in mourning. In her hand is a felted top hat. Across her waist is the chain of the gold pocket watch that once belonged to my father. She must have saved it from the fire for me.

I take her hand and yank her into an embrace. Celine draws us both close. In our arms, Odette's body sags. I hear a single sob.

"Was it the Brotherhood?" I say.

Odette nods against my shoulder.

"Was anyone injured?" Celine asks.

Odette pulls away, her gloved hand swiping at the blood tears trickling down her cheeks. She shakes her head. "Nicodemus wasn't here. He was in New York. The rest of us—including all the mortals who worked here—managed to escape before the blaze consumed the building." Her smile is bleak. "Even Toussaint made it out unscathed, though the poor little snake refuses to come into the light, no matter the enticement."

Rage riots through me, hot and fast. All at once it turns to ice in my veins. I think back on the fire that took my sister, Émilie, from me. The Brotherhood should know better than to do such a thing to my family. "And Jae?" I ask softly.

"Madeleine freed him from his silver prison." Her sad smile widens, her eyes tremulous. "We haven't seen him since, though I suspect he is still in the city. Our family has taken refuge at the Hotel Dumaine. Ifan has made certain none but we are allowed access."

"Why would the Brotherhood do such a thing?" Celine asks, her voice breaking.

"Both the Fallen and the Brotherhood have been searching for a reason to strike out at each other for the last decade," I say. "If it hadn't been this, it would have been something else." I glide forward, kicking aside a brick and watching half of it disintegrate to dust. Determination takes root in my bones. I stand tall, my eyes blazing. "All that matters is that none of our family was harmed. Jacques' can be rebuilt. But I refuse to lose someone else I love."

Odette nods, her gloved hands—the fingertips stained pink with blood tears—slipping into her pockets. "I come here every night. Perhaps it's because I keep hoping I'll find something in the rubble." She sniffs. "Or perhaps it is merely an excuse."

"And the Brotherhood?"

Odette looks around. "They must see this as retaliation for the death of Antonio Grimaldi that night in the cemetery."

"Have they attacked since then?" I press.

She shakes her head. "None of their ranks have been seen since the fire." Her nostrils flare. "Believe me, we've looked."

My eyes scan the rubble, taking note of anything unusual.

But all I see are the burned tapestries, the piles of fine linen blackened by smoke, the shards of glass glittering in the twilit moon.

Celine pauses before the remains of a crystal chandelier, the brass partially melted, the crystals covered with soot. Her smile is wistful. "The first time I saw this place, I thought it was magic."

"What do you mean?" I ask.

"It felt like I'd crossed into another world."

Odette rests her head on Celine's shoulder, her sable hair shining. "And you did, mon amie," she said. "And I'm happy to see your memories have returned." She glances my way and extends her right arm. In her hand is my father's gold pocket watch.

"Thank you, Odette," I say as I take it from her. "I would have mourned its loss."

"I did not go back for it," Odette says. "Jae did. He left it with the front desk at the Hotel Dumaine."

I nod once, a knot gathering in my throat. Despite what Jae has done, he will always be my brother. I pause to pry open the lid of the watch with my thumb. It has not been wound for an age. The times I wore it in recent years, it was merely a decoration. On the inside, I read the inscription:

IL Y A TOUJOURS DU TEMPS POUR L'AMOUR.

—*PHILOMÈNE*

There is always time for love.

My mother gifted this to my father on their wedding day. I close the watch and place it in my trouser pocket, the knot in my throat pulling taut.

"It was unpardonable of you both to be gone so long," Odette says, her fingers lacing through Celine's.

I move closer to them, my eyes continuing to scan the ashes of our former home. For an instant, I think I hear whispers of tinkling glass and catch a glimmer of silver service dishes. Of Kassamir clapping his hands, the servers standing at attention like soldiers.

"If you could do it over again," I say to Celine, "knowing what you know now, would you have crossed the threshold of Jacques'?"

She takes a sharp breath. "A wise woman would say no. But I can't regret it, because this is the life I chose. It is mine and no one else's."

"Even if Celine hadn't crossed that threshold," Odette says, "I think she would have found her way to us. She was as inevitable as the dawn."

I take a breath of the soot-tinged air. The heat of a New Orleans summer evening has begun to thicken around us, the cicadas droning in the trees. As I step over another pile of rubble, my foot brushes a stack of discarded paper. "Far be it from me to—" I stop short, the air knocked from my lungs.

"Bastien?" Odette blurs toward me, her eyes like sharpened daggers.

I say nothing as I stare at the ground. At the sheaves of scattered paper, their corners curling upward. At the unmarred sheet in the center, anchored by a white marble rook.

A piece of my uncle's chess set.

The rook. A carrion bird that feasts on the dead. A word synonymous with swindling.

Celine reaches for the piece of pristine paper. I do nothing as she stands, her expression quizzical. She unfolds the note.

"'Mon petit lion,'" she reads, "'our family left me to burn. Consider the favor returned.'" She pauses, her eyes going wide. "'If you ever wish to see our uncle again, find us on the *Crown Jewel of the Mississippi*. Yours in life and in death, Émilie.'" Shock settles on her face. "Émilie?" she breathes. "Isn't that your—"

"Sister," I say, the world beginning to spin around me. I take the letter from Celine, the blood roaring through my body. "My sister," I mutter as I reread the note. "My sister."

Mon petit lion. My little lion. I hated that nickname. Only Émilie called me that.

Odette's shoulders shake with incredulity. "Comment est-ce possible?"

I stare out at the remains of my fire-ravaged home, a flurry of images aligning in my mind. Everything that has happened to us in the last few months shifts. Nothing seems random. It all has a purpose. The murders along the docks close to Jacques', attributed to Nigel. The attack on Celine at Saint Louis Cathedral. How surprised we all were to know that our lanky, card-loving brother, Nigel Fitzroy, had been the mastermind behind it all.

Perhaps it was not surprise. Perhaps it was disbelief.

The rook. A swindling carrion bird.

"My uncle loves chess," I say, the words ashen on my tongue. "He's been a student of it for centuries."

"He told me that once," Celine says, "at the masquerade ball."

"I never play with him, and he never asks me to play with him. It was something he did with Émilie. She was a prodigy, even at a young age. But still she only beat him once. It was the week before she died . . ." My voice fades into silence.

Odette's hands fly to her mouth. "Mon Dieu," she whispers. And I know she understands.

"Bastien, what happened?" Celine asks. "You never told me how she died."

"It was my fault," I say, my voice hollow. "As a child, I enjoyed playing with sunlight. Creating prisms with the crystals I found throughout the house. I would collect these pieces of glass, even from the chandeliers. In the bright heat of the afternoon, I would stack them until a pattern of rainbows formed along the wall. My father would reproach me for it. He kept saying I would start a fire one day. But I didn't listen, and no one enforced the rules with me. Even as a boy, I was coddled and given everything I could ever want.

"That afternoon, I left my collection of crystals on my bed upstairs after arranging them just so. Then I went down to the kitchen to bother Émilie. When I returned to my room, a blanket in the corner was smoldering. A small fire had been lit. I was young and afraid of getting in trouble, so I threw the smoldering blanket into my closet and shut the door. You can guess what happened after that. I couldn't see. I was scared. So I ran to a hall closet upstairs and hid." I close my eyes, remembering how I'd started to choke. How I'd struggled to see or call out to anyone. "Émilie was the one who ran up the stairs, through the blaze. By the time she found me, the fire had consumed the second-floor landing." I stop, feeling almost human as I recall that moment. That feeling of powerlessness. "I don't remember much of what happened next. I was told she wrapped me in a blanket and pushed me out the window so that I could land in the center of a sheet the fire brigade was holding. She never made it out."

I say nothing for a time, and then a dark burst of laughter flies from my lips. "They never found a body. The fire brigade said it was likely the heat of the blaze had consumed all traces of my sister. For weeks, I hoped someone had rescued her. Found her. I begged my uncle and both my parents to check all the hospitals. To ask all the doctors. I didn't believe she was dead. I thought if she was dead, I would have known it. There would be some kind of proof. A body, a feeling of loss. I was so sure she was still alive. The only thing my parents did was collect all our belongings and move across the city. They knew—even though no one told me—that we were being targeted by Nicodemus' enemies. Not long after that, my mother was turned into a vampire. That fire—the one I caused that day—was the beginning of the end for my family."

"Ce n'est pas possible," Odette mutters to herself. "Émilie . . . is alive?"

Anguish tugs at the corners of Celine's mouth. "If she's alive, why would she turn on her own family?"

"I don't know. She seems to believe Nicodemus left her to die, though I can't imagine what would cause her to think that." My expression hardens. "But I intend to ask her why."

Odette grips me by the wrist. "And you will not be alone when you do."

I nod and crumple my sister's note in my fist.

MICHAEL

———— ≈ ————

A cross the way, on the second floor of a deserted pied-à-terre, Michael Grimaldi watched the trio depart from the charred ruins of Jacques'. He waited until they moved out of sight. Then he stood from his chair, his heart pounding like the beat of a drum.

He'd expected to see Odette Valmont. She came here each night just after sundown. Only to leave after kicking through the rubble, as if she expected to uncover something she'd missed in the days prior.

But Michael had not expected to see the girl he loved . . . with the boyhood friend who'd betrayed him so many years ago.

Sébastien Saint Germain.

Michael bit back the bitter taste in his mouth, his arms shaking. Bastien and Celine had disappeared more than seven weeks ago. Not once had they been sighted in the days since. Most of the other officers in the New Orleans Metropolitan Police believed the two young lovers had left the city to elope.

Michael alone argued with them. Insisted that these officers continue to be stationed around Jacques' and the Hotel Dumaine. Not once had he thought it possible for Celine to do such a thing as leave without a word. The day before she vanished, she'd told Michael she wanted to build a life together. That she wanted to be with him. She'd meant it. Of that Michael was certain.

If something had happened to Celine, it had been done against her will.

At first Michael's superiors humored him. They allowed him to place officers around all the establishments frequented by the members of La Cour des Lions. After a month passed without any sightings or any new clues, they'd quietly pulled back their resources, against Michael's renewed protests.

Even after the fire at Jacques' last week, Michael had been unable to convince his fellow officers that something was afoot. Not so privately, many of his colleagues had asserted that he was no more than a jilted lover, incapable of accepting the obvious fact that the girl he loved had fallen for another man.

Michael thought he might go mad.

If Luca were here, Luca would have believed him. Michael's cousin was due to return from his European honeymoon any day now. And just because Celine had appeared alive and safe in the company of Sébastien Saint Germain did not mean that she'd turned her back on Michael. It was possible Odette Valmont had helped keep her trapped all this time. Perhaps Celine was still their prisoner, yearning to be set free.

His fists clenched at his sides. No matter what, he would clear his name of this despicable stain. He was not a jilted lover. Nor was he a cuckolded fool. If Bastien had taken Celine away against her will, the fiend would pay for it. And if . . . if Celine had chosen the bloodthirsty bastard over Michael, he would not turn his cheek and wait for the other slap.

No. He would be the one to decide what happened next.

Michael moved from the shadows of the abandoned flat and onto the darkened street. With haste, he began striding toward police headquarters in Jackson Square. He needed to send for a recruit so that they could follow Bastien, Celine, and Odette to Hotel Dumaine, where the rest of their fallen court of vampires lurked.

After all, there was a reason Michael Grimaldi had been chosen as the city's youngest police detective. And he would not allow his instincts to be ignored any longer.

II

———— ≈ ————

Along the nearby street corner, a gentleman in a bowler hat watched Celine Rousseau, Sébastien Saint Germain, and an unidentified young man leave the destroyed building that had once housed the city's best-known dining establishment. He cracked his knuckles and smoothed his immaculate mustache. Then he removed his notebook. Jotted down his observations. And began striding toward the Hotel Dumaine.

Soon he would have all the information his client needed.

Soon he would be able to serve justice on a murderess.

ÉMILIE

———≈———

Émilie had often dreamed of the sight before her now. All around the boat deck, her brother and sister wolves from Texas, from Arkansas, from Kansas, from Oklahoma, from Georgia, from the Carolinas were gathered. Here they all stood, ready to listen. Ready to learn.

Ready to unite.

They mingled, waiting for the sun to rise over their shoulders. For its light to seep into the sky and take the place of night. The riverboat churned at their backs, the giant red wheel tossing a constant spray of water, the banks of the Mississippi guiding their path forward. Newfangled electric lanterns blazed brightly, strung through the wooden rafters, bathing the polished wooden decks in a soft glow.

Beer and moonshine and table wine were poured liberally. Everywhere Émilie looked, she saw men and women laughing together. Occasionally children would dart between them, weaving through the crowd like the reeds of a basket.

It was all so different from the world in which Émilie had been raised. Here, among the wolves, there was no pretense. Men were not given unfettered authority, and women were not relegated to roles of subservience. Even the children were allowed seats at the table, their voices valued.

Among the vampires—among Nicodemus' ilk—decorum had been sacrosanct. Her uncle had expected all his children, mortal and immortal alike, to bow before him. In that world, there had been no place for Émilie. All eyes had been on her younger brother, Bastien, the scion of the Saint Germain family.

Émilie breathed in through her nose and closed her eyes.

Her uncle would pay for this. She'd waited for this dawn for ten years. When the sun rose from its berth, Nicodemus would be there to receive his reckoning.

Émilie caught the eye of another young wolf. A girl with hair the color of flaxseed. The girl grinned at Émilie, her brown eyes flickering in the darkness, caught on a beam of starlight. In her warm gold stare, Émilie saw endless possibilities. A future in which she could be whoever she wished to be and love whomever she wished to love.

"Happy?" Luca asked behind Émilie, his large hands pulling her close.

Émilie nodded. "This is what I always dreamed of. A world in which we are all united."

"Then I am pleased."

She turned toward him, her arms looping about her husband's neck as she stood on her toes. He'd always been tall. Taller and stronger than any other wolf in the whole of Louisiana. "You should be more than pleased. Tonight you made my greatest dream come true."

Luca wrapped his arms around her. A smile touched his lips. "Are you ready to make my dreams come true in return?"

"Of course." She pressed a kiss to his chin. "You saved me, after all."

It was true, in a way. As Luca held her tightly—a contented sigh rumbling from his chest—Émilie's mind drifted back to the day of her human death at the age of fifteen. How she'd spent the morning playing with Sébastien, then left him to his own devices so she might read a book. Émilie had been sure to leave him in his room within shouting distance. She could have read in the room with him, but the light was better in the downstairs nook, and Émilie wanted to enjoy *Le Vicomte de Bragelonne* without any distractions.

Passersby had noticed the fire from outside. A Créole maid had screamed as she raced for the stairs, Émilie in tow.

The fire had already spread to the first landing. Unbeknownst to all, Bastien had hidden himself in a hall closet. No one had been able to find him before they'd raced out the doors, choking on the acrid smoke.

Émilie had known it would be too late.

She'd taken the stairs two at a time, the fire thrashing at her skirts, singeing through her stockings. She stifled a shriek and rolled across the floor to put out the flames along the hem of her muslin dress. Her actions had been taken without thought. Without consideration for the risk they posed to herself. Her baby brother was trapped, and she would rather die than watch him burn. He was only a boy of six, after all.

"Bastien?" Émilie had said in a level voice. "You have to come downstairs with me."

"No!" he'd shouted from the hall closet. "The fire will burn me. If I stay here, it will leave me alone."

"If we don't go now, we will get even more hurt."

He'd said nothing for a time. Smoke had begun to choke the air around Émilie.

"Bastien?" She'd tried the knob and found it locked, the metal hot in her palm.

"I'm sorry, Émilie," he said so softly she could barely hear him. "It's my fault. It's all my fault."

"Just open the door, mon amour, and all will be forgiven."

Bastien turned the handle, and Émilie would never forget the stark look in his grey eyes. As if he'd aged a decade in a matter of a few short moments. She swept him up in her arms and turned back for the stairs.

A gasp in her throat, she stopped in her tracks. There was no way to use the stairs anymore. The fire had caught along the balustrade and begun to lick at the expensive wallpaper. It was already reaching for the crown molding around the ceiling, the paint starting to bubble.

Émilie knew she could not panic in front of her little brother. So she raced toward the back of the home and put him down. "Stay right here," she ordered as she threw open a window sash.

Another mistake. A breeze tore through the open window, fanning the flames. The smoke began billowing higher, the fire moving ever closer to them.

Still Émilie refused to be daunted. She began shouting and flailing her arms.

It was an act of God that had drawn the fire brigade toward them. That had granted the men the wherewithal to create a makeshift landing space below, two windows over. Émilie had seen her uncle staring up at them from the crowd, a bleak expression on his face, as if he were resigned to their deaths.

Hang his resignation. Émilie refused to give up.

Coughing all the while, she ripped a piece of her petticoat and threw it over Bastien's protesting head. In the nick of time, she managed to hurl him out the window, watching—her heart in her throat—as he landed in the center of the blanket, to cheers from the crowd. To her uncle's awaiting arms. As soon as Nicodemus lifted Bastien from the center of the bedsheet, he'd turned his back on the fire. Turned his back on her.

A fit of coughing overtook Émilie in that moment. Caused her eyes to water and her body to fold in on itself. She backed away, clutching both hands to her throat, feeling the heat burn into her lungs. When she regained her bearings, precious moments had been lost.

The window was no longer an option.

The fire surrounded her on all sides.

A fresh slew of tears coursed down her cheeks. She crouched toward the floor, seeking clean air, realizing the flames would close in on her soon, hoping the smoke would choke her before the fire burned her skin.

Something rustled through the flames. A blur of motion coming from above, descending as if from the attic.

The instant before Émilie succumbed to the smoke and the despair, a set of clear, inhuman eyes—rings of blown-out black pupils surrounded by ochre—stared down at her as strong hands snatched her through the smoke.

When she woke, her lungs were burned. The skin on her right hand and along the right side of her neck was singed. It took her only a moment to agree to their terms. To agree to serve whoever had saved her. To honor the one who swore to put an end to her pain. Who vowed never to turn his back on her.

With every promise, Émilie recalled the sight of her uncle watching their home as it burned. The relief in his eyes when Sébastien landed in the center of the fire brigade. How he turned away from the burning building. Away from her.

In life, Nicodemus had never concerned himself much with her welfare. In death, he left Émilie to burn. He would burn everything to the ground if it meant saving his legacy.

Which was why Émilie took it from him. Why Émilie lied to everyone. Even the ones she purported to love.

She grinned up at Luca Grimaldi.

Everything Émilie had worked for all these years was about to come to pass. She'd already made one part of Luca's dreams come true. She married him. At her behest, they eloped and traveled to Europe for a honeymoon. One in which Émilie had spent an inordinate amount of time speaking with some of the elder wolves in the Greek archives. The next part of Luca's dream would never come to pass, though he did not know it.

Émilie had no interest in having children. She never had. And the notion that she simply must in order to have value as a woman had always chafed her sensibilities.

One of the most lasting lessons her uncle had taught her was the weakness of love. It was something Émilie had marveled at over the course of the last decade. Many of the men, women, vampires, werewolves, and other fey creatures she encountered were beings capable of great evil. Interestingly they were also capable of great love.

And so many of them loved their families with an inordinate amount of ferocity. Their loved ones were often their greatest weakness. It was for their families that they did their worst.

Émilie wasn't interested in that kind of weakness. In that kind of excuse.

She fought for herself and for herself alone. The family she had now was one of survival. She loved them because they gave her the strength of numbers. But her love was conditional. And she always made certain her conditions were met.

"The leeches are almost here," a voice announced through the din.

Émilie refrained from going to the edge of the deck to peer at the sight she'd longed to see for so many years. Instead she walked toward the bow, to the dais reserved for musicians. The electric lanterns glowed beneath her. Along the horizon, a faint light began to bleed into the night sky. The first signs of dawn.

Luca came to stand beside her. He reached for her hand. Émilie wove her fingers through his. Something roared through her with the force of a summer storm when her brother stepped over the railing, a blank expression on his face.

Sébastien looked so much like their father. Handsome. Chiseled. Strong.

Émilie almost flinched.

A lie. In the end, Rafael Ferrer had been weak. So very weak.

When Bastien saw her, he stopped, a look of shock and dismay on his face. In the blink of an eye, he schooled his expression into one of calculated ambivalence. A part of Émilie was impressed. The little brother she remembered was far more ruled by the tides of emotion. He reached behind him to offer his hand to the young woman accompanying him.

Celine Rousseau, who disregarded her brother's help and held the hem of her long skirts high before planting her booted toes on the deck. Émilie's gaze narrowed. Odette Valmont, Shin Jaehyuk, Boone Ravenel, and Madeleine de Morny moved into position as all the wolves formed a protective semicircle around Émilie and Luca.

Émilie removed her hand from Luca's and stepped toward Bastien.

"I appreciate you responding to my invitation, Monsieur Saint Germain. Though I'll admit I expected your arrival a bit sooner," Émilie said in a pleasant tone.

Bastien took in a breath as if he meant to speak, then stopped himself. Again Émilie found herself admiring his restraint.

"I'm certain you wish to ask me how I came to be here, mon petit lion." She grinned.

"I do," he replied. "But does it matter?"

"I suppose not."

"Where is Nicodemus?"

"He came to me of his own volition, just as you have."

"I am not here because I wish to be here, Émilie." His piercing grey eyes cut through her. In another life, she might have been intimidated. "I am here because I was not given a choice."

"You were given choices, Sébastien. You chose to come here to save our undeserving uncle, for reasons I am certain I will never understand," she replied. "You could have left him to his fate, one he deserves more than most villains, to be sure."

Bastien paused as if in thought. "I suppose it depends on how one defines a villain, does it not?"

"You sound so much like him," Émilie said, her words taunting. "How proud he must be of you."

"I am nothing like Nicodemus." He frowned, a muscle ticking in his jaw.

Delight warmed through Émilie. Finally she'd managed to strike a nerve with her little brother. Before Émilie had a chance to react, Celine Rousseau stepped toward her, her eyes flashing. "Enough of this. You asked Bastien to come if he ever wished to see his uncle again. What do you want from us?"

A formidable opponent, as Émilie had surmised. "Marceline Rousseau," she murmured, appraising her slowly. "I'm happy to finally make your acquaintance."

"You came to my shop once. I remember you asking Pippa about a mourning gown."

"I did. I could not help myself. Tell me . . . how does it feel to realize you will one day destroy the boy you love? That your kind will forever be plotting to put an end to his kind?" It was deliberate of Émilie to bait this girl. She wanted to see what the half fey could do. What kind of Vale magic might flow through her veins.

"I don't know what you hope to accomplish by provoking me," Celine said softly. "But it won't work. You won't goad me to anger, though you are most deserving of it. The anger I feel for you is deep and strong. But I will not let it control me, as it has controlled you. I will not allow hate to define my actions."

Something pricked at Émilie's skin. Like a drove of ants crawling down her back. She laughed, letting the sound carry into the sky. All around her she felt the wolves stir, restless in the shadows. Eager to be unleashed, just as she was. How much Émilie longed to tear Celine Rousseau's words from her pretty, pale throat. To watch her brother fall to his knees at the sight of his lost love.

But the wretched girl was right. Émilie's hate should not define her actions. And Émilie had greater things in store today. From her periphery, she saw the rest of the vampires draw together in a tighter circle around Celine. She marked how Bastien made no move to silence his woman or stop her from taking charge, though he angled himself nearby, his grey eyes glittering.

They loved her. Every one of these fallen leeches would kill for the half-fey daughter of the Lady of the Vale. It was almost enough to make Émilie laugh even louder.

The wolves growled as they tightened their own circle. They would be less powerful in the daylight. Émilie knew this, though she nonetheless waited for the dawn. Because Émilie could not leash her emotions in the face of this wretched half-fey creature—this girl who had stolen her brother's heart—she laughed again.

"Where is Nicodemus, Émilie?" Bastien asked, his voice cold.

Émilie turned to the young man who used to be her brother. She took her time, wishing to savor the moment. The rays of sunlight reached ever higher in the sky. Dawn was fast approaching.

It was time.

"Luca," she said softly. "Please see that our esteemed guest is escorted to the boat deck."

Bastien's eyes narrowed as Luca Grimaldi gestured toward the stairs leading below. Her brother's shoulders rolled back as he followed Émilie's earlier gaze toward the horizon. Then he murmured something.

As if he knew what Émilie intended to do.

Immediately Jae stepped forward, his long jacket falling from his back, his posture like that of a coiled asp.

"Don't move," Émilie said loudly. "If any vampire makes any sudden moves, I will not lift a finger to save you or yours, Sébastien."

"And if any harm befalls Nicodemus, I offer you the same promise," Bastien replied without missing a beat.

He thought her the sort to throw a chained victim helplessly on the boat deck and watch him burn. Of course he did. That was the elegant, brutal world in which they had been raised.

So of course it gave them pause when Nicodemus walked up the stairs of his own volition, neither chained nor bound. Two werewolves flanked him. The only sign that he was anything less than an esteemed guest were the long spears tipped in solid silver in each of the wolves' right hands.

Émilie watched confusion flicker across Bastien's face, quickly replaced by cool indifference. Nicodemus nodded at his progeny, his expression unreadable. He strode across the boat deck with purpose, the wolves continuing to flank him. He paused for only an instant before Sébastien and the rest of his immortal children.

"It was good of you to come," he said with a small smile. "Mademoiselle Rousseau." He offered the girl a bow.

Bastien nodded once in acknowledgment. Nicodemus continued making his way toward Émilie. Once his back was turned from his children, his features sobered. He slowed his footsteps the closer he came to Émilie. In the distance, the sun had begun its careful rise.

"I knew you would not disappoint, Uncle," she said with a pointed grin.

"What do you want in order for us to depart with Nicodemus?" Bastien asked from where he stood.

"You are free to leave now," Émilie replied, her grin widening.

Nicodemus stared at her, twirling the signet ring on his right hand.

"What games are you playing, Émilie?" Bastien asked.

"I asked for Nicodemus to come so that we might clear the air between us," Émilie replied. "He obliged me. Through the course of our conversation, I believe he has come to understand my way of thought," she continued. "To fully realize what it will take to forge a lasting peace between the Fallen and the Brotherhood."

Nicodemus continued to meet her gaze, his eyes unblinking. He inhaled as if he meant to speak. Over his shoulder, Bastien took another step toward them, stayed only by Celine's hand on his arm.

"She is correct, Sébastien," Nicodemus said without turning around. "There is indeed a way to spare everyone present the bloodshed of years ago."

"No," Odette murmured. "No." She shook her head as understanding dawned on them all. Bastien blurred into motion, Jae rushing from one side.

Nicodemus removed his signet ring and closed his eyes. The flames alighted on his exposed skin. Émilie watched him grimace in agony, though he made no sound. A pang unfurled around her heart. Once she'd loved him. Seen him as her protector.

Nicodemus Saint Germain. The oldest, most powerful vampire in the American South.

Her brother shouted like a demon possessed. Screams of outrage rang through the throng of vampires present. Still Émilie did not turn away from her uncle's demise. She watched him fall to his knees, the signet ring striking the deck with a metallic ping.

Soon he was nothing more than a pile of ash.

Émilie looked at the young man who had once been her brother. Saw the hate ripple across his face, his fingers intertwined with those of his half-fey love. Snarls ripped from Boone Ravenel's chest.

A grin tugged at the edges of Émilie's mouth. She gazed at Celine. "Leave now, or face your—"

The shot that rang out next surprised her. Almost as much as the bullet that tore into her shoulder, nearly knocking her off her feet. The resulting burn caused her to gasp in pain. Typical bullets did not do that.

Which meant this bullet had been tipped in silver by someone who knew what they were.

Michael

―――≈―――

He'd taken the shot despite the consequences, out of worry for Celine. Though he knew it meant he was firing upon one of his own. But Michael Grimaldi had watched for long enough. He thought it would give him satisfaction to see the end of Nicodemus Saint Germain.

The reality was the complete opposite.

The next instant, Michael dispatched his fellow officers of the Metropolitan Police. They mounted the railing of the riverboat, their whistles blowing in the dawn light. For an instant, everyone on the deck—the werewolves Michael had known from childhood, his own cousin, the vampires in the Court of the Lions—did not move. Then pandemonium erupted.

Michael had thought the presence of the police would deter the violence from escalating.

He was wrong.

The most powerful of the wolves, those able to transform in daylight, quickly changed shape, their clothes ripping to shreds, their growls tearing through the crowd. Several vampires blurred along the edges of the deck. It was impossible to know who struck first, but a wolf yelped, its jaw torn from its mooring. Its body fell to the deck, lifeless. The next instant, cries of rage littered the dawn sky.

For a moment, Michael's fellow officers froze in shock, unsure of what to do.

Who was their enemy in this fight?

A shrill whistle blared from the opposite end of the deck as an officer fired at a wolf charging toward him. The next instant, the rest of the police force took aim, two of them moving to protect Celine and the other women close by.

Though Michael carried a revolver loaded with solid silver bullets, he tore the dagger from his side, refusing to fire again on one of his own. But he did not hesitate to fire a warning shot at Jae's head when the vampire moved toward Luca, who fought back to back with his new wife. Neither had shifted into their animal forms, though Michael knew Luca was powerful enough to do so at any time of day.

Those who could not shift fled to the other side of the riverboat. The rest of the wolves attacked at random, their lack of organization obvious. Luca yelled over the din, trying his best to rally those who remained to his side.

Bastien and Odette stood before Celine, knocking any wolf that charged out of the way. Michael did not miss how Bastien avoided using lethal force. When Celine shouted, Bastien turned in place in the same moment two wolves descended on Odette, knocking her from her feet. One wolf buried its fangs in Odette's throat.

Bastien hurled himself against the wolf's side, knocking the second attacking wolf away from Odette with a swipe of his arm. Michael watched as the wolf slid backward, then moved to attack Celine, who held a pistol and a knife in each of her hands. She fired, and the wolf dodged the shot just as Boone came to her aid.

From nowhere, the werewolf Michael shot—the girl Luca had recently married—stepped into the light, her expression one of triumph.

"Celine!" Bastien shouted as Celine brandished her silver dagger and heaved it with all her might at Luca's wife, the blade sinking into the werewolf's shoulder. The girl sent Celine a savage smile before grabbing her by the throat.

Without a second thought, Michael shoved aside the officer and the wolf in his path. He rested his pistol on his forearm and fired at Luca's bride. Unlike the first time, he shot to kill.

His cousin stepped between them.

Michael's silver bullet hit Luca square in the chest.

BASTIEN

———— ≈ ————

My sister's scream pierces the chaos. Its echo rises into a sky on fire, the sun rising at her back.

Émilie falls to her knees beside Luca's lifeless body, blood slipping down her arms from injuries to her neck and shoulder. She looks as she sounds. Like a wounded creature. An animal for whom nothing matters but putting an end to the pain.

I feel the pull of her anguish. I take a step forward, then stop myself. It seems unreal that I should see her once more, alive and whole. Has it really been a single night since I received her note? After years without her, a part of me still has trouble believing the sight before me. The boy in me wants to run to her, embrace her, soothe the lines of agony on her brow, just as she'd done for me on more than one occasion.

But the man I am becoming knows better.

I think of my uncle's final directive. The one Nicodemus shared with me just before he met the sun, his unspoken words ringing through my head, maker to immortal child.

Do not let them win, Sébastien. Take back the Horned Throne. Fix what has been broken.

Be better than I was.

I stand still, watching Émilie shriek at those around her, tears coursing down her cheeks, her arms cradling Luca's head, his blood soaking through the front of her dress, mingling with that of her own wounds. For a breath of time, no one on board moves, save for the restless stirring of those succumbing to their own injuries.

I understand the pain of her loss. It is the type of pain I knew in the wake of our parents' deaths. In the wake of my sister's death. And I want nothing more than to comfort her. But Émilie isn't the sister I knew. Anger has filled her with hate. Anger has driven the course of her life. It has made her strong. Proud. It has left her alone.

She is more like my uncle than she will ever know.

My sister catches my gaze. She cradles Luca's head to her breast and lifts her chin.

"Help me," she says beseechingly. "Brother."

I take a step. Stop myself, uncertain yet again. Untrusting of what I see. What I feel.

"Sébastien," she implores. "Please."

Several members of Luca's pack move forward. Before I can make a decision, Odette glides toward Émilie, her hands raised, her intentions clear—only to help. Her face is wan, her expression subdued. The wound along her neck from the wolf who attacked her has barely begun to heal.

There is such kindness in Odette. Out of us all, her dead heart feels keenly for those around her. It's what drives her to fight for the ones she loves with such fierceness. She knew Émilie as a child. There is sorrow on her face at watching someone she once cared for suffer before her very eyes.

I swallow around the tightness in my throat. Steel myself to help, despite my misgivings. Celine takes a hesitant step, her head quirked at a tentative angle. Odette crouches beside Émilie as my sister extricates the blade from where it is buried in her shoulder. With utmost caution, Odette moves to press a hand to Émilie's wound, reaching for something with which to fashion a tourniquet.

She never sees the dagger in Émilie's hand slice toward the side of her injured neck. A flash of metal. A stunned silence. A jubilant cry.

"Odette!" Celine screams.

For a dreaded moment, I fail to understand what has happened. I only see Odette fall to one knee, a look of surprise across her brow. Then she folds over like an accordion, her throat cut through to the bone, a torrent of crimson cascading like a waterfall toward the sun-warmed deck beside her feet.

I blur into movement. The next instant, the fingers of my right hand are wrapped around my sister's neck, my left hand ripping the glistening silver blade from her grasp. She meets my gaze, her face devoid of emotion, her eyes like chips of ice.

Behind me, I hear a flurry of motion. I listen as Jae curses once and Boone wails. As Madeleine yanks Odette's slumped figure away from everyone else. I know without seeing that Odette's body will soon begin to dry like a husk, then blow away, like discarded bits of paper. Even if we call Ifan now and promise him an exorbitant price, there is little chance he could save her. Outrage scalds through my blood, washing everything in crimson tones. I try to tamp down my fury. Try to silence my need for retribution. Blood for blood. My pound of flesh.

"Why?" My vision swims. My voice is dry. Brittle.

"Because I could," Émilie says.

"No. That's not enough of a reason. *Why?*"

"It's the reason I choose to give." She wraps her bloody fingers around my wrist. "Are you angry, mon petit lion?"

I say nothing.

A corner of her mouth kicks up. "Do what Uncle Nico taught you to do."

I swallow, my fingers tightening around her throat.

"Take your revenge, little brother. Today I've taken much from you. Take this. You've earned it." Her smile widens, her teeth pressed together, flashing like ivory. Low growls emanate from behind her, the pack hoping to rally behind its new alpha.

I study her in silence, trying to find a point of clarity through a haze of sadness. Why does she want me to kill her? Is it simply because she wants to ensure the rivalry between the Fallen and the Brotherhood will ignite anew?

What happens next is subtle. A blink and I might have missed it.

Émilie flinches.

My rage abates, a tide retreating from the shore.

"Regret?" I say softly. "For what?"

Her upper lip curls into the beginning of a snarl. "Regret is for fools." Her laughter is like dried leaves caught in a twist of wind. "Do it. Lash out. If you don't, I'll destroy everything you love." Émilie looks behind my shoulder. I do not need to guess where she has turned her attention. "The half blood is next."

The rage flows to my fingertips once more. I can take the blade in my hand and sever her head from her neck, just as she's done to Odette. Bury the knife in her heart, all the way to the hilt, twisting it deeper than her betrayal. The demon in me is delighted at the prospect. My bloodlust longs for the satisfaction.

Unshed tears glimmer in Émilie's eyes, but she blinks them back, her teeth bared.

"Bastien." Celine's voice comes from behind me. "Don't."

It isn't what I am. It is who I hope to become.

Be better than I was.

I think about my uncle, who used violence for centuries to protect the ones he loved. I think about Sunan, and the promise I held so close to my chest, of finding a way to be unmade.

Maybe this is my unmaking. Not from a demon to a man. But into a better version of myself.

I drop my hand from Émilie's throat and step aside.

I will not stand in the path of an unstoppable force. That is the way of disaster. The way of Death. Power isn't about deciding who lives or dies. It is having the strength to walk away.

"Madeleine and Boone," I say through clenched teeth. "Take Odette to Ifan."

"It's too late," Madeleine says through her tears. "She is gone, my dearest. We must—"

"Take her. Now," I command, my tone weary.

When Émilie lunges at me once more, she is immediately restrained by Jae. The wolves in the shadows stir, preparing to resume what they started, despite their losses.

I sense their hesitation before I see it. I know that—without a leader—they will be hard-pressed to rally together. Before they have a chance to regroup, I let my voice carry across the deck. "Make a single move, and I'll ensure that the Brotherhood dies here and now."

The growls grow louder.

"Do as I ask, and I'll let you leave to bury your dead and mourn," I continue. "This"—I glance about—"is not the way forward."

Boone's nostrils flare. "She killed Odette, Bastien. Someone must answer for that. She cannot be allowed to find her way back to us or lead any more of her kind against us. That is foolish."

Jae's attention settles on me. "There is another way. I can take her to Lady Silla and ask that she be banished to the Wastelands."

I consider this a moment before I nod in agreement.

"And what if she is able to escape? What if she seeks another way to wreak her revenge?" Madeleine says.

Jae's eyes flash. "You know what must be done. An alpha that cannot run at the head of its pack is an alpha no more."

A sharp spate of laughter fills the air. "They turn to you, little brother, to lead in the absence of our uncle. Set the right example," Émilie says, her tone jeering.

I inhale deeply. Then I nod at Jae. "Do it."

The next instant, Jae cuts off Émilie's left hand at the wrist.

BASTIEN

———— ≈ ————

Celine and I are the last to make our way back to the Hotel Dumaine.

I know both of us are stalling. Neither of us wishes to cross the threshold and discover that Odette is lost to us forever.

"Do you think there's any chance?" Celine asks as we pause half a block away from the entrance to the hotel.

I know there isn't. Her blood loss was too great, the wound too deep. "Maybe," I say.

"Perhaps if I speak to my mother," Celine says. "If I make her a promise."

"If there's anything to be learned from our time in the Vale, it's the danger of too many promises." I catch her hand in mine and pull her close.

Her voice wavers in my shoulder. "I'll make any promise if it means Odette will live."

I hold her tighter. Then I feel her stiffen against me. My nostrils flare as the scent of gunpowder is carried on the wind. I turn at once.

A man with an elegant mustache stands several paces away, a

bowler hat in hand. His eyes are narrowed, his posture ramrod straight. In a second I recognize that he must have served in the military.

"Mademoiselle Rousseau," he says, his accent unmistakably French. "I am Agent Boucher of the French National Gendarmerie in Paris."

I move in front of her, my gaze locked on his.

"I represent the Marquis de Fénelon," he continues.

Celine gasps behind my back, her fingers digging into my shoulder.

Agent Boucher sniffs. "He is quite certain you can tell him what happened to his son, François." He takes a step forward. "I have in my hand a notice that you are to accompany me back to Paris for questioning."

"No," Celine whispers. Her hands shake.

It is all I need to hear. In a ripple of movement, I grab the French police officer and drag him into the alley beside the hotel. He struggles, but my arms close around his throat, choking the life out of him.

"Bastien," Celine says, tears streaming down her face. "Please don't kill him."

"He's here to take you to Paris. They will hang you for murdering that boy, Celine."

"If you kill him, the marquis will simply send someone else." Her voice trembles. "I need to disappear. I need to wait until he gives up."

I tighten my grip.

"Stop," Celine cries, her fingers on my arm. She holds up the hand with the gold ring her mother gifted her. "I'll return to the Sylvan Vale. Leave him here. Let him go."

I stare at her, my fangs lengthening. The demon within me taking control.

"Come with me," she says.

Epilogue

The Grimaldi family had a bloody past.

From the time the first Antonio Grimaldi ruled his village six hundred years ago in the heart of Sicily to the moment Michael's great-grandfather boarded a ship bound for the New World, theirs was a path lined with bodies. As with their archenemies, werewolves were made in blood. A bite from a werewolf often resulted in death, which was why it was rarely attempted among their ranks. The risk was too great. The Grimaldis had learned this truth the hard way. It wasn't enough to be born into a family of wolves. You had to forge your own path. One surefire way of ensuring the change was sinister in construct: take the life of one of your own. A wolf for a wolf.

Like Michael had taken Luca's life. Even though it had been by mistake. The cost of the magic was clear.

One must die so the other may live.

It began with the shifting of the clouds.

Michael had known to expect it. Nevertheless the first ripple down his spine set his teeth on edge. A pang unfolded in his chest. He bowed his head, noting the sudden race of his pulse.

The way every tendon in his arms stretched, his neck lengthened, his chin tilted toward the moon.

He stared at it. Studied its mottled surface, his skin bathing in its cool light. Blood rushed through his veins. His face turned hot. Though he fought it—a sad attempt to cling to the vestiges of his humanity—Michael fell to his knees, his hands reaching for the soft loam before him, his fingers curling into the soil.

He was changing. He was becoming. Never again would he be what he once was.

The truth rattled through his bones. He yelled and no one was there to hear it. He'd made certain of that when he'd slogged his way to the heart of the bayou, far from his fellow man, knowing he would emerge an altogether different kind of creature.

His yells became snarls. His fingers sharpened into claws. The four chambers of his heart burst in his chest, his veins filling with liquid fire. He remembered being a boy of ten, jealous of Luca, who'd taken the life of his own father at his father's behest. It had been a mercy killing. Luca's father had been injured in the Brotherhood's war with the Fallen. Moments away from his own death, he'd given Luca a pistol. Told him what to do.

Tears in his eyes, Luca had sworn vengeance on the leeches for what they'd done.

He, in turn, had also given his life for it.

The pain peaked through Michael's body. He'd known to expect it, but that did not make it any less intense. Like a thousand needles stabbing through to his bones. He cried out once more and the sound burgeoned into a howl.

No. He would not seek revenge for what he had lost. That was a lesson for fools.

He would seek purpose. He would go back to where it all began.

And he would make sure the generations to follow never knew this kind of pain.

⤚∾⤙

From where she sat in the bog, the frogs croaking at her feet, Pippa listened to Michael's screams. She heard the way his bones broke, the sound like the snapping of twigs. When his cries became inhuman, she covered her ears, tears streaming down her cheeks. Twice she stopped herself from stepping from the shadows. It was a blessing that Michael was distracted by his suffering. Fortunate she could move so quietly. Years of training with her fencing tutor had taught her to stay light on her feet.

What was happening to him? Had she erred in following him into the bayou? When his cries began to shift into the howls of an animal, she stopped short, her heartbeat thundering in her ears.

She didn't know much. She wanted to help him.

But whatever he'd become was dangerous.

And it did not sound as if he would be able to tell her where Celine and Bastien had gone.

The next instant, Pippa moved from where she was crouched in the bog and began to hurry home.

There were entirely too many unanswered questions around

everyone involved with Jacques' and the Court of the Lions. Pippa knew they were not at all what they seemed. At home in Yorkshire, she'd lived a life tainted by secrets, the ones she kept and the ones that were kept from her.

Pippa despised secrets. Almost as much as she despised being kept in the dark. Her wedding was in less than a month. In her mind, that meant she had a little more than three weeks to find out where her best friend had gone. What kind of secrets Celine continued to keep.

If Michael wouldn't lead her to the truth, Pippa would begin hounding someone else from Jacques'. Someone who'd already infiltrated their circle. Someone she was bound to understand, especially since they'd journeyed to New Orleans from the same country.

Yes. Arjun Desai would be her next mark.

YOUR GUIDE TO RENÉE AHDIEH:

SEE WHERE
CELINE AND
BASTIEN'S STORY
BEGAN

Excerpt on Page 404

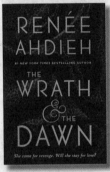

CHECK OUT
RENÉE AHDIEH'S
FIRST SERIES

Excerpt on Page 413

STILL CRAVING
MORE RENÉE
AHDIEH?

Excerpt on Page 423

Excerpt on Page 431

THE
BEAUTIFUL

"It's true: Vampires are back, and they're more seductive than ever."
—*BUSTLE*

RENÉE AHDIEH

#1 *NEW YORK TIMES* BESTSELLING AUTHOR

———◆◇◆◇◆———

N ew Orleans is a city ruled by the dead.

I remember the moment I first heard someone say this. The old man meant to frighten me. He said there was a time when coffins sprang from the ground following a heavy rain, the dead flooding the city streets. He claimed to know of a Créole woman on Rue Dauphine who could commune with spirits from the afterlife.

I believe in magic. In a city rife with illusionists, it's impossible to doubt its existence. But I didn't believe this man. *Be faithful,* he warned. *For the faithless are alone in death, blind and terrified.*

I feigned shock at his words. In truth, I found him amusing. He was the sort to scare errant young souls with stories of a shadowy creature lurking in darkened alcoves. But I was also intrigued, for I possess an errant young soul of my own. From childhood, I hid it beneath pressed garments and polished words, but it persisted in plaguing me. It called to me like a Siren, driving me to dash all pretense against the rocks and surrender to my true nature.

It drove me to where I am now. But I am not ungrateful.

For it brought to bear two of my deepest truths: I will always possess an errant young soul, no matter my age.

And I will always be the shadowy creature in darkened alcoves, waiting . . .

For you, my love. For you.

Not What It Seemed

———◦◇◇◇◦———

The *Aramis* was supposed to arrive at first light, like it did in Celine's dreams.

She would wake beneath a sunlit sky, the brine of the ocean winding through her nose, the city looming bright on the horizon.

Filled with promise. And absolution.

Instead the brass bell on the bow of the *Aramis* tolled in the twilight hour, the time of day her friend Pippa called "the gloaming." It was—in Celine's mind—a very British thing to say.

She'd begun collecting these phrases not long after she'd met Pippa four weeks ago, when the *Aramis* had docked for two days in Liverpool. Her favorite so far was "not bloody likely." Celine didn't know why they mattered to her at the time. Perhaps it was because she thought Very British Things would serve her better in America than the Very French Things she was apt to say.

The moment Celine heard the bell clang, she made her way portside, Pippa's light footsteps trailing in her wake. Inky tendrils of darkness fanned out across the sky, a ghostly mist shrouding the Crescent City. The air thickened as the two girls listened to the *Aramis* sluice through the waters of the Mississippi, drawing closer to New Orleans. Farther from the lives they'd left behind.

Pippa sniffed and rubbed her nose. In that instant, she looked younger than her sixteen years. "For all the stories, it's not as pretty as I thought it would be."

"It's exactly what I thought it would be," Celine said in a reassuring tone.

"Don't lie." Pippa glanced at her sidelong. "It won't make me feel better."

A smile curled up Celine's face. "Maybe I'm lying for me as much as I'm lying for you."

"In any case, lying is a sin."

"So is being obnoxious."

"That's not in the Bible."

"But it should be."

Pippa coughed, trying to mask her amusement. "You're terrible. The sisters at the Ursuline convent won't know what to do with you."

"They'll do the same thing they do with every unmarried girl who disembarks in New Orleans, carrying with her all her worldly possessions: they'll find me a husband." Celine refrained from frowning. This had been her choice. The best of the worst.

"If you strike them as ungodly, they'll match you with the ugliest fool in Christendom. Definitely someone with a bulbous nose and a paunch."

"Better an ugly man than a boring one. And a paunch means he eats well, so . . ." Celine canted her head to one side.

"Really, Celine." Pippa laughed, her Yorkshire accent weaving through the words like fine Chantilly lace. "You're the most incorrigible French girl I've ever met."

Celine smiled at her friend. "I'd wager you haven't met many French girls."

"At least not ones who speak English as well as you do. As if you were born to it."

"My father thought it was important for me to learn." Celine lifted one shoulder, as though this were the whole of it, instead of barely half. At the mention of her father—a staid Frenchman who'd studied linguistics at Oxford—a shadow threatened to descend. A sadness with a weight Celine could not yet bear. She fixed a wry grin on her face.

Pippa crossed her arms as though she were hugging herself. Worry gathered beneath the fringe of blond on her forehead as the two girls continued studying the city in the distance. Every young woman on board had heard the whispered accounts. At sea, the myths they'd shared over cups of gritty, bitter coffee had taken on lives of their own. They'd blended with the stories of the Old World to form richer, darker tales. New Orleans was haunted. Cursed by pirates. Prowled by scalawags. A last refuge for those who believed in magic and mysticism. Why, there was even talk of women possessing as much power and influence as that of any man.

Celine had laughed at this. As she'd dared to hope. Perhaps New Orleans was not what it seemed at first glance. Fittingly, neither was she.

And if anything could be said about the young travelers

aboard the *Aramis*, it was that the possibility of magic like this—a world like this—had become a vital thing. Especially for those who wished to shed the specter of their pasts. To become something better and brighter.

And especially for those who wanted to escape.

Pippa and Celine watched as they drew closer to the unknown. To their futures.

"I'm frightened," Pippa said softly.

Celine did not respond. Night had seeped through the water, like a dark stain across organza. A scraggly sailor balanced along a wooden beam with all the grace of an aerialist while lighting a lamp on the ship's prow. As if in response, tongues of fire leapt to life across the water, rendering the city in even more ghoulishly green tones.

The bell of the *Aramis* pealed once more, telling those along the port how far the ship had left to travel. Other passengers made their way from below deck, coming to stand alongside Celine and Pippa, muttering in Portuguese and Spanish, English and French, German and Dutch. Young women who'd taken leaps of faith and left their homelands for new opportunities. Their words melted into a soft cacophony of sound that would—under normal circumstances—soothe Celine.

Not anymore.

Ever since that fateful night amid the silks in the atelier, Celine had longed for comfortable silence. It had been weeks since she'd felt safe in the presence of others. Safe with the riot of her own thoughts. The closest she'd ever come to wading through calmer waters had been in the presence of Pippa.

When the ship drew near enough to dock, Pippa took sudden hold of Celine's wrist, as though to steel herself. Celine gasped. Flinched at the unexpected touch. Like a spray of blood had shot across her face, the salt of it staining her lips.

"Celine?" Pippa asked, her blue eyes wide. "What's wrong?"

Breathing through her nose to steady her pulse, Celine wrapped both hands around Pippa's cold fingers. "I'm frightened, too."

TURN THE PAGE FOR AN EXCERPT OF:

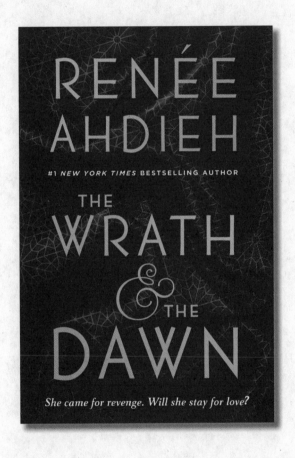

MEDITATIONS
ON GOSSAMER AND GOLD

T HEY WERE NOT GENTLE. AND WHY SHOULD THEY BE?
After all, they did not expect her to live past the next morning.

The hands that tugged ivory combs through Shahrzad's waist-length hair and scrubbed sandalwood paste on her bronze arms did so with a brutal kind of detachment.

Shahrzad watched one young servant girl dust her bare shoulders with flakes of gold that caught the light from the setting sun.

A breeze gusted along the gossamer curtains lining the walls of the chamber. The sweet scent of citrus blossoms wafted through the carved wooden screens leading to the terrace, whispering of a freedom now beyond reach.

This was my choice. Remember Shiva.

"I don't wear necklaces," Shahrzad said when another girl began to fasten a jewel-encrusted behemoth around her throat.

"It is a gift from the caliph. You must wear it, my lady."

Shahrzad stared down at the slight girl in amused disbelief. "And if I don't? Will he kill me?"

"Please, my lady, I—"

Shahrzad sighed. "I suppose now is not the time to make this point."

"Yes, my lady."

"My name is Shahrzad."

"I know, my lady." The girl glanced away in discomfort before turning to assist with Shahrzad's gilded mantle. As the two young women eased the weighty garment onto her glittering shoulders, Shahrzad studied the finished product in the mirror before her.

Her midnight tresses gleamed like polished obsidian, and her hazel eyes were edged in alternating strokes of black kohl and liquid gold. At the center of her brow hung a teardrop ruby the size of her thumb; its mate dangled from a thin chain around her bare waist, grazing the silk sash of her trowsers. The mantle itself was pale damask and threaded with silver and gold in an intricate pattern that grew ever chaotic as it flared by her feet.

I look like a gilded peacock.

"Do they all look this ridiculous?" Shahrzad asked.

Again, the two young women averted their gazes with unease.

I'm sure Shiva didn't look this ridiculous . . .

Shahrzad's expression hardened.

Shiva would have looked beautiful. Beautiful and strong.

Her fingernails dug into her palms; tiny crescents of steely resolve.

At the sound of a quiet knock at the door, three heads turned—their collective breaths bated.

In spite of her newfound mettle, Shahrzad's heart began to pound.

"May I come in?" The soft voice of her father broke through the silence, pleading and laced in tacit apology.

Shahrzad exhaled slowly . . . carefully.

"Baba, what are you doing here?" Her words were patient, yet wary.

Jahandar al-Khayzuran shuffled into the chamber. His beard and temples were streaked with grey, and the myriad colors in his hazel eyes shimmered and shifted like the sea in the midst of a storm.

In his hand was a single budding rose, its center leached of color, and the tips of its petals tinged a beautiful, blushing mauve.

"Where is Irsa?" Shahrzad asked, alarm seeping into her tone.

Her father smiled sadly. "She is at home. I did not allow her to come with me, though she fought and raged until the last possible moment."

At least in this he has not ignored my wishes.

"You should be with her. She needs you tonight. Please do this for me, Baba? Do as we discussed?" She reached out and took his free hand, squeezing tightly, beseeching him in her grip to follow the plans she had laid out in the days before.

"I—I can't, my child." Jahandar lowered his head, a sob rising in his chest, his thin shoulders trembling with grief. "Shahrzad—"

"Be strong. For Irsa. I promise you, everything will be fine." Shahrzad raised her palm to his weathered face and brushed away the smattering of tears from his cheek.

"I cannot. The thought that this may be your last sunset—"

"It will not be the last. I will see tomorrow's sunset. This I swear to you."

Jahandar nodded, his misery nowhere close to mollified. He held out the rose in his hand. "The last from my garden; it has not yet bloomed fully, but I wanted to give you one remembrance of home."

She smiled as she reached for it, the love between them far past mere gratitude, but he stopped her. When she realized the reason, she began to protest.

"No. At least in this, I might do something for you," he muttered, almost to himself. He stared at the rose, his brow furrowed and his mouth drawn. One servant girl coughed in her fist while the other looked to the floor.

Shahrzad waited patiently. Knowingly.

The rose started to unfurl. Its petals twisted open, prodded to life by an invisible hand. As it expanded, a delicious perfume filled the space between them, sweet and perfect for an instant . . . but soon, it became overpowering. Cloying. The edges of the flower changed from a brilliant, deep pink to a shadowy rust in the blink of an eye.

And then the flower began to wither and die.

Dismayed, Jahandar watched its dried petals wilt to the white marble at their feet.

"I—I'm sorry, Shahrzad," he cried.

"It doesn't matter. I will never forget how beautiful it was for that moment, Baba." She wrapped her arms around his neck and pulled him close. By his ear, in a voice so low only he could hear, she said, "Go to Tariq, as you promised. Take Irsa and go."

He nodded, his eyes shimmering once more. "I love you, my child."

"And I love you. I will keep my promises. All of them."

Overcome, Jahandar blinked down at his elder daughter in silence.

This time, the knock at the door demanded attention rather than requested it.

Shahrzad's forehead whipped back in its direction, the bloodred ruby swinging in tandem. She squared her shoulders and lifted her pointed chin.

Jahandar stood to the side, covering his face with his hands, as his daughter marched forward.

"I'm sorry—so very sorry," she whispered to him before striding across the threshold to follow the contingent of guards leading the processional. Jahandar slid to his knees and sobbed as Shahrzad turned the corner and disappeared.

With her father's grief resounding through the halls, Shahrzad's feet refused to carry her but a few steps down the cavernous corridors of the palace. She halted, her knees shaking beneath the thin silk of her voluminous *sirwal* trowsers.

"My lady?" one of the guards prompted in a bored tone.

"He can wait," Shahrzad gasped.

The guards exchanged glances.

Her own tears threatening to blaze a telltale trail down her cheeks, Shahrzad pressed a hand to her chest. Unwittingly, her fingertips brushed the edge of the thick gold necklace clasped around her throat, festooned with gems of outlandish size and untold variety. It felt heavy . . . stifling. Like a bejeweled fetter. She allowed her fingers to wrap around the offending instrument, thinking for a moment to rip it from her body.

The rage was comforting. A friendly reminder.

Shiva.

Her dearest friend. Her closest confidante.

She curled her toes within their sandals of braided bullion and threw back her shoulders once more. Without a word, she resumed her march.

Again, the guards looked to one another for an instant.

When they reached the massive double doors leading into the throne room, Shahrzad realized her heart was racing at twice its normal speed. The doors swung open with a distended groan, and she focused on her target, ignoring all else around her.

At the very end of the immense space stood Khalid Ibn al-Rashid, the Caliph of Khorasan.

The King of Kings.

The monster from my nightmares.

With every step she took, Shahrzad felt the hate rise in her blood, along with the clarity of purpose. She stared at him, her eyes never wavering. His proud carriage stood out amongst the men in his retinue, and details began to emerge the closer she drew to his side.

He was tall and trim, with the build of a young man proficient in warfare. His dark hair was straight and styled in a manner suggesting a desire for order in all things.

As she strode onto the dais, she looked up at him, refusing to balk, even in the face of her king.

His thick eyebrows raised a fraction. They framed eyes so pale a shade of brown they appeared amber in certain flashes of light, like those of a tiger. His profile was an artist's study in angles, and he remained motionless as he returned her watchful scrutiny.

A face that cut; a gaze that pierced.

He reached a hand out to her.

Just as she extended her palm to grasp it, she remembered to bow.

The wrath seethed below the surface, bringing a flush to her cheeks.

When she met his eyes again, he blinked once.

"Wife." He nodded.

"My king."

I will live to see tomorrow's sunset. Make no mistake. I swear I will live to see as many sunsets as it takes.

And I will kill you.

With my own hands.

TURN THE PAGE FOR AN EXCERPT OF:

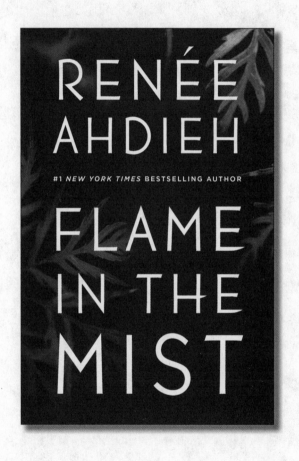

RENÉE
AHDIEH

#1 *NEW YORK TIMES* BESTSELLING AUTHOR

FLAME
IN THE
MIST

The Beginning

———✦———

In the beginning, there were two suns and two moons.

The boy's sight blurred before him, seeing past the truth. Past the shame. He focused on the story his *uba* had told him the night before. A story of good and evil, light and dark. A story where the triumphant sun rose high above its enemies.

On instinct, his fingers reached for the calloused warmth of his *uba*'s hand. The nursemaid from Kisun had been with him since before he could remember, but now—like everything else—she was gone.

Now there was no one left.

Against his will, the boy's vision cleared, locking on the clear blue of the noon sky above. His fingers curled around the stiff linen of his shirtsleeves.

Don't look away. If they see you looking away, they will say you are weak.

Once more, his *uba*'s words echoed in his ears.

He lowered his gaze.

The courtyard before him was draped in fluttering white, surrounded on three sides by rice-paper screens. Pennants flying the golden crest of the emperor danced in a passing breeze. To the left and right stood grim-faced onlookers—samurai dressed in the dark silks of their formal *hakama*.

In the center of the courtyard was the boy's father, kneeling on a small tatami mat covered in bleached canvas. He, too, was draped in white, his features etched in stone. Before him sat a low table with a short blade. At his side stood the man who had once been his best friend.

The boy sought his father's eyes. For a moment, he thought his father looked his way, but it could have been a trick of the wind. A trick of the perfumed smoke curling above the squat brass braziers.

His father would not want to look into his son's eyes. The boy knew this. The shame was too great. And his father would die before passing the shame of tears along to his son.

The drums began to pound out a slow beat. A dirge.

In the distance beyond the gates, the boy caught the muffled sound of small children laughing and playing. They were soon silenced by a terse shout.

Without hesitation, his father loosened the knot from around his waist and pushed open his white robe, exposing the skin of his stomach and chest. Then he tucked his sleeves beneath his knees to prevent himself from falling backward.

For even a disgraced samurai should die well.

The boy watched his father reach for the short *tantō* blade on the small table before him. He wanted to cry for him to stop. Cry for a moment more. A single look more.

Just one.

But the boy remained silent, his fingers turning bloodless in his fists. He swallowed.

Don't look away.

His father took hold of the blade, wrapping his hands around the skein of white silk near its base. He plunged the sword into his stomach, cutting slowly to the left, then up to the right. His features remained passive. No hint of suffering could be detected, though the boy searched for it—felt it—despite his father's best efforts.

Never look away.

Finally, when his father stretched his neck forward, the boy saw it. A small flicker, a grimace. In the same instant, the boy's heart shuddered in his chest. A hot burst of pain glimmered beneath it.

The man who had been his father's best friend took two long strides, then swung a gleaming *katana* in a perfect arc toward his father's exposed neck. The thud of his father's head hitting the tatami mat silenced the drumbeats in a hollow start.

Still the boy did not look away. He watched the crimson spurt from his father's folded body, past the edge of the mat and onto the grey stones beyond. The tang of the fresh blood caught in his nose—warm metal and sea salt. He waited until his father's body was carried in one direction, his head in another, to be displayed as a warning.

No hint of treason would be tolerated. Not even a whisper.

All the while, no one came to the boy's side. No one dared to look him in the eye.

The burden of shame took shape in the boy's chest, heavier than any weight he could ever bear.

When the boy finally turned to leave the empty courtyard, his eyes fell upon the creaking door nearby. A nursemaid met his unflinching stare, one hand sliding off the latch, the other clenched around two toy swords. Her skin flushed pink for an instant.

Never look away.

The nursemaid dropped her eyes in discomfort. The boy watched as she quickly ushered a boy and a girl through the wooden gate. They were a few years younger than he and obviously from a wealthy family. Perhaps the children of one of the samurai in attendance today. The younger boy straightened the fine silk of his kimono collar and darted past his nursemaid, never once pausing to acknowledge the presence of a traitor's son.

The girl, however, stopped. She looked straight at him, her pert features in constant motion. Rubbing her nose with the heel of one hand, she blinked, letting her eyes run the length of him before pausing on his face.

He held her gaze.

"Mariko-*sama*!" the nursemaid scolded. She whispered in the girl's ear, then tugged her away by the elbow.

Still the girl's eyes did not waver. Even when she passed

the pool of blood darkening the stones. Even when her eyes narrowed in understanding.

The boy was grateful he saw no sympathy in her expression. Instead the girl continued studying him until her nursemaid urged her around the corner.

His gaze returned to the sky, his chin in high disregard of his tears.

In the beginning, there were two suns and two moons.

One day, the victorious son would rise—

And set fire to all his father's enemies.

TURN THE PAGE FOR AN EXCERPT OF:

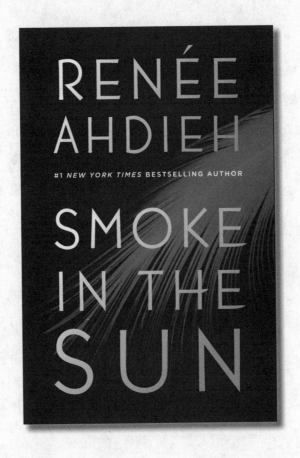

RENÉE
AHDIEH

#1 *NEW YORK TIMES* BESTSELLING AUTHOR

SMOKE
IN THE
SUN

A Good Death

———✶———

Somber clouds waited above, like specters.

Most of the people had donned funereal grey. Their heads were lowered in respect, their voices hushed. Even the smallest of children knew better than to ask why.

This was the honor afforded their recently deceased emperor. The honor of their extreme reverence and their unwavering love. A reverence—a love—the girl did not feel in her heart.

Nevertheless, she kept silent. Appeared to follow suit, though her hands were balled at her sides. She watched from the corner of her eye as the funeral procession wound through the muted streets of Inako. As a light rain began to fall from a dreary silver sky. Her woven sandals soon became wet. The fabric of her plain trousers clutched at her calves.

Her left fist tightened around the rock in her hand.

The drums marching out the processional beat drew closer, their low thunder reverberating in her ears. The reedy melody of the *hichiriki* split through the rising din of the rain.

When the imperial guards posted along the lane turned their gazes toward the crowd, the people bowed with haste, afraid they might be disciplined for any slight, however small. Those in the girl's vicinity bowed lower as the spirit tablet leading the procession shifted into view. Tendrils of smoke from the agarwood incense suffused the air with the scent of burning cedar and warm sandalwood. Etched on the tablet's stone surface were the names of many past emperors—the deceased heavenly sovereigns of the Minamoto clan.

The girl did not bow. She kept her eyes lifted. Locked on the spirit tablet.

If she was caught, it would be tantamount to a death sentence. It would be the height of disrespect—a stain of dis-honor on her family and all those who followed in their footsteps. But honor had never held much weight for her.

Especially not in the face of injustice.

For a final time, the girl clenched her fingers around the rock. Rubbed the sweat from her palm into its roughened surface. Took aim.

And launched it at the spirit tablet.

It struck the center of the grey stone with a sharp *crack*.

A stunned silence descended upon the crowd as those bearing the tablet swayed for a suspended moment. They watched in horror when the tablet crashed to the dirt in several pieces.

A single cry of outrage bled into many. Though there was no love lost between the fallen emperor and the people of the Iwakura ward, this act was an affront to the gods themselves. The samurai guarding the procession reared their horses and charged into the crowd. A collective stammer arose from the people, much like the drone of a beehive on the cusp of exploding. Trembling fingers pointed in all directions, stabbing accusations anywhere and everywhere.

But the girl was already on the move.

She lunged into the shadows behind a small apothecary shop. Her hands shook from the energy pulsing beneath her skin as she yanked a mask above the lower portion of her face. Then the girl grabbed the edge of a pine eave and braced her foot against a stained plaster wall. With lightning precision, she vaulted onto the tiled rooftop.

The shouts from below grew louder.

"There he is."

"That's the one who threw the rock."

"That boy over there!"

The girl almost smiled to herself. But she did not have time for the luxury of emotion. With fleet-footed steps, she raced toward the ridgeline of the roof, then slid down the sloping tile on the other side. The pounding of hooves to her right drove the girl toward the rooftop at her left. She leapt over the yawning space between the two structures and tucked her body into a roll. Even with these cautionary measures, a painful shudder rippled from her heels up her spine.

As she flew across the curved tiles—using the arches of

her feet to grip their damp surface—an arrow hissed by her ear. Like a cascade of water, the girl slid to the roof's edge and dropped into the shadows below.

A quick beat was spent in contemplation. Her chest heaved as she took in one breath. Then two. She needed to get more distance. Blinking back the rain, the girl darted into an alleyway, skirting a discarded cabbage cart in the process.

A sudden rush of footfall rose from her left.

"There he is."

"Over by the alley next to the forge!"

Her heartbeat crashed through her ears as she tore around the corner, the clatter of footsteps drawing closer. There was no place to hide, save for a rain barrel propped against a wall of the dilapidated forge. She would be caught if she lingered for even a moment longer.

Her eyes darting to the four corners of the earth, the girl made a quick decision. As nimble as a cat, she levered her back against a wooden post and kicked upward once, twice. Her body quaking from the effort, she wedged a foot into the crook of a support beam. Then the girl flipped over, pressing her shoulders into the rough straw of the roof's underbelly.

Her sight blurred from fear as a soldier came into view just beneath her. If he looked up, all would be undone. The soldier glanced around before shoving his sandaled foot against the rain barrel. It tumbled aside with a thud, the rain within it joining the mud in a delayed splash. Frustration forced a huff of air past the soldier's lips.

Close by, an unintelligible shout of fury rang out into the sky.

As the soldier's ire grew, the girl squeezed her body tight, the effort straining her core. She was lucky the training she undertook daily had honed her limbs into such lithe lines. Had made her aware of every muscle, every gesture. She held her breath, locking her fingers and feet into place.

The soldier kicked the barrel a final time before racing back into the streets.

After several moments had passed, the girl finally allowed herself to relax. Permitted her body to seek a more comfortable position. She stayed hovering in the shadows until the sounds of tumult melted into the pounding rain. Then—with deliberate care—she reached for the wooden post and let her feet sink into the muck with a muffled thud. The girl straightened, removing the mask from her face.

As she turned to leave, the door leading to the enclosed portion of the forge slid open. Startled by the sound, the girl let the mask fall from her hand into the mud.

Before her stood a woman with greying temples and an unforgiving stare.

Though the girl's features remained expressionless, her heartbeat faltered in her chest.

The woman would be near her mother's age, if the girl had to guess. If she shouted a single word, the girl would be caught. Fear keeping her immobile, the girl stayed silent as the woman inhaled slowly, her eyes narrowing in understanding.

Then she jerked her chin to the left, directing the girl to flee.

Bowing with gratitude, the girl vanished into the rain.

She doubled back countless times as she wove through the rain-slicked streets of the Iwakura ward, ensuring no one could follow her footsteps. When she neared an arched stone bridge—crossing into a grove of snow-white dogwood and pale pink cherry trees—her gait took on a different cadence. Her shoulders dropped, and her neck lengthened. It was automatic, the moment the scent of night-blooming jasmine curled into her nostrils.

Still she did not use any of the main thoroughfares, save for the bridge itself. Concealed beneath a shower of dying petals, she hailed a *jinrikisha* and settled under its worn canvas canopy. Her eyes shuddered closed, and her lips parted as they silently counted each of her breaths.

Ichi.

Ni.

San.

Shi.

Then the girl lifted her chin. With deft motions, she restored her disheveled clothing until nothing appeared amiss. Reformed the topknot at the crown of her head into an elegant coif. Like the gifted quick-change artist she'd been trained to be, the girl transformed from a daring boy into a demure mystery. When she finally arrived at the teahouse gate, she knocked twice, pausing for a beat before rapping her fist five more times in quick succession. A shuffle of feet and a series of whispers emanated from beyond the gate door before it swung open.

Though these servants knew to unlatch the door at this series of knocks, no one was there to meet the girl, as she'd expressly requested. So none of them would ever be forced to lie about having seen her. The girl's misfortunes were not worth the lives of all the young women here, and the cost of asking them to harbor her secrets was far too great.

She made her way across the polished stones of the garden, past the burbling brook and its three miniature waterfalls, into a music of tinkling laughter and lilting *shamisen*. Then she floated by the elegant bonsai garden to walk behind the teahouse itself, toward a smaller structure nearby. Outside an intricately carved sliding door, her trusted maidservant, Kirin, stood waiting, a carafe of clean water in her hands.

Kirin bowed. The girl returned the gesture.

As the girl removed her sandals, the freckled maidservant pushed open the silk-screened sliding door leading into a chamber flanked by two large *tansu* chests crafted of red cedar and black iron. The girl stepped over the raised threshold and took a seat before a polished silver surface positioned behind rows of dainty cosmetics and glass vials.

She stared at her reflection. At the elegant lines of her face. The ones that concealed her so well within these walls.

"Would you care to have a bath drawn?" Kirin asked.

"Yes, please," the girl replied without looking away.

The maidservant bowed once more. Turned to leave.

"Kirin?" The girl swiveled in place. "Has anything been delivered to the *okiya* in my absence?"

"I'm sorry." Kirin shook her head. "But no messages have come for you today, Yumi-*sama*."

Asano Yumi nodded. Returned her gaze to her mirror.

Her brother, Tsuneoki. would seek her out soon. She was certain of it. Following Ōkami's surrender in the forest three days ago, she and Tsuneoki could no longer afford to remain idle, darting between shadows, leaving whispers in their wake. Nor could they continue to allow their painful past to direct the course of their future. It was true Yumi's elder brother had hurt her. Deeply. With his lies about who he was. With his blind insistence that he alone possessed the answers. That he alone made the choices.

Though his choices left Yumi alone and apart, always.

Years ago, Tsuneoki's negligence had driven Yumi to scale the walls of her perfumed prison and take flight across the curved tiles. Her brother's stubborn conceit had given her wings. And with them, she would fly, anywhere and everywhere.

Absentmindedly, Yumi toyed with the alabaster lid of a jar filled with beeswax and crushed rose petals.

Her brother wore his smiles like she wore these paints. A grinning mask, concealing fury and heartbreak. Their mother used to say they should be careful of the masks they chose to wear. For one day, those masks could become their faces. At this warning, Tsuneoki would often cross his eyes and slide his tongue between his bared teeth, like a snake. Yumi would double over with laughter at the sight. When they were young, her brother had always made her laugh. Always made her believe.

Before the day it all ended, like a flame being doused in the wind.

The lid clattered off the top of the cosmetics jar, startling Yumi from her thoughts. She met her gaze in the mirror. Blinked back the suggestion of tears. Set her jaw.

It was time for the Asano clan to mete out their justice.

A justice ten years in the making.

Yumi thought again of the rock she'd held in her hand. Though the incident had occurred only this morning, it felt like a world away. She recalled the cries of outrage emanating from the crowd. They saw her actions as foolish. But they were afraid, and they'd built their lives upon this fear. It was time to dismantle it from within. Strike it down at its very foundation.

So Yumi had begun with a rock. The sound it had made as it struck the emperor's spirit tablet reverberated through her ears. The first of many battle cries to come.

She could still feel the grit on her palm.

It was time for the Asano clan to restore justice to the Empire of Wa.

Or die trying.

Acknowledgments

———≈———

I wrote this book in the middle of many life changes, and it reminded me so much of how cathartic artistic expression can be. It's easy to lose sight of that in all the deadlines, the social media posts, and the frenetic energy of each passing day. To write is such a gift, and it is a gift made possible by so many, including each and every one of my readers. I have the best readers in the world. You make me laugh and cry and experience joy and sorrow in the fullest measure. To me, that is the stuff that makes life worth living.

To my agent, Barbara: thank you for always being the mast of the ship in any storm.

To my editor, Stacey: thank you for always having the best questions and the best laugh in the world. The owner of Count Saint Germain's home will never be the same after crossing paths with us.

To the tireless team of dream makers at Penguin: thank you for loving and championing my stories with such unabashed enthusiasm. Special thanks to my publicist, Olivia, for all your amazing work. To Tessa for the tireless planning and for midnight tacos in the middle of nowhere. Thank you to Caitlin Tutterow for your patience and professionalism. A huge thank-you to Carmela Iaria, Venessa Carson, Doni Kay, Felicia Frazier, Shanta Newlin, Christina Colangelo, the entire marketing team, and the wonderful book lovers in school and library. Special shout-out to Kara Brammer and Felicity Vallence for being The Best™.

To Cindy and Anne for the notes and meticulous edits and for keeping my days of the week straight. Anne, thank you for sharing your love and expertise on our favorite city.

To Carrie and Brendan: it is such a gift to have you both so close by. I especially like how everyone at Cantina just knows to leave us alone. For hours. As long as we have chips.

To Jessica Khoury for the map. It never fails to take my breath away.

To Alwyn, Rosh, JJ, and Lemon: I am so lucky to have you in my life. CMC forever.

To Baa: you are more than a friend. You are family. Every day I am thankful for you.

To Emily Williams: thank you so much for keeping me on track and making sense out of the chaos.

To everyone at IGLA: thank you for everything you do to get my work in the hands of readers everywhere.

To Elaine: isn't it such a comfort to know you will never, ever be rid of me? ;-) If the Spanish in this book is wrong, I'm telling everyone to @ you.

To Erica, Chris, Ian, and Izzy: I am so excited for everything the future will bring us. Here's to lots of Disney. To Umma, Dad, Mama Joon, and Baba Joon: thank you for all your love and support. To Omid, Julie, Navid, Jinda, Evelyn, Ella, Lily, Isabelle, and Andrew: I am so thankful for each of you. To Mushu for being my constant writing buddy and for all the kisses and cuddling.

And to Vic: I think this next chapter will be our best chapter. There is no one I would rather write this story with than you.

RENÉE AHDIEH is a graduate of the University of North Carolina at Chapel Hill. In her spare time, she likes to dance salsa and collect shoes. She is passionate about all kinds of curry, rescue dogs, and college basketball. The first few years of her life were spent in a high-rise in South Korea; consequently, Renée enjoys having her head in the clouds. She lives in Charlotte, North Carolina. She is the #1 *New York Times* and international bestselling author of the Wrath and the Dawn series, the Flame in the Mist series, and *The Beautiful*.

You can visit Renée Ahdieh at
reneeahdieh.com